REVENGE OF THE DRAGON

MATT MEMEMARO

To Autumn,

For all of the hard work you do. It's about time you had a dedication.

ALSO BY MATT MEMEMARO

Ironrock
Windrise
Talon's Peak
Bloodstone
The Haven
Travion's roost
Desacourt
Nestlewood
Ashenfort
Sinibad's Lair
Thornton Grove
The Tomb of Chilijo
The Obelisk
The Dragon's Gore
Kressin
Gatestone
Montemayor
The Commonwealth

ONE

The dragon's roar split the air, louder than any thunder that Ayr had ever heard. He checked over his shoulder, half expecting to see the mighty golden dragon hot on his and Azura's tail. There would be nothing that could stop the golden dragon; not even the mighty black behemoth, Evor that flew with them. The cave around Ayr shuddered as Sinibad, the golden dragon took each step. Would the cave even be large enough for it to extend its wings to fly out of? He didn't want to think about the gargantuan, unnatural size of the elder dragon that was lumbering out of the cave behind them. How had it grown so big? Was it a result of the magic that ran through its veins?

Ayr could feel Azura underneath him, her entire body quivering with fear as she flew. Hopefully it wasn't affecting her ability to power through the air. Ayr did whatever he could to calm her nerves as he urged her on. Would they have to keep fleeing once they made it out of the cave? How far would the dragon chase them until they were far enough away from its wrath?

With Azura panicking, Ayr could do little more than hang on. His hands were firmly in the saddle grips, and his body snug against Azura's ashen scales. She had never flown this fast before. There had been no need. Beside them, Evor was pulling away. The black dragon was still over twice the size of Azura and much faster than her. Ayr caught a glimpse of his rider, Elanor Sunfire, who was pinned against him just as

Ayr was on Azura. There was no conversing between the two of them as they flew.

Slowly, more light spilled in from above as the entrance to the cave came more into view. The ground was shaking less now, either Sinibad was no longer chasing them, or the giant was taking to the air. It did not stop Ayr from pushing Azura to go faster so that they might escape the dragon's lair. Ayr felt like he had been sprinting as a result of Azura's efforts. Yet still they pushed on, despite his dry mouth and exhaustion. Bugs flew into his face and Ayr was grateful for the protective mask adorning it.

Evor was the first to burst out of the cave, the outside, early morning sunlight reflecting off his black scales. Azura was not far behind, desperation radiating through her body as she tried to keep up with her promised. Her breath came in ragged gasps that Ayr could barely hear over the sound of her wings beating on either side of him. There was little that he could do to calm her down, as the sounds of Sinibad moving filled the air once again.

As they flew down into the valley beneath the massive cave entrance, the world continued to shake around them. Just how big was Sinibad? Ayr turned his head, seeing how much distance they had put between them and felt panic shoot through his chest. Rising from the depths of the cave like an enraged serpent, Sinibad's mighty, golden head was the first part of his body to come into view.

Azura felt the panic that surged through Ayr's body and reacted accordingly. She skipped a beat and stumbled, losing altitude. Ayr lurched forward; however, he was secure in the saddle and did not go far. He regained his composure and tried to calm Azura, rubbing her back through the saddle.

Sinibad let out a roar that ripped through the sky like a shockwave. "Yes! Flee, riders! You will not be able to escape my wrath! I come for the Obelisk!"

Ayr went to cover his ears from the booming sound that erupted from the chest of the golden dragon, but by the time he had removed his hands from the saddle, it was already too late. Each sound that the dragon made sounded like a giant thunderclap, echoing in Ayr's ears, making his head spin. If not for Azura, he would have been completely disoriented. Despite his time at the Seminary of Fire as well as the Obelisk, Ayr was still not used to roars of this magnitude.

Sinibad stopped roaring and for a time, the only sounds that reached Ayr was that of the wind that whipped around Azura, along with her wingbeats. If not for the looming presence somewhere behind them, the flight would have been peaceful. Ayr didn't want to disturb Azura as she focused on speed alone. She was almost matching Evor, but the larger black dragon still flew ahead. It was not until the sun began to dip in the afternoon that Evor and Azura slowed down.

Ayr could feel how exhausted Azura was. Despite her size and her capability for long flights, this had been the longest and fastest she had ever travelled. They were still in the middle of nowhere, countless mountains and never-ending forests as far as the eye can see. Thankfully, there was also no sign of Sinibad. Ayr tried to sustain Azura, but by comparison the energy that he could summon was nothing compared to what she brought. Azura nudged him away as Evor started to descend.

Seeing this, Azura hummed in her mind, and followed him, dropping quickly through the sky. Ayr's stomach rose in his chest as a result of the rapid descent, but he quickly steeled himself, allowing his body to go with Azura on the downward spiral. He could see where she was going. Ahead of them was a clearing that barely looked large enough to house Evor. It would do for now. They all needed rest.

Azura was the first to near the ground, her lighter frame and more agile movement allowing her to turn into a steep dive. The ground raced up at them and Ayr held on for his life. As they neared the ground, Azura slowed only for the thunderous wingbeats of Evor to drown out any noise from overhead.

Azura touched down with a gentle ease, a soft thud echoing around the clearing. Evor landed beside them moments later, however his landing was the opposite. The earth beneath his feet started to rumble much like it had done when Sinibad had stalked them through the cave. Only when he had settled did the sound stop. The massive dragon turned his head to stare at Ayr and Azura.

"We will rest here. You should dismount and let Azura rest properly, Ashbourne."

Ayr glanced up at the sky, fearing that Sinibad would appear to block out the sun at any moment. "Should we dismount here? Is it safe?"

Evor chortled as he sniffed the air around them. "I cannot smell the monster. We should be safe for now. I will alert you if that should change. Elanor needs to speak with you, Ashbourne. Now!"

Before Evor finished speaking, Elanor was dismounting from the black dragon's back. It was the same manoeuvre that Ayr had seen her do a dozen times already. She pointed at the ground, gesturing for Ayr to dismount as well. With no choice but to comply, Ayr followed suit. Elanor pointed her feet at the ground as she sat on the back of Evor's neck. She gracefully touched down to the ground a moment later with an insignificant thud, bending at the knees. She stood up to her full height as Ayr was lowering himself off Azura. He had significantly less distance to travel.

In one smooth motion, Elanor stormed across the gap separating them, ripping her mask from her face and throwing it on the ground in anger. Her hand flew to her hip, grabbing at her sword. She thrust it forward towards Ayr, thrusting it at his throat. "What the fuck was that Ashbourne!"

Ayr threw his hands up beside his face in surrender with no time to grab his sword. Instead, he ripped his mask from his face so that Elanor could see him clearly. "What was what? I have no idea what you're talking about!"

Elanor jammed the sword closer to him. "No idea what I'm talking about? Really? After all of the time, effort and energy I've put into you, only to get close to you, you turn around and spit in my face! That was your father in that cave!"

"I know who it was, Elanor! I'm not blind, but I'm not entirely sure what you expected me to do about it!"

"Dalton Ashbourne has a fucking elder dragon at his disposal! Did you know about this?"

"No! I knew nothing about it! Nothing! I swear to you on my father's life!"

"That doesn't mean shit to me!" Elanor's words struck him like a whip.

"Elanor! I don't know what you want me to tell you! I had nothing to do with this! Dalton is his own man and I am my own. I came to the Seminary and the Obelisk to become a rider. I've bonded with Azura. I've bonded with you!"

"Fuck!" Elanor threw her sword to the ground in frustration. She buried her head in her hands as she sank to the ground in a squat. "Fuck! This is exactly what we didn't want to happen! Father!"

Ayr didn't know what to do. He wanted to approach her and console her, through the guidance of Azura. However, at the same time, Elanor could have reacted negatively. Instead, Ayr stayed back and folded his arms.

"You seem concerned, Elanor."

"I am, Ashbourne! You don't understand what this has done!"

Ayr shrugged. "I am confused. My father has been alive my entire life. I'm not sure exactly how we can fix this. It's not like you can strip a dragon from a non-rider, is it?"

Elanor sucked in a deep breath of air and removed her hands from her head. "Your father still lurks out there somewhere beyond my reach, with a threat bigger than you or I can contain. The whole purpose of stripping Dalton Ashbourne's dragon from him was so that he would never threaten us with them again."

"He almost brought down the Commonwealth without a dragon of his own. Imagine what he will be able to do with an elder dragon under his control." Ayr frowned. "But wait, elder dragons are untamed, aren't they?"

Elanor ran her hand over her head. "You're thick, aren't you Ashbourne? Didn't you hear him speak to it? Clearly there's an arrangement there."

Ayr puffed out his lips. "So, what could the elder dragon want? What's it's grudge against the Commonwealth?"

Evor lowered his head over Elanor. "It could be anything. They deem themselves superior, not serving the Commonwealth and their riders. I dare say that a dragon of that size was vexed by the Commonwealth many years ago and not deemed suitable to serve, just after the first war."

Ayr put his hands on his hips. "And how are we going to verify this information? You're not just going to ask it are you?"

Evor scoffed, a puff of smoke jettisoning out from his nostrils. "You're funny, Ashbourne, but no; unless Sinibad comes down from the mountains himself to tell us, we will have to speculate. Any dragon is killable, but I wonder at what cost. Sinibad is old and powerful. Even a dozen skilled riders and their dragons would not be able to destroy him."

"Evor." Elanor raised her hand. "That's enough. We can't do anything more today. We faced it down, now we need to return to the Obelisk. Standing around here pouting won't do us any good, now will it?"

"You're quite right, Elanor. We must report this. Your father will want to know. Dalton Ashbourne cannot be allowed to roam the world unchecked with a dragon."

Elanor knelt to pick her sword up with a disgusted expression across her face. She slid it back into its sheath where it belonged, and similarly recovered her mask from the ground. Elanor dusted it off without looking at Ayr before pulling it back over her face.

"Get a move on Ashbourne. Unless you and Azura plan on becoming snack food for an elder dragon."

"I don't have a death wish, despite what the watchers might think."

Azura cut into his mind as pointed as Elanor's sword.

Rider. Now is not the time. Surely you can see that, can't you?

Well, it's not our fault that the watchers chose to send us on this mission.

No, it is not. Did you stop to consider that they may have done that for a reason? Everything is connected at the Obelisk. Elanor has plans for you and it would be foolish to think otherwise.

Plans? For me?

Yes. Despite your family lineage, you are going to be a perfectly serviceable rider. Those don't come along all that often. Elanor would be foolish to throw that away. Now work with her, and if your father wishes to upset your new way of life and allegiances, then we will do everything in our power to stop him.

"Finished?" Elanor had put her hands on her hips. "You really need to get better at multitasking, Ashbourne."

"Apologies, Azura is all encompassing."

A slight curve stretched across Elanor's lips. "I'm well aware. Now come on, I don't want to leave you behind."

TWO

It would have been too easy to scold Ashbourne and punish him for something he had no part in. How could he have known that Dalton was planning something as diabolical as that? There would have been a sign. So far, he had been honest and if anything was amiss, Azura would have known. Doubts accumulated in Elanor's mind like a dark rain cloud ready to open above her head. Her thoughts were mirrored by Evor as he entered her mind.

I don't know if I trust Ashbourne.

Evor! How could he have known that his father was planning on doing this.

You're well aware of the Lord Chairman's plans, are you not, Elanor?

I have a good relationship with my father.

What's to say that Ashbourne isn't in the same situation? We know nothing about what he was like before he stepped through the black gate and into the Seminary. You need to be wary of who you trust, Elanor. Even if his dragon is promised to me.

Then I need to find out more about him. These past few months have been insightful, but we need to reveal his true character.

I will trust you to investigate then.

I will once we are back at the Obelisk.

Very well, Elanor.

Evor groaned as he laid himself down on the ground. Whilst he was as large as a small castle, his scales did not provide the best platform for Elanor to climb up onto his back. However, with their practiced ease, Elanor quickly found herself in the saddle, gazing down at Azura and Ashbourne.

"Let us know when you're ready!"

Elanor laughed down at Ashbourne. "Even though it takes me longer to mount Evor, I'm always ready. You two fly ahead. We'll catch up. There's still no sign of Sinibad."

Azura reared her head as she looked to the sky. "Thank Chilijo for that. We will see you back at the Obelisk, Elanor."

Evor readied himself underneath her as Azura spread her wings and kicked off from the ground. As always, watching the smaller white dragon take flight was a spectacle. From where the sun was shining, it collected underneath her wings, making them glow of all colours of the rainbow. Azura let out an excited bark as she took flight with Ashbourne secured firmly on her back. Once Azura was clear, Elanor leant forward in her saddle.

Decades had passed since her first flight with Evor, and by now they did not need to communicate what the other wanted; as if they were physically joined. In the years since, Evor had reached his full size, only growing marginally year by year as time dragged on. Whilst he would never reach the size of Sinibad, it was possible that given enough time, he would come close. Dragons of old that had lived for centuries before the first war would reach similar sizes. However, due to Dalton Ashbourne's guile and cunning, they were among the first to fall.

Decades, if not centuries of wisdom

It won't happen again, Elanor. We won't allow it to happen.

I know. But what if? He will be even more powerful now, even if he doesn't have an army.

We can stop him before he raises one. We just need time, Elanor.

Well, we're running out. You need to hurry.

Of course, Elanor.

Evor leapt into the air, making Elanor's stomach rise to her throat. Despite the years that she had spent riding him, the feeling of inertia was all still too familiar. There was no amount of magic within the Commonwealth that could help the riders overcome the forces of physics like that. Regardless, her stomach settled quickly, and within a dozen furious wingbeats, Evor was drawing level with the clouds. If not for the threat looming somewhere behind them, they would have been able to enjoy the beautiful day.

Thin cloud cover rolled slowly across the sky like a wave rolling onto the blue shores that awaited its arrival. It blew in from the north, but Elanor knew that elder dragons couldn't control the weather. The first war would have been a lot more dangerous if they could. As Evor soared over the forests and lakes, it was near impossible to think about the worries and terrors that would await them once they got back to the Obelisk. In the moment, it did not matter if Dalton Ashbourne had an elder dragon or what the Lord Chairman would say, all that mattered was the air pushing through her mask and the enjoyment of being on Evor's back.

Evor swayed as the currents rose up off the lakes, using them to what little advantage he could. Whilst he was a magical creature, and powerful in his own right, Evor was far too large to be affected by the elements on such a stable day like today. It did not take him long to catch Azura either. The white dragon was still climbing through the air as Evor soared past her. Elanor glared down at Ashbourne, who was looking back at her, his face hidden behind his fanged black and white mask.

Elanor shook her head, enjoying the ride, pretending that he wasn't there. There was no denying Azura's presence, however, nor did she want to ignore her. Elanor wanted to reach out and speak to her, however the only way would be through Evor. Content, Evor pushed into her mind, asking the question but Elanor pushed him away.

There was still a long journey before them, and with each minute that passed, Elanor grew more wary. Life in the saddle for extended periods of time was draining, but Evor provided her with the strength that she needed. Before long the afternoon turned into night, and Elanor was still on edge. Dragons had excellent night vision and considering the urgency of their discovery, Elanor wanted to push on for as long as possible. She could sleep in the saddle and laid her head down against it. It did not take long into the night journey for Evor to drift into her mind once again.

Elanor. Azura is requesting that we stop.

Ugh! What for? Does Ashbourne want a break?

I understand your frustration, but we need to remember that Azura does not have the stamina for a journey this long yet. We should rest briefly and let her regain her strength.

It's not Azura's doing! You know this is Ashbourne. I wouldn't be surprised if Sinibad is going to catch us now.

Elanor... my promised would not lie to me. We will not be long. I could feel you going to sleep. You could do with the rest as well. I will keep us safe tonight.

Fine.

Elanor barely had time to protest before Evor began his descent into the mountains below. It was not far removed from where they had stayed the previous night. However, without a map or any landmarks nearby, she had no idea of where she was. As he touched down in the mountains, they rumbled underneath his weight. In the dim light, Elanor could not see if they had disturbed anything, nor did she care. She patted Evor as she removed her hands from the saddle. Evor lowered himself closer to the ground and Elanor slid down his leg.

The dark ground rushed up at her as she landed with a sigh. Whilst she was used to long hours, sometimes spending days in the saddle, Elanor was always grateful for a reprieve. Azura landed moments later, and Elanor tore the mask from her face.

Azura squatted down, resting on her forward legs, allowing Ashbourne an easier path down her body. He rolled off her and collapsed to the ground. There was no effort or self-preservation, making it look like he had died in the saddle. Azura was too large to pick up his crumpled body without incredible care.

"That tired, huh, Ashbourne?" She had half a mind to walk over and kick him, but that would have proven counterintuitive. "What happened to your bond with Azura? I thought you were meant to be bonded."

He stirred slowly, groaning at first and then rolling over, glancing up at her with dead eyes that were almost invisible in the dark. "Give me a break."

Elanor scoffed at him. "Be thankful that Sinibad isn't tracking us now, otherwise you wouldn't get one. We can't stay long here, can we, Evor?"

The massive black dragon shook his head. "I would not advise it. Take your rest, Ashbourne. You will need it. I expect you back in the saddle by the time the moon reaches its peak."

"But it's almost there."

Elanor could feel Evor smiling inside her head. "Exactly, Ashbourne. Now get moving, or I will make you move."

With a sigh so loud, it could wake the dead, Ashbourne clambered to his feet with considerable effort. Azura made herself available to him, undoubtedly giving him energy to help him along in the process. Once he was back in the saddle, Evor turned his head to Azura.

"Stay with me, little one. We are almost there."

"I know, I can feel it."

Evor turned, hearing something. Elanor snapped her head around in the same direction, her ears not yet picking up the sound. Despite her eyes not being as finely tuned in the dark as Evor's, she could still make out the looming shadow on the horizon. The hairs stuck up on the back of her neck. As they watched, the once solid figure multiplied.

"Ashbourne! Get a move on! Wyverns! Come on! Azura, get in the air!"

"What, here?"

"Yes, here!" Elanor waved her hands over her head.

"There's no need to tell me, Elanor."

"Come, little one! Let us burn the rodents!" Evor turned his head towards the sky with a roar.

Evor pushed off the ground and began to gain altitude. Azura rose beside him like a silent phantom in the night. She turned with him, both dragons turning to face the threat coming from the north. Elanor knew that Evor was more than capable of tearing wyverns out of the sky, and with Azura's assistance, they would be unstoppable. The wyverns drew nearer, and Elanor sat back in the saddle, her arms no longer secured in it. She readied her sword, her hand on her hip waiting until one of the wyverns drew close enough for her to strike.

The true battle against the wyverns would be in the air. Wyverns only grew to be half the size of Azura, but enough of them could still pose a problem to a dragon the size of Evor. The two-legged fiends could latch onto his wings or other extremities, tearing not only him, but Elanor from the sky as well. Elanor, being a much smaller target if she ran along Evor's back would prove to be a more enticing meal, providing a distraction.

Considering the size of the wyverns, Elanor was more than capable of fending them off, as long as they didn't all rush them at once. It was hard to tell exactly how many wyverns flew at them, but as they neared, she could feel Evor tense underneath her. Evor charged the wyverns

with vigour. As they neared, Elanor could finally count the number of
wyverns. There were eight total, at least for the moment. But wyverns
bred like rabbits and where there was one, hundreds could follow.

Two had split away from the rest of the pack whilst half a dozen
continued flying at her and Evor. She patted Evor gently, urging him
on, a smile playing on her lips. Evor's booming roar ripped through
the night sky in an attempt to scatter the smaller monsters. They
were undeterred, and Elanor knew what was coming as Evor's neck
underneath her started to heat up. She could feel his glands swelling as
the fire built.

A rumbling thunder filled the air, building to a crescendo. The
wyverns were almost within range. Azura let out a roar of her own
beside them, and the fire rising in Evor's belly erupted as he opened his
mouth, turning the night sky ablaze. The sight was something Elanor
never tired of. A wave of red and orange fire swept across the darkness,
engulfing the first of the creatures. The wyvern howled as its body was
immersed in the flames, but it was only one of many.

Despite how widespread Evor's wall of flame was, it was easily
avoided by the other five wyverns. Elanor waited for the clash of scales
and talons that was to come. Evor readied another fireball and spat
it towards the nearest wyvern. The monster spun in the air, twirling
over the fireball like it was just any other obstacle. Thankfully, unlike
dragons, the wyverns were unable to breathe fire, however they were
no less of a threat.

The first wyvern changed its angle of attack, opting to soar over
Evor's head. However, the change in the attack made it open to a strike
from Elanor. Against the blackness that was Evor, Elanor knew that
she was all but invisible. She rose up, still protected from the wyvern
by Evor's head. With her sword extended, Elanor struck at the wyvern,
as it attempted to dig its talons into Evor's back.

The wyvern shrieked a blood curdling cry that almost deafened Elanor. She withdrew her sword and felt a splatter of blood spray onto her mask. She flicked her head back and saw her victim smash into Evor's back, only then to tumble from sight, falling into the darkness that enshrouded them. With one wyvern gone, there were still more than half a dozen in the air. Evor lashed out, biting through one of the wyverns. Pieces of it fell to either side of him, limbs and scales indistinguishable from each other.

Evor reared around as the other wyverns zoomed overhead, missing him entirely. More fire spilled from his jaws, catching the slowest of the wyverns as it tried to turn to attack. The creature howled as flames engulfed it, and it too began to fall from the sky. There were four wyverns left surrounding them. Elanor leapt up from the saddle as another wyvern passed overhead. It met the same fate as the first as it went tumbling into the darkness, its soft belly opened by her blade. Elanor revelled in the blood that spilled onto her and she could feel Evor's admiration coursing through her veins.

These rodents are no match for us, Elanor. They will burn.

Evor spun through the air again, catching another wyvern by its spindly tail. It howled much like the others had done only moments ago. Evor ripped and tore at the screeching wyvern's tail pulling it back towards him. Once it was close enough, he let it go momentarily, then surged forward to catch more of the wyvern in his mouth. Elanor felt the force of the bite, as Evor bit down on their prey. The bones of the wyvern cracked instantly, the bite force of Evor stronger than almost anything else in the world. He was the true master of the sky, and the wyverns were beneath him.

As he bit down again on the wyvern, devouring the half that was left of it, the two remaining creatures howled as if they had also been struck in pain. Then, as one they darted below Evor, faster than he could turn. Evor tracked them with the grace of an eagle, but when he had turned again, the three remaining wyverns were fleeing back to the north. Elanor glanced up and saw Azura above them, as part of a wyvern wing fell from her mouth. She had manage to kill one, as the second that attacked her was following its kin.

Evor let loose a tremendous roar, one that could have rivalled Sinibad's, shaking the air around them. With a single wingbeat, he pushed his body higher into the sky, drawing level with Azura and Ashbourne, whose faint outline appeared to have his sword in hand, but in the darkness it was impossible to see if there was blood on it.

Elanor lowered her sword and swung it over Evor's shoulder, flicking most of the blood from it. She slid her sword back into its sheath and waved.

"Sinibad must have sent them! Elder dragons have an affinity with wyverns. Get a move on, Ashbourne! There's no rest for the wicked!"

THREE

The golden rays of the morning sun continued to brighten as the leagues passed by underneath Azura's wings. He could have fallen out of the saddle at any moment, but as the morning sun rose over the mountains and the surrounding landscapes, Ayr let out a sigh of relief. His eyes felt ready to roll back in his head. The wyvern attack had certainly energized him, but most of that energy had come from Azura.

Do not give up on me yet, rider. We are almost home. I can smell it.
I'm not, Azura. You give me strength.

Azura beat her wings and surged upwards again, gaining more altitude. Ayr lurched backwards in the saddle, as she rose higher. He caught his stomach in his throat as Azura levelled out, and for the first time in hours, he felt alive. On the horizon, he could make out the all too familiar sight that he had longed for since encountering Sinibad.

An enormous shadow loomed in the distance, the only place that Ayr had experienced true safety in, the entire time he had been with Azura and finally, Ayr felt somewhat at ease. He relaxed the closer they drew to the Obelisk; the towering, blackened structure growing by the minute as they neared the horizon. It had only been a little over two days, but with everything that he had seen in that time, Ayr was ready for some well-earned rest and relaxation. He had a funny feeling that this was only the beginning.

We will need to report to the Lord Chairman, rider. This is a signif-icant discovery.

Ayr laughed at Azura and patted her beside the saddle grip. *You don't say. I could have gone without it.*

This is what our jobs entail. I will do whatever I can to keep you safe.

Thank you, Azura.

The outskirts of the Obelisk city were beginning to pass under them, and Ayr sat up in the saddle. He stole a glance at Elanor out of the corner of his eye. She was stoic, leaning forward in the saddle, seemingly anxious to get back within the walls of the Obelisk. As they neared the enormous structure, Ayr could now pick out dragons by their individual colours against the pristine blue sky. The sight of the dragons soaring overhead was as beautiful and calming as it had been the first time he had seen it. There were less clouds in the sky than there were thoughts in his head. What would they say to the chairman?

Can you ask Evor what she's thinking?

No rider, I cannot. If Evor does not want to divulge information about Elanor, he will not. That information has to be given willingly. I know that we are promised, but unlike the bond between us, I cannot see everything inside his head yet.

Ayr sighed and leaned back in the saddle again. At last, they were underneath the shadow of the Obelisk. Ayr stole one final glance be-hind him, checking the sky for the monster that could have very well been chasing them. Evor flew ahead, Elanor taking charge as per usual. They flew up and underneath the Obelisk into where the landing platforms awaited them.

Today, there was no sign of any other riders or dragons awaiting them. Instead, the insides of the Obelisk seemed somewhat aban-doned. Whilst there had been dragons outside, these platforms were usually occupied by dragons and their riders in some form. To see them this empty was highly unusual. Ayr frowned as Azura came into land on the platform beside Evor. She lowered herself to the ground, allowing Ayr a comfortable dismount.

As he slid down her body, Ayr realized he had not stood on solid ground in hours. His regret was almost immediate. He hit the ground, and his knees buckled, the inner of his thighs burning like the fire that raged inside Azura. Even her calming presence was not enough to ease it entirely. Ayr rubbed his thighs as he took his first step away from Azura, being careful not to fall from the platform.

He stretched out his legs and turned back towards Azura, whose neck was coiling slowly around him. Ayr laughed softly as she slid her head underneath his hand, as if asking for a pat.

"It's nice to be back."

Azura cooed at him as he rubbed his hand along her cheek. She half closed her eyes as her tongue rolled out of her head. "I'm glad we are not dead. Next time, you might get to slay a wyvern on your own, rider."

"I'd rather not face them again, Azura. They were terrifying."

"Yet we are stronger from the experience. You should go. You wouldn't want to keep Lady Sunfire waiting, would you?"

Ayr sighed heavily and glanced past Azura. Elanor was patting Evor on the side of the leg, not paying him any attention. Ayr refocused his gaze on Azura. Staring into her big blue eyes was like losing himself in a pool of water. He sighed again.

"I know what you're thinking, rider. I don't need my eyes to know that."

Ayr raised a closed fist to his forehead. "I want to trust her. I want to trust the other riders here, but they're going to treat me differently because of my last name. You'll stay with me, won't you?"

A puff of smoke exited Azura's nostrils. "Always, rider. Now, go! I will be there."

Ayr shook his head and turned away from Azura, rubbing his hand over her scales one last time. As Ayr lowered his mask, he saw Elanor mimicking his movements on her platform, however without the thigh rubbing. She looked as composed and as stoic as ever, her eyes locked onto him as she flicked her auburn hair out from underneath her mask. Elanor closed the gap, and the two of them met before the doors leading to the rest of the Obelisk.

"So, you survived, Ashbourne."

Ayr raised an eyebrow. "You seem surprised, Elanor."

"Surprised that more wyverns didn't catch us." She jerked her head to the side. "Let's go. We need to find the Lord Chairman."

"And what are we going to tell him?"

Elanor rolled her eyes. "The truth. Come."

Elanor turned and pushed on the wide black door that stood before them. It scraped across the floor as it slowly opened just enough for the two of them to slip through. After having been out in the wilderness for so long, it was a strange feeling coming back into such an enclosed space. Even though the hallways were still large enough to accommodate most dragons, there was still a roof over his head, which Ayr was grateful for.

Ayr followed Elanor through the passageways that he was unfamiliar with. Despite having been in the Obelisk for weeks, he was still learning the layout. Azura was a wealth of knowledge, slowly filling his mind, ensuring that the gaps that were there were filled in. Whilst Azura was knowledgeable she could not provide all of the answers to his questions. As they continued to traverse the Obelisk, Ayr frowned, wondering why it was so abandoned. The halls were quiet and even this early in the morning, they were usually packed.

They had been walking for several minutes when Elanor finally turned down another hallway. It was only half the height and width of the previous one, with more than ample space for plenty of humans, but not for dragons. As they moved down the hallway, Ayr felt like the walls were closing in. There were no windows here or any sign of the outside world. They were in the heart of the Obelisk.

Elanor turned another corner and stood before a door, this one only as wide as they were. The heavy wood was laden with metal studs in a pattern in the shape of a cross. Elanor touched her forehead and then her left and right shoulders respectively. The metal studs retracted into the door and became flush with the wood. The door started to slide open and let out a loud hiss once it stood fully ajar. Behind the door was a simple metal platform and tube.

Elanor raised her hand as she stood to the side. "After you, Ashbourne."

"What is this place?" Ayr glanced up at the tube above him.

"I thought you'd have figured it out by now. This is the entrance to the Lord Chairman's chambers."

Elanor turned her back to him and repeated the gesture she used to open the room. As the door hissed shut, Ayr felt a jerk under his feet, as the platform started to move upwards. It was a similar movement to when Azura took off from the ground. Ayr stumbled, and almost put his hand against the wall, but Elanor slapped it away. The journey was short, only seeming to last a few seconds before it slowed to a stop. There was an identical door in front of them and Elanor repeated the cross gesture.

As the door began to open, light spilled in from outside. The area was a courtyard the size of a small village; however, rather than the empty space being as green as grass, it was covered in black tiles. Ayr raised his hands to cover his eyes. As he lowered his hand, and his eyes refocused, an enormous stationary figure came into view just outside of the elevator room.

Apart from Sinibad, this dragon matched and beat every other that he had seen for size. The end of the dragon's tail that was coiled on the ground started as a deep emerald green. The tip of the tail was thicker than Azura's body. As Ayr followed the tail up towards its owner, the green melded with patches of scales blotching against each other to create a multilayered camouflage pattern.

The dragon was curled around the spires that enclosed the courtyard, the tall, blackened walls protecting this part of the Obelisk from the outside world. It was much like where the Bonding had taken place, with ample space for a dragon to fly in and out of. The green dragon kept extending over the entire roof that was in sight, looping around in an almost horseshoe shape. It reared its head upon seeing them, snarling as they approached. Elanor raised her hand and beckoned for Ayr to follow her.

He felt stupid for following her but felt compelled to do so. "Elanor, what are you doing! That dragon is about to attack!"

Elanor continued to walk straight towards the dragon, undeterred. Ayr could not believe what he was seeing. Surely, Elanor was not giving up her life just to walk at this dragon. She must have had a plan. The dragon arched up. As the dragon opened it's mouth, Ayr heard wingbeats overhead.

He looked up and in the morning sunlight, he saw Azura and Evor both swooping overhead. They were headed for the courtyard, both dragons in unison as they flew towards the riders. The green dragon raised its head to the sky, letting out a low roar that echoed up towards the clouds. Evor and Azura returned the call, and the dragon sank back down onto the roof without another grumble.

Elanor turned and smiled at Ayr as he stared in shock. Evor and Azura made their way into land and crashed into the ground at the feet of the giant green dragon. Baindussa grumbled at both new arrivals, but was otherwise complacent, barely raising his head.

"Baindussa? Attack me? As long as Evor is nearby the chance of that is extremely low."

Ayr was not convinced. "So, it senses our dragons and lets us pass? I've never heard of anything more convoluted."

Elanor shrugged. "That is Baindussa's condition of entry. If anyone attempts to circumnavigate the security protocols to see the Lord Chairman, they will have him to answer to. You can't get in here without permission from him or my father."

"Does Baindussa not recognise riders? Surely, if he is your father's dragon, you'd be able to come in here when you please."

"If you look closely, you might be able to see that Baindussa is blind. Baindussa allows entry to the Lord Charmain's chambers based off the smell of a rider's dragon."

Ayr squinted up at the massive green dragon. "What's wrong with it?" He paused and could see Baindussa's eyes. There was no light in them, and unlike most other dragons, Ayr could see that they were sunken. "Oh, I see. So how does someone see the Lord Chairman if they don't have a dragon?"

"Someone will accompany them. Come on Ashbourne, do you really think anyone can get up here without one?"

Ayr shrugged. The Obelisk was an obstacle in and of itself. Nobody could get into it without a dragon of their own, let alone onto the peak of the enormous structure. Ayr had heard stories of far away lands that had access to giant metal birds that could rise into the air and compete with dragons. Somehow, he did not believe that anything outside Sinibad would be able to compete with Baindussa.

Evor and Azura fell in behind their respective riders, and Ayr felt like there was an earthquake following him with each step. The doorway to the Lord Chairman's chambers was as tall as Baindussa, easily able to fit even the largest of dragons inside. As Ayr passed underneath the tip of Baindussa's tail, he took one final glance up at the enormous beast. He had so many questions.

"How does Baindussa feed?"

Elanor didn't break her stride. "What?"

Ayr was not sure how to rephrase his question. As they walked, he reformulated it in his mind. He could feel Azura pressing against him, trying to help him. "Well, Baindussa is blind, right? So, how does such a large dragon actively feed? He wouldn't be able to fit into the halls of the Obelisk, would he?"

Elanor shook her head and laughed. "When there is a will, there is a way. Baindussa is blind because he once fought an elder dragon."

"And he couldn't heal himself?"

Elanor shook her head again. "Baindussa's promised was killed in the fight. There was no going back once he lost his eyes. Baindussa does not need his eyes to see, however. There is more magic in his body than most of the Obelisk. Baindussa sees through my father's eyes."

Ayr nodded in understanding. "I see. Where is your father? Is he that powerful?"

Elanor pointed at the looming black door in front of them. "He is. Through here, Ashbourne."

They slowed as they approached the door until Elanor stopped completely. Ayr went to press against it, but Elanor stopped him. With her outstretched hand, Elanor pressed against the door, straight in front of her face. In the dim light, Ayr saw a flicker as a panel that Elanor had pressed upon sunk into the metal, much like it had done in the previous room. The door began to slide open, and standing before them was an old man that Ayr had not seen in several weeks.

Kaiser stood before them with his hands behind his back. He was dressed in a freshly pressed uniform, with what little of his greying hair remained brushed gently to the back of his head.

"Lady Sunfire. Ashbourne." Kaiser barely paid Ayr any attention. "It's good to see that some of you survived the elder dragon."

Elanor went to push past him, but Kaiser threw out his arm, catching her. "What happened out there, Elanor?"

"Get off me Kaiser. Is my father in his study?"

Kaiser nodded. "He is."

"Good, we need to speak to him immediately. I won't have a word spoken about what we saw outside the chambers."

Kaiser extended his hand towards the next closed door. "Yes, I can see the distress on your faces. Very well, come with me."

FOUR

Without any more words spoken between them, Kaiser turned and started towards the next door. It was already beginning to swing open, whether by magic or other means, Ayr could not tell. He stared in awe as the door opened to reveal a majestic room that stretched far into the distance. It was clear that the Lord Chairman was a man that indulged in luxury, but Ayr realised that he needed the space for the massive green dragon that was outside.

The black tiled floor was complicated by the equally dark roof, which gave Ayr the impression that he was inside the depths of a dark cave. There were few specks of differing colour throughout the room. In these chambers, there were no windows, the only light coming from braziers that hung from the columns which held the structure upright. The braziers were as large as Azura's head, with all of them high towards the ceiling, and requiring a large dragon to light them.

As they passed under the braziers, Ayr could feel the heat radiating from them and he felt more comfortable than he had been in the past few days. Whilst his eyes still wanted to roll back in his head, Ayr kept his vision focused on the wide desk that appeared to be almost as long as Azura in the middle of the chamber. There were gaps along its length, enough room for a human to squeeze past. Otherwise, the desk in most places was overcrowded by piles of cream coloured paper. The only space that was free from the paper was a small section of desk space that had a quill rising from it.

In front of the clear desk space sat four high back leather chairs that melded with the colour of the floor and the desk, with one sitting behind it. The chair behind the desk was unlike the others. It was much taller than the other chairs, with an elaborate backing that rose up towards the ceiling. The backing looked like it was fit for a serpent to rest upon. It was clear that it was where Kaiser was taking them.

Ayr looked to the left of the desk and saw rows of towering bookshelves all racing towards the back of the room. There looked to be enough material for a large library, all at the disposal of the Lord Chairman. Ayr marvelled at the wealth of knowledge before him within the thousands of tomes that occupied the room. As Ayr ogled at the bookshelves, another presence was making themselves known.

A familiar rider and purple dragon were walking towards them from behind the desk, coming into his vision from a side room of the main chamber. Ayr groaned. It was none other than Major Kaladin and his vicious dragon, Gundrag. Kaladin wore a frown on his face, his eyebrows furrowed together, almost in annoyance. He was dressed in his own black uniform, matching Kaiser in his presentation.

"Ah, Lady Sunfire, Lord Ashbourne, welcome back. I heard about your mission. Many of us did not think that you would be returning to the Obelisk."

Elanor sneered at Kaladin as he approached. Gundrag lumbered behind him, before setting down underneath one of the braziers, stretching out. "You owe me, Kaladin."

A wicked grin spread across Kaladin's face as he gestured to the seats in front of the desk. "Sunfire, Ashbourne. Take a seat. He will be with you shortly. We are most eager to hear your report."

Elanor glared at Kaladin again, as Kaiser moved around the mountain of papers on the desk and vanished from sight. He reappeared a moment later before vanishing again to where Kaladin and Gundrag had appeared from. Elanor gestured towards the seats before taking the one on the right. As Ayr had nowhere else to be, what was the harm in joining her. He pulled the chair out from the desk and flopped beside Elanor. He could see Kaladin, now leaning back on a nearby column.

A moment later, Ayr heard more footsteps coming from one of the offside rooms. They were too heavy to be a human, but too light to be a dragon. Ayr watched, listening as the footsteps grew closer. From the same place that Kaladin and Gundrag had emerged, was a smaller dragon, that would have only been as tall as Ayr was. The dragon was a strange pale hue that seemed to shift and fade with the background of the chambers as it walked. Without a word, the dragon approached the desk and looked up at the cutout.

In the next motion, the dragon glanced up at Gundrag and leapt into the air. The dragon coiled around the back of the chair before digging its way into the cutout. Its snout and tail overhung the shoulders of the chair, the latter swaying gently from side to side as it blended into the wood behind it.

Ayr leaned forward into Elanor's ear and whispered. "If that's your father's dragon outside, then who's dragon is this?"

"That's my mother's, Draxion. Do you think that watchers, whilst magical, don't have a source somewhere? Nobody in your intake was paired with a dragon that has the ability of foresight. Those dragons are few and far between. We keep them sheltered away from the world. The safest place in the world for Draxion is here."

"Why is she so small if she's bonded to your mother? She's smaller than Azura was only a few weeks after we bonded."

Elanor tutted at him. "No two dragons are the same, Ashbourne. Watchers are not combative, even their dragons. It stunts their growth despite the connection they will have with their riders. They typically only grow big enough to be ridden. The only dragon I know of that was both a watcher and combative was Chilijo himself. Now shut up. Crassus comes."

More footsteps filled the room. This time, they were certainly from a human. Ayr sat upright in his chair, and a moment later, the Lord Chairman came into view. He walked forward slowly, deep in conversation with Kaiser. As Crassus Sunfire approached the chair with Draxion inside it, they stopped speaking and Kaiser bowed his head, moving away. Crassus took each step slowly before finally sitting in the chair. Once seated, Crassus raised his hand to scratch the near camouflaged dragon that was almost wrapped around his shoulders as she sat perched on the chair. He stared straight ahead at Ayr and Elanor before speaking.

"Hello, daughter. I assume you have come to report your findings regarding the elder dragon task. I hope you're bringing me good news."

Elanor sat back and puffed out her lips. "I would like to be the bearer of good news, father, but I am afraid not."

Kaladin folded his arms across his chest. "Did you find the elder dragon or not?"

Elanor took a deep breath and glared at him. "We did. But we also found something else of greater concern." She didn't pause, turning her attention to Crassus. "We found Dalton Ashbourne. He was hiding in a cave with the elder dragon."

"What! I didn't hear you correctly, Elanor." Crassus turned a deep shade of red.

"You did hear me. Dalton Ashbourne is back amongst the living."

Crassus' face was still reddening. "How? He's been dead for almost twenty years."

"When you try and drown a man, you should tie a weight to his ankles so he can't free himself."

Crassus slammed his fist down on the desk. "Did you know about this?"

Ayr shook his head. "I did not know that he had an elder dragon at his disposal."

"But you knew he was going to resurface?" Crassus' tone was flat.

"No! I knew nothing of the sort. I haven't seen him in months. Dalton Ashbourne is my father in name only. I do not endorse any of his actions! I am here to help you!"

Crassus snorted. "How am I supposed to ascertain whether or not you're here at the wishes of Dalton Ashbourne?"

Ayr bowed his head. "I'm not. I swore an oath. I took Azura as my dragon, or she chose me. What am I meant to say? You'll either believe me or you won't. Dalton caused you many issues years ago and I wasn't involved in it."

"I can vouch for Ashbourne." Elanor was nodding beside him. "Considering his bond with Azura, I doubt that he wants to do anything to harm the Obelisk or the Seminary. Considering his bond to me."

Crassus leaned back in his chair. "Ah, of course. Azura and Evor. The promised that waited. I should have known." Crassus' gaze darkened in light of the revelation. "Elanor. There is also the matter regarding your student. Don't think that just because Dalton Ashbourne has resurfaced that you'll be able to get away with it."

"What matter?"

"The matter in which he took the life of another young rider, only within the past fourty-eight hours. Do you know anything about this, Elanor?"

Elanor turned her head and took in a deep breath of air before quickly releasing it. She then turned straight to stare back at Crassus. "No, no I do not, Lord Chairman."

"Elanor." Crassus' tone was flat. "Do not lie to me. You are too precious to me for a rift to come between us over something like this. We have stripped dragons from riders for less and I know how much Evor means to you."

Elanor licked her lips and sighed. "I'm sorry, father, but yes, Ashbourne killed the recruit, Bradley Owens. I saw the body."

A slow pained expression washed over Crassus' face. On the other hand, a smirk grew on Kaladin's lips. "I knew it. I told you, Lord Chairman, the Ashbourne boy was not to be trusted. His father sent him here to weaken the riders."

Ayr lurched forward in his seat. "If I wanted to weaken the riders, don't you think I would have killed someone higher than just a lowly recruit? Someone like you perhaps, Kaladin."

A loud boisterous laugh came from Kaladin, echoed by Gundrag over him. "Boy! You think that you could kill me? Gundrag would rip both you and Azura to pieces before you had chance to slip a blade between my shoulder blades."

Ayr raised his hands slowly and put them on the table as he glared at Kaladin. "You wouldn't know. I haven't tried, Major."

Kaladin continued to laugh; however, his tone was softer this time. His fist clenched beside him. "An Ashbourne's already tried to kill me once. I think I'll live. What challenge would the rebel king's pup present?"

A snarl escaped Ayr's lips and a wave of anger washed over him. He pushed up from the table, ready to charge at Kaladin. Nobody else in the room moved as Crassus raised his hand, each of his fingers spread out.

A roar filled the room, coming from both him and Baindussa. "Sit! I did not release you, Ashbourne!"

As Crassus spoke, Ayr felt a cold chill overtake his entire body all at once, like the aftershock was coming back with a vengeance. This magic was stronger, and Ayr wanted nothing more than to sink back into the chair, defeated. He fought against the magic, feeling that his temples were going to explode. Cold sweats were breaking out all over his body, and Ayr was unable to do anything to contain them. He wanted to scratch, he wanted to crawl around on the floor, but even as he felt Azura enter his mind to try and calm him, Ayr realized she was not having any effect on him.

Rider!

What is happening to me?

Crassus is powered by Baindussa. He is one of the strongest magic wielders in the Commonwealth. We cannot compete!

Help me, Azura!

He is too strong rider! I can't resist him! He will break me!

"Sit, Ashbourne!"

Rider!

At last, Ayr gave up. He felt like his mind was breaking in two, even with Azura's support. Ayr let go of his magic and let the rush of power overwhelm him. He let out a loud sigh of pain as he sank back into the chair. Crassus lowered himself back into his seat, shaking his head. He lowered his hand as he sat and then glanced over his shoulder at Kaladin.

"If this boy threatens you again, Kaladin, you have permission to end his life." Kaladin nodded as Crassus turned back to face Ayr with a frown on his face. "There's something about you that I can't quite put my finger on. You're as powerful as your uncle. It would be a shame to see that talent go to waste."

"Then don't waste it." Ayr was rubbing his temple trying to remain calm.

Crassus leaned forward again. "I'm afraid you've left us no choice, Ashbourne. You've killed a rider and tried to resist a probe. Major, how many void cells are occupied at this moment?"

Kaladin was quick with his answer. "None of them, sir. There will be plenty of room for the boy and his dragon."

If Ayr could have leapt to his feet, he would have. "Void cell? Where are you sending me? Why are you sending Azura?"

"If the rider is imprisoned, the dragon is as well. There will be no contact between the two of you for the foreseeable future. You can sit and contemplate your actions whilst we investigate the death of Bradley Owens and what Dalton Ashbourne returning to the world with a dragon means."

Ayr gasped, his mouth hanging wide open. The effects of Crassus' magic were still hanging over him. They were washing away, but ever so slowly. Ayr tried to turn in his seat to look at Elanor who was silent, just shaking her head.

"Father, you're making the wrong decision. Ashbourne would not cross me."

Crassus turned his head and touched Draxion behind his head again. "What have you got for me? Can you see Ashbourne's fate?"

Draxion raised her head slowly and nestled down into Crassus' hand. "No, Crassus. I cannot see anything about his future yet. It is still unclear."

"For everyone's safety, I would like to move both Ashbourne and Azura into a void cell for the time being. Elanor, I need you to investigate the elder dragon. Take however many riders you need to destroy it."

"Is that a smart idea, father? I'm not sure that seeking out the elder dragon right now, even with as many riders as we can muster would be feasible. We need to recall riders from across the world to deal with it. I'd like to request some time to study it."

Crassus frowned again, but Draxion slid down from her roost. "I think that is a reasonable request, Crassus. Elder dragons are not something we should take lightly."

Crassus frowned and gestured at Kaladin, calling him to the front. Kaladin grunted and pushed himself off the column. He strode across the room and made his way through the gap in the desk. He cracked his knuckles as he sneered down at Ayr. Kaladin approached Ayr and placed his hand on his shoulder.

"Come on, Ashbourne. Time to get up. Don't make this any harder than it needs to be."

Don't fight him, rider.

I can't, even if I wanted to.

Kaladin was waiting for any sign of hostile movement from Ayr. It was almost as if he was egging him on to attack him. Ayr glanced at Elanor who sat back in her chair, unable to do anything. What could she do? Move against the Lord Chairman of the Obelisk? Moving as slowly as he could, Ayr rose from his seat, with his head lowered. Elanor looked up at him with sadness in her eyes.

"You'll be out soon enough. I'll get this sorted. Just bear with me. The void cell will be rough. Just meditate and you'll get through it!"

"I know."

Gundrag was now moving as well. Kaladin could only contain Ayr. The larger purple dragon moved over the desk and cut between Evor and Azura. His proximity made Azura shrink away. Even if she wanted to, she would not be able to overpower the giant on her own. Ayr wasn't moving fast enough for Kaladin's liking, and he was pulled violently. Ayr almost stumbled off his feet, but for all of his flaws, Kaladin kept him steady.

"Come on Ashbourne. I'll take you to your new home."

"Elanor." Crassus was speaking again. "Stay a while. I'd like to speak to you alone, please."

"Yes, father."

FIVE

Everything is going to be fine rider.

How can you say that? We're being transported towards a jail cell. What are they going to do to us?

Nothing, just remain calm.

Ayr was still being pushed through the Obelisk. He had never been this far into the depths of the enormous structure. No light filled the corridors apart from the few braziers that were scattered along the hallways. Kaladin's footsteps echoed in Ayr's ears as they walked, feeling like a weight bearing down upon him. Not even Azura could help him. He could barely feel where she was.

Where are you, Azura?

I'm at the top of the Obelisk. I can see everything. Gundrag is taking me to a void cell for dragons.

What's going to happen in the void cell?

It will stop us from communicating with each other. Void cells block all magic going in and out of them.

That sounds like torture. I have not been without you since we were bonded.

Just do what Elanor told you to do. You will get through this, rider.

Are you going to be okay?

Yes, rider. Practice your thoughtfulness and we will succeed. I am almost at my cell. I will not be able to speak to you anymore, rider. Good luck.

Azura! Wait!

For the first time since he had called her to him, Ayr's mind was completely silent. There was no buzz and no feeling that Azura was nearby. An emptiness filled Ayr, one that he felt hard to describe. It felt like a wave of despair that sucked the soul from his body. Kaladin's footsteps continued to echo in his ears, the only thing that kept him pushing forward.

They were nearing the end of a corridor, one that did not have a door at the other side. Instead, every few feet that they walked past was an empty black pit from the ceiling to the floor. Kaladin kept pushing Ayr forward until they reached the last of the pits in the wall. Kaladin was rough, holding Ayr by the collar. He turned to face one of the pits and pushed Ayr forward again.

"In you go, Ashbourne."

Ayr turned and laughed softly. "I'm not going in there."

He was pushed again, now only inches away from the pit. "Azura has been put in her cell, there's nobody coming to save you, Ashbourne. Go in, or I'll throw your corpse in there instead."

Ayr gulped. With his back to Kaladin, there was no position that he could fight out of. If he had been smarter, he may have been able to fight Kaladin before his back was against the wall. Unfortunately, he also had more than just himself to think about. With another shove, Ayr could not push back anymore. He took a step and pushed into the blackness of the void cell.

It felt like a liquid that enshrouded him completely, sticking to his body. There was a coolness to it, however it felt damp, and clouded his brain. Ayr wanted to back out, but there was a force pulling him forwards, further into the cell. He took what only seemed like half a dozen steps and then could no longer walk forward. Ayr heard the sound of a gate slamming shut behind him, and he tried to turn, but was suspended in place.

"Good luck in there, Ashbourne. Don't try to escape. The void cell will stop any magic that you try and use. Without access to Azura, you're going to struggle."

"Wow, thanks for the words of encouragement."

Kaladin sniggered and started to walk away. "Oh, and Ashbourne, one more thing. If by some miracle you do manage to get out, there will be guards waiting for you. So please, try your luck."

No further word was spoken between the two of them as Kaladin's footsteps started to fade from earshot. As soon as he was gone, Ayr began struggling against his bonds. There was nothing holding him from moving, but he felt sluggish and immobile regardless. He tried to turn back towards where he had just walked in but was unable to complete the motion. Panic was starting to set in. Ayr shook violently, to see if there was any way that he could free himself. His legs were beginning to feel weak. The more he moved, the weaker he became.

Time continued to slip away from Ayr. Without Azura or any connection to the outside world, he was unsure of just how much time was passing. It felt like he had been trapped for no time at all, but at the same time, the exhaustion and the emptiness of the cell made it feel like it had been days. Ayr slumped as much as he could, trying to conserve energy, but it had no effect. He kept slowly spinning in the cell, unable to move freely. Knowing that his physical efforts were only tiring him out, Ayr wanted to try a different approach.

His fingers bent slowly under the pressure of the cell, and he almost managed to close his hands. He had no Azura to draw on, and no way of accessing her immense magical reserve, but he would try nonetheless. Ayr tightened his fist and felt the magic surging through his body. Whether it was the void cell around him, or the lack of Azura, no sooner than it had surged through him it fizzled out.

Not wanting to be deterred, Ayr tried again, summoning the magic into his fist. This time, he managed to hold it for a few seconds later before it fizzled out as his first attempt. Ayr jolted involuntarily, as a sharp pain zapped through his body. Ayr groaned, unable to identify the source of the pain, but it was clear that he should stop producing magic, especially without assistance.

Azura. Azura. Azura

Unbroken silence filled his ears. Ayr grumbled again, unable to reach her. Since he had bonded with her, he had taken her for granted. Azura never left him, constantly in his head steering his thoughts or providing him with clarity. Now that there was this silence, combined with his immobility, Ayr was beginning to lose his mind. Any situation he had been in, Azura had been with him. It felt like an itch that he could not scratch square in the middle of his back that was running up and down his spine.

The scratch was slowly eating away at his mind. As he continued to rotate, there was nothing that Ayr could do to stop it. He sighed, and closed his eyes again, remembering what Elanor had told him. Ayr tried to relax as much as possible, much like he had done outside Zenender's Ranch. If he could channel his energy, perhaps he could slip through a crack in the void cell and call Azura to him. He slipped into a rhythm and more time passed before a voice broke his concentration.

"Are you alright, Ashbourne? Ashbourne!"

Ayr gasped. He wasn't hearing things. "Elanor? Elanor! What are you doing here? Aren't you supposed to be going after the elder dragon? How long has it been?"

Elanor's laugh came through the void cell. "You haven't been meditating, have you, Ashbourne?"

"How could you tell?"

"If you had, you wouldn't care about the amount of time you've been in here. You're predictable, Ashbourne. I knew you would not follow my instructions."

Ayr sighed. "Can't you let me out?"

"No. Kaladin needs to be the one to do that."

"I miss her already. Everything feels so closed off, and I feel so alone. There's a part of me missing."

"I hope I never have to go through that pain."

"It's torture."

Elanor clicked her tongue. "I know, that's why I told you to meditate. Focus on something positive."

Ayr sighed again. "I don't have anything to be positive about, Elanor."

He heard a soft change in Elanor's voice. She must have only been on the other side of the black liquid that kept him in place. "I haven't forgotten last night, you know."

A shiver that wasn't from the void cell ran down Ayr's spine. It felt like eons since they had shared their first kiss under the moonlight in the mountains to the sounds of Evor and Azura's love making. He remembered the warmth of her lips against his and how they had held each other by the fire as Evor and Azura had roared in the background.

"If it wasn't for this cage, Elanor, I'd have you already."

"Careful, Ashbourne. I know our dragons are promised to each other, but there's a very good reason why you're locked in this cage."

Ayr drew in another deep breath and sighed. Up until this point, Azura had been the only other being occupying his mind, but now it was Elanor. All he wanted to do was to stretch out and find her in his arms. This emotion also clearly was not driven by the dragon. "She misses him. She longs for his touch."

"And we long for yours, Ashbourne."

Another shiver shot down his back. "Then set me free."

"If I could, I would. I'd rather have you out there hunting Dalton Ashbourne than half a dozen other riders."

Ayr raised an eyebrow even though Elanor could not see it. "Why me?"

Elanor scoffed. "It's always good to have a meat shield, Ashbourne."

"Right, so I have no other value to you?"

"Do you really think that I would have taken you on as my student if you did not? You've already sorted out someone that was going to be a problem for the Commonwealth in the future in Owens."

"Great, so you can use me to murder your enemies."

Elanor laughed. "I didn't say that. But I just came to check on you, Ashbourne. You should seriously consider meditating. You won't be able to move much until Kaladin unlocks the cell, and I don't imagine that will be until the trial happens."

"Trial? What trial?"

"Your trial for killing Owens. That's what my father wanted to speak to me about. Since you're not longer in the Seminary of Fire, unless it's deemed as absolutely necessary, killing Owens will get you booted from the Obelisk. I can make a defence case for you, but it will take time. If the jury finds you guilty, you will also have to face Owens' dragon, Bersos, in a trial by combat."

"You can't be serious! He's huge! Azura wouldn't even be able to fight him alone."

"You'll have your sword and access to any magic that you can conjure. I didn't say that the trial by combat would be easy. It's a punishment - usually one given to someone who has wronged a dragon."

Ayr wanted to kick the ground. "What are my chances of not being found guilty?"

"Slim, but I want you to survive. Nobody has to know that I've helped you."

"How exactly are you going to help me fight a dragon?"

"I've slain a few in my time, Ashbourne. I happen to have some tricks up my sleeve."

Ayr laughed gently. "Great. Well, I'm glad I've got you in my corner. Let's just hope it doesn't come to that. Bersos is not a small dragon after all."

"No, he's not." Ayr could almost hear Elanor shaking her head. "But even giants fall. Anyway, I need to get going. I just came to check on you. Do you remember how to meditate?"

Ayr rolled his eyes. "Of course. It's not a skill that I could easily forget. I called Azura to me in only a few days."

"Excellent, so you should be able to keep yourself occupied without me then?"

"That might be a stretch. How long are you going to be?"

"Hard to say. I could be gone for a week or a month. Your father has eluded us for twenty years, give or take. As for Sinibad, that's a whole different story."

Ayr groaned. "So, I guess that Azura and I will just be stuck here until you've completed your investigation. I'm glad that I'll have nothing to do in that time."

"Just stay put Ashbourne. You won't know how long has passed. I'll have you out of here in no time."

SIX

He's ungrateful. He should be glad that Crassus did not squash his head like a bug.

He's frustrated, Evor. There's nothing he can do. You and I would be no different if we were in that situation.

It has been days, Elanor. Nothing seems to be getting better. I would not go much longer without being able to speak to my promised.

What do you do when you don't have her to talk to?

Evor snorted. *I talk to you. We are wasting precious days. She should be free so that she may soar the skies with me.*

All in due time, Evor.

So, what is your plan today, Elanor? Yesterday and the day before was research. Is it due to be the same again today?

Yes, of course. I won't rest until I have found the information that I am looking for.

Your concern is well founded, but you and I both know that information on elder dragons is rare. Information on Dalton Ashbourne is even rarer.

I need to find it. If I can also find a way to keep Ashbourne out of Bersos' clutches, we might be making progress.

You can call him Ayr at any point, Elanor.

It doesn't feel right. I still don't trust him completely. I know he's bonded with Azura, but I know you feel it too.

Yes, but it is up to us to guide him. I can sense your feelings, Elanor. But we cannot turn our back on Azura, despite who her rider is.

I made an oath, the same as you, Evor.

Elanor cut the communication with Evor and refocused on her surroundings. She was moving quickly through the halls just below where the void cells were. There was nothing for her to feel in the cells, so she moved on towards her destination. Evor was already on top of the Obelisk where Azura sat in her void cell.

With a growing pit of anger in the back of her mind, and a staunch walk to match, now with a full belly, Elanor made her way towards the library. Realistically, she should not have left it, but she still needed to eat, sleep and spend time with Evor. Despite being almost as old as she was, the dragon was much like a child, unable to go too long without attention from her. It was part of the sacrifice of being a rider, having another living being connected to her for life. As long as they weren't separated by too great of a distance or locked in a void cell, everything would be fine. The torture that Ashbourne and Azura would be going through was unimaginable, but at least Azura was being kept company.

Elanor stormed into the library. There were half a dozen other riders, most of whom she knew on sight were already moving amongst the shelves. Each of them seemed content, slowly browsing through the wealth of knowledge before her. So far, the last two days had seen her research attempts bear no fruit and she was getting sick of waiting. Elanor leaned across the front counter, tapping her fingers on the marble tabletop as she waited for the librarian to appear.

He took his time, finally appearing from between the furthest row of bookshelves. The librarian was old, and he mimicked the other man that managed the knowledge within this room, Norman. A shiver ran down Elanor's spine as she had remembered how flirtatious she had been with the mutilated skeleton. Thankfully today, she would not need to seduce this librarian, nor was he mutilated, having all of his limbs and digits. A dragon rested on his shoulder, a small black and green assistant, that helped him go about his work.

"Ah, Lady Sunfire. Norman warned me that you might come in today. He may or may not have taken the day off sick as a result."

Elanor shook her head, glaring at the frail man. "Lazurus, don't mess me around today. Norman has been unable to provide me with the answers I seek the past two days and your dragons have proven less than useful. Have you found any information on the elder dragon, Sinibad?"

Lazurus nodded slowly as he moved in behind the counter. His crimson robe caught on the corner of the desk as he rounded it and Elanor shook her head as he tried to free himself. Lazurus adjusted himself and made his way over to her.

"Sinibad is a name that I have not heard in a very long time, Elanor. I heard the rumours that this is the dragon that Dalton Ashbourne has at his command. Please tell me that Ashbourne does not have a dragon."

Elanor nodded. "It's true. I'm going to hunt it."

A pale wave of fear washed over Lazurus' face. "Chilijo save us!"

"Why? I know this elder dragon is enormous, but we can kill it."

"Give me a moment." Lazurus puffed out his lips and bent to retrieve something from underneath the table. He scrambled underneath the counter, the only thing visible to Elanor was his robed behind. Lazurus emerged a moment later, huffing with a heavy golden tome in his hands. "It took the dragons hours to find this last night."

Elanor placed her hand on it, glaring at the librarian unimpressed. "What's this, exactly?"

Lazurus raised an eyebrow as the dragon on his shoulder stood up on its hind legs. "This is what you've been searching for is it not? This is the book holding the information regarding the golden elder dragon, Sinibad."

"And what about Ashbourne?"

Lazurus looked confused. "What about Ashbourne? I've have sent requests to every library within the Commonwealth. With any luck, we may get a response back in a few days."

"A few days! How long do the dragons take to ferry a book back from Desacourt? Surely your assistants move faster than wyverns?"

Lazurus snorted. "You think that I just sent envoys to Desacourt? I thought you were smarter than this, Elanor. The records of Sinibad came from Desacourt, but the annals regarding Dalton Ashbourne were buried deep in a vault. We did not think that we would be needing them."

"Why would you not have gotten them out the moment I mentioned Dalton Ashbourne upon my return to the Obelisk?"

"These things take time, Lady Sunfire. I put the request in and sent the envoys out as soon as I heard. I can't do anything else for you I am afraid. It may take several days for the tome on Dalton Ashbourne to come back."

Elanor tightened her grip on the golden tome at her fingertips. She scowled at Lazurus before taking it off the counter. "Thank you for your time."

Lazurus bowed his head. "Anything for you, Lady Sunfire."

His eyes didn't leave Elanor's as she walked away. She could feel him following her until she had left his vision as she turned down the first row of bookshelves to the left. The only figures in sight now were the few draconic library assistants that glided overhead. Their wings beat slowly, able to hold their small bodies in the air without too much effort. They paid her no attention as she walked underneath them. They would only come when called.

The library was peaceful. Despite the other riders moving through the shelves, calling out requests from the dragon assistants above, there was a strange tranquillity in the library air. It made for a peaceful adventure anytime that Elanor wanted to come and read a book. How-ever, this time would not be so peaceful. The contents within her arms felt heavy, but she soon spotted an unoccupied table that had a chair with its back to the wall. From there, Elanor would be able to see anyone approaching her.

She crossed the room with a spark in her step, more than ready to throw the heavy golden tome on the table in front of her. It landed on the table with a loud dull thud that made another rider in a nearby shelf peer through the gap in the books. Once they say everything was fine, they returned to what they were doing. Elanor threw herself down in the chair and with a heavy sigh, flipped open the front page of the book.

Elanor frowned as she inspected the first page. Not that she expect-ed much, but she thought that there would be some kind of introduc-tory page, outlining the author and what qualifications they had. In-stead, she was greeted with white paper. Annoyed, Elanor flipped over the page to once again find it blank. Elanor began frantically flipping through the pages until she at last found an image that resembled the giant golden dragon she had seen in the cave.

The sketch was gorgeous, in full colour and appeared to be to scale. Elanor ran her thumb over the tiny black spot that would have represented a human on the page. Was that what she looked like to the dragon? Nothing more than an ant that could be squashed without a slither of effort? She shuddered at the thought of facing the beast again. Whilst she and Evor had faced an elder dragon before, that had cost the lives of many riders. Sinibad seemed even more indomitable.

Yet, when they had attempted to hunt the previous dragon, there had been an entire book of knowledge for the riders. Everything was listed from birthplace and hatchmates, but for Sinibad there was noth-ing. It was as if someone had previously ripped the pages out and had meticulously replaced the pages with blank ones. There was no information and what was there was nothing short of wanting. She knew just how big Sinibad was from looking at him. There had to be an explanation. Glancing up at the ceiling, Elanor spoke through her gritted teeth.

"Davari! I require assistance."

A moment later and the familiar draconic assistant broke from the sky and had landed on the table in front of her. He kept his wings curled up as he stalked around the tome that was as long as his body.

"Hello Lady Sunfire, is everything to your satisfaction?"

Elanor shut the book at his feet. "No, it's not. Where is all the information on the elder dragon I requested? This is not a finished book. There's no birth, no family lineage, no roosting sites. We are supposed to know."

Davari peered under the hardcover of the tome, attempting to read the pages. Elanor flicked open the book again to allow him to view it. With a careful precision, Davari flicked through the pages, his expression darkening with each page that he turned. Eventually when he was satisfied that he had seen enough he looked up at Elanor.

"This is absurd. Someone has altered this record!"

"Then what are you going to do about it."

Davari looked up at the ceiling. "Excuse me a moment, whilst I consult with the librarian."

In the blink of an eye, Davari was gone, lost somewhere up in the ceiling, no doubt zooming to wherever Lazurus was mulling around. Elanor sunk back in the chair, defeated. It had taken three days to get the information on this elder dragon and almost none of it was useful. What more did she have to do? It was not like Lazurus would know any better either. Who was in charge of quality control?

Elanor heard a deep laugh near her and looked up. It was no dragon, but instead, from behind one of the nearby bookshelves, Kaladin was emerging. He looked smug, like he knew a secret that Elanor did not. Elanor rolled her eyes at him.

"What do you want, Kaladin?"

"How's your research going, Elanor?"

"Why is it of any concern to you? It's not like the head of security at the Obelisk will be sent to hunt down an elder dragon."

"Can't I know what you're doing?"

"Kaladin, just because you and I used to fuck doesn't mean you're entitled to having me or any of my time. Evor has made you very unattractive since Azura has been bonded to Ashbourne. I don't know why exactly you're still trying."

Kaladin laughed softly. "You told me you loved me, Elanor. Or was that a lie as well?"

"You're old Kaladin. Surely there's another woman out there for you."

Kaladin snorted. "Any woman that did not die in the Ashbourne rebellion is far too young apart from you. I need someone with that experience."

"I guess you're out of luck then, Major. There might be a rider in the northern reaches if you go searching."

"My place is here, at the Obelisk. I know that Gundrag and Evor are not promised, but I'm sure once he rips out Azura's throat and Ashbourne dies, there won't be anything to stop you coming back to me."

Elanor scoffed and returned her eyes to the book. "We're done here."

Kaladin barked as he rammed both fists down on the table, jolting it forward. Elanor grunted as she was slammed back into the wall, the wooden edge of the table digging into her gut. She put her hands on the table, trying to push Kaladin back.

"We're done when I saw we're done. Why are you protecting the Ashbourne boy, Elanor?"

"Azura is promised to Evor! You know that, Kaladin. I have no other reason."

"If he turns on us, I won't hesitate to kill him."

Tears started to form in Elanor's eyes as she suffered under the strength of Kaladin who was still pushing against her. "Then don't give him a reason to. Azura is a special dragon. She will bring him in line."

"And what about his father?"

"Why do you think I'm here? This is the golden dragon that we saw."

Kaladin grunted and pushed against the table one more time. Elanor gasped as she felt her ribs almost crack under the pressure. She coughed and collapsed forward into the empty pages of the book. Elanor only allowed herself to take a breath before she forced herself up to face Kaladin.

"Is that all you have for me, Kaladin?"

Kaladin ran his hand across the table as if teasing her with it before gently tapping it. "I won't be as gentle next time, dear Elanor."

Through gritted teeth, Elanor laughed softly. "Ashbourne has more bite than you, Kaladin."

"We'll see how much bite he has when I make him swallow his own teeth."

Kaladin turned on his heel with a snarl that sounded like it came from Gundrag and disappeared back behind the bookshelves. Ensuring that he was gone, Elanor finally allowed herself to breathe properly again. She needed to get Ashbourne out of that void cell somehow.

SEVEN

This book was worthless to her. There was no point in sitting here reading through the rest of the book. It would sit here in the library until she needed it again, if she needed it again. Fuming, Elanor closed the book, slamming the cover shut against the cream pages. She stood up from the table and placed the book underneath her arm before storming from the quiet recluse of the library, through the rows of leather-bound books back towards the front counter where Lazurus stood speaking to his assistant.

He spotted Elanor and stood up straight. "Ah, Lady Elanor, is everything to your satisfaction?"

The book was coming at his face before he finished the question. "Fucking useless!"

Elanor didn't stop to hear his excuses and continued to storm out of the library. Her ribs were still throbbing with pain as a result of Kaladin's attack. With her frustration running rampart through her mind, she finally let Evor into her head. It was better that he had been kept out of the confrontation with Kaladin.

I saw the whole thing, Elanor. Are you alright?

I'm fine, Evor. Kaladin is becoming more and more of a child as the days go past.

I can speak to Gundrag on your behalf if you wish.

No, no, there's no need. The sooner my father calls this trial for Ashbourne, the better. We need closure and we need to move on. I'd rather have him and Azura by our side if we need to face down Sinibad or Dalton Ashbourne again.

For what purpose, Elanor? Azura is small and can barely hold her own in a fight. The same as the boy.

Leverage, Evor. Do you really think that Dalton Ashbourne would strike down his own son straight away?

No… But Major Kaladin has a point. What if Ashbourne does turn on us?

We can't let that happen. You have a hold on Azura, do you not?

She is mine, as promised when we were hatched. Considering the hold, I have on her, she is likely to keep Ashbourne tethered to us. Clear your mind of future problems. Get our promised out of their cells and see Ashbourne through his trial. I will tend to Azura.

Elanor drew in a deep breath, setting her sights set on her new goal. Three days would have been enough time to call Owens' parents to the Obelisk from most places within the Commonwealth, so long as they came by dragon back. With Evor still inside her head, however timid and quiet. Elanor charged through the hallways of the Obelisk, heading back towards her father's chambers. She had not been here since Ashbourne was taken to the void cell, but now was the time. She wanted him for the elder dragon hunt.

Elanor approached the corridor that housed the safe entrance to the Lord Chairman's chambers and found both Kaiser and Kaladin in the doorway. She frowned, but as she rounded the corner, she could see that they were speaking with a male and a female. They were older and of a natural life span. It was clear that they were the parents of Bradley Owens. They disappeared into the elevator before Elanor had walked halfway down the corridor.

When she reached the elevator, she waited for a moment before the door reset itself. She followed the cross motion across her chest and the door slid open. Elanor willed for it to hurry, not wanting to miss out on anything that the Owens' family would say. Where was Bersos? Had he been summoned by Crassus?

Eager to find out just what was happening inside the Lord Chairman's chambers, Elanor burst out of the elevator the moment the door opened and strode across the courtyard underneath the watchful gaze of Baindussa. She waved up at the dragon, and he raised his head slowly. However, Kaladin, Kaiser and the Owens' parents were crossing the courtyard. Gundrag stood nearby as a watchful sentry and with that, the group's entry to the chambers was granted. Elanor quickened her pace to ensure that she would not be left alone, as Evor was still with Azura.

Do you need me, Elanor?

No, Evor. I will be fine. Keep tending to the little one.

As you command, Elanor. Good luck.

Elanor managed to catch up with Gundrag before he slinked inside the chamber walls. She was underneath the tip of his tail, masking her figure from Baindussa. She scoffed to herself as the giant emerald dragon reared his head. The guardian could hardly tell friend from foe and this was testament to that. The downside of her father still caring for his blind dragon.

Despite catching up to Gundrag, the dragon quickly left her behind. It did not matter, as Elanor was inside. The second door was being opened by Kaiser, and Elanor waited until they were over the threshold before continuing. She could already see Crassus, seated behind his desk, with Draxion draped over his shoulders, and a midnight blue dragon standing over both of them like a silent guardian. Bersos.

Crassus rose from his chair and got the proceedings underway, gesturing for the parents to sit. They appeared to do as they were told, but as they did so, both Kaiser and Kaladin were moving again. Kaiser was moving around behind the desk, closer to Bersos, whilst Kaladin had turned on his heel and was now coming towards her. He smiled as he approached.

"Elanor, good to see you didn't want to miss out on the fun."

"What are you doing, Kaladin?"

"Going to collect Ashbourne. Your father has deemed that it was time he faced trial."

"Already?" Elanor flung out her arm trying to stop him from moving past her.

Kaladin smirked as he moved past her, treating her no differently than if she was an ant in his path. "Perhaps if you had spent more time preparing him for what was about to come, you wouldn't be in this situation, Elanor. I hope that book on the elder dragon had everything you were looking for."

"You can't do this, it's not time yet!"

Kaladin continued to shove past her as she tried to stop him. He completely removed her arm from his grip as he shrugged her off. "It's done. The boy's parents are here, as is his dragon who can verify the attack. Why wait?"

Elanor groaned as Kaladin stormed off into the outside world. Short of ramming her sword into his back, there was nothing she could do to stop him. Frustrated, Elanor bundled her fists and stormed into the Chairman's chambers, where he was addressing his two guests.

"I must deeply apologise for your son's death. I know you were quite proud that he had bonded with a dragon and passed his trials."

Owens' father leaned forward at the desk. "Yes, so then why was he killed if it was outside the Seminary of Fire?"

Elanor quickly cut over the top of him. "Excuse me, Lord Chairman. But what the fuck is this? Are you starting the trial of my student without letting me know?"

Owens' parents spun in their seats as Crassus shook his head at her. "Not the time, Elanor."

Elanor put her foot down. "No, this is exactly the time. You're accusing my student of murdering another student. You're going to bring him out of the void cell, and you had full intention of having the trial private without any defence present. Do you want to tell the parents what their ungrateful shit of a child tried to do? How he attacked my student in the library after dark."

Crassus continued to shake his head. "I've already told you, this is not the time, Elanor!"

Elanor stormed forward and placed her hands on either one of the chairs. "If you don't want to hear what I have to say then this is not a trial. You're choosing to convict Ashbourne regardless."

Crassus nodded slowly at her. "That's correct. I intend to strip his dragon from him as well."

"Do you have any idea who that dragon is? That's Azura. She was supposed to be mine. Do you remember? Then she passed on me in favour of Evor who she is promised to. What happens if you strip that dragon from her rider? Evor is the last of his bloodline. He needs her fully capable so that they can fulfill their promise to each other."

Crassus sat down again and snorted. "You should have taught her rider how to act in polite society. His punishment is already decided. He killed another rider."

Smoke poured down on them from above, and Elanor glanced up to see Bersos looming over them. The midnight blue dragon had not moved from his position at the back of the room, carefully watching over the proceedings. He spoke with a loud, yet calm hiss, one that Elanor could hear venom dripping from. "He killed my rider, Crassus. I would have revenge."

"Your rider went to attack another rider within the confides of the library. If your rider was a better fighter, we would not be having this conversation. You are angry and are in mourning because of what happened. What if it had happened to Evor, or Azura?"

More smoke shot out of Bersos' snout. "That is not my concern. Neither of them are of my bloodline, nor is Azura a suitable match. Lord Chairman, why do you humour your daughter? I would have my revenge, sooner rather than later."

"And you shall have it, Bersos."

"No! You can't do this. Father, please I beg you. Think about Azura. Think about Evor's bloodline!"

"It is done!" Crassus waved his hand in the air as if dismissing her. "Ayr Ashbourne will be taken to the Amphitheatre where he will face Bersos in a trial by combat. This will be no quarter given. Bersos will feast on the bones of Ashbourne."

"When does the trial by combat begin?"

Crassus smirked at her. "Kaladin takes him to the Amphitheatre now. His end draws near. We will have Azura above the arena watching his demise."

Bersos grumbled, something that sounded halfway between happiness and contentment. "If you will excuse me, Lord Chairman, I must ready myself to feast on the human."

Bersos stretched his neck out as he stepped over the table and made his way towards the entrance of the chambers. Apart from the dragon's loud footsteps there was an uneasy silence that filled the room as he exited. Shaking her head, Elanor had no choice but to follow him.

Evor, is Gundrag with you yet?

Not yet, Elanor, but he is coming. Are they moving them to the Amphitheatre?

They are; and thank Chilijo that Azura is being made to watch. Without access to her, Ashbourne would struggle for magic.

Thank Chilijo indeed. I will begin advising Azura of what she needs to do to help him succeed.

I don't know if even with Azura's help he can do it. Bersos is no longer a small dragon, Evor.

Yet he is inexperienced. With Azura's guidance, Ashbourne will be able to make something happen.

For both of our sakes, I hope so.

Here comes Gundrag now.

There's nothing you can do for Azura. Ensure that she is let out of the void cell properly. Best of luck.

Elanor was almost already outside of the chambers when she saw Baindussa's claw drop down from above. The dragon rarely, if even moved from his roost, only to eat and perhaps to sleep. Whilst Crassus dealt with business, he'd remain in the one place, on guard, ensuring that he was not disturbed. Elanor glanced up at Baindussa as she walked underneath him and quickly made her way back into the Obelisk once again. She needed to find Kaladin, and with him Ashbourne. Elanor shook her head. No, there'd be no point in trying to speak to him in Kaladin's presence.

Evor, come to me.

What about Azura?

There's nothing you can do for her. We know where she is going. Gundrag is not going to kill her today.

As you wish, Lady Elanor.

Elanor closed her eyes as she stood in the courtyard, focusing on what Evor could see. He launched into the air, moving away from the void cell that was attached to the roof of the Obelisk. Unlike the cells designed for humans, the dragon void cells appeared to be nothing more than swirling black holes, removed from reality. She saw Gundrag move underneath Evor and with a sigh of relief, she could hear his wings approaching. Elanor opened her eyes and saw him angling down towards the courtyard.

Retrieving her mask from her pocket, she pulled it over her head with a deep sigh. Evor landed in front of her with an earth-shattering thud. He lowered his body to the ground, allowing Elanor an easier passage onto his back. Once she was in place, Evor looked back at her and let out a huff of his own.

I can sense your fear, Elanor. They will be fine.

EIGHT

Ayr jolted from his slumber as he felt a coarse hand grip him around the back of his throat. Before he had any time to protest or struggle against the new force, he could feel himself being pulled back involuntarily. Unable to move and unable to struggle against whatever was pulling him. There was a silver lining, however. The darkness of the void cell was now growing brighter and for the first time in what felt like months, Ayr took a step.

Despite his muscles having been upright for so long, there was no cramping or exhaustion. He had gotten used to the suspended state that he had been in. Now that light was filtering back into his eyes, Ayr tried to rub them but found he still could not move his arms. His legs were slowly coming back to him, and he was now making the steps himself.

Ayr kept blinking as more light entered his eyes, the sudden shift catching him off guard. With one final pull, he was flung free from the void cell and back into reality. The rough hand that grabbed him still had not let go. Ayr was flung backwards, unable to stand up on his own. He crashed to the floor as his feet were taken out from under him, his head falling dangerously close to the cold tiles beneath. Ayr blinked again and saw none other than Kaladin standing over him.

"Get up you guttershite!"

A boot came, striking him in the stomach. Ayr groaned as the pain radiated through him. He crumpled up, trying to get away from the strike. Kaladin brought his boot forward again, but instead of lashing out with another vicious kick, Kaladin held back at the last second and laughed.

"Come on, Ashbourne. Stop being pathetic. It's time for your trial."

Kaladin's iron grip settled on his shoulder. There would be no escaping from the larger man. Ayr was powerless to resist him as Kaladin picked him up with one muscular arm. In an instance he was at a standing base, with Kaladin still very much in control of him.

"My trial? I didn't realise that I had already been found guilty. Do I not get a chance to defend myself?"

"Nope. Unlucky. Now come on. We've got someone that wants to see you."

Kaladin pushed him forward again, and with nowhere else to go, Ayr complied. He walked with the ever-looming presence of Kaladin over his shoulders. If he ran, Kaladin would no doubt catch him. The head of security knew these corridors like the back of his hand. They walked until they reached a corridor that filtered light in from outside. The light at the end of the corridor was suddenly covered in darkness.

An all too familiar purple giant stepped across their path, his taloned foot crashing down onto the courtyard outside. There was no turning back as Gundrag loomed before him. The massive purple dragon lowered his head and huffed at Ayr, smoke exuding from his nostrils.

"Long time, no see, Ashbourne. Glad you could join us."

"It's not like I had a choice."

Kaladin laughed heartedly behind him. "No, you did not. Get in his claw."

Ayr turned around only to receive another palm square in his back. He staggered forward as Gundrag raised his paw enough to allow Ayr to stand under it. With no choice but to walk into the creature's grasp, Ayr held his breath, waiting for the worst to happen. Instead of Gundrag's claw closing around him like a vice, the dragon carefully scooped Ayr off his feet.

"Don't think about trying to escape unless you want to fall to your death, Ashbourne."

A moment later, with only the smallest glimpse into the outside world, Ayr felt Gundrag take off. The force was nothing like being on the back of the dragon, but he still felt rocked. Ayr had nowhere to move unless he wanted to be crushed by Gundrag and he had no idea where the dragon was going. The flight lasted only a few minutes before Gundrag was coming into land again.

The dragon slowed, and Ayr still could not see where he was. Gundrag also had not landed yet. Gundrag's descent was slow and before he came to a stop, Ayr was falling towards the ground. His arms splayed out as he tried to grab onto Gundrag, but the fall was short and violent. Ayr hit the ground and pain shot through his body. He gasped for air as he stared at the sky above him. Gundrag stared down at him. If the dragon wanted to send his fiery hot breath towards Ayr there would be nothing he could do. Ayr continued to lay on his back, trying to move. He coughed and spluttered as the warm sun beat down on his face.

There was a wall in front of his feet that reminded him of the void cell. However, instead of being all-encompassing, it reached to the point where Gundrag dropped him from. As he looked around, he could see that he was in a cage with the other three walls nothing more than steel beams that he could not slip through to escape into the outside world. Tall dark rock walls as high as the cage itself.

Ayr groaned as he slowly rolled over. Nothing felt broken, but his entire body ached. Sucking in a deep breath of air, he pushed himself up off the ground. Each inch of movement was an effort, and he struggled to get himself to a vertical base. Taking another gasp of air, he tried to push himself to his feet again, but slumped face first into the dirt.

Rider!

Azura!

I can feel your anguish and pain. Let me help you.

No, Azura I need to do this.

Do you know what they're making you do? You have to fight Bersos. Let me help you. I will give you my strength. I will not need it.

As she was speaking, Ayr felt an all too familiar surge of energy washing over him. It was calming and as he continued to breathe deeply, he could feel more of her magical power pushing into his system. As the moments passed by, Ayr was beginning to feel more alive as the soreness left his body. Finally, he had enough strength to push himself up off the ground and into a squat.

Rider. She comes.

Ayr heard footsteps approaching as he glanced up. He still had one hand on the ground clenched in a fist. As the footsteps neared, Ayr was delighted to see that it was none other than Elanor. Ayr felt a rush of emotion come over him as she came into view. Was it from Azura? Either way, he was grateful to see her. Perhaps she was his ticket out of here.

"Elanor! What are you doing here?"

"I came to see you, Ashbourne. Did Azura tell you what your task is?" Ayr nodded in response. "Then you know what you need to do, don't you?"

Ayr scampered over to the cell wall. "I can't fight a dragon on my own, even with Azura's power. Where am I?"

Elanor shook her head. "Where you are is not important. It's the Amphitheatre where we hold all entertainment activities. I told you; they're giving you a sword and you're allowed to use whatever magic you know. I'm sorry you've had no time to prepare."

"Can I use Azura?"

Elanor nodded and squatted down to his height, inching closer to the cell. "Did Gundrag drop you in here? There's no way that Kaladin would have put you on his back."

"Gundrag carried me here, yes."

"So, you didn't see what you're in for then? I don't imagine the view from inside his claws was a pleasant one. You've got a labyrinth out there. The Amphitheatre is usually a rocky, built-up maze perfect for dragons to stalk their prey in. Bersos will hunt you."

Ayr clenched his fist. "I'm ready, but why are you helping me, exactly?"

"I don't want you to die, Ashbourne."

"I don't want to die either. I have too much to live for. Azura, you."

Elanor shook her head, a smirk coming to her lips. "You don't mean that, Ashbourne. That's Azura speaking through you."

Ayr glanced down at the dirt floor at his feet. There was no extra wave of emotion from Azura surging through him. "No, it isn't."

Elanor snaked her hand through the gap in the steel bars. Her fingers found his as they traced around the ground, and reacting to her touch, Ayr closed his gently around hers. He raised his eyes to meet hers through the bars.

"I shouldn't trust you, but I find myself unable to control myself."

Ayr looked down at Elanor's hand that was now entwined with his. "You don't have to."

He tightened his grip and pulled her forward into the steel. Elanor let out a little yelp, but otherwise didn't resist. Ayr pushed his head against the bar as he pulled Elanor towards him. Their lips met in a warm touch that was reminiscent of their first kiss on the night that they had spent in the wilderness. Ayr longed for the kiss, trying to get deeper, pulling Elanor tighter in his arms. The steel bars intruded on their space and there was little he could do. After what seemed like no time at all, Elanor broke the embrace.

"I did not know you had that fire in you, Ashbourne."

"I'm not going to die today."

Elanor raised her gaze and glanced towards the sky. Ayr followed her eyes towards the sky. His mouth opened slightly. From the Obelisk it appeared that dozens, if not hundreds of dragons were descending from the sky, coming into land around them. Due to the overhang of the cell, and the surrounding rocky walls, Ayr could only see their descent so far.

"Looks like they're getting a big crowd in." Elanor clicked her tongue.

"What for?"

"Do you really think that word isn't spreading about what's going to happen? How many people in the Commonwealth do you think want to witness the demise of the son of Dalton Ashbourne?"

Ayr shrugged. "Yeah, you're right. "What's the best way to kill a dragon?"

"Stab it through the head if you can. You're going to need to get lucky."

Ayr puffed out his lips and an uneasy grin curled his lips. Sarcasm was the only defence mechanism here. "Great. Got to get close to his mouth. Well, this will be a piece of cake."

"Be careful, don't take any unnecessary risks."

Elanor pressed herself against the bars and pulled Ayr to her. This time they lingered for longer. If only she could have been inside the bars with him. This time he was the one that broke the embrace.

"Good luck, Ayr. Use Azura, she can help you and help you find your strength."

"Ayr?" He raised an eyebrow. "That's the second time now."

Elanor winked at him as she pulled away. "Maybe if you're lucky there'll be a third time. Go and kill that dragon."

She walked away from the cage, and still silence began to fill Ayr's immediate surroundings once again. All he could do was watch as dragons dropped from the sky. With Elanor gone, Azura began to come back into his mind. She was nothing more than the ever-soothing presence that he was growing to love. Ayr slumped against the far wall of the cell as he let her into his mind. With Azura pushing him gently, he sat down to conserve his strength.

More and more dragons fell from the sky, all of them entering the Amphitheatre overhead. The flapping of wings was filling his ears and as Ayr brought his legs across his body to sit cross legged. He heard a sound from behind the black wall. He wasn't sure what it was, the audio distorted and unclear, but what followed was a rapturous roar from both riders and dragons alike.

Get ready to make your entrance, rider.

There was another short dialogue from whoever was inside the Amphitheatre, followed by another thunderous roar. Ayr continued to breathe deeply, waiting for whatever was about to happen. Azura flooded his mind with visions of what was happening in the Amphitheatre outside. Bersos was waiting for him, with Azura's vantage point being somewhere high above the floor. If she was suspended or in a cage, she would be unable to help him. The roar was dying down and Ayr felt the heat from a new light enter his cell.

Ayr opened his eyes with care and a whole new world was now open to him. It was just as Elanor had described. The Amphitheatre rose up into a sky-like a stairway to the gods of old, with tiered seating for both riders and dragons to gather around where the action would be taking place. Ayr squinted as he tried to count the individual riders, but there were simply too many.

The terrain inside of the Amphitheatre was as tiered as the seats surrounding it. Level with Ayr was what appeared to be a deep cavern that ran into the ground underneath the seats. The ravine rose all the way up to the base of the seating in the distance. Rocky outcrops and otherwise barren terrain littered the surface. None of it would serve to make for a good escape; if Bersos was hunting him, there would be nowhere to hide. Ayr could make out a box approximately halfway up in the seating. In the box, whilst there was no Baindussa lurking nearby, there was certainly Draxion along with both Kaladin and Crassus. Ayr shook his head up at them.

As he stared at the box, a small black dragon, no larger than a cat was cutting across from the seating towards him. The dragon was struggling to maintain altitude and it was easy for Ayr to see why. Clutched in the dragon's claws was a sword longer than its body and more than likely just as heavy. The dragon continued to maintain altitude but was quickly being dragged down. It reached Ayr and dropped the sword at his feet before flying off.

Crassus stood from his seat, gesturing to the crowd. "Ayr Ashbourne! You have been found guilty of murder and have therefore been sentenced to a trial by combat. Bersos! Come forward!"

For Crassus to have been that loud, there was no doubt that he had used magic to amplify his voice. But that was not Ayr's main concern. As Crassus spoke, a rumbling rolled out from the dark ravine in front of Ayr.

Emerging with a formidable presence from the depths of the ravine before him was none other than Bersos, the dragon cloaked in scales of deep midnight blue. Smoke curled and twisted like ethereal tendrils from his expansive nostrils, casting a smoky haze that mingled with the surrounding air. The dragon's eyes glowed with an intense luminescence, a stark contrast to the dark, glossy sheen of his colossal body, making his appearance both majestic and terrifying.

He loomed over Ayr like a massive shadow, though even his immense form was dwarfed by the towering walls of the ravine. His eyes glowed with an intense, piercing gaze, as if they could see straight into Ayr's very soul. The air crackled with tension, for although Bersos was not yet within striking range, the threat was palpable. All it would take was a single, fiery torrent from his gaping maw to reduce everything to ashes and bring the battle to a swift, devastating end.

However, Ayr had a feeling with the amount of theatrics that had gone into getting him this far, Crassus did not want his time to come to an end so soon. With another sigh, Ayr took a step forward and reached for the sword that was at his feet. He picked it up, careful not to take his eyes off Bersos in case he wanted to make a move. When Ayr was back in a standing position, a loud horn sounded overhead.

NINE

Ayr groaned. The sword they had given him was blunt. It was clear that they wanted for Bersos to win. The dragon's life was more valuable than his. What was he compared to a dragon? Ayr shook his head and began to assess his options. He felt far too exposed here; the dragon would be able to come out from the ravine and swallow him without a second thought. The Amphitheatre had plenty of options available to him.Still, Azura was pushing him towards the ravine. A roar erupted from the ravine and Bersos started towards him.

Are you crazy?

He's large, rider, that will be your best chance of success. You can force him into a narrow area of the underground.

How far back does it go?

Far enough that I can't get into it. Now run!

Where was she? It was clear that she could see the Amphitheatre from the vision that she had sent Ayr, but she was nowhere in sight. Regardless, Ayr surged forward with the sword in hand. As he took his first step, he could see Bersos rising from the ravine even more. Ayr was closing the distance between himself and the ravine, but Bersos being as large as he was stood in the way.

Gritting his teeth, Ayr rose up to his full height, not wanting to be intimidated by the blue dragon. Bersos grinned down at him as fire started to fill his mouth. Thinking that Ayr was within striking range, Bersos shot forward like a striking serpent. Ayr anticipated the movement and held back, causing Bersos to miss him by inches.

Ayr dashed past Bersos' head before he could strike again. As he ran forward, Bersos' foot came crashing down beside him. Ayr narrowly avoided the dragon's tectonic weight. Whatever information Azura was feeding him from her elevated position was working. Bersos wrapped around like a snake, his tail lashing out in a sidelong arc at Ayr. Ayr ducked under it, dropping into a slide on his knees. A roar erupted from the crowd, the spectators all buying into the action below.

"Come here, Ashbourne!" Bersos roared in annoyance.

Ayr did not look back. He imagined the dragon's angry monstrous head behind him. Instead, he launched himself into the ravine, regardless of the consequences. Azura would not lead him astray. His feet pounded against the dirt as the cliff walls on either side of him closed in. Azura was right. Even she would have a hard time manoeuvring in here. The ground was uneven, slowing Ayr down, but he continued to navigate it.

He could hear the angry footsteps of Bersos behind him. As Ayr leapt over the first pile of scree, he wondered why Bersos had not set him on fire already. The dragon was nearing the ravine, and once again would be within striking distance. Curiosity finally got the better of Ayr despite the warning from Azura. He turned over his shoulder and saw Bersos arcing up with more fire spilling from his jaws.

Rider! Duck!

For not the first time today, Ayr fell forward. As he did, a heat more intense than he had ever felt before filled the sky above him. He could feel the hairs on the back of his neck melting and with his free left hand he tried to cover them. The stream of heat dissipated as fast as it had come over him, and he was grateful for the reprieve.

Get up! Run!

Bersos roared overhead again, and Ayr pushed himself up from the dirt, almost leaving the sword behind him. The ground which was more uneven here with more piled up rock for Ayr to scramble over. Bersos was still coming after him, but as he moved past the next pile of rocks, Ayr started to see more narrow pathways breaking off the further he went. He could feel Bersos behind him, lining up again to unleash another torrent of fire.

Ayr ducked into the first crack he found, praying that it would be large enough for him to fit down. Thankfully, as he turned the corner, he found that it was not only wide enough for him, but long enough to hopefully get away from Bersos and his fiery breath. The path kept angling down and away from where he currently was. Bersos was hot on his trail and Ayr turned to see the dragon rearing his head.

"You can't outrun me forever, Ashbourne!"

Fire spilled from his jaws again and Ayr used every second that he could to create separation between the two of them. He was descending the path at a rapid pace, but would it be far enough away. He heard Bersos breathe in and hit the ground once again, diving forward. Due to the differences in elevation the heat from the fire stream this time was not as bad, some distance above Ayr's head. It shot past him, lighting up the ravine in an orange and red glow. Knowing that he was safe for the moment, Ayr focused on the blunt sword in his hand. If he was going to kill Bersos it needed to be more than just a blunt object.

With a grunt, Ayr pushed himself onto his knees and laid the sword before him. He focused on the blunt edge of the sword and extended his palm out towards it. Ayr began to move his hand along the blade, ensuring that he was hovering over every inch of it. Behind him, Bersos was growing frustrated, scraping at the side of the ravine to widen it.

"Ashbourne!"

Ayr ignored him, continuing to apply magic to the sword. As he moved his hand along it, the blade continued to get sharper along the edge, just as he envisioned. However, there was one voice that he could hear and not drown out as easily as Bersos.'

That's not a spell that Elanor or I taught you!

Now isn't the time, Azura! Is there more than one way out of here?

To your left.

Ayr double checked his sword, ensuring that it was sharp enough. Satisfied that it was, he raised his hands and clutched the sword in his right. Bersos had vanished from the gap that he had originally stood watch over and Ayr was left with a strange pit in his stomach. If he could have kept his eyes on the dragon, he would not have been as nervous, but now that Bersos could drop on him out of nowhere.

Ayr heeded Azura's directions and quickly found the pathway that she was talking about. It was a similar width to the last passage but with almost none of the height between the ground and the blue sky above. Vines hung down between the gap in the rock, almost like a canopy that blotted out the sky even more. The sound of Bersos' footsteps approaching filled the air again, but now they were coming from above with small pebbles of dirt falling in front of him.

"I can smell you Ashbourne!"

Ayr kept moving, keeping one eye on the path in front of him and the other above him. More black and sharp rocks continued to fall around him, and he quickened his pace. Azura was no longer speaking to him, but her presence still filled his body with magic. Ayr kept one fist closed, beginning to coil the magic around it, ready to lash out as soon as he saw Bersos.

The rumbling above his head continued as he ran along the path, and once he reached the end, Ayr waited for direction from Azura. She nudged him towards the left path towards what must have been the centre of the Amphitheatre. The ravine above him was more open with a view of some of the seats in the grandstand high above. The crowd roared with excitement and Ayr heard the sound of wingbeats coming near. He lifted his head and saw Bersos flying above him.

Bersos roared; from his adjusted body movements, it was clear that he had spotted his opponent. Bersos soared ahead of him, circled back around, and then landed in front of Ayr. He was so wide that he could stand on either side of the gap. The dragon sneered down at Ayr before he took a step into the open space.

Using his left paw, Bersos slid down the rocky surface of the cliffs and came to land in front of Ayr. There was no fire in his mouth and Ayr cocked his hand, ready to unleash the torrent of magic that was still coiled around his fist. It glowed with an aura that reflected Azura's scales when the sunlight caught it. She was still feeding him, and his hunger was nearly satisfied.

Rider! What are you doing?

What must be done!

Bersos growled and took another step forward, his head inching closer to Ayr, ready to open his mouth and swallow him whole. Feeling that the dragon was drawing too close for comfort, Ayr slowly raised his arm. Bersos laughed at him, clearly thinking it was a feeble attempt to ward him off.

"What's this, Ashbourne? A feeble spell to frighten me? Something that your master has taught you in the last few weeks?"

For the first time since the horn had sounded, Ayr smirked up at Bersos. "You wish."

Bersos surged forward, his mouth opening, ready to swallow him whole. Ayr drew himself up to his full height, not wanting to be intimidated by Bersos. The dragon roared as Ayr directed all of the magic in his body towards him. The burst of energy was stronger than anything Ayr had ever felt before, like a phantom had rushed through his body. Ayr jerked backwards, almost falling to the ground.

Rider! Get up! What are you doing? How did you know how to cast a netting spell?

I read it in a book!

No, you did not.

I need to sustain it! Give me magic! Quickly!

Despite the spell being effective, Bersos was still coming towards him at a slower pace. Ayr grinned; his trap had worked just as intended. The netting spell spread out like a spider's web, but it was not large enough to entirely trap Bersos. His tail lashed around his body with the ferocity of a whirlwind, each movement powerful and swift. Yet, despite its relentless energy, the tail's chaotic dance was largely halted by the shimmering barrier of Ayr's spell. He smirked, watching it come nowhere near him, but as he took a step forward, Bersos battered the net again and this time his tail broke through.

Ayr was too late in raising his sword. The tip of Bersos' tail smashed through the net and struck him across the chest. The net had done it's job, holding Bersos back, but Ayr still recoiled. He touched his hand to his chest and felt the deep gash that was now hot with fresh blood. However, that was not his most pressing concern. Bersos was pulling his head back at full speed. Ayr tried to refocus his energy on the spell as it slipped away from him, but it was too late. The spell was crumbling around Bersos as he began to thrash in anger.

"Release me Ashbourne! Release me from this prison!"

Ayr was running out of time. Adrenaline surged through his veins, but it was not enough to keep the pain in check. He needed to end this quickly. Some of the energy from Azura lingered inside Ayr, like a bubble rising up from his chest. Knowing that he was hurt, Azura continued to support him. Sucking in a deep breath, Ayr rose to his full height and let out a roar that echoed Azura's as she channelled power into him. Ayr charged towards Bersos, who was breaking through his spell and almost moving at full pace again.

Ayr raised his arm again as he ran forward, expelling what energy remained. The existing spell flourished with the extra power, slowing Bersos again. However, despite being slowed, the dragon was still more than dangerous. He was crazy, but he had to get close enough to strike a killing blow. With another shout, Ayr ran up onto Bersos who was low enough to the ground. The dragon was large enough that Ayr found easy footholds, little more than steps on his scales.

Bersos opened his mouth, but it was not fast enough to catch Ayr who moved with fast feet over the reptile's nose. He rode the momentum like a shockwave, racing towards one of the few places that he knew this sword could penetrate. He was so close, but he could feel Bersos turning underneath his feet with each step that he took. There was no avoiding the dragon, staring straight into his angry yellow eye.

Ayr roared, Azura copying his sound, filling his mind with rage. He would not lose her. With one final bound, Ayr clambered onto Bersos' cheekbone, just within reach of his eye. Ayr raised the sword as Bersos began to utter the beginnings of a roar. Ayr thrust the sword into the fleshy eye socket just above him. Bersos' roar started with vigour as Ayr clung on for dear life. The sword was in just enough as Bersos started swinging his head. The dragon was in agony, but Ayr needed to end it.

Azura! Please!

How, rider?

The magic flowed through him quickly and Ayr used it to help him shimmy the sword further into Bersos' eye. All it needed was a little encouragement. The dragon continued to roar and the more he threw his head around, the closer Ayr's blade was getting to his brain. As Ayr went to adjust the sword at the wrong time, he felt his hand slip. His stomach rose in his throat as Bersos turned his head the other way, causing Ayr's remaining hand to slip from the hilt.

He was mid gasp as his hand fell away from the hilt. Ayr hit the ground, faster than in the time it took him to blink. For the second time within a matter of hours, he had crashed into the earth. Ayr was slow to rise, his body afire with pain. Bersos continued to stomp and flail about. As he did, one of Bersos' claws came down into Ayr's leg. The claw went straight through his flesh, tearing through the muscle. Ayr let out a bloodcurdling scream as Bersos retracted the claw, spinning in circles as he went.

His hands sprung straight to the wound, a gaping hole in the side of his thigh that left his bone exposed. If it had been more in the centre of his leg, Ayr would have lost it. Azura's magic was still flowing into his body, but what was her limit? Bersos was toying with him. The pain of his torn thigh kept Ayr on the ground, breathing heavily as he tried to work through it. He held his right hand over the injury, not that it was doing much. Ayr groaned as he tried to stand; his leg did not want to cooperate. He put all of his weight onto the other leg, and with a scream, finally pushed himself to a standing base.

The spell he had cast on the sword was still doing it what he wanted it to do. The more that Bersos flailed around, the more the sword dug into his head. Ayr could only watch as the sword was nearing the hilt, burying its way into Bersos' eye. Blood pooled around the wound and the sword finally was almost lost apart from the hilt. Bersos thrashed his head to either side twice more before collapsing onto his side.

It was almost as if he had fallen into Ayr's now defunct spell and was falling in slow motion. With a thunderous roar, Bersos smashed his head into the cliff behind him and finally fell silent. His body slumped to the ground and Ayr stared, unable to believe his eyes. Smoke swirled above his nostrils as the flame was dying from within him. Ayr grunted as he started towards the still body of Bersos.

He half expected the dragon to spring back to life to strike at him again. As Ayr limped towards Bersos, his thigh slowed him down, his right leg shaky and weak. It was clear that Azura was keeping him upright. He could feel her magic all but holding his wound together, the need for her tears was prevalent. With each shaky step that he took, the sound of anticipation from the Amphitheatre above grew stronger.

Ayr reached Bersos and collapsed beside the dragon. He laughed as he realised that his presence against the dragon was not bothering him. Bersos must have been dead. Taking a moment to recover, Ayr groaned as he tried to pull himself up the dragon towards his eye. The blood was already everywhere on Bersos' face. Hooking his fingers underneath the scales one at a time, Ayr climbed up onto Bersos which was easier now that the dragon was unmoving.

He clambered under to where the hilt of the sword sat inside Bersos' eye. His hands were covered in the dragon's red blood, but it was not the prize that he wanted. As Ayr reached the sword, he glanced down into Bersos' eye. There was no light in the eye anymore, no anger, just a glassy, empty vessel. Wanting the sword with him, in case of more danger, Ayr slowly pulled it from Bersos with a loud squelch.

Ayr gritted his teeth as he ripped the sword out fully. He glanced up at the Amphitheatre that was growing louder by the second. Ayr slid back down Bersos and made his way back down the ravine he had first stepped into. Each step was a mission, one that he could only complete with Azura's assistance. Whilst hanging onto his thigh, Ayr pushed through the pain, using the sword as a crutch. If it was not for Azura and her magic, he would have collapsed. As he rose out of the ravine, a hushed silence fell over the Amphitheatre. He limped towards where Crassus, Kaladin and Elanor were all waiting, watching the proceedings in the small box.

Azura, can I have a little more of your strength?

What are you doing now, rider?

Addressing Crassus.

You should not. How are you still able to handle the transference of energy?

Azura, please. Just one more favour.

Rider, how do you know all this magic we have not yet learned?

I will tell you later, Azura.

Ayr felt her reluctance in surrendering more of her magical reserve. He raised his index finger to his throat and pressed against it. He felt his ears pop, which could only mean that this particular spell had been a success. He keeled over, almost falling forward into the dirt, keeping his finger to his throat as he allowed his voice to disperse over the stunned Amphitheatre.

"I killed the recruit Owens! And I killed his dragon! What have you got next for me, Lord Chairman? I swore fealty to the Seminary, the Obelisk, the Commonwealth and most importantly, my dragon, yet I am treated unjustly! I have passed your test, Crassus. Release me, as was the agreement!"

Crassus sat forward in his seat. Behind him, Ayr could make out Elanor in the box, her eyes fixed firmly upon him. He wanted to smile, but something told him that Crassus would not take kindly to the gesture. Kaladin leaned in towards Crassus and they exchanged several words before Crassus raised his hand, dismissing Kaladin. Kaladin moved away and Crassus rose to his feet.

He held out his arms, gesturing to the crowd, calling for silence. "Ayr Ashbourne, it would appear that you have won your trial by combat. Release his dragon and return them to the skies if he lives. There's nothing more for them here. Head back through the cage, Ashbourne."

TEN

Crassus slumped back in his chair in disgust. He kicked at the table that stood in front of him, sending it toppling over onto its side. With an angry snarl, Crassus snapped towards Elanor. "He is powerful enough to slay a dragon by himself. Did you know about this?"

Elanor tried to hide her smile as Crassus rounded on her. She stood to attention, keeping her eyes fixed upon the floor of the Amphitheatre where Ashbourne was limping back towards the cell. It was clear that he was hurt, and he needed Azura sooner rather than later to help him heal. Already, she could see the dragon assistants cutting at the ropes that held Azura suspended in place. Ashbourne had dropped his sword where he stood as he waited for the verdict from Crassus.

Elanor shook her head. "I suspected it when he summoned Azura to him in only a matter of days, but I did not think he would be anywhere near the level of competency of Dalton. That was incredible. Bersos is not a small dragon. For a human alone to defeat one, even with assistance from their dragon is rare."

Kaladin leaned in to whisper loudly in Crassus' ear. "He shouldn't have survived. How did he defeat a dragon like Bersos, even if he is only just a hatchling?"

Crassus raised his hands to underneath his chin and bit down on his bottom lip in annoyance. "Perhaps Elanor has taught him more than she has let on. A recruit that has been with us for that period of time should not have been able to do what he did."

Kaladin's angry gaze found her. "Well?"

How had he done it? Since returning from the cave with Sinibad and Dalton, they had spent no time together. He would not have learned anything in the void cell either. Was it all by Azura's guidance that he had managed to slay Bersos?

"I taught Ashbourne the basics. I will need to investigate further. Azura is powerful in her own right. If you'll allow me, I will put them to the test." She nodded down at Crassus. "Father, if you'll excuse me."

Crassus waved his hand at her with annoyance. "I expect your findings by tomorrow."

"It may take a little while longer to get to the bottom of this."

Kaladin sneered at her. "Find out, Lady Sunfire. Tomorrow."

Not one for formalities, Elanor returned the sneer and gave Kaladin a sloppy salute. She shook her head and exited the curator's box, leaving both Kaladin and her father behind. Once she left the box, Elanor could finally let her true feelings out. A rush of happiness came to her head as Evor filled her mind.

They are letting the little one out now.

Is she safe?

She is, but she is gravely concerned for Ashbourne.

Of course she is. He looks half dead. Bring her to the cage. She will need to heal him.

As you wish, Elanor.

With a renewed quickness in her step and a fresh smile on her face, Elanor made her way back down to the cage Ashbourne had been held in prior to the trial. The beating of wings resonated throughout the Amphitheatre, and she wondered how many dragons and riders would be disappointed in the result. All of them, she imagined. Elanor laughed to herself as she started down the narrow staircase that led to the underbelly of the Amphitheatre. She retraced her steps to where she had been only a short time ago, passing nobody in the dark depths of the enormous structure. Elanor's boots scuffed against the dirt with each step she took as she approached the cage.

Are you near, Elanor?

I am, is she there?

We are about to be.

The steel walls of the Amphitheatre were beginning to give way to the tall natural rocky ones that made up the actual arena. She was nearing the cell and could feel Evor's presence, quite literally on the other side of the wall. She smiled as she neared, and a few steps later, the steel bars came into view.

"That was incredible, Ayr! Oh, Chilijo!"

He was on the ground, laying down with his legs stretched out in front of him, with both Azura and Evor standing over him. Their shadows kept him out of any direct sunlight, Azura with her head lowered near his leg. Elanor had been at the Obelisk long enough and had seen plenty of gory wounds. This ranked up there with them. How had he been able to stand and climb his way back out of the pit. Was Azura really that strong?

"Ashbourne! Ayr! Ayr! Are you okay?"

Ayr raised his head slightly and gave her an unconvincing thumbs up. "Once Azura heals me I'll be fine."

"Can she still do that? It sounds like she expended a lot of energy for you to get over the top of Bersos."

Azura nodded and she lowered her head, turning it so that one of her eyes was directly over Ayr's wound. "Of course, I can heal this, Elanor. It may take some time. Growing back muscle is different than fixing a bone that is still in place."

All Elanor wanted to do was console Ayr. Dragon riding was not a risk-free business and Elanor had plenty of her own wounds as proof.

Thankfully, Evor had been able to heal each one, some with considerable time and effort. This would be one of those wounds. Growing back flesh and muscle was not easy, even for a dragon's tears.

Azura cooed as she tried to lower her head to Ayr's leg. "Elanor, I will need you to hold the rider down. I do not want to cause any more damage."

"Well, I need to wait for whoever has the key before I can get in there."

She pressed herself against the cage in case there was a chance that she could slip between the steel. As she stretched through the bars, she heard the jiggling clatter of keys behind her. Elanor turned and saw Kaladin trudging through the Amphitheatre behind her. He held the keys in his hand as they set on his belt.

"Do you need to get inside, Lady Sunfire? Have you got a dragon that you have wronged, perhaps? Like student, like teacher. Correct?"

"I'd prefer that Ashbourne be let out. He is my student, after all and my father gave you an instruction that I'd suggest you follow."

Kaladin shrugged. "He did, but he did not specify when. It could be before I set Gundrag loose in the Amphitheatre."

"And then you would have Azura to deal with."

Kaladin snorted and grinned at the smaller white dragon. "I don't think that she would be an issue."

"She's more than what she looks, Major." Ayr raised his head again. "And I've already killed one dragon today. I don't imagine you want me adding a second to my belt anytime soon."

With a grunt and a fumble at his belt, Kaladin grunted and removed the set of silver keys. He held them out, suspended in the air. "Set your boy free, Elanor. I'd suggest you keep him away from me unless you want us to come to blows. Just because he won a trial by combat does not mean anything in my eyes. His father still roams at large."

"Dalton Ashbourne will be brought to justice soon."

Kaladin sniggered as he took a step back. "Whatever you say, Lady Sunfire. Just return those to your father when you return to the Obelisk."

"That was stupid of you. What if I don't?"

"Then Gundrag and I will be hunting for you. Gundrag!"

As Gundrag's wingbeats filled the air, Elanor glanced down at the set of keys that she had just received. Kaladin had not made it easy on her. There was no description of what any of the keys were or what they unlocked. As the head of security, Kaladin would know, not that he wanted to be of assistance. Gundrag landed outside the Amphitheatre. Whilst Elanor could not see him, she could feel his presence. She kept fiddling with the keys until she found one that looked to be a similar size to the lock. There was no point in repositioning in the Amphitheatre to a place where Evor could land and take off safely. Even with the number of keys that were in her hands, Elanor would be faster.

She tried the first key which did not even fit in the lock. Shaking her head, Elanor shuffled through the keys again and found a smaller key. This one fit into the lock but did not turn it. Frustrated, Elanor found a similar key, and on this attempt, it actually worked. Relieved, Elanor flung the gate open and raced to Ayr's side. He was lying down with his head in his hands.

"I'm here, Ayr."

A smile came to his lips. "Ayr? That's new."

Elanor realised her mistake and rolled her eyes. "Oh, shut up. Let me hold your leg."

Ayr groaned as he tried to move it, but Elanor placed her hands on it at the knee. "Hold it still."

"Are you ready, rider?"

Ayr's only response was to nod as he closed his eyes. Azura lowered her head over the gaping wound. One by one, tears fell from her eye in an attempt to heal Ayr. Elanor watched as she knew the pain that Ayr would be going through. The dragon tears were cold at the best of times, undoubtedly making him feel like he had jumped headfirst into an ice bath. Ayr gritted his teeth and started to scratch his fingernails into his forehead. Elanor pushed down on his leg, keeping it in place. Azura had only placed a handful of tears on Ayr's leg, but Elanor could already see the change.

The muscles were tightening where they were exposed to the tears and the air around them. Otherwise, there was no change yet. Azura continued to pour more tears into the wound, and slowly, Elanor was beginning to see some changes as muscle growth began a moment later. Ayr continued to twitch, but there was nothing more that she could do for him. It was in the hands of the magic. In order to prevent the wound from any possible infection, Elanor lifted her hands off of Ayr's leg and began to unbutton her overcoat with a frown.

Ayr raised an eyebrow at her.

"We should cover it so nothing gets into your leg."

"Don't we need to treat it more?" Ayr groaned as he tried to raise his leg again.

"No, the tears will suffice. We need to get you back to the Obelisk though. You'll need to rest."

"I can feel it. It's not every day that you get to kill a dragon."

Elanor smiled down at him. "No, it is not. You did well today, Ayr. Azura, can you get him back to your chambers?"

Azura nodded in response at her underneath the shadow of Evor. "Of course, Elanor."

"Can you stand, Ashbourne?"

Ayr laughed and nodded. "After everything that we've been through, are you still going to call me that?"

Elanor laughed in return and smiled at him, extending her hand. Evor was standoffish, not wanting to give Elanor any wayward emotions, but he was still inherently proud of Azura's efforts. It was that pride that pushed Elanor over the edge. She took Ayr's hand in her own helped him to his feet; intentionally over pulling him into half a stuttered step towards her. Elanor caught him, stopping him from stumbling over.

Ayr pulled back. "Elanor. What are you doing?"

"You need support!"

"I can stand."

"Fine." Elanor let go of him and Ayr could not even take a step before he stumbled. He leaned forward into Elanor who caught him again. She laughed. "I thought you were good, Ashbourne?"

Ayr shook his head as he tried to stagger backwards. Elanor grabbed him and held him steady. Evor was silent overhead, urging her to take no action. Ayr was still reeling, his eyes telling Elanor that the story that he was not all there. He was not focused, but Ayr blinked and steadied himself, his eyes focusing on her lips. Elanor bit her lower lip as she took in the sight of him, his scent reeking of dragon's blood. Ayr stood only a little taller than she did, and he stooped down towards her. Was he being pushed by Azura?

They tightened their embrace as their lips met. Evor's emotions ran through her, not wanting her to push forward, but Elanor ignored her. Despite the sweat, blood and grime that she could feel on him, Ayr tasted salty. Considering what he had just done, by no stretch of the imagination was it a bad taste. Elanor revelled in it, leaning more into the kiss with her eyes closed. Not only were his lips soft, but there was a coarseness to his chin and a firmness that had not been there in their previous encounter. They held their embrace, and it felt like no time had passed as Ayr fell away.

Elanor caught him and pulled him back close to her. She could feel his heartbeat racing against her chest. "Azura, he needs you."

Azura bowed her head and put it against the ground so that Ayr could put his arm over it. Almost instantly, Elanor shook her head and pulled him off her. She was too big now to have Ayr cradled around her neck.

"Put your paw out, Azura. You'll have to carry him gently."

"I will be gentle, Elanor."

Elanor nodded as she clicked her tongue. "Good. I will come see you both later."

ELEVEN

yr groaned as he slowly opened his eyes. It was too early. His head was throbbing and the entirety of his right leg felt like it was on fire. He was in his own bed as the sun filtered in from the stained windows, yet it felt like he had not seen the sun in days. When he had fallen asleep, his leg had still been completely mutilated with only the smallest amount of muscle growing back. Now, it was almost completely healed. Where the chunk had been removed from his thigh, in its place was now a thick scar, as wide as his finger. What had Azura done to him?

Ayr breathed in, still feeling the effects of Azura's magical tears in the wound. Whilst the freezing pain was not as prevalent, it was clear that she had recently put more tears onto his leg. Strangely, Ayr was no longer in his uniform and had been dressed in nothing but his undergarments. Azura was far too big to be able to undress him with such precision, considering there was no clothing scattered around him.

Still breathing deeply, Ayr rolled over onto his side and sure Azura nestled beside him in the large open straw pit that was her bed. This morning, she was curled up in a ball, her wings folded neatly on her back. As she heard him stir, she raised her head to greet him with a warm smile.

"Good morning, rider. How are you feeling?"

Ayr laughed softly as he flopped back onto his back. "Can you tell?"

"The magic that I used was very powerful. It is not so easy to grow back a person from nothing. Even one as special as you."

Ayr rubbed his eyes with the palms of his hands. "How long have I been asleep?"

"Two days, rider."

"Two days?"

"Be calm. The Lady Elanor was here after you went to sleep and helped you change. Other than that, the outside world has passed us by."

Ayr grunted as he sat up and exhaled. "Did she say anything about the fight?"

Azura shook her head. "Nothing, she came and dressed you. She said that I should alert her once you awake."

"I see." Ayr placed his hand over his stomach as it started to rumble. "I should probably get up and get something to eat."

"That may be wise, rider."

Still groaning, Ayr pulled himself out of bed and headed to the dresser. He flung it open to find over half a dozen identical black uniforms waiting for him. Whatever one he must have worn in the Amphitheatre had either been replaced or disposed of. Pulling the jacket over his undergarments quickly, he heard Azura raise her head.

"I've been meaning to speak with you, rider." A shot of fear ran down Ayr's back like a trickle of water. "There is no need to be frightened."

"What did you want to talk about, Azura?"

" The skills you used in the Amphitheatre. Elanor did not teach you that magic. Did she?"

Ayr sighed, wondering when this question was going to come. He had expected it, but not this soon. "No, she did not. I know plenty of magic." He had finished putting on his jacket and was now pulling on his pants. A fresh pair of boots in his size also sat in the bottom of the dresser.

"If you can perform magic, why were you sent here and not to one of the mage schools within the Commonwealth?"

Ayr laughed with a light tone as he fastened his belt. "And have my talents wasted, Azura? My father sent me here so that I could bond with a dragon."

"I've heard the stories about your father. I know what he did to the Commonwealth. Did he send you here to finish what he started?"

Ayr sighed and left the boots in the dresser. He crossed the room to where Azura lay, her gaze apprehensive. Ayr cupped his hand to the side of her face. "I'm not here to make the same mistakes that he did. I want to forge my own legacy."

"That's what I am concerned about, rider."

Ayr removed his hand from her face. "What do you mean?"

"You're powerful, rider. That is abundantly obvious to me and now to everyone else inside the Commonwealth. The Lord Chairman will have sent letters to the Overlord and others in positions of status who have a vested interest in ensuring that Dalton Ashbourne does not attempt to overthrow them again. You did not need all of my power to complete those feats that you did against Bersos in the Amphitheatre. How do you know that magic?"

Ayr bowed his head. "My father taught me."

Now it was Azura's turn to pull away, both physically and mentally. "There was something dark in you that I could not see. Is that what you've been hiding from me? You must have discipline to be able to do that."

"I have not hidden anything from you, Azura, you just needed to go deeper. We are in this together."

"We are dragon and rider, but this is not something that I can keep secret. Even for you, rider." Azura lowered her gaze, her blue eyes searching deep within his soul. "I trusted you."

Ayr held his hands out. "You heard me did you not? In the cage?"

"I hear everything you say, rider."

"Then you would have heard me saying that I have too much to live for now. My father gave me no instructions, except to obtain a dragon. It is clear to me that he has become hostile towards me and, by proxy, you. Azura, you mean more than anything in the world to me and I will do anything to protect you."

Azura's gaze softened. "You would?"

Ayr nodded his confirmation. "Absolutely. You should have no reason to doubt me, Azura."

"Hmm. I have to consider what you've said, rider. Go and get yourself some food and then come back to me."

Ayr returned to the dresser and quickly pulled the boots onto his feet. They were a new pair, free of any grime or dirt. With a sigh, he grabbed the sword that sat in the sheath on top of the dresser and made his way towards the door. As he went to push on the handle, he turned back to look at Azura again. She was nestled back down to where she had previously been laying. Ayr closed the door behind him and silence filled his mind. Azura was zoning out as she returned to slumber. With another sigh, Ayr set off in the direction of the mess hall. There was nothing he could do for the time being, especially with no direction from Elanor. The halls at this time of day for whatever reason were almost empty. Had something happened in the past two days?

Ayr entered the mess hall unopposed and found it sparsely populated. There was only a total of four riders and their dragons, all watching over the riders as they ate. One by one, the riders looked up from the table. The closest rider glanced up at his dragon and something passed between them. Ayr sat down at the nearest point on the table that had any left-over food on it. He was famished, but with the looks he was receiving, he did not want to get any closer to the riders or their dragons.

Ayr dug into the food that sat in front of him, despite it being cold. There was ham and an arrangement of other scraps of meat, scattered amongst what few remnants of fruit were still littered across the table. He picked at them, swallowing each bite before picking something else to grab. There were no plates nearby and Ayr could not be bothered walking to the end of the hall to get one. As he ate, the hairs on the back of his neck rose. He glanced over his shoulder and saw the other riders now all staring at him. Two sat together, both burly, older men, easily in their late twenties.

They were bulkier and all dressed in their identical uniforms. Ayr's eyes met the one staring at him from underneath a mop of almost wet black hair.

"Is that him?"

The rider sitting beside him grunted as he stood up in a flash. "Yeah, that's him. Spitting image of his old man. Get him!"

Ayr dropped the grape that he was eating onto the table and flung his legs over the bench he sat on. The riders already had closed the distance and were almost upon him. Ayr was still nimble enough, but as he started towards the mess hall door, another rider cut him off. This fifth man was just as large as the others, the hint of a blackened tattoo on his wrist underneath the cuff of his jacket. With the width and seemingly overpowering strength of this rider there was no feasible way that Ayr would be able to squeeze past him.

"Yeah, this is Dalton's seed, alright. I'd know those eyes anywhere."

"If this is the right rider, Arthur, are we doing it?"

The man that had been identified smirked and cracked his knuckles. "Yep. Do him in."

Ayr had no time to defend himself as he was rocked by a clubbing blow to the back of the head. He staggered, almost folding completely underneath the strike. It felt like a hammer, but the sound of the meaty smack that filled his ears told him it was nothing more than a closed fist. Ayr tried to swing his fist back to meet his attacker but was interrupted by another strike in his side.

Ayr reached for his sword and was stopped by half a dozen grabbing hands, all trying to pin him in place. There was nothing he could do, except take the punishment as he writhed in pain. The other riders all towered over him, as their hands pummelled him from the sides. Blow after blow landed upon him from every angle, and eventually, Ayr was looking through one almost closed eye. He groaned as Arthur raised his hand, placing it under Ayr's chin, smirking at him.

"Send a message to your father, will you?"

"I don't speak to him."

Arthur's smirk widened. "You will once he sees what we'll do to you."

"Gentlemen!" Elanor's voice cracked across the room. "What the fuck do you think you're doing to my student?"

Ayr opened his eyes and saw Arthur's closed fist being held above his head. His wrist was being held by Elanor who was staring deftly at him, shaking his head.

"Lady Sunfire, we're conducting Commonwealth business. Ashbourne should not have walked out of the Amphitheatre alive."

"That's unfortunate that you feel that way, Arthur. But what is done is done. Release him or you will have to deal with me."

A moment passed between the two of them before Arthur's fist softened and became an open hand once again. There was a look of disgust on his face as he glared down at Ayr. Arthur signalled at the other riders and at long last, Ayr felt his limbs go limp. He sunk to the ground as he listened to the footsteps moving away from him as the riders left the room, their dragons not far behind.

Elanor tutted as she crouched down beside him. "Good to see you're awake, Ashbourne. I don't imagine that experience was pleasant for you."

She reached out tried to touch his face, but Ayr recoiled. Through his swollen eyes and cracked lips, Ayr grimaced at her.

"I don't know why I keep doing this. I'm keeping my head barely above water as it is. Sticking my neck out for you has no benefit to me whatsoever. Arthur and his colleagues are not to be trifled with. What did you do to provoke them?"

"I sat down and ate."

Elanor snorted. "They wouldn't have done anything unpro-voked." She then groaned and laughed softly. "Actually, who am I kidding. Yes, they would have. It was a good thing I stepped in then."

"I appreciate it."

Elanor chortled again, this time louder than the last. "Oh, you ap-preciate it? I'm glad that I've got some reassurance that I'm appreciated despite almost killing myself for you on multiple occasions!"

Ayr brushed his hands together and pushed off the ground, his bottom lip quivering. He held back tears and rubbed his face in frus-tration. He groaned and looked up at Elanor again. "It's just hard. I am trying to make my own path in this world, yet nobody can or will separate me from my father."

"Then you need to become better than he ever was."

Ayr felt sadness washing over him. "How?"

Elanor frowned for a moment and then smiled. "There has been no further word from my mother about the whereabouts of Dalton Ashbourne, but I have an idea. Pack your bags and clean yourself up. We're going to get out of here for a few days. It's clear that you need more training, and I don't think that remaining here is going to provide you with any benefit. Just make sure you bring a coat. I'll bring Evor to your room when we are ready."

TWELVE

Retreating to his room like an errant pup with his tail between his legs, Ayr finally woke Azura. She was immediately apologetic, not being there for him, even at a time when he should have been safe. With Azura now awake, the pain that Ayr felt was slowly going away.

I am so sorry, rider. I should have been there for you.

It's okay, Azura. I need to learn to deal with these problems on my own.

Rider, we are bonded. We are never alone anymore.

I know, but I need to be able to defend myself from those kinds of threats. I need to become more powerful.

You killed a dragon on your own, rider. You are more than powerful enough. Don't let yourself be ambushed next time. I won't be far away either. You are as much of my responsibility as I am yours.

Thanks for the advice, Azura. I'll be back soon.

With her inside his head, Ayr was now moving faster than before with his injuries subsiding. The attack by Arthur and the other riders had been fast and brutal, but nothing that was bothering him to the point of not being able to function. Thankfully, Elanor had stepped in before it got to that point. Ayr reached the door to his chambers and pushed it open gently, to find Azura waiting for him inside. Her bright blue eyes were all-consuming, staring into Ayr's soul, making him feel smaller than he already was.

"I'm sorry that happened to you, rider."

Ayr shrugged, unable to contain his disappointment. "She saved me. I'm fine now."

Azura's eyes matched his and her gaze softened. "You're still hurt. Rider, let me heal you. I heard what Elanor said. If we're going somewhere I need you to be in peak physical condition."

"Azura..."

"Come here, rider."

The compulsion was strong, and Ayr was powerless to resist her. He took one shaky step forward and was covered by her overwhelming power. Azura extended her neck and lowered it over Ayr. A solitary tear fell from her onto him, and the all too familiar freezing sensation washed over Ayr again. He was already beginning to feel rejuvenated, his soreness fading.

Azura cooed and moved away, returning to her straw bed in the middle of the room. She let out one of the loudest huffs that Ayr had ever heard, threatening to blow him over with a hurricane-like wind. Ayr regained his footing and made his way deeper into the chambers. What would Elanor want him to bring?

If Evor is correct Elanor intends to take us into the wilderness.
You will not need food. I can take care of that for you.
So, then I just need my riding equipment and your saddle.

Ayr walked further into the room, passing Azura's long, coiled body as she watched him. He made his way to the drawer and eagerly retrieved a large empty leather satchel from within. He crossed to the desk where his spell book sat waiting for him. Ayr packed it into his satchel and retrieved his sword laying on the desk beside it. He strapped it to his belt and puffed out his lips with a heavy sigh.

Ayr ducked down, opening the larger bottom drawer of the desk and withdrew another pouch that would slip in beside the spell book. This contained a small rucksack, that would fold out and provide him with a thin layer of comfort when sleeping on the ground. Once the rucksack was inside, there was little room left. It would only be enough for a change of clothes. Ayr went to the wardrobe again and pulled one vest and pair of pants from it.

There was a soft knock on the door. Ayr turned his head. "Was that you?"

Azura shook her head in return. "That was the door, rider."

"It can't be Elanor already, can it? We've barely had five minutes together. I'm not ready yet, are you?"

"I am always ready. You need to saddle me."

Ayr clicked his tongue. "Of course. I don't want to tear my legs up again, do I?"

Elanor knocked on the door again and Azura moved towards it. Ayr called her back with another click of his tongue. A few seconds passed before Elanor rapped on the door again.

"Ashbourne! I know you're in there. Are you ready?"

"Almost!"

"Open the door, we're coming in!"

Ayr sighed and crossed the room before unlocking the latch on the door. He didn't have time to step back before the door smacked him in the face. Ayr winced as his head vibrated as a result of the blow. He stepped away and Elanor pushed her way into the room.

"Oh shit, sorry, I didn't know you'd be right behind it."

"Well, I had to open it, didn't I?"

Elanor pouted at him. "Aww, poor baby. Do you need me to kiss it better?"

"That would be great if you could." Ayr grinned at her.

In response, Elanor rapped him over the head which only added to his pain. "We're in a hurry here. Don't you want to get out of here sooner rather than later? Is that satchel what you've packed?"

"Yes, of course. What else do I need?"

"You don't need anything else. Where we're going everything will be provided to us."

Ayr retrieved the spell book from within the satchel. "Not even this?"

Elanor's eyes lit up. "I'll give you credit, you're smart, Ashbourne, even if you've got a slight concussion. Doing what I told you to do. Anywhere we go that isn't into the mouth of an elder dragon could be a good learning opportunity." She narrowed her eyes at him in the next breath. "Something tells me you don't need it though, do you? Who are you trying to fool?"

Ayr froze. She had not forgotten his efforts in the Amphitheatre.

Azura, please don't throw me underneath the cart. She can't know the truth.

You should not be lying to your promised.

This is for both our sakes.

I understand, rider.

"Azura helped me. She understands more magic than I could. Without her I could not have defeated Bersos."

Elanor leaned back, assessing his answer. Part of Ayr made him feel like that she was not impressed. She glanced up at Azura. "Is this true?"

Ayr held his breath. He could feel Azura struggling with her answer, and he pushed her towards where he wanted her to go. Azura resisted at first, and then gave way, submitting to his will.

"Every word of it, Elanor."

Evor was not so easily convinced. His giant head poked through the door as he glowered at Azura. "Little one? Answer me."

Azura bowed her head and Ayr sensed fear rising from her. "It's true."

"So, we've got raw talent on our hands then." Elanor nodded her approval. "That means we have a lot to work with then. Are you two ready to go?"

"I just need to saddle Azura."

Elanor shook her head. "You've had how long? Hurry up!"

Azura already had the saddle in her mouth but was unable to strap it to herself. That would be Ayr's job. Over the last few months, he had gotten used to Azura growing and moved his body around hers, strapping the saddle securely onto her back. He didn't cause any discomfort to her, and within minutes, Azura was ready and safe to ride. Ayr patted her leg and Azura cooed. Elanor had been watching the entire process.

"Good. Now come on, we've got somewhere to be."

"Where are we going?"

Elanor smirked at him. "It's a surprise. Don't you want to find out?"

Elanor turned, swung onto Evor's leg, and began climbing up him. When Elanor was seated in her saddle, Evor took a step forward into the room and filled it entirely. He stepped across the room, past Azura and stood before the open windows, swishing his tail as if beckoning to her. Elanor pulled her mask out from her vest and pulled it over her head.

"Are you coming, little one?"

Rider, come on.

With his chest feeling lighter than before, and the prospect of flight just ahead, Ayr was eager to climb into his saddle. Evor turned and took another step out of the giant window that led to the outside sky before plummeting from view. Ayr could feel Azura's excitement building, as she made her way towards the window. He removed his mask from his vest. Seconds later, he was staring through the fabric of it.

Come on Azura!

In the next breath, Azura leapt into the air, following her promised. Ayr clung onto the handholds inside the saddle as Azura rocketed through the air, eager to catch up to the larger black dragon.

It was clear that Evor was in no hurry, his massive black wings moved at a quarter of the pace that they had when escaping from Dalton and Sinibad. Azura had to work hard to catch up, but within a matter of minutes, she drew level with her larger counterpart.

As Azura glanced at Evor, Ayr mirrored her gaze and found himself staring at Elanor. She leaned forward in the saddle. Evor began to edge ahead of them. Unable to read Elanor's face, it seemed that from her stance she was challenging them to a race. It would be no contest, but still fun.

Are you up for it?

I'm already racing him, rider.

Ayr laughed as he sunk forward into his saddle. There was nothing he could do apart from enjoy the ride. He kept stealing glances at Elanor who remained locked in on wherever their destination was. They quickly left the Obelisk behind, and the mountains that they had only retreated from days ago were now starting to take command in the foreground. Thankfully, Elanor was not leading them back towards Sinibad's lair, but rather to the east. It was not long until they had flown over the Seminary of Fire and the expansive plains.

The plains were once again bordered by gargantuan mountains on the other side, however, seemed much more forgiving than what had awaited them to the north. Azura flew wordlessly, following Evor's flight, almost matching him wingbeat for wingbeat. The mountains began to swallow them, and Ayr had no idea where Elanor and Evor were taking them. The afternoon sun was past its peak, causing the shadows of the mountains to grow longer.

Evor is slowing down, rider.

Excellent. I wonder what our destination is.

I have heard rumours of a place near here that may be where Elanor is going. It's said to be beautiful.

What is it? Where are we going?

They call it the Dragon's Gore. I have never seen it with my own eyes. We will discover it together, rider.

Evor has not shared it with you?

He wanted to keep it as a surprise.

Ayr looked ahead and and saw that Evor was indeed slowing down, Azura matched his movements. There was one sole mountain ahead of them, one that split a gulley between two higher peaks. Evor soared through the left-hand path while Azura took the right. As Azura came around the peak on the right, Ayr's jaw dropped underneath his mask.

The yellow glow of the sun illuminated a vast open area that was similar in size to the Seminary of Fire. However, rather than being covered by forests and grassy plains, this area was unlike anything he had seen before. The sunlight gave the area the illusion of being sunburnt, with nothing but sand and dust covering it. As they drew nearer, Ayr began to see different streaks of colour throughout the otherwise seemingly barren landscape.

They travelled further, and as the distance passed under the dragons' wings, Ayr's eyes widened as he beheld enormous dome-shaped structures erupting from the earth. They loomed in the landscape, a surreal sight of vibrant green, so flawlessly round that they seemed to defy nature itself, as if they were conjured by some powerful sorcery or forged by Chilijo himself. Evor was headed towards an area where many of them were gathered like a forest. They were far enough apart that Ayr could see the gaps between them, but close enough together to provide shade for one such as Evor.

Behind the forest was a body of water. Whether it was a large lake or part of an ocean, Ayr could not tell as Azura continued her descent. Evor landed heavily on the ground below them, the edge of his wings, grazing against the trees. They were unmoving, even against the massive weight of Evor as he made himself comfortable on the ground. Azura came down in front of him, her much smaller frame not touching the trees. Ayr lurched forward in his saddle as she landed.

Ayr glanced over at Elanor who was already looking at him. He saw the slight nod of her head as she removed her hands from the saddle and began dismounting from Evor. Knowing that she was getting off, Ayr mimicked her movements and climbed down from Azura. Ayr hit the ground first and pulled the mask from his face as he waited for her. A moment later, Elanor touched the ground and was removing her own mask.

"Welcome to the Dragon's Gore, you two."

Ayr raised an eyebrow. "The Dragon's Gore? What is this place?"

"This once was a battleground, many years ago in the first war. The violence here was so potent that it stained the trees for eternity."

"The trees?" Ayr turned to the nearest tree, staring at it, perplexed. "What's wrong with them?"

Elanor shook out her auburn hair and slid her sword from its sheath. She strode over to the tree before she raised her sword and jabbed it into the tree like it was a needle. Elanor pushed the blade in for a moment, before she withdrew it. Ayr was shocked to see it lathered in a liquid that looked like blood.

"They are called dracaena cinnabari, also known as the dragon's blood tree. The books say it was Chilijo himself that bled into the ground here and his blood is now the lifeblood of this area."

"How exactly does that work?"

Elanor wiped the sword free of the blood before placing it back in her sheath. She shrugged. "I was not around when the legends of old were forged. If I'm lucky enough, I might be able to see some forged in my lifetime."

"It's hard to believe that somewhere so beautiful was tainted by such a travesty."

"It is, but the land has healed for over a thousand years. I thought it would be smart for us to get away from the Obelisk for a few days."

Ayr was still curious and pressed her further. "So, what are we doing here?"

Elanor sighed and looked up at the dragon's blood trees around her. "You're a danger to yourself when you're in the Obelisk, Ayr, especially after everything that has transpired. I'm in no better situation either. This is something we can both use to our advantage."

"So, we come here to what exactly? Train? There's nothing here."

Elanor rolled her eyes. "You need to open your mind, Ashbourne. There's plenty here for us. Peace and quiet being first among them if you'd stop asking so many questions." She smiled and turned away from him. "Come on, there's plenty to do here."

THIRTEEN

*P*lenty *to do here?*

That is what Evor is telling me.

The larger black dragon was already leaning over Azura, his indomitable figure casting an even larger shadow over them than the trees. Ayr could feel Azura leaning into him, merely wanting to be in Evor's presence. Her vision was clouded, Evor clearly overpowering her emotions. She swayed between Evor and the large tree that Elanor was now moving underneath.

Are you okay, Azura?

Yes, rider. Evor and I will remain here. I am sure that Elanor wants to test you.

Test me?

Yes. Now go.

Azura nudged him to follow Elanor as she was swallowed by the trees. Without waiting around to be left behind, Ayr took off after Elanor, sprinting to catch up with her. As he caught her, Ayr wanted to reach out and grab Elanor's hand, but he pulled away at the last second. Thankfully, she did not turn and notice him.

The Dragon's Gore was a peculiar place, with twisted trees casting long shadows and eerie mist swirling at ankle height. As he wandered deeper into the area, the air seemed to thicken around him, and a chill crept up his spine. The rustling of unseen creatures in the underbrush made his heart race, and an inexplicable tingling began at the back of his neck, slowly spreading throughout his body. There was no influence from Azura, nor was Elanor displaying any signs of using magic. His abilities were still not where Dalton wanted them to be, but he had a chance to show Elanor what he knew.

It was clear that the area itself was full of magic. If the trees bled, what other secrets did this place hold? Ayr followed Elanor deeper into the Dragon's Gore underneath the shade of the larger dracaena cinnabari that grew out of the ground on either side of them. Underneath the shade of the dragon's blood trees, there was an array of colour as the undergrowth came to life.

There was no indication from the sky that the Dragon's Gore was filled with this much life and abundant colour, but as they moved underneath the trees, Ayr was more shocked by the second. Whilst the outside world of the Gore was mostly an orange glow that matched the sun, underneath the shade of the enormous trees was another world entirely.

There was still sand and dirt covering the ground, but as Ayr followed Elanor deeper into the forest, the white and brown covering was slowly changing colour. Green became the predominant colour of the floor; whether it was moss or grass, Ayr could not tell. Elanor was moving too quickly for him to stop and investigate further. Not that it mattered. He heard a roar overhead and looked up to see both Azura and Evor passing overhead through a gap in the trees.

Where are you going, Azura?

Evor is taking me somewhere. He says it will be beneficial for my flying. I will be back soon, rider. Focus on your training. Impress Elanor.

I will. Take care, Azura.

Another thunderous roar came from Evor; however it was already growing fainter as the dragons must have been vanishing somewhere on the horizon. With this roar, Elanor also looked up at the sky and smiled.

"They're adorable together."

Ayr smiled in response, though Elanor could not see it. Azura was filling his mind with images of Evor and all of the happy emotions that came along with it. They had a job to do, but Ayr more than welcomed the happiness that she was experiencing.

"I can feel it. She's telling me everything."

"I know, Evor is doing the same thing to me. If not, I'd assume something was wrong. There's a training ground not far from here. That's where they're going. It's a natural rock formation that dragons can use to help increase their manoeuvrability in the air. Since Azura is going to be a smaller dragon regardless, that will only help her if she ever has to fight against bigger ones."

"I get the feeling that all the manoeuvrability in the world won't help against Sinibad."

Elanor stopped walking and put her hands on her hips as she spun to face him. "You should have more faith in your dragon, you know. There's a reason why she chose you... and it's part of the reason why we came here."

Ayr folded his arms over his chest. "Why are we here then?"

A blue and orange butterfly floated in front of their faces; its wings gently carrying past them. It was unlike any that Ayr had ever seen before. With each wingbeat, specks of silver and gold showered the surrounding area. Ayr stood transfixed, watching as it flew past, rising towards the tops of the trees. The butterfly crested the tree and was gone from sight.

"The Dragon's Gore is a magical place, Ayr. I know you can feel it."

"I can feel something, but I did not realise that it was magic."

Elanor scoffed at him and grinned, her tongue running along the top row of her teeth. "Don't bullshit me, Ashbourne. Your skill with magic is evident, even if Azura was helping you. You know exactly what magic feels like. Come on."

Elanor turned back and started leading him down a gravel path between what appeared to be like two large split rocks on either side of it. The light was beginning to dim, as the trunk of an extremely large dragon's blood tree loomed overhead. The trunk itself thicker than Evor's body was tall, and Ayr could not make out the branches high above him, as they were blocked by the relatively smaller trees. The shade kept the area cool and, with limited lighting, gave it an ethereal atmosphere.

Ayr's body was tingling, but he was not sure if it was from excitement, the magic in the air, or Azura. He could sense the magic in the air, hanging heavily over him like a cloud, but it very well could have been a combination of all three. He knew Azura was contributing heavily to his mood, but this new and pristine area of the Dragon's Gore had drawn his eye as well. Even though it was shaded, towards the tops of the larger dragon's blood trees were what appeared to be orange lights.

They glowed like embers in a dying fire, some winking in and out of existence. From this far beneath them, Ayr could not make out what was making the light even whilst squinting.

"What are those lights, Elanor? Are they natural."

Elanor followed his finger towards where he was pointing. "Fireflies. They watch over this grove."

"Why does this grove need watching over?"

Now it was Elanor's turn to point. "They say that tree was the first to be planted here and it was planted by none other than Chilijo himself."

Ayr raised an eyebrow, skeptical of what he was hearing. "A dragon planted a giant tree in a magical wasteland. How is that possible?"

"Don't let anyone at the Obelisk hear you questioning Chilijo. That dragon is the reason why we exist."

Ayr laughed. "Or what? They'll beat me? What's new?"

Elanor stopped and knelt, her hands rummaging through one of the small shrubs that were right beside the path. Ayr heard leaves breaking and twigs snapping as she appeared to be gathering from it. Elanor finished foraging through the shrub and her hands reemerged with handfuls of kindling.

"What are you doing with that?"

"I'm not doing anything with it. You will be, Ashbourne. Come on."

They were nearing their destination. The path continued down into the grove a little further before it split into a fork. Elanor took the right path that angled slightly upwards towards a large flat moss-covered rock. Ayr followed Elanor until she stopped on the open surface. The dragon's blood trees loomed over them like silent sentries looming in the distance.

"What are we doing here?"

"What do you think, Ashbourne? I need to test you." Elanor placed the kindling she had in her hands on the ground and shrugged. "You're the magically gifted one between the two of us, after all."

Ayr snorted and squatted down beside the kindling, raising his hands towards it. "It seems self-explanatory. I just don't know if the spell will take hold or not."

"Evor is taking Azura away, so you won't be able to rely on her for her power. I want to see what you can do."

Azura.

Yes, rider?

What do I do? I don't want to show her my full capabilities, but I also don't want to lie to her.

I will not be able to help you. What does your heart say? You've unlocked something since we've been bonded together, and you know she will report back.

I can't hide it anymore.

Then be true to yourself, rider. Good luck.

Ayr inhaled, closing his eyes as he took a deep breath. The forest air was richer than it had ever smelt before, or was it because of the magic in the air? He opened his eyes to see Elanor staring at him. She clicked her fingers over his nose.

"Hello, Ashbourne. Are you with us?"

"Yes, Elanor. I'm just trying to focus."

The kindling was bundled appropriately in between them. Elanor had moulded it into a pinnacle like a normal campfire. The kindling looked wet, but this was clearly a test. Ayr readied his hands down over it, trying to focus on the energy he would need to control to keep the fire burning.

"Have you still got any contact with Azura?"

"Let me check." *Azura.*

Yes, rider? What is wrong?

Nothing. Don't tell Evor that we are conversing.

Why, rider? You should not be doing magic if you need my power to help you. She wants to see what you can do on your own.

I know, that's why I'm telling you. I can find you anywhere, Azura. Going away from me won't change that.

You can, but fine. I will not tell him. For you.

Thank you, Azura

"No, I cannot."

Elanor stood up. She folded her arms over her chest and frowned down at him. "That was a long time talking to her."

"Can you still talk to Evor?"

Elanor shook her head in response. "No, he has gone out of range."

"Exactly, I had to be thorough. You want to see what I can do with this, correct?"

Elanor gestured towards the kindling and raised an eyebrow. "Whenever you're ready."

Ayr breathed in again and felt the magic in the air around him. Creating fire was a simple enough spell, evident by the fact that Elanor had made him do it in the cave when he had first met her. What was she looking for this time? Sustainably and control? There was not enough kindling to keep the fire alight for any more than a few minutes, so he would need to use his energy to ensure that it did not burn all of the wood straight away. The spell snapped to life with a wave of his hand. Ayr willed the flitting flame into existence, using his magic to fuel the fire. It was a slow feed, much like a tap that had barely been turned on.

"I'm assuming you want to see how long I can sustain this?"

Elanor nodded with an approving expression on her face. "You catch on quickly, Ayr. Yes, I would like to see your control with simple spells. Anyone can have their dragon help them with spells beyond their level."

"How do you know that's not what Azura did in the Amphitheatre?"

"My father heard reports back from the groundskeepers. The way that you broke through Bersos' eye would have taken both precision and power, something that every other rider would not expect you to have. Don't let the flame falter."

Ayr, who had been watching Elanor and not paying attention to his spell, gasped as he ignited the flame once again. He held it steady, not allowing it to grow outside of his control. Elanor took a step towards him and placed a hand with a delicate touch on his shoulder. A wave of excitement flew at him from Azura and Ayr almost let the spell slip again.

"Sorry, that wasn't my intention. My magic is at its best when I am passionate."

"What about the Amphitheatre? Was that passion?"

Ayr shook his head. "What would you have done in my position, Elanor? Grovelling before the dragon, begging for forgiveness? We don't live in that kind of world. I had to kill Bersos otherwise he would have used my bones for toothpicks."

"Ah, so it was rage then." Elanor's other hand snaked around behind his neck as she took another step. She was now directly behind him, and he could feel more heat than what was coming from the fire. "The most primal of our instincts."

"It was kill or be killed."

"Hmm." Ayr froze as Elanor's lips graced the back of his neck. Instantly the small hairs stood up on the back of his neck. "I understand completely. Thankfully, I have never been in that exact situation before."

"Your father is the Lord Chairman of the Seminary of Fire and the Obelisk. Why would you ever be?" Ayr felt another burning sensation on the left-hand side of his neck as Elanor moved around it, kissing him again. He still had not recovered from the first. Another landed a moment later no more than a fingernail away. Shivers ran down Ayr's spine. "Elanor, what in Chilijo's name are you doing?"

"You can stop the spell now. I've seen enough."

Ayr was confused. "I've barely started. What did you need to see?"

"That you could keep your focus, even with distractions. Knowing what Azura would have been doing for you in the Amphitheatre was enough to raise suspicion. But I can tell that even without her you would have pulled it off."

"That's hard for you to say."

Elanor tutted. "It is clear to me that you're dangerous, Ashbourne, but there is something about you that I find alluring. It's not just Evor's influence either."

"What is it then?"

Elanor grunted as she sat down on the rock beside him. "Put the fire out, please."

A smirk played on the edges of Ayr's mouth. "There's no need. I have control of it."

Striking like a serpent, Elanor snatched Ayr's hand, wrapping her fingers around it like vices. He could not pull away. Ayr narrowed his eyes at her.

"Let me go."

"Or what, Ashbourne?"

"I have my strength; you have your magic. Why are you fighting against me?"

"You want me to serve you, and I won't allow that."

Ayr extended his hand out towards the flames that were still crackling away on top of the kindling. They responded to him rising at his command. Elanor gripped Ayr's left hand harder, and pivoted her body around his so that she could lash out again and snatch at him. Ayr thought he had pulled back far enough, but Elanor was all over him. She grabbed his hand and for a moment he let the flame go. It almost died before he caught it again.

Elanor's eyes widened in shock. "What the fuck?"

Ayr grinned at her. "What, did you expect me to just let go of the spell? I'm not a novice, Elanor."

"I can see that. So, now what? What do you want with me? Was this just a ploy to get close to me so that your father could strike out at mine? Why didn't you just kill me in the cave?"

Ayr tried to suppress his delight but seeing her this vulnerable was a new sensation. For the first time since he had known her, Elanor was panicked.

"I don't want to kill you, Elanor. Far from it. I made a promise to you and made an oath to the Commonwealth. The power I possess is mine. Azura is mine and I am hers."

Elanor leaned back and frowned. She still had not let go of his hands or even tried to get away. "Then why does it seem like it is only you pulling the strings?"

"I'm pulling the strings? I'm not the one sitting in an ivory tower, commanding. The watchers have a lot to answer for."

"Yet, they are the ones that guide our actions."

"Do you ever think that they shouldn't?"

"The dragons did, Ashbourne. Again, I thought you were loyal to the Commonwealth."

Ayr nodded. "I took my oath, but you can't tell me that you don't think the same thing, Elanor. What good did your mother sending us to Dalton and Sinibad achieve?"

"We know that Dalton is out there now."

Ayr tried to hold back a chortle. "I knew he was out there. You could have just asked me."

"You wouldn't betray your own blood." Elanor raised her eyes to his.

"I took an oath to the Commonwealth."

Elanor was quick with her response. "Oaths can be broken."

"And blood can be betrayed."

FOURTEEN

Ayr leaned in before she could stop him. He was not fast with his movement and Elanor could have moved with plenty of time to spare if she so chose it. Their lips met once more, and Elanor found herself surrendering to him. How could she possibly compete with this magical power? Ayr gently pulled her closer to him, and she went willingly. The fire was still glowing, the moment of passion causing the flames to leap higher into the air.

Elanor moaned softly as her lips explored Ayr's further, and he gave into her. Elanor used her strength to push him backwards, and regardless of safety or the magic that would have been waiting at his beck and call, Ayr went with her body. The moss-covered rock was entirely flat against his back, and there was no danger that they could slip from it. Elanor twisted her hands, at last trying to free herself from him. As she did, she pushed more weight onto him, the movement of her mouth quickened.

As Elanor moved her hands, they slowly ran down to his wrists where she grabbed him. Unable to do anything to prevent the movement, Elanor raised both of his hands above his head and placed them gently on the ground. She removed one hand, holding both of his wrists in the one. Even her singular hand was enough to keep him pinned; not that he wanted to go anywhere.

Elanor started to shift on top of him. It was gentle at first, until she turned his head to the side. Breathing heavily, Ayr opened his eyes, wondering what she was doing. Elanor nuzzled her lips to him, kissing him on every bit of bare skin that was available to her. Ayr moaned again, now clearly relishing in the delight and warmth of her touch. He was responding through the fabric of their uniforms, but it still was not where Elanor wanted it to be.

Rather than waiting for him to take the initiative, Elanor was on the front foot. She took pressure off his groin and sat back, more onto his thighs. Letting him know that she was looking at him by taking a long, hard stare, Elanor smirked.

"Are you going to get a move on?"

"Why, have we got somewhere to be?"

Elanor had half a mind to reach out and slap him across the face. Now he was being a sarcastic asshole at the wrong time. Instead, Elanor just rolled her eyes and stood up slowly. Ayr's eyes were transfixed on her. She had him in the palm of her hand. It was the same result every time. This was the moment she had waited over thirty years for. At last, Evor's promised had grown to maturity with a rider of her own. Her mother had often said that the connection between the two of them was unlike anything she had ever experienced.

As she began to remove her uniform, Ayr had also begun to remove articles of clothing. He'd begun with his boots, but by the time that Elanor had shed her vest, Ayr had also removed his pants. They were still wrapped around his ankles and Elanor let out a sigh of annoyance. If they were going to do this, it would be properly. Considering how otherwise desolate the Dragon's Gore was there would be absolutely no chance that they would be interrupted.

"Everything."

With little to no hesitation, Ayr began stripping what little remained of his uniform from his body. In the time that Elanor had looked away, by the time she looked back at him, Ayr was laying before her naked. His eyes were tracing her figure and Elanor knelt and placed herself on top of him. She felt him quiver underneath her as she leaned down to initiate contact with him again.

Their lips met again in a fiery exchange, their body heat just adding to the tension. Elanor's hands found her way to Ayr's chest, and she could feel every breath that he took as they grew rapidly faster. He pressed against her. It was clear his only desire was to be as close as possible to her. They continued to kiss, Ayr taking charge and guiding her where he wanted her. Elanor was no novice herself, and needed little direction, but she paid attention to his wants and desires.

They were close as she started to kiss his neck again. Ayr breathed heavier, his hand snaking its way to the back of her head. His direction was nothing more than a gentle tug. He wanted a turn. Elanor moaned as he began to kiss her neck, albeit it with a little more force than she had done to him. He was growing longer and harder as the moment passed and it was not long before Elanor could feel his wetness against the inside of her thigh. She revelled in it, wanting to do nothing more than please him. How many ladies had he been with before? Elanor tried to clear her head. Why was that important? It did not matter. Their dragons were promised to each other.

Ayr began to nip at her neck harder with more excitement and Elanor knew it was time. She shifted her weight as Ayr thrust up slightly with his hips. The effect was immediate. Elanor moaned again as she felt his shaft enter her. The motion was simple, one that she had experienced many times with the likes of Kaladin, who by all measures was larger than Ayr, but as he moved deeper inside her, Elanor felt a surge of energy course through her body.

It was unlike anything she had ever experienced before. Ayr must have felt it as well. His eyes and mouth were as wide open as they embraced each other in perfect symmetry. He moaned along with her, and as Elanor started to bring herself down onto him, he began to shiver. Elanor grabbed his jaw and held him tight to her. She lowered her mouth to his again, bucking her hips to urge him on. Ayr was responsive, as they kissed, seemingly eager to please her.

He thrust up again and again, his hands working their way down her back. His touch was electric, sending shockwaves through her body with every thrust. They kept close together, and Elanor continued to move with his motion. Elanor sat up and licked two of her fingers before running them down her body and touching herself. With the added stimulation, she was quickly reaching a climax.

Elanor continued to grind against Ayr, her fingers working away, bringing her to the edge. Ayr was thrusting faster and faster, almost in time with her moans. Elanor rose as she reached her climax, both of her hands grabbing at Ayr's chest. He groaned as she finished on him and a moment later, Ayr's eyes were rolling in the back of his head. Elanor felt warm liquid shoot into her, and she let out a loud sigh of relief, laughing gently. Everything was tingling from her head to her toes as she tried to pull herself off him.

Her legs shook as she tried to stand. Her first attempt was less than futile, stumbling forward, almost falling to her knees again and on top of Ayr. He put his hands up to stabilise her. Elanor pushed his hands away and rose under her own merit, her legs still quivering. She could still feel him inside her, and for some reason, she still wanted more from him. Not that he could know yet.

"Fuck you, Ashbourne."

"Fuck me? Why? You wanted that just as much as I did."

Elanor stared down at the ground and shook her head. "Evor pushed me over the edge."

Ayr pushed himself up onto his elbows and started to laugh. "Evor? Don't bullshit me, Elanor. Evor did not influence you directly in the moment. The dragons are nowhere near us."

"And how do you know that exactly?" Ayr went to answer, but Elanor cut him off. "Fuck you! How have you got a better connection with Azura?"

Ayr could no longer hide his smirk. "I called her to me in a record time. What made you think any different?"

Elanor shook her head in disbelief. She had been deceived when the evidence had been right in front of her the whole time. "I was naïve. You're a shrewd operator, Ashbourne, and I gave you the benefit of the doubt. We should not have done that."

"Why not? I can't think of a good reason. It was going to happen eventually."

Elanor paused. She couldn't be that mad. Even if it had not just happened, their dragons would have brought them together eventually. That was the problem with promised dragons. Always wanting to bring their riders together like family. If the option to continue the rider's line was there as well, eventually they would follow the path of the dragons too. She sighed again, still feeling him inside her.

"You're not wrong. I don't regret it, but no doubt Evor will help push us together more."

"Evor is all that Azura thinks about."

Elanor snorted. "Of course he is. They've been waiting decades for Azura's rider to arrive. I hope that she will have many eggs one day."

"Is Azura having eggs going to affect our progress?"

"No, dragons are magical creatures, Ayr. Azura's body will do things over time that amaze you."

"She already has. She's beautiful."

Elanor glanced up at the canopy of dragon's blood trees overhead. There was no sign of the sky above them. "Can you still hear her?"

Ayr nodded. "They're coming back to us now. She's very happy."

"As she should be. This helps her as much as us. You now have more of a reason to support each other. Not that you needed anymore reason."

Ayr smiled at her and the smile warmed her heart. She felt another flutter in her stomach. "So, what else did you plan on doing whilst we're here Elanor?"

"Training. The fire was just the first test. I want to push you to your limits out here. We've got nobody near us here, so there will be no judgement and you'll be safe."

"I'll be judged by you though. What's worse, you'll report everything to your father!"

Elanor folded her arms over her chest. "You know what. If you don't want me to, I won't."

"Are you feeling ill?"

"No, why would I be?"

"You're not going to report me to your father? I thought you reported everything to him."

"I can lie."

Ayr raised an eyebrow. "You'd betray your blood for me?"

Elanor tried to contain a smile. "For Azura, mainly. But if you're lucky, it will end up being for you."

"Well, I'm honoured."

"I keep saying there's something about you, Ayr. I am slowly piecing it together, brick by brick. I hope that I will one day soon be able to have the full picture laid out in front of me."

"I feel the same way."

They smiled at each other again as the sound of wingbeats filled the air around them. Ayr frowned and looked up at the organic ceiling above them. The fireflies were still glowing their bright orange lights against the brown and green of the tree. Everything appeared normal apart from the growing sound of wings around them. The wingbeats were soft, far too small, and too numerous to be either Azura or Evor. One by one the wingbeats started to fall silent and the trees around them shook as something large landed upon them.

"Do you hear that, Ayr?

Ayr nodded at Elanor, and judging by the blank expression that fell over his face, he was trying to reach Azura..

Evor, are you close?

Elanor... you are in danger. I am coming.

"That's not Evor and Azura, is it?"

Ayr shook his head. "Can you hear Evor yet?"

"The connection is faint. He won't be far away. Did you speak to Azura?"

"I did, but we're alone for now."

"We need to hide. Get your clothes, quickly!"

Elanor had no eyes for Ayr anymore, opting to scramble for her uniform that she had discarded only a short time ago. There was no time to dust it off or ensure it was clean. Her riding pants were pulled on first, followed by her boots. If she needed to run, she could at least manage it with her boots on. As one boot came on, a vicious snarl could be heard from high above. As Elanor pulled her second boot on, the danger became apparent.

Against the glows of the fireflies high in the dragon's blood trees, Elanor saw the first signs of movement. Branches were being pushed apart on the canopy that shrouded them in darkness. There was no sign of Evor that she hoped, but instead, his visage was replaced with something much smaller, but just as deadly. Were they here by chance? The wyvern's head poked out of the canopy, snarling as it came. Elanor half expected to see it breathing fire, clearing its way through the tree faster.

With her second boot on her foot, she finally checked on Ayr who had everything but his vest on. His eyes widened as he too saw the wyvern descending out of the dragon's blood tree. She was dressed enough. Elanor threw her coat over her shoulders, and double checked to ensure her sword was strapped to her hip.

"Let's go!"

"Where?"

"Follow me!"

The topography of the Dragon's Gore meant that they had ample opportunity to find a hiding place before they were spotted, but something told Elanor with the number of wings that had fallen silent around them, that this wyvern was not hunting alone. Ayr picked himself up off the ground and ran beside her. Elanor threw one final look over her shoulder as the bottom of the tree began to shake. Her suspicions were confirmed when another head began to emerge from the green undergrowth. This head was much larger, easily able to swallow the wyvern whole, much like Evor would have been able to.

"Ayr! Come on!"

Elanor squinted at the dragon that was now coming into view. For some reason, this dragon looked familiar, yet she had never seen a large red one like this before. With no time to ponder, upon seeing the even greater threat, Elanor led Ayr away from the moss-covered rock and towards somewhere that might be more protected.

There was a smaller cluster of trees only a short sprint away. As they ran towards them, more and more wyverns began to descend through the canopy, all of them chomping and gnawing at the branches around them. All it would take would be for one of them to look in the right direction and they would see two ant sized riders running for their lives. There was at least a dozen, all climbing their way through the trees.

Elanor gasped as she averted her eyes to where she was running. Whilst what seemed like most of the wyvern and the dragon were descending through the trees, one black monster was coming at them head on, streaking through the air like an arrow. Thankfully it was otherwise occupied and had not seen them yet.

"Ayr! Drop!"

Elanor threw herself face down into the dirt and prayed that Ayr did the same. She grunted in pain as she hit the ground, her chest taking the brunt of the force. She wished she'd been able to do the buttons up on her vest, at least giving her some protection against the elements. The wyvern soared overhead a moment later, an ear-splitting roar echoing from its belly. As soon as the wind from the wyvern had passed, Elanor was back on her feet. There was still no time to ensure her clothing, but the smaller dragon's blood trees were just within reach.

She glanced back over her shoulder and saw Ayr scrambling to his feet. Seconds later and Elanor had at last reached the relative safety of the smaller trees. She did not stop running until she had at least past three trees, each that she passed under feeling like an added layer of protection. She hit the fourth tree trunk, clinging to it for safety. Ayr was a step behind her. He looked worse for wear, a small cut just underneath his right eye and a small trickle of blood already running down his face.

Elanor took a breath and tutted, raising her hand to wipe the blood clear. He went to flinch away, but Elanor wrapped one arm around his shoulder, keeping him close. "What did you do?"

"It was when we hit the ground. What are we going to do against all of these wyverns?"

Elanor sighed and peered out from underneath the safety of the dragon's blood tree. The area was crawling with the wyverns and the red dragon was almost completely out of the tree. What was the method behind descending from above? More importantly, who had sent these wyverns and why were they here?

FIFTEEN

Elanor puffed out her lips with a heavy sigh as she stared out from underneath the protection of the small trees. "We must wait for our dragons. I can hear Evor properly again. They must be close."

Azura?

Yes, rider. I am nearby.

Can you see where we are yet?

Almost, rider. Chilijo's tree should not be far away.

Ayr's hand went to his sword hilt on his hip, as did Elanor's. She drew it slowly, attempting not to make any sound with it.

"We've been attacked once already by a group of wyvern. I do not think that is a coincidence."

Ayr nodded his agreement. "I saw a rider on that dragon which looks familiar."

"Why does it look familiar? Are you saying it's somebody from the Obelisk."

"No. I didn't say that I saw it recently. We'll have to investigate."

Elanor held her arm out. "I know that you're confident after killing Bersos, but come on Ayr. You want to just walk out there to the jaws of that dragon just because you think it looks familiar?"

"I didn't say it was a good familiar. I'm happy to wait here for Evor and Azura to arrive."

"I don't think we're going to have the choice, Ayr."

Ayr froze as he heard a loud grumbling from behind him. Elanor raised her sword; her eyes open wide in fear. She pulled Ayr towards her, and he retrieved his own sword from its sheath as well. The snarling continued, and as Ayr turned, he saw the red angry eyes of the wyvern staring at him. It was peering under the trees, the tallest of which was only an arm's reach above Ayr's head. This wyvern was small, but no less deadly than the others.

"Stay very still."

"Why, it can see us."

"Wyverns are primitive creatures, Ayr. If we are not a threat to it, then it should not be to us."

"And if it's been sent here to hunt us, specifically?"

Elanor groaned beside him and the wyvern took a step forward. "I don't think it's going to leave us alone."

"Can they breathe fire?"

"Some can."

The wyvern reared back its head and let out an ear-splitting screech. It was no roar like the dragons, but more of a high-pitched wail. With how the wyvern turned and looked up at the canopy, it was clearly calling to the others that were nearby. The wail was short and sharp, and they were trapped with nowhere to go. Azura was drawing closer. He could feel her presence starting to wash over him again, but there were too many wyverns.

"We can't stay here, Elanor!"

"You're right. If you've got any of that magic, now would be the time."

Azura!

I am with you rider!

Ayr just needed to figure out what would be the best way to deal with the wyvern. Could they move past this one quickly and find a new hiding place? Would the other wyverns heed the call of their kin and flock towards them? There were too many questions as Azura sent a surge of energy through his body. Not that he particularly needed it. Ayr raised his hand. If the wyvern was anything like Bersos, killing it would take too long. They needed something that would have immediate effect. As the wyvern came back around, Ayr focused his energy at its eyes. That was all that he needed. With a flick of his wrist, he shot the magic at the wyvern's eyes. The wyvern roared in anger as two blinding lights shot at it.

Ayr stuck out his hand towards Elanor. "Quick! Let's go! The spell won't last long."

The wyvern writhed and contorted as Ayr held the bright lights in place, hovering around its head. He was distracted with holding the spell and Elanor took over the lead. They were racing towards the next cluster of dragon's blood trees that would provide what appeared to be more shelter from the black monsters. Unfortunately, the first wyvern was not the only one that had now spotted them.

At least a dozen more wyverns were working their way through the canopy. Their heads were pointed towards Ayr and Elanor. There would be no way for him to blind all of them simultaneously. The next cluster of dragon's blood trees may have provided more shelter. As they ran into them, grey rocks rose up on either side, many of the dozens present that created a wall.

The wyvern was still roaring behind them, and as Ayr glanced over his shoulder once more, he could see at least half a dozen of the creatures landing around the one that he had blinded. There was concern amongst the creatures, each of them around the original like a pack of wolves. The blinded wyvern continued to roar, and Ayr realised he needed to drop the spell.

He was a step behind Elanor as she slid into the trees, not repeating the same mistake of last time. Elanor hit the ground, making herself as small as possible. Ayr dove in as well, lowering himself to the ground beside her. The trees loomed over their heads as the wyverns started to split up, taking off in the air in every direction. As Ayr turned, he heard a monstrous thud.

Elanor groaned. "That's a big dragon. And it's got a rider."

"A rider? How?"

Ayr completed his turn on his belly and stared back towards where the blinded wyvern was now recovering. Standing over it was the enormous red dragon that had also broken its way through the canopy. The red dragon's head was as large as the size of the entirety of the wyvern, making it dwarfed by comparison. Even Evor would have difficulty dealing with a dragon of this size.

"Find them! We are not to leave without them."

Ayr frowned. The voice sounded familiar, but once again, he could not place it. It could have been any rider at the Obelisk from any period of time. Their face was obscured by a mask. The smaller wyvern took off from the ground, leaving only the red dragon and its rider behind. The red dragon surveyed the immediate area, turning its head in all directions, as the rider placed his palm towards the ground. A moment later, the dragon started in their direction. With no Azura by his side or Evor to protect him, Ayr began to panic.

Azura! Where are you?

There is an army with them, rider.

She shared her vision with him, a haze coming over him. What he saw was Chilijo's tree from outside, as grand as it was from the ground. Azura was flying towards it at pace, with a wyvern between her teeth. She tore at its neck, before letting it fall to the ground far below. That one wyvern was not the only one in the air. Chilijo's tree was swarming with them.

Evor flew ahead like a battering ram as he tore through dozens of wyverns. Once they realised what was headed towards them, they found themselves unable to move out of the way. Evor tore through three wyvern in a matter of seconds as they swarmed him, while he burnt half a dozen more to a crisp with a fiery breath, one that's roar filled Ayr's ears.

"Ayr! Ayr!"

Ayr brushed Azura's vision to the side and he returned fully to where he was hiding underneath the dragon's blood trees. Elanor was nudging him with her elbow. As Ayr came to, he saw the red dragon coming closer to them. Its footsteps sounded like Evor storming across the ground. The rider on the dragon's shoulder still had their hand out as he guided the dragon forward.

Elanor grit her teeth and grunted as she pushed herself up off the ground. "Fuck it. Evor is almost here."

"Where are you going?"

"We need to know who it is. Come on."

Ayr grunted, but not because of the physical movement. It was more out of annoyance. They had hidden twice already, yet Elanor was walking towards the red dragon. It knew where they were. There was no mistaking the way that it carried its head as it was aimed straight towards their cluster of dragon's blood trees. As Elanor emerged from between the trees, the rider lowered their hand. Now that the rider was closer, Ayr could make out what they were wearing. It was like his riding uniform, but there was clear difference. The leather was more studded and the vest that the rider wore appeared to be made of a strange material that shifted in the low light.

Ayr was still apprehensive about showing himself but saw no other option. The wyvern still had not circled back around for the time being. The rider shifted in their saddle and peered down at Elanor. The mask on their face was marred with no visible distinct pattern, almost as if there had been no love and care that had gone into it.

"Ah so, Dalton's information was correct. I did not think that we would find you here. Word got out that the two of you had decided to leave the Obelisk, but I expected to see your dragon, Ashbourne. Where is she?"

"Fighting through the wyverns outside. You wouldn't know anything about that would you?"

The rider laughed softly. "Sinibad's dragonflight hunts you. You should not have angered him."

A chill shot down Ayr's spine. "Who are you?"

"You don't recognise my dragon, do you, Ashbourne?"

The voice sounded familiar, but Ayr could not place where he had heard it. The rider leaned back in his saddle and raised his hands to his head. With another swift motion he removed the mask from his face. Another shiver shot down Ayr's spine as he recognised the face that was coming out from underneath the mask. It was pale, and slim with high cheekbones. A face that Ayr thought he would never see again. He recoiled in shock. With the mask removed, Stephen Gable leaned back in his saddle, a smile coming to the edges of his lips. "Didn't think you'd see me again, did you, Ashbourne? It's amazing what a little fall can do to change someone's life."

Elanor gasped, a hiss escaping her lips. "That dragon is Onoss. What happened to you when you fell from the Catalyst?"

"You should investigate the death of recruits more thoroughly, Elanor. When I fell from the Catalyst, Onoss saved me and took me to his father."

"His father?"

Gable leaned forward and rubbed his hand on Onoss' shoulder. "Show them."

For the first time since he had landed, Onoss spoke. "Yes, rider."

Onoss raised his head and shook himself like a dog after a bath. Then, like a slow wave washing over him, Onoss' red scales started to fade away piece by piece. The fade started from the dragon's tail, the red becoming a soft gold colour. Onoss' scales continued to change and melt into the soft gold colour that was on the tip of his tail until all of his scales had been replaced. There was a red glow underneath the golden scales, making Onoss appear to swell in size.

"Onoss is the true spawn of Sinibad! An elder dragon in his own right!"

Elanor hissed beside Ayr again. "That's not possible. We vet all dragons before they are given the chance to stand before recruits."

Gable's wicked smile returned. "It appears that your due diligence failed and now that will cost you. Who do you think removed the pages of Sinibad from the book?"

"How long have you been working with Dalton Ashbourne?"

"Long enough. Ever since his son decided to throw me off the side of the Catalyst. Onoss showed me the error of my ways. You will now come with me."

Elanor shook her head. "We're not going anywhere with you, Gable."

"That's fine, I thought you'd say that. Your dragons will not return to you."

Gable raised his fist to the sky and Onoss responded with a shriek that was akin to the wyvern's calls earlier. Ayr wanted to charge at the dragon, but considering how large it was, even with his magic, he doubted that he would be able to do anything more than anger him. It was not like the last time that they had met. As Onoss' shriek became quieter, Ayr heard the unwelcome beating of smaller wings around them. He looked up to see at least half a dozen wyverns all circling above.

Azura...

I am coming, rider!

Another image flashed into Ayr's mind. Azura was getting closer. Chilijo's tree was almost filled her vision. The cloud of wyverns around it was diminishing quickly. Evor shot a jet of fire into the sky beside her and a handful of wyverns started to fall towards the ground, their wings scorched, smoke rising from the ends of their tails. Ayr's heart fluttered as he returned to the present, feeling Azura wash over him completely.

"Dalton wanted you alive, Ashbourne, but he said nothing about Elanor."

Ayr stepped between them and held his sword out. "I wouldn't think about it if I were you, Gable. Remember what happened last time we crossed swords?"

Gable sneered down at him. "You're a fool, Ashbourne. Dalton held you in much higher regards. Are you forgetting that I'm on the back of a dragon? You might not have heard the news. I've killed one."

Gable let out a loud laugh. "Bersos was still a hatchling by comparison. He also no longer had a rider. Your magic won't be able to bring down Onoss so easily, especially not without your dragon."

"She is close."

Gable waved his hand in the air and kept a nonchalant expression as he gazed around at the wyvern in the air. "Onoss. Deal with these two."

"Yes, rider."

Onoss reared his head back, and Ayr could see the flame building inside his body. Azura let out a scream in his mind as she surged forward, desperate to save both him and Elanor. She appeared to be too far away as she made a last-ditch effort to get between them and Onoss. As Onoss opened his mouth, a torrent of flame shot down from above. Ayr covered his eyes and darted backwards as the flames met. He could feel Azura's rage and anger as she tried desperately to defend him with the only weapon that she could. Ayr flung his hand out, seeing his position through her eyes and aimed his magic towards Onoss.

The effect was immediate. With nothing more than a surge of unspecified energy, Ayr was able to shift Onoss' flame upwards. Azura capitalised on the movement, her breath surging underneath Onoss' lifting flame. Onoss was forced to take a step back.

I am with you, rider. Stand strong.

Roaring filled the air around them. This was louder than Onoss or any of the wyvern that had come into the Dragon's Gore thus far. The thunderous roar could have only been Evor. He streaked across the sky underneath the canopy, launching himself at Onoss. Onoss turned at the last moment as Azura's breath continued to rain down on him from above. The two gargantuan dragons collided in a maelstrom of fire that included fangs, claws and roaring.

Azura stopped launching her fiery breath at Onoss as they collided, beating her wings and taking off into the air again. The wyverns all shrieked in unison as Azura charged them down. The fight was on. Evor roared as Onoss ripped and tore at him, both of the dragons claws and fangs gouging the other. Ayr winced as he ducked out of the way, imagining what they could do to Azura if she was caught up in a fight with either of them. Instead she had other things to worry about.

Rider, take cover! Give me your strength.

Ayr yearned to be nearer to her, able to help her in the fight. He did not want to be cowering away somewhere whilst the fire breathing monsters battled it out above. Yet there was only so much he could do with his magic and sword whilst being on the ground. Elanor's hand found his in the next heartbeat and without even looking at each other, they were both racing towards the relative shelter of the tree line.

Elanor was not present, clearly fighting in her mind with Evor, giving him the strength to attack Onoss. The black dragon should have had the edge on the younger gold, but there was no telling who truly had the advantage. Sparks flew through the air as the dragons rolled and turned over. Evor was fighting from underneath Onoss, trying to scrape at his belly.

They reached the tree line as Azura was now finally engaging the wyvern. The wyverns flew around her like a pack of wild dogs, shrieking and snapping their fangs. Azura had grown quickly into an expert of the skies. The wyverns shot their fiery breath at her, and whilst not as impressive as hers, if it caught her, the fire would have still done damage.

In return, Azura launched her own fireball at the first wyvern in the way. The wyvern shrieked as it was shot down from the sky, Azura soaring past it without sparing a second thought to the creature. The other wyvern in the vicinity all wanted revenge for their fallen comrade. Four of them flew after Azura, while one made its way towards Evor.

Azura! Behind you!

I know, rider!

Please be careful.

With your fire burning inside me, these runts do not stand a chance.

Another pained roar came from Evor and Onoss' direction as Azura spun in the sky, faster than a creature of her size had any right to. The wyvern were caught off guard as she came at them; tightening together in their flight pattern, almost hitting their wings against each other. Azura reared her head back, unleashing a torrent of fire. Her opponents scattered at the last second, but it was too late for the lowest wyvern that perished in the flames.

Azura suddenly roared in pain, and Ayr winced, feeling a slicing sensation across his shoulder blades. A wyvern had raked its talons across her and a splatter of Azura's blood fell from the sky. Ayr grimaced as he straightened his back, urging Azura on. Azura roared as she passed over the fight of the two larger dragons on the ground. The lone wyvern that had snuck up on Evor, was dangerously close to his hind leg. Before Azura could open fire on the wyvern, it opened its mouth and bit into Evor.

Unopposed and not expecting the bite, Evor let loose a vicious roar, one that echoed around the Dragon's Gore. He tried to kick at it, but couldn't reach. The wyvern whilst small was still inflicting damage as Elanor screamed beside him, unable to do anything. Ayr continued to push more power through his body and into Azura. She had no other choice. Azura reared her head back and launched a fireball at the wyvern. Without wanting to catch Evor, as the fireball rocketed towards the ground, she turned and unleashed another torrent at Onoss.

The first fireball melted the wyvern, as it engulfed it in flames. The wyvern let go of Evor and began howling as it died. Onoss on the other hand saw the jet coming, and unlocked Evor from his jaws and stood up, fleeing. With no advantage or time to counter Azura's breath, Onoss leapt into the air, taking flight as Elanor continued to scream beside Ayr. The giant gold dragon and what remained of its smaller black companions were all fleeing, with Azura hot on their tail. Ayr continued to provide her with the energy that she needed to sustain the fire, until Onoss and the wyvern were almost out from underneath the forest.

With no pressure on him, Evor finally rose from his prone position. He was worse for wear, however Elanor stopped screaming at last as he rose to his feet. Evor was shaky and he grumbled like an old man rising from his seat. He glanced up at Azura chasing Onoss through the sky, and a grin spread to his lips. Evor let out another heavy sigh and then sunk back to the ground.

"Evor!"

Azura was still in the air as she spoke to Ayr once again.

Thank you for your assistance, rider. That was exhilarating.

You looked like you were having a good time. Come quickly, I think Evor needs you.

Yes, rider.

Elanor had left his side and was sprinting across the open ground towards Evor. Evor groaned again, this time sounding more pained. Had the wyvern and Onoss hurt him that badly? There were scratches and an array of wounds all along his body, but from this distance, they looked like they paled in comparison to the size of the great beast. Realising that Elanor might need him, Ayr picked up speed and started sprinting towards where Evor lay as well.

He crossed the few hundred meters quickly and by the time he was slowing down, Elanor was already hugging the bottom of Evor's jaw. Her sobs were uncontrollable.

"Come on, Evor, get up."

"That young rodent was powerful Elanor. Combined with the wyvern, I need rest."

"No, what if they come back, we need to go."

"I feel weak, Elanor. Every mark that the monster landed upon me stings. It is unlike anything that I have felt before." His breath was coming in short gasps. "Elanor, where is Azura?"

"I am here, Evor."

Azura circled above, looking for a place to land. She landed with a crash on the far side of Evor's body. Evor's breath was growing even faster, his body shaking as he laid upon the ground. Azura rested her head over Evor, examining him with a careful blue eye. She took a deep breath in.

Elanor finally drew her eyes away from Evor. "What's wrong with him. Azura? Can you heal him?"

"I can heal him, but these wounds will take some time. It would appear that Sinibad's dragonflight are employing ancient weapons."

Ayr frowned, confused. "How? I thought you could only heal your rider. What weapons are they?"

Azura lowered her head closer to Evor with a faint smile. "I won't discuss it now, I need to heal, Evor. Promised dragons are the same as our riders. The connection is almost the same. My tears will work. Stay with me and lend me your strength, again. Elanor, Evor will be whole again."

SIXTEEN

Seeing Elanor in such pain was unnatural. Ayr knew what it was like. He could feel Azura all through him, more so now that they were reunited. Ayr wanted to help her as much as possible, Evor still short of breath in front of him. With her head over Evor, Azura was in the perfect place to lower tears onto his massive body.

Ayr could feel the power swelling in her body as the first tear fell. He was taken aback by the amount of magical energy that she was using on Evor's wound. It was more than anything she had expended upon him, or in any of the spells that he had asked her for assistance with. It was clearly needed. As Elanor continued to hug the jaw of Evor, stroking him with assurance, Azura drew back, waiting for the magic of her tear to work. For a moment there was no change in Evor's breath.

"He needs more. Rider, can you help me?"

"I am with you, Azura."

"No, come closer. I know you are powerful. Give me everything that you can spare."

Ayr shuddered, stepping around both Elanor and Evor. Evor's ragged breath threatened to blow him away as he walked around in front of the massive dragon's head. Azura cooed, watching over her promised with her own bated breath. Ayr reached her a moment later and outstretched his hand towards her.

"How can I give you everything?"

"Do not worry, rider. I will take it."

There was no warning before Ayr felt something hit him like he had run into a wall. Ayr struggled to breathe, and he felt his power being depleted by the second. He wanted to let go, take his hand away from Azura, but he could not let her down. With the number of times, she had helped him so far, he would have been a poor excuse of a rider. Ayr clung to Azura as she continued to siphon energy from him.

His legs were beginning to shake from the abundance of energy that Azura was sapping from him. Just as Ayr was ready to let go, Azura finally cut the connection and stopped siphoning energy from Ayr. He keeled over. Azura cooed overhead and she brought her head down, nuzzling into Evor. Evor groaned again and his breath started to return to normal, slowing down, becoming deeper.

"Little one." Evor's low groan filled the air.

"Yes, Evor!"

Evor sighed and his chest settled at last. He fell silent, even with Azura's prodding. His upper wing beat one more time, before finally falling to the ground behind them.

"Evor!"

"He's asleep!" Elanor yelled from the other side of his head. "How much magic did you put into him, Azura?"

"Enough. He most likely needs more."

There was silence from the other side and moments later, Elanor appeared around the top side of Evor's head with her hands on her hips. "How long will he be asleep for?"

Azura shook her head. "I do not know, Elanor."

A frown came across Elanor's face, and she glanced at Evor again. "Then we need to protect ourselves. If you don't know how long he will be asleep for, we are in danger until we can return to the Obelisk."

"Yes, we are."

Elanor shook her head in frustration and scratched the back of her head. "Fuck. I feel weak. I also don't know what to do. What if they come back?"

Trying to be light-hearted in the moment, Ayr laughed softly. "Not likely. Did you see what Evor did to him? Azura will also take care of the wyverns."

Elanor glared at him. "Did you see what that dragon did to Evor? Azura is not equipped to take down that many wyverns. One mistake could be fatal to one or both of our dragons."

"Then we will protect them."

"We can't hide Evor. Look at how large he is."

"Then we need to watch over him and pray that he wakes up soon. What do you think Azura?"

Azura bowed her head, resting it again on Evor. "Yes, this is the best course of action. I need to recover after expending that much energy."

Elanor kicked the ground in frustration. "Great, we have two drag-ons that are seemingly out of commission and an enemy that could come back at any point in time. Guess, we'll set up a camp."

She turned her back and started walking back around behind Evor and out of sight. Azura raised her head from Evor's shoulder and looked down at Ayr. He felt small under her gaze, even though he could feel her presence waning. She was fading as well. Ayr touched her leg with a heavy sigh.

"Come on, I'll take care of it from here."

They followed Elanor, who was walking back towards the trees nearby. The hairs on the back of Ayr's neck stood up as he reached the tree line, Elanor already on her hands and knees gathering pieces of wood together that she could light a fire on.

By the time that Ayr approached her, Elanor already had the wood together and was placing her hands over it. She was competent with magic in her own right, but it was clear from the frustration that was once again growing on her face that something was wrong. Elanor waved her hands over the stack of wood. The first time there was a small spark, but it was not enough to catch the wood and light it.

Elanor swore under her breath and tried again. Ayr stood behind her, his hand by his sides as he watched her attempt the spell. The second attempt was much like the first, with the slightest spark coming from Elanor's fingertips. On the third attempt, there was nothing at all. Elanor sat back, huffing and puffing as she shook her hands as if wringing them free of water.

Ayr stepped up behind her. Elanor threw her hands out again and for the fourth time, no magic sprung from them. She groaned as she failed, but Ayr stepped past her. Still feeling some magical energy with him, Ayr stretched out his hand and sent a spark towards the wood. His spark travelled more distance and did not flicker out upon contact. At Ayr's command the fire roared to life, reaching its full potential. Elanor darted back upon seeing the flames shoot up in front of her.

"Fuck you, Ashbourne!" Elanor shot to her feet and spun around at him. Ayr backed away with his hands held up by his side. "I get it. Evor is no longer here to support me! Don't rub it in my face! Have you ever lost your life partner?"

Ayr was taken aback. "What are you talking about? He's not here? He's recovering! You're not the only one that has a recovering dragon. I just so happen to have access to a larger reservoir of magic. Would you prefer that I didn't light the fire? What else are we going to do whilst we wait for Evor to rise?"

Elanor's scowl softened as she glanced out of the trees towards Evor. A sadness came over her face. She was spacing out, all of her attention on her fallen companion. Was she trying to wake him up again? Ayr did not know what magic was inside dragon's tears, despite having felt her power flow through his body before. All he had hoped was that whatever power he had given her would be enough to heal Evor in a hurry.

Elanor turned back towards him. "I shouldn't be blaming you for everything that has happened to us so far. It's not your fault, and you're just trying to help."

Ayr smiled at her. "I feel like it is. If it wasn't for me, we wouldn't be here."

"Not necessarily, Ayr. Evor and I used to come here often once we had been given permission to leave from our master. If I had decided to come here without you, there would be every chance that I was out here alone when they decided to attack. My mother still would have sent Evor and I after Dalton and Sinibad."

Ayr reached down and found her hand wrapping around his. "As long as I'm not being a hinderance."

Elanor squeezed his hand back. "You're not. I'm just anxious."

"I can't imagine how you must feel. Is it like he's gone?"

Elanor nodded. "Evor's ember has always burned bright. When I couldn't use magic just then I felt useless and out of place. Like there was nothing for me in this world."

Azura cooed overhead again as she turned her body to rest beside Evor, but closer to the riders and the forest. She crashed down into the ground, clearly exhausted. Her tongue rolled out of her open mouth and her eyes half shut as she yawned. "He will come back to you. He may already be on the way. I sedated him to help his breathing and to help expel the toxin from his body."

"How long will that take?" Ayr peered out from underneath the trees, examining the area around them. As the minutes passed, he was beginning to get more paranoid, even with Azura by his side. She was trying to calm him, as she herself curled onto the ground in an enormous white ball. With her relaxed, Ayr was coming down too and he finally let go of Elanor's hand. She glanced at him before pulling away completely.

"We need to prepare. Come on."

"Prepare? What for? Elanor, we have our swords, and our dragons will be strong again soon. Can't we just wait?"

Elanor kicked at the ground. "I'm not used to just waiting around. There has to be something that we can do."

"We wait, Elanor. Shouldn't we have patience in a situation like this?"

Ayr went to sit by the fire, flopping down on the ground beside it. He slipped his sword from his sheath and turned it over in his hands. With a careful eye, Ayr inspected the blade, but considering his use had been minimal, there was no real need to sharpen it. It was just something for him to do. Hopefully Elanor would join him. Ayr reached into his vest, only to realise that he had not brought a whetstone with him.

Instead, he set about picking at the one foil he found in the sword, tutting at himself, for not having found it when he was back at the Obelisk. As he worked at the foil with his thumb, Elanor finally sat down beside him in a huff. Even though she was on edge, now that she was seated, her presence calmed him.

"I suppose there's nothing better to do."

The two of them sat in a comfortable silence beside the fire as Ayr continued to control it. It had died down, as to not burn through the wood so quickly. Ayr listened as the wood crackled underneath the flames but was quickly growing bored with trying to smoothen out the foil in his blade. He glanced to his right and saw that Elanor's blade was practically perfect. She must have felt him looking at her and her eyes met his.

"Fuck this."

Elanor cast her sword beside the fire, the steel clanging to the ground. She reached out and grabbed at Ayr's hand pushing his sword away from his body. It too fell to the ground as Ayr wrapped his arm around Elanor. She pushed him back into the dirt, and they collapsed together as their lips met.

They rolled in the dirt beside the fire, and under Ayr's control, the flames rose. Elanor pulled away from Ayr, turning towards the fire. "What do you think you're doing?"

Ayr laughed. "Sorry, lost control."

Elanor's hand came down on his chest with a soft thud. "Didn't think that would be something you'd do."

Ayr shrugged. "Yeah well, it's not every day that you get a beautiful rider straddling you, wanting your attention."

With a roll of her eyes, Elanor slid off him. "Don't inflate your ego, Ashbourne. It's got nothing to do with you. We're only being drawn together because of our dragons."

Ayr raised an eyebrow as he turned his head towards the dragons. Both were still soundly asleep. "Are you sure about that?"

He could hear Elanor grinding her teeth in annoyance and he allowed himself a small smile. "Don't get ahead of yourself, Ashbourne."

There was a sense of sarcasm in her voice and as she stood up, Elanor gasped. She keeled over just as a low groan emanated from Evor. It was little more than a rumble, but it showed that the massive black dragon was coming back to life. Elanor stood up once more and ran out from underneath the tree line. Azura stirred in front of her and Ayr followed Elanor out into the open area. Evor continued to rumble as Elanor ran towards him, only stopping when she reached him.

Azura was rising from her slumber as well. *I hope that Evor is healing.*

Me too, Azura.

"Elanor. I am weak. The damage done to me has been mostly healed by Azura. I can still feel a poison lingering within my blood."

Elanor touched her hand to his face. "I know, I can feel it. What is it?"

Evor groaned as he tried to raise his head. "I do not know. It feels unnatural, almost like it is magic. It is unlike anything I have ever experienced before."

"We need to return to the Obelisk."

"Yes, Elanor, we do. But I do not think I can fly at the moment."

Elanor scratched Evor's leg with affection. "Can you at least stand?"

Another groan escaped Evor. "I can try, Elanor."

Evor sucked in a large breath of air as his legs shifted underneath his massive frame. The motion was slow, much slower than any other he had made before, and it was clear that he was suffering. Evor's head at last rose off the ground and he shuddered again. Ayr thought that he was going to collapse again, but instead, Evor shakily rose to his feet.

Beside him, Elanor breathed her own sign of relief. A rush of gratitude and pride surged through Azura into Ayr as Evor took his first step like a newborn hatchling, stepping out of his egg for the first time. Evor took his second step and found himself on more stable footing. With another groan he raised his head, stretching towards the sky.

"Give me a moment, Elanor. We will be able to return to the Obelisk."

"I'm glad to see you're okay!"

Evor sighed and shook his magnificent head. "I can still feel the poison within me, but I am still healing. The sooner we leave the better."

Azura was less sure of the situation. "Evor, you should not rush it. I don't know how quickly my tears will work."

"Do not worry little one, I will be able to fly. Come, Elanor. Let us make our way home."

SEVENTEEN

Their return to the Obelisk was slow, hindered by Evor's ability to fly at his fullest capacity. As they soared through the air, Ayr kept scanning the horizon, looking for any sign of potential danger. Evor limped through the air, his wings not operating at optimal capacity. He was forced to keep low to the ground, his enormous frame barely scraping his feet over the tall trees in the forests below.

It was not until the mountains that Evor finally started to gain altitude. The progress he made was painstakingly slow, eventually climbing to the altitude that would see him safely over any ridges or outcrops. Azura's concern for him was weighing heavily on his mind as well. As Evor continued to gain altitude, he faltered in mid-flight, almost falling from the sky.

What did you do, Azura?

Evor needs my support. I am there for him.

You're doing amazing. Are you okay?

My strength still has not fully returned to me, but we can recover now. We are safe.

Ayr felt a magic blast cascade into Evor. It caught him as he stumbled, and in the next wingbeat, Evor was making up for the lost altitude. It was clear that Elanor was directing him towards the roof. She needed to speak with her father. Ayr's worst fears still had not been imagined, but until Azura and Evor touched down in the safety of the

Obelisk, Ayr would not feel safe. Azura's nerves were beginning to calm once they crossed the threshold of the Obelisk.

As they neared the Lord Chairman's chambers, more of the Obelisk was coming quickly into sight. Azura overtook Evor, diving towards the courtyard that housed the entrance to the Crassus' quarters. The giant green silhouette of Baindussa greeted them momentarily as they came into view of the top of the Obelisk. Baindussa glared up at them, almost with disdain in his dead, empty eyes. The blind, emerald dragon could not see them but seemed anything but impressed.

Baindussa's deep rumbling voice echoed through the sky like thunder. "Evor... Azura... why have you returned? Why are your riders not going through the passageway?"

Evor was the loudest of the two dragons and took control. "There was an incident in the Dragon's Gore, Baindussa. Let us pass so the riders can speak to Lord Crassus."

"The Dragon's Gore? That place has no concern to me. Why do you need to speak to Crassus?"

"It has to do with the elder dragon, Sinibad, Baindussa. Let us pass. If the riders can speak to Crassus, then this affair may be over sooner rather than later."

The scales on Baindussa's forehead pressed together as the dragon frowned. "The elder dragon? The one that Crassus asked you to hunt? You've been in the Dragon's Gore this whole time?" Baindussa was growing frustrated, but in the next breath settled himself. "Land and seek Crassus, riders. Pray that he will be more forgiving than I. Evor, Azura, remain me with me."

What is he going to want with you?

I'm not sure, rider. Baindussa rarely wishes for other dragons to remain with him on his roost.

Could you be in danger?

Unlikely. It is my guess that he will interrogate us at the same time as Crassus questions you to ensure the events are the same.

We're bonded, why would we have different answers?

Baindussa would use his magic, rider. You've felt it before.

Ayr nodded, remembering the overwhelming force that Crassus had used against him. With a sigh he leaned back in the saddle as the Obelisk raced up to meet Azura. She touched down on the ground, resulting only in Ayr slightly rocking in the saddle. As she came to a stop, Ayr slid down her front leg and touched down onto the tiled floor of the courtyard. He was grateful to be on solid footing once more, even if it meant leaving Azura temporarily. Ayr removed his mask from his face and tucked it into the pocket of his vest. He ran his hand across Azura's leg, giving her the reassurance she needed to hear.

We won't be long.

I know. I want nothing more than to be resting with you, rider. Answer the Lord Chairman's questions and return to me, quickly.

I will, Azura.

Ayr left her side and glanced over at Evor who was nestling on the tiles, trying to make himself as comfortable as possible. He was still groaning as he settled down, and as she sat, he glanced up at Baindussa.

"Hurry up, Baindussa. I do not have the time or energy to speak with you for long."

Baindussa hissed at Evor as he slinked around the reaching black spires of the Obelisk. Elanor darted out from beside Evor, removing her mask, also staring up at Baindussa.

"Baindussa! Can you not sense that Evor is hurt?"

"All I can sense is a weak dragon who was too weak to fly with his own wings."

If Elanor's rage was backed up by Evor, it still would have paled in comparison to the oversized green monster. "A weak dragon! Evor faced down the spawn of an elder dragon while you lounge here acting as my father's keeper."

Baindussa's head swung down with a thunderous snarl stopping just shy of Elanor's. Evor, despite being in his weakened state, stood up to the equally as large Baindussa with a loud snarl of his own. Evor bore his fangs at Baindussa, and the two dragons stood in a stalemate. Evor was the first dragon to break his stare, and he took a step back.

"Riders, you can pass."

Elanor bowed her head out of respect. "Thank you, Baindussa."

She tilted her head towards the door, gesturing for Ayr to follow her. She stepped out from underneath Evor and crossed the courtyard. The shadows of the spires loomed over them as they made their way towards the open door. Ayr quickly passed from being under the shadow of Baindussa to being under the protection of the high ceilings that led towards the Crassus' chambers. Elanor fell into step beside him without a word and they walked down the hallway.

They stood before the closed doors to Crassus' chambers a moment later and like much of his existence, Ayr felt dwarfed again. As Elanor went to raise her hand to the doors, they opened of their own accord. Kaiser's head popped out from the door and his stern expression was present.

"Kaiser."

Kaiser bowed his head. "Lady Elanor. Ashbourne. Baindussa has informed your father that you are here. Come in, quickly."

Kaiser stepped back from the door, holding it ajar, waiting for both of them to cross the threshold. With both inside the room, he closed the door behind them with a loud thud. Ayr stared straight ahead at the long desk that sat in the centre of the room. Crassus stood behind it, dressed in a long, elegant robe that matched the colour of Baindussa's scales.

He had his face down, buried in what appeared to be a stack of paperwork. On the chair behind him was none other than Draxion, curled into a ball. The smaller female dragon opened her right eye and began to stretch out across the back of Crassus' chair. Crassus remained unphased until Kaiser approached the desk and spoke.

"Lord Chairman. Your daughter and Ashbourne are here to speak to you."

Crassus dismissed him with a wave of his hand. "Yes, thank you, Kaiser. I can see that. You can stay if you wish."

Kaiser bowed his head. "Yes, Lord Crassus."

At last Crassus looked up from his paperwork and threw it down on the table in disgust. "Anton Ashbourne is nothing more than a thorn in my side. He requests more assistance to the Haven when we are simply stretched too thin thanks to the Watchers."

"Is there anything that we can help with, father?"

Crassus shook his head, still reeling with disgust. "Where were the two of you the past day?" He touched the side of his head and grunted. "Oh wait, don't tell. The Dragon's Gore. Why were you there?"

"Is that any of your concern? If you noticed more ongoings than what happens inside your chamber, perhaps you'd notice that not all is well within the Obelisk?"

Crassus' fist visibly tightened by his side. "Yes. You were needed here."

Elanor raised an eyebrow. "Why? If my pupil is in danger, it was my duty to take him somewhere that he was not. Not that it helped."

"What happened? Baindussa says you were attacked."

"We were. A spawn of Sinibad that infiltrated the Seminary of Fire under our noses with a rider of its own. They also had a flock of wyvern with them. You need to take this threat seriously, father. We were lucky to be able to fight them off. Evor was almost killed during the encounter. If it was not for Ayr and Azura, he may be lying in the Dragon's Gore right now."

Crassus leaned forward and frowned. "Ashbourne helped you, did he? That's interesting."

"Yes, without him, the chances are I would not be alive."

"Yet without him, you would not have gone to the Dragon's Gore, now, would you? I don't exactly know what you were thinking taking him on as your student, Elanor, but it is clear to me that you have made a mistake."

"There was no mistake. I have chosen Ayr Ashbourne as my student because of his dragon. Azura is the only dragon capable of helping Evor with continuing his bloodline. Something that I was not able to find on the elder dragon."

"Our records are complete, Elanor. The information should be available to you."

Elanor shook her head. "If it was, I would not have been shocked to discover Sinibad's child when it attacked us. You say that Anton Ashbourne is sending you messages regarding more assistance, maybe it's time we asked for something back. Outside of Baindussa, Drementhol is one of the few dragons that would be capable of taking it on. Perhaps he needs to retreat from the Haven for a time to help us here. If an elder dragon gets out of control, it is everyone's problem."

Crassus' hand hit the desk with a loud thud, sending the papers scattering in every direction. "Anton is an Ashbourne, just like the rest of them! He's stubborn and unyielding. If he believes that there are other dragons that can defeat the elder dragon, he will not contribute."

Elanor chortled loudly. "Who then father? What dragon and riders are powerful enough to destroy an elder dragon with a rider of its own?"

"With a rider of their own? Especially one as powerful as Dalton Ashbourne?" Crassus' eyes darkened. "None of them. We will need assistance. You need to rally whatever riders have not been given instructions by the watchers. This was your mission given to you by your mother, was it not?"

"It was. Therefore, it is my responsibility, but it is not something that I can do alone. Do what needs to be done, father."

"I will not request that Anton or others assist you with your mission, Elanor. Find riders here. Anton will not be swayed from the Haven for this. Not even for his brother."

There was an uneasy silence as Elanor froze in her tracks. She stared at Crassus with a look that could have stabbed him through the heart. Ayr saw her fist clenching by her side, and as he went to interfere, Azura reached through to him.

Tell Elanor not to be concerned. We have Evor and there are allies here that we can use here at the Obelisk.

Thank you, Azura.

Ayr reached out and gently touched Elanor's forearm. She shrugged him away with a grunt. "Elanor!"

Elanor snapped around to face him. "What?"

"We have other options. My uncle is not the be all and end all when it comes to riders and their dragons. We can figure this out, together."

There was another silence before Elanor finally nodded in response. "Come on, Ayr. Our dragons need tending to."

EIGHTEEN

Elanor knew that he was right, though she did not want him to be. There had to be a way to find dragons and their riders from the Haven. Short of going against Crassus' orders and flying there on their own, their hands were tied. As she turned away from Crassus, she beckoned Ayr to follow her. Once they were in the corridor outside of Crassus' chambers, Elanor finally turned to Ayr.

"He's going senile. Someone needs to light a fire up his rear end. I'll have to spread the word amongst the riders at the Obelisk. There will be the riders that want glory, but Sinibad is even larger than the one that Evor and I faced already. That dragon also did not have a rider."

"And this one does. My father."

"I'm not excited to see what an elder dragon, and a lunatic can do together."

Ayr cut across her. "Hey, watch it."

Elanor rolled her eyes again and pointed towards where Evor lay, still conversing with Baindussa. "You cannot seriously tell me after everything that has happened that you're still defending him. It's his fault that Evor is out there in pain."

"Dalton is not responsible for injuring Evor."

"No, but he sent Onoss and the wyvern. Now hurry up, I want to see my dragon."

She quickened her step, anxious to lay her eyes on Evor again. Whilst it had only been a few moments, she could feel his pain inside her head. She was doing what she could to comfort him, but Evor was not trying to give any indication of just how hurt he was. She needed to help heal him, yet the top of the Obelisk, just outside Crassus' quarters, was not the place.

As the pair of riders neared the entrance, a shadow loomed over the doorway. As they rounded the corner, Elanor saw a flash of purple as a smaller figure cut their way into the door. The figure removed their mask and revealed the all too familiar face of Kaladin as he stormed towards them.

"Great, here we go."

"I need to speak with you, Elanor."

"Can we do it some other time, Kaladin? I've just had a long flight and I can't be bothered dealing with your shit right now."

"No, it can't. What are you playing at?"

Elanor shook her head. She knew this had been coming. It was just much faster than she had expected. "You go on without me, Ayr. Take Azura and rest. I'll deal with this."

"Are you sure?"

Elanor nodded in response. "You don't need to be here for this."

Ayr insisted. "Are you sure?"

Now Elanor was stern. "I'll be fine. Go. Get some rest."

She continued to stare at Kaladin until Ayr's footsteps had completely faded from earshot. Then she gave it longer, allowing Ayr to leave the courtyard behind entirely. Kaladin stared back at her, his face carrying his all too familiar smirk.

"What do you want, Kaladin?"

Striking like a serpent, Kaladin lashed out, his forearm smacking into Elanor's throat. He was strong, with all of the fury of Gundrag behind his movements. Caught unawares, Elanor gasped as she was slammed into the wall behind her. Evor let loose with a roar that shook the walls, stepping towards them. Even though she could not see him, she could feel his presence.

Be calm, Evor!

Elanor, you are in danger!

No! But if he harms me, remove Gundrag's head from his body.

Yes, Elanor.

Evor went silent inside her mind with a low growl that resonated throughout the area overhead. Kaladin continued to apply pressure to her throat and leaned in.

"You fucked him, didn't you, Elanor?"

"Like that's any of your concern, Kaladin."

Kaladin's eyes flashed red with a shade of jealous anger. "It is my concern when the security of the Obelisk is at risk, Elanor. What did you just see your father about? What happened out there?"

"You have no reason not to trust him. Ayr could have handed me to his father's servant at any point whilst we were in the Dragon's Gore. If he was going to do something, that would have been the time."

Kaladin was flat. "I don't care. He is still an Ashbourne at the end of the day. If he had sprung from Anton's balls, I might think differently about him."

Elanor scoffed. "You're jealous, aren't you? Imagine that. A young rider comes in here, regardless of his name and the great Major Kaladin, hero of the Ashbourne rebellion, is jealous. You're pathetic."

"I'd watch your mouth if I was you, Elanor."

"Or what, Kaladin? You can't touch me. Gundrag wishes that he could stand up to Evor. You've been envious of me the moment that Evor and I became dragon and rider. You always wanted him, everyone knows it."

Kaladin's eyes narrowed at her. "Pray that I don't find Ashbourne guilty of any wrongdoing. I know what happens when two promised dragon riders get together. If anything was to happen to him, that would destroy you."

"Don't you dare threaten him."

A smirk spread across Kaladin's lips. "If I want to, you won't be able to stop me. Despite our history and despite your father. Everyone here but you wants him dead."

Elanor was defiant. "And that's enough. We've had this discussion before. Lay a hand on him, and you'll face my wrath."

Kaladin drew back with the smirk still across his face. "I don't fear you, Elanor."

"You should."

"Evor will only be able to protect you so much, Elanor."

"We're done here, Kaladin. There are bigger things to worry about in this world. You're not one of them."

Kaladin grunted and thrust his hand forward, applying more pressure to her throat. "I loved you."

"And I loved you. Some things are not meant to be. Now go, or Crassus will hear of this."

With a grunt, Kaladin removed his hand from her throat. He scowled at her one final time before backing away without another word. Elanor swallowed deeply, not massaging her throat until Kaladin had turned his back on her, opting to walk towards Crassus' chambers. Elanor shook her head at his retreating back and made her way back out towards the courtyard and towards Evor.

Evor was still laying in front of Baindussa, but the green dragon had backed off somewhat. Azura was nowhere in sight, but in her place stood the purple Gundrag. He sneered down at her much like Kaladin had.

"Are you having trouble finding riders coming with you to destroy the elder dragon, Lady Sunfire?"

"I haven't even started looking. We're beginning the process short-ly."

Gundrag hissed at her. "I have always wanted to face down an elder dragon. I could convince Kaladin to come with you on your journey."

Elanor looked down her nose as much as she could at the dragon. An extremely hard task to achieve considering his size. "If I wanted help from your master, I would have just asked him. You and Kaladin would offer no value to the hunt."

Gundrag sat on his hind legs and began to laugh. "No value? I am one of the largest dragons available here at the Obelisk. If Crassus does not ask the Haven or other areas for assistance, you do not have much choice."

"Then we'll work with what we have."

Evor grunted at Gundrag. "If you're not wanted, you're not want-ed. Stay at home, hatchling."

Gundrag turned and snarled. "Hatchling? I was fighting in wars before you were born."

Baindussa had heard enough and finally spoke up, his voice ripping through the air "Silence!" Immediately the two younger dragons bick-ering stopped and silence fell over the Obelisk. "Elanor, if you wish to slay this elder dragon, you will need all the help you can get. I do not doubt yours or Evors abilities, but Gundrag is a valuable asset. If you need the Major's assistance, you must do so by any means necessary."

"Is that you or my father talking, Baindussa?"

"We are one."

Elanor retrieved her mask from the inner folds of her vest and scoffed. "So you give me nothing whilst I am speaking to you, but use your dragon as a voice of reason."

"You would hear it better from I than Crassus."

Elanor shook her head as she pulled her mask over her face. "I'll hear nothing more about Gundrag and Kaladin joining my hunt. I'll be the one that decides who comes with us and who doesn't."

Gundrag snorted above her. "You will fail in your quest without us."

"We will see about that." Evor went to extend his neck but groaned as more pain shot through his body. "Come, Elanor, we should leave this place. Gundrag, Baindussa, I bid you a good day."

Are you okay? I can feel everything.

Yes, Elanor. I will be able to reach our quarters. Once the little one has regained some of her strength, we should send for her again. She will be able to help healing me back to full strength.

And what do we do in the meantime whilst you rest?

It sounds to me like you have a hunt to prepare for, Elanor. This is not something that can wait. We are in danger. The longer that Ayr is near us without his father being brought in, the worse off we will be.

Elanor was amused. *Ayr? You've never called him that before.*

Who has changed my mind on the boy? We are one, Elanor.

Yes, yes we are. Let's get out of here.

Elanor clambered up Evor's leg before either of the other dragons could say anything. Once she was onboard Evor, Elanor thought about securing herself in the saddle. There was no need to with how slow Evor was and just how close their destination was it seemed fruitless. Without uttering a word to him, Evor lifted himself off from the ground with considerable effort. It may have been worth just leaving him here. Evor was determined. He groaned as he rose, Gundrag issuing a snort beside him. Evor paid the purple dragon no attention and stretched his wings out above him. As he stretched, Evor reached out to Elanor again.

Rider... I do not feel well.

I know, we're going to get you the help that you need.

No, Elanor. I...

Without another word, Evor went from stretching out to falling forwards. Elanor went to strap herself into the saddle, but it was too late. There was no place for her to go. Evor's head fell, and she did along with it. The ground was racing up to meet her, before everything went black.

NINETEEN

Elanor blinked once and the world was still black in front of her. She blinked again and it finally started coming into existence. She frowned, trying to protect her eyes as a sharp burst of light shot into the room. Her head was throbbing and everything else in her body ached. She tried to move but was restrained. Elanor went to let out a scream but was silent. Where was she?

As she calmed herself, her first thought was to reach Evor, but he too, was silent. What had happened to him? She struggled remembering the events of what had transpired before she had blacked out. She remembered him falling over, is that what had caused this? As she tried to piece everything together, she heard a loud thud from somewhere in the distance. Another soon followed it, but it was much closer as the door to the room she was in swung open. She was in the medical ward. Elanor tried to groan but nothing came out.

"No! Evor cannot remain where he is!"

"He has to, Lord Chairman! We have no tools, nor the magical power to remove him. He is still very much alive, it is not like we can begin disposing of his body!"

Elanor wanted to leap up from her position and strangle Crassus. Something had happened to Evor and rather than keeping him safe, all he wanted to do was move him because it was inconvenient? Her invisible bonds still remained in place and she tried to struggle against them to no avail. She heard Crassus and who she could only assume was Kaiser approaching.

"Look, Lord Chairman. She's awake."

Their footsteps scattered across the tiled floors and within seconds, Crassus came into view, peering down at her like she was in an observatory. Concern was written all over Crassus' face. Maybe now he would take her seriously.

"Hello, Elanor. I'm sorry. You've been in a terrible accident. I have tried to reverse your injuries as much as possible. Bear with me."

Crassus went to work, running his hands over her. She could feel the magic exuding from his body, no doubt aided by Baindussa. As Crassus placed his hand over her chest, Elanor felt the invisible chain that was keeping her in place starting to lift. It was as if Crassus was drawing the magic away from her. There was no doubt he was the most powerful rider in the Commonwealth, perhaps with the exception of Anton Ashbourne. The skill and dedication it took to master the magical talents that Crassus had was immense, even with a dragon as powerful as Baindussa. The dragon could provide all the power and some of the focus, but the dedication required for the spell to work was up to the rider. Crassus had always been powerful, yet rarely showcased his magical abilities to the world. Even with Evor's help, Elanor could barely heal a scratch on her arm, yet here was Crassus able to hold her in stasis whilst he worked over her.

Kaiser came into her vision a moment later, as did Ayr standing beside both older men. His eyes met hers and she wanted to stretch her hand up towards him. Ayr refocused on what Crassus was doing, and Elanor could see him concentrating as if following the movements. As Crassus' hands reached her feet, Elanor was finally feeling strong enough to sit up.

"Not yet. Remain calm. Can you speak, Elanor?"

This time there was no restriction on her voice. "Yes, father."

"Good. Do you know why you're here?"

"Yes. Evor had an accident, and I fell from his back. Why?"

"Baindussa has examined Evor thoroughly. Evor has been poisoned."

"No shit. How?"

"It is an ancient magic, one that either the wyvern or that elder dragon spawn would have been able to put on their talon or fang. Did you notice anything different when they struck Evor?"

Elanor shook her head. "It was in the heat of a battle, how could I? What is the ancient magic?"

Crassus lowered his head and his eyes darkened. "You need to remain calm, Elanor. I've seen it once before." He raised his hand to hover above her chest. "No sudden movements. The poison is the scalebane."

"The scalebane. I thought that was a myth!"

"I thought the same thing, until the Ashbourne rebellion. If it was not for Baindussa, Draxion would be nothing more than a withered husk in a graveyard near the Tomb of Chilijo."

"Draxion suffered from the scalebane? Why did you never think to tell me?"

"It was not considered important until now. In her reduced state, it is quite easy for Baindussa to keep her healthy, her powers also help her."

Elanor frowned. "Is she even a watcher dragon?"

Crassus nodded. "She is, that much is clear. With the amount of scalebane that has infected her, Baindussa can stop it having any further effects on her body. Evor on the other hand will suffer."

"We need to help him!" Elanor tried to jolt up from the bed, but Crassus' hand snapped shut and Elanor froze. She couldn't move against his power.

"I told you, no sudden movements, Elanor. We will help Evor. Ashbourne's dragon is healing him when she can, but it is clearly not enough. She does not have the power to sustain him yet, especially for a dragon of his size. Any efforts are only pausing the effects of the scalebane, not eliminating it completely."

"Then what do we do?"

A grin spread across Crassus' face as he held his hand out.

A piece of parchment rustled somewhere in the room, and it appeared the next moment in Crassus' hand. He handed the paper down towards her, but still held his arm out, guarding her. "No sudden movements, Elanor."

Elanor glared at him as she stretched up slowly to take the piece of parchment from him. It was full of hastily scribbled, barely legible wording that had clearly been copied down in a hurry with almost no thought to its presentation. Elanor squinted as she tried to decipher it. She read through the notes quickly, before handing it back to Crassus. Warmth radiated through her soul.

"The Tomb of Chilijo! Of course. Where else would a precious treasure be? Especially with the ability to cure such an evil."

Crassus tutted. "Read it again. Not in the tomb, *near* the tomb. This is a rash decision, Elanor."

"The tomb is surrounded by thousands of other potential gravesites. Where did you get the information from?"

"I found it in the library, Elanor. One of the old books. We've been searching for days."

Elanor would have shot up from her prone position if it not for Crassus. "Days! I've been out for days?"

Crassus nodded. "Your fall was significant. Ashbourne has barely left your side the whole time."

Elanor raised an eyebrow. "Really?"

"He was insistent. Wanted to be here in case you woke up."

"Well, I'm awake and we have a heading. I need to save Evor. Are you going to let me out of bed?"

Crassus cast a concerned eye over her again and shook his head. "It's against my better judgement, but yes, if you feel like you are able to stand, you may begin making preparations."

Elanor grunted as she felt Crassus' spell finally lift off her and her bodily movements started to return to her. She started to move her limbs, feeling the blood rush back into them. With a sigh, she sat upright, now able to grasp the edge of the bed. Her legs were beginning to feel more solid. She pushed herself up and went to swing her legs around. Crassus, Kaiser and Ayr moved out of the way.

She glanced down at her body, seeing that she was wearing a tan medical robe, one that the doctors within the Obelisk would issue patients. She felt uncomfortable as the fabric draped around her knees, wishing to be back in her vest and riding pants. Elanor held out her hand and Ayr was the first one to take it.

"How do you feel?"

"Alive..."

Elanor slid her feet onto the tiled floor and groaned as she took all of her weight at last. She stood still for a moment before taking her first step. Everything seemed normal, but the lack of Evor's presence was noticeable.

"Get me a uniform. The longer Evor waits, the more in danger he is. How far is the tomb from here?"

Crassus pursed his lips. "You have no dragon, Elanor. How are you going to get to the tomb?"

"Azura could carry us both!"

Elanor smiled at Ayr. "Riding on that dragon is something that I have wanted to do for as long as I've known her. She would need to be agreeable of course. Kaiser, fetch me a uniform, please. The sooner I'm dressed, the sooner we can leave."

Kaiser bowed his head and exited the room. Elanor sat back down onto the edge of the bed with another loud sigh. She continued to rotate her feet until Kaiser returned with a uniform in her size in hand. Elanor took it from him and gestured for the men to leave her.

"I need to get changed, gentlemen. Can you give me some privacy?"

Crassus bowed his head. "Of course, Elanor. Come, Kaiser, Ashbourne."

Elanor held her arm out. "Ayr, you can stay. I need to speak with you."

"I don't think so Elanor. There is no reason. If you want to head out as quickly as you are suggesting, then Ashbourne should ready himself as well."

"There's no need. Leave us, father. May your dragon always breathe fire."

"And may his wings carry you forward."

Crassus cast a steely glance at Ayr that made Elanor want to step between the two of them. Each wanted what was best for her in his own way. She had to commend Ayr for wanting to step up to her father. Even riders like Kaladin would not have dared, even if they had been seeing each other. Kaiser laid the uniform down on the bed beside her and made his way out of the room along with Crassus. They shut the door behind them and left Elanor and Ayr in a still silence. Ayr's hands found hers and they coupled each other.

"You don't have to do this. I don't know how long we will be."

"I've spoken to Azura, and she is more than happy to take us to the tomb. She wants to stay here to help heal Evor, but she understands that this is the only possible way to cure him."

"Who got that information out of the book, Ayr?"

Ayr's eyes narrowed. "Why do you ask? It was me. Kaiser brought me the book and I researched. I was here the whole time."

A smile came to Elanor's lips. "That's sweet of you."

"I didn't want to leave you and Azura didn't want to leave Evor."

"She is a good dragon." She lowered her hands from his. "Should we get going?"

Ayr nodded. "Time is of the essence."

"Great, take this, then."

Elanor stood up from the bed and began to undo her robe. Ayr had not taken his eyes off her as she lowered it to the floor. Elanor allowed him to look, but she was in a hurry and anxious to get in the air. She threw on the uniform, once again feeling like she belonged. As she pulled on her boots, she felt Evor's presence nearby. He was stirring, but weak. Elanor reached out to him, easing him back into sleep.

Elanor...

I know, we're going to get you help. You've been poisoned.

Save me...

"Hey! Hey! Elanor, are you good?"

Elanor blinked. Ayr was grabbing her wrist and waving his hand in front of her face. Her eyes refocused on him, the blinding pain from Evor rocketing into her body. She winced and stabilised herself, grabbing Ayr's hand.

"Yeah, we need to go. Come on. Where's Azura?"

"Still with Evor."

Elanor took her first step, finally able to put one foot in front of the other. Ayr let go of her hand as she gained more confidence in walking, and they left the medical room together. Ayr led out her outside, down the winding, long corridor towards the platform that would take them towards Crassus' chambers. From where he had called out, Evor had not been able to move.

As they approached the rising platform, they found Crassus and Kaiser already waiting for it. The door was open, and they stepped into the tube. Elanor quickened her pace and Crassus saw her coming, holding it open for them.

"Thank you, father."

"Good to see you return to form, Elanor."

"I am not whole without Evor."

"You'd best get a move on then."

There were no further words exchanged until they reached the top of the Obelisk. Elanor felt Crassus' hand on her shoulder.

"Good luck, Elanor. I know how much he means to you."

"Thank you, father."

Elanor took a deep breath as the doors slid open in front of her. There, laying across the walkway towards Crassus' chambers in the middle of the courtyard was Evor. He was sprawled unevenly, with one of his legs stretching out towards the entryway. His head was on the ground, and the only sign of life came from the very slow rising and falling of his enormous chest. Baindussa watched over him from above like an owl standing sentry on a nearby tree. Azura also stood over Evor, much closer, with her head almost level with his. A single, solitary tear fell from her face onto his. Azura looked up at them as they approached.

"He's sleeping now. I've just put him under again. How long do you think we will be?"

Elanor shrugged. "How quickly can you get us to the Tomb? Have you recovered enough to be able to fly?"

"Yes, I have been waiting for the moment that Ayr said it would be a possibility. Evor is stable for now. We will need to hurry."

Baindussa raised his head high above the courtyard. "Take the time that you need. I will hold Evor in a stable condition until you return. You will not lose the dragon that you once knew."

"Thank you, Baindussa."

Baindussa hummed at her, lowering his head. "It is my pleasure. Evor has been a great servant of the Commonwealth. I will keep him healthy while Azura cannot."

Now that Azura had finished shedding her tears over Evor, she moved around his prone body towards the riders. Crassus and Kaiser walked past her with no comments, and Elanor breathed a sigh of relief as she saw two saddles already strapped in place on her back. Ayr moved past her and was pulling on his mask in anticipation, ready for flight.

"We've had her ready to go at a moment's notice. I had Kaiser fetch another saddle for her."

Elanor grinned at him as she went to reach into the pocket of her vest. "Good thinking, Ashbourne. Ah, I don't have my mask."

"Good thing we got it off you after you fell. It protected your face too." With a flick of his wrist, Ayr produced her mask and held it in front of her.

With another small smile, Elanor took it and began pulling it over her face. "Thanks. I'm ready now." She glanced up at Azura. "Am I able to ride her?"

Azura cooed as she nestled herself close to the ground to allow the riders to board her. "Yes, I will allow you to ride me as well, Elanor. It would be an honour to have the rider of my promised upon my back."

TWENTY

Ayr climbed up Azura with a sense of urgency. He could tell just from her body language that she was most eager to leave. The fate of her promised was relying on her speed and their ability to find the scalebane cure. Elanor was right behind him, and as Ayr found his balance in the saddle, he reached down with one arm, extending it towards Elanor. She graciously accepted the offer and Ayr helped pull her onto Azura's back.

The saddle behind Ayr was tied into his and helped secure it in place. There were half a dozen small satchels all hanging from it, each of them filled with items that they would need for this journey. Once he felt Elanor sit down behind him, Ayr braced himself. There was no time between Elanor being secure and Azura kicking off from the courtyard. She jolted into the air and Elanor let out a yelp behind him. Azura was wordless as she rose into the air, quickly making Baindussa and Evor smaller beneath them.

"By Chilijo's grace, I hope you find what you are looking for, Azura."

Azura let out a roar as she continued to rise high above the Obelisk. She was heading west and towards the south. The tall mountains loomed large before them, standing like silent sentries watching over them. As the sun continued to rise at their back, Ayr sat back in the saddle and grabbed at one of the waterskins in the first pouch behind him. He then shook his head, realizing it would not be an intelligent decision to drink whilst Azura was still in the air, especially at this height.

The cold air was ripping through his uniform, but thankfully Azura's head was deflecting some of it. She was beginning to level out and her speed was increasing. She felt strong underneath him as her wings beat evenly on either side of him. Even though Azura had expended copious amounts of energy the two days of rest had been beneficial. Any time that she had not spent with Evor, had been time spent resting and eating to ensure that she could be ready if they needed to depart at a moment's notice.

What do you think she's thinking about, rider?

I'm not sure. I know how I would feel if I was in her position.

How would you feel, rider?

Empty. You know that. I would not want to exist in a world where you are not by my side anymore, Azura.

Then you'd best pray I never leave it.

If you're curious to hear what Elanor has to say, slow down so that I can ask her.

If I slow down, it will take us longer to reach the Tomb. We must save Evor.

I understand, Azura. Do you know where you're going?

Yes, rider. I studied the map.

The flight continued, dragging into the late afternoon. The landscapes had changed from the mountains to a rich forest and back again. From this height, Ayr could sparsely make out the details outside the cluster of trees, or the jagged tips of the mountains below. There were few small settlements scattered amongst the trees and the mountains, but there was nothing substantial directly underneath their flight path.

As the sun started to set on the horizon, a flicker of orange light caught Ayr's eye. Just within the horizon was a city sitting just within the clutches of another mountain range. The tall spires of the dozen towers that stood watch over the city rose above the surrounding mountain tops, but the rest of the city was hidden below the heights of the raw and rugged peaks, even from this elevation.

I know that place. That's where I grew up.

What place?

The city, Azura. Look at it. It's beautiful.

Azura grunted and shook her head with distain. *There is nothing I dislike more in this world than human civilization. It is an eyesore.*

What about the Obelisk?

That is my home. That was necessary for my survival.

Yet my home was not?

Your home is beautiful, Ayr. What did you call it?

Dominion, but the locals call it by another name. Kressin. It was not my ancestral home, but it was the one that my father raised me in. I will return to it upon a day.

We shall do so together, rider.

Ayr continued to watch night overcome them as they flew past Kressin. The city was equipped with its own small station of dragon riders, yet thankfully none of them had come to investigate their presence in the area. Dalton had done a good job of keeping their identities secret in the years that they had lived there before eventually moving throughout the rest of the Commonwealth. A sliver of fear shot down Ayr's spine and the hairs on the back of his neck stood up. Was Dalton still residing in the city? If so, where was Sinibad? Why had they come this way? It wasn't Azura's fault.

I cannot sense any strange dragons, rider. Calm yourself.

Are you going to land tonight, Azura?

No, Evor is in danger. I will continue flying into the night as far as it will take me.

Is that safe?

I cannot let Evor wither away to nothing. Your magic will sustain me, rider.

With the last rays of sunlight still on the horizon, Ayr turned to Elanor in the saddle behind him. He stuck his thumb up at her, and Elanor's only response was a nod of her head. She sat firmly in her saddle, her head fixed straight ahead. Darkness slowly overtook them, and Azura continued to fly into the night.

Now that he was used to her speed, Ayr had taken the liberty of having something to eat and drink. By no means was the jerky and water enough to sustain him for a long period of time, but considering this was an in and out mission. If Azura landed they would have been able to hunt for food. Ayr was getting sore in the saddle, but there was not much he could do to alleviate the soreness. The saddle was comfortable enough and as the moon neared its peak, Ayr started to yawn.

You can sleep, rider. I won't let you fall.

Ayr looked over his shoulder at Elanor. She was slumped forward in her saddle, both of her arms locked in underneath it. Her head was rolled to the left, her mask shining underneath the moonlight. Feeling the same need, Ayr adjusted his grip, ensuring that his own arms were tied in correctly. The top of the saddle was curved ever so slightly, giving Ayr just enough room to place his head. There was little cushioning, but with Azura's level movements, he was not being tossed around too much.

Azura started to sing to him, humming gently, pushing the quiet melody into his mind. Ayr started to relax and allowed his body to loosen. Ayr fell in and out of sleep, the sounds of the wind mitigated by Azura's song. As he started to fall asleep, Azura's song slowed, only for Ayr to slowly wake again.

Each time he rose, Azura continued her song only for him to slowly fall asleep again. Ayr would wonder how Elanor was faring, but between Azura and his almost immediate return to sleep, could not check on her in time. The process would repeat until the early hours of the morning when the moon began to slip behind the mountains and the first light of dawn showed itself. As the light started to intensify, Azura was no longer as persistent with her song.

Ayr at last rose from his sleep, feeling refreshed and less sore, despite not having moved in the saddle. As he rubbed his eyes underneath his mask, he felt a tap on his shoulder. He turned and saw Elanor waving at him. He waved back as she retrieved a water skin from one of the pouches. She leaned back in the saddle and drank quickly before lowering her mask again and stashing the water skin away.

The morning continued to wash away, with time slipping away from them. Ayr ate again in the saddle as the sun roared in full above them to the north. The open landscape was now beginning to change too. Instead of there being lush greenery and scattered forests amongst the mountains, the scenery was replaced with an increasingly desolate wasteland. The greens gave way to what was at first earthy brown and greys, and then to an almost black soil.

Are you sure we're going the right way?

Yes, rider. This is the way to the Tomb of Chilijo. This ground was destroyed in the first war, yet it is where Chilijo wished to be buried.

Where is the tomb?

Just ahead, rider. Look.

Ayr shifted in his saddle and peered over Azura's head as she started to dip towards the ground. Ayr gasped in shock, thinking that what loomed before him was another entrance to the cavern that they had found Sinibad in. Upon closer inspection, rather than there being a massive opening that was fit to hide an elder dragon, the entrance was much smaller. The mountain itself on the other hand was just as large, with a curve towards the horizon. The spires of the mountain were strangely only in the direct middle of the mountain range, almost like they formed part of a spine.

Azura. What is that?

That is the Tomb of Chilijo. Brace for landing, rider.

Azura angled herself towards the entrance of the tomb and it quickly rose up towards them. As Azura neared the ground, the tomb grew clearer, with more intricate details becoming more apparent. As they neared the ground, the Tomb of Chilijo began to tower above them. Once she touched down onto the ground, Ayr was blown away by its sheer size. Taking a moment to relish in the glory of the structure in front of them, he finally removed his mask.

It was the longest time that he had ever had it on for. Not that it was uncomfortable, but it was nice to breath wholly once again. The mask provided a thin layer of protection from the elements, but it was still breathable considering the speeds that Azura would get to mid-flight.

Ayr heard Elanor draw breath behind him. "Where are we? Is this the Tomb?"

Azura turned and shook her magnificent white head over the two of them. "Yes, Elanor. I can sense magic ahead, but there is something stopping me from taking flight now that I have landed."

Elanor keened her head with an eyebrow raised. "What's stopping you?"

"I am not sure, Elanor. The Tomb of Chilijo has not been visited for many years - to my knowledge."

"Ayr, did you find anything else in your research?"

Ayr packed the pocket of his vest where he had stored the page of parchment that held all of the notes he had pulled from the book. Now that they were back on solid ground, it was now the time to review it again. The parchment was double sided, faint ink stains bleeding through on either side almost made some of the letters illegible. He squinted as he unfolded the paper trying to understand his messy handwriting.

"It says that there has been a store of scalebane ether somewhere here. There was no further description."

"The Tomb of Chilijo hides many treasures, Ayr. The Commonwealth thought it would be best to lock some secrets away in here. I'm glad Kaiser found that book for you, but you didn't think to loan it out of the library?"

Ayr shook the piece of parchment in front of him again. "I'm honestly not seeing anything here that eludes to the location of the scalebane ether though."

"Let me look."

Elanor took the parchment from him, but Ayr was still trying to decipher the hastily scribbled words on the page. Elanor held it out in front of her and a frown came over her face.

"Did you get all the information from the book?"

Ayr groaned. "There wasn't really enough time."

Elanor tutted and tossed the parchment to the side. "So then what was the point? That page might as well be useless."

Ayr scrambled after the page, desperate to keep it in his possession before the wind claimed it. "Hey! What did you do that for?"

"If you can't be both attentive to detail and retain it, what good are you? We're now out in the wilderness with only a loose idea of where an ether that can save my dragon is!"

Ayr held up his hands in defence. "We're here aren't we? We'll find it."

Elanor grunted and shook her head. "Every second we waste here is a second longer that Evor is in danger. Now we're going to need to venture into that tomb and uncover something that might not even exist. I hope you're happy, Ashbourne."

Azura cut her off. "Elanor. I'm sure that the rider did not mean for this to happen."

"Azura. You want Evor to retain his form, do you not?"

"I do, Elanor."

"Then we'd best get looking immediately."

Something in the distance caught Ayr's eye. It was a smaller figure, coming towards them against the indomitable backdrop of the Tomb of Chilijo. It was definitely human and as the figure neared, Ayr could make out that they had a significant limp.

"Azura. I thought you said nobody had explored here in years."

"To my knowledge, no dragon has been here. I did not say the same for any humans."

"Should we go investigate then?"

The figure was not intimidated by Azura's presence as it continued towards them. Ayr's hand fell to his waist, ready to engage the figure should they get too close. As the figure strolled towards them, it slowed, only to pull back on its hood. It was an old man, withered and worn with shaggy, greying hair that ran down to his shoulders. His face was covered by a thick, bushy beard and underneath all of the hair, Ayr could make out his small black eyes.

The man held his hands up in the air as a sign that he carried no weapons. "Greetings mighty dragon riders! What brings you to my home?"

Ayr raised an eyebrow. "You live here? What's your name?"

"Aye, I am Harmon. I live here and watch over this place. It is my duty."

"Do you know what this place is?" Elanor raised her arms and folded them over her chest. Her frown punctuated her face.

"Yes ma'am. This is the Tomb of Chilijo. I'll ask again. What brings you here?"

Elanor took a step forward. "We're looking for the cure to a poison we believe to be stored here. The scalebane."

Harmon's small eyes lit up. "Yes, I know the scalebane. A man came here not too long ago looking for it."

"What was his name?" Ayr felt a lump rising in his throat.

Harmon paused, glancing down at the ground, searching for the name. "Ashbourne."

"Can you take us to the scalebane?"

Harmon put his hands on his hips and started to laugh. "You're a fool if you think I take just anyone into the Tomb of Chilijo. What makes you so important?"

"I am his son."

Harmon exhaled and then turned on his heel, starting to limp back to where he had come from. "You'd best come with me then, Ashbourne."

TWENTY-ONE

With Harmon leading the way, Ayr did not feel any more secure than he had done before. The man's limp was off-putting, with Harmon swaying left and right, looking like he might fall over at any point. The Tomb of Chilijo loomed before them, as tall and imposing as the Obelisk itself. As they approached the side of the mountain, Harmon slowed to a waddle, He turned over his shoulder and smiled, seeing that they were still following them.

"This is the way. Come through here."

I do not trust Harmon, rider.

Neither do I, Azura. But this is the only way to get the scalebane ether..., do you not want to follow through with it?

I want nothing more than to embrace Evor again. This must be done.

Okay. Keep a lookout.

I will be vigilant, rider.

Ayr frowned as they came before a seemingly impassible rock wall. As Harmon approached, he raised a gloved hand to the wall. With the hand about to press against it, Harmon ripped the glove off, to reveal a withered, blackened hand underneath it. None of his fingers were straight, and only his index finger possessed a nail.

Ayr recoiled as he watched Harmon press his hand into the wall. The effect was immediate. A smaller section of the wall started to shift around them, moving out of place like a door. It was only as high as Azura's head, but it was wide enough so that two dragons of her size could walk side by side. The section of wall then began to shift to the side, moving much like the hidden door that led to Crassus' chambers. A few moments later, it came to a stop.

Ayr glanced at Elanor with a hushed tone. "Is this smart to be following him?"

Elanor drew her sword with a shot at Harmon. "As long as the scalebane ether is in there I don't care. I'm going to get it one way or another."

Ayr drew his sword and was calmed by Azura's presence. Despite not being able to fly, she kept him focused on the task ahead. Harmon took a step into the tomb and as he did, two fires shot up on either side of him that ran from the floor up to the ceiling, illuminating the surrounding area in orange light. There was a third fire coming from the ceiling, suspended high above them in a brazier. Ayr suspected it was only there for decoration as it served no obvious functional purpose.

Harmon thrust his arms out in front of him, and one by one, more columns of fire roared into existence. The structure that they stood in continued back as far as the eye could see, with a new column of fire erupting to life every second. The floor and walls were black as if they had been scorched by dragon fire.

"Welcome to the Tomb of Chilijo. This is where he fell centuries ago."

"Where he fell? Are we inside Chilijo right now?"

"You stand inside Chilijo. We are inside his head at the moment."

Azura circled Harmon and hissed at him. "This is sacrilege."

Harmon laughed up at her and Ayr felt a surge of rage shoot through his body. "Do not speak to me about sacrilege, dragon. There is a reason that riders and their dragons do not come here. Which one of you thought it would be a good idea?" His eyes found Elanor and he nodded slowly. "Of course. I can see your pain. That was a rash decision."

"Where is the scalebane ether?" Elanor was beginning to get frustrated.

"The treasures that are hidden within this tomb are not readily available. We have a long way to go yet."

"Do you live here, Harmon?"

Harmon nodded in response. "I do. It is my duty to safeguard this tomb and all that resides within it. The curse has been passed down to me through my father."

Now it was Ayr's turn to question the old man. "Curse? Just how old are you?"

"My grandfather was Chilijo's rider if that answers your question."

Azura was internally shocked. Ayr felt the surge of surprise wash through him like a cold wave as she filled his brain with knowledge. The legend of Chilijo was centuries old, older than the riders as an organisation. The first war had almost ended dragons in the world until his brave sacrifice had saved them. This man appeared to be only as old as Crassus. Despite his limp he was in good physical health.

"I know what you're thinking. When my father died, the burden of this place was placed upon me. The riders should have given this place more thought if it meant so much to them. Chilijo's magic is powerful. Did you notice the blackened earth upon your arrival? There is a reason why we walk across flat ground now."

"We were told to not come here unless under the gravest of circumstances. I decided that now was the time that a rider should venture to the tomb. I don't know what I would do without my dragon."

"Regardless of what you might believe, Chilijo was a false god. Yes, he won the first war, but there was more to it than anyone alive realises today. He is not the saviour that the Commonwealth believed him to be, nor was he on their side."

"Why are you telling us all this?" Elanor's voice was firm and deep. "Chilijo has been considered an deity by the riders for centuries."

"Because even the best stories are diluted in fiction. The victors are the ones who write history. Just like how I imagine it was described in whatever book you found that brought you here."

Ayr shook his head. "How did you know I found it in a book?"

Harmon scoffed. "Who do you think controlled the flow of information from this place? Anything that has left these walls within the last fifty years has been because of me. I put those books into the world."

Ask him about the scalebane.

"Great. So, then what can you tell us about the scalebane?"

"I make it here in the depths of the tomb. "

Elanor rolled her eyes. "Here? With what tools? There's nothing here Harmon."

"You have seen nothing of Chilijo yet. Follow me."

Chilijo's head and the columns that they were walking between seemed endless. If the dragon had been alive, they would have been walking along his tongue. The fires kept burning, and Ayr could clearly make out the roof of Chilijo's enormous mouth.

The path before them narrowed; Chilijo's neck was still almost just as wide and as deep as his head had been, still giving Azura plenty of room to manoeuvre within. As they walked down Chilijo's throat, more fire columns continued to light up, illuminating the path ahead. Here however, the walls seemed to be sturdier as if they were almost in something that was not the remains of the world's most decorated dragon. They seemed more concrete and more akin to the makeup of the Obelisk. On these walls, Ayr could make out strange runes that ran along them, all within standing height. He went to open his mouth before Harmon cut him off.

"That's our story. It is the duty of my family to ensure we keep this place sacred, and this history intact. We're nowhere near the scalebane yet. Please keep following me."

Can you sense the magic, rider?

Ayr flicked his tongue out like a dragon. *Yes, it doesn't seem right. I refuse to turn back.*

So do I, rider.

They walked in silence for what seemed like leagues. If Azura had been able to fly they could have covered this distance in a matter of seconds. Instead, Ayr was forced to continue following this strange man with the limp, further into the darkness. It was not until the neck began to thicken out and lead into the body of Chilijo, that the true enormity of the ancient beast was made apparent. The cavern that they were now in rose high, massive stone platforms also were suspended in the air, held up either on stilts that disappeared into the depths below, or by large beams suspended from the ceiling.

As more and more fire flickered to light, Ayr was dumbstruck by what he was witnessing rising around him. "Who built all of this?"

"My forefathers and I have preserved both Chilijo and his tomb since his death. Everything you see here was crafted by our hands and our hands alone."

"Where did you get the materials and magic from?"

Harmon turned and grinned at Elanor. "You really don't understand Chilijo's power, do you?"

"No, nor do I care. I'm here for one reason and one reason only, Harmon. Hurry up and take us to the scalebane."

"Patience, dragon rider. The tomb does not take kindly to the demands of outsiders. You will have your scalebane."

Harmon extended his arms again, much like he had done when he had called the flames up. Then as he moved his arms, platforms started to move and transform. Some of the platforms above them were cut in half and shifted into the surrounding platforms, creating some smaller and some larger. Even the one that the three of them stood on started to shift and change.

"Ayr!"

At first the platform was split in half, separating Elanor from him. Once the platform detached, it moved with enough speed to cut off any chance Ayr had of joining Elanor. As soon as the first split in the platform took hold, another shattered the ground behind him. He shot up towards the ceiling, and it was now Azura that was left behind. She squealed as the platform was taken out from underneath her, and without being able to use her wings, as Ayr ascended away from her, there was no way for her to catch up.

"What have you done, Harmon?!"

The old man turned, with his hands still in the air as he directed the platforms to follow his will. If Ayr interrupted him now, there may well have been no way that he could regroup with Elanor and Azura. They were ascending rapidly through the darkness, heading back towards the head of Chilijo, but only higher. Ayr peered over the edge of the platform as they flew. There was no sign of Azura or Elanor.

Rider! I will find you! Do not panic!

I'm not. Stay close to me.

I always will, rider. Find out what is going on.

Ayr rejoined the world, still with his head over the side of the platform. Harmon had his back to him and Ayr could have easily pushed him off. "Where are you taking me?"

"There's someone that would like to see you, Ashbourne."

"Who?"

A grin came to Harmon's lips. "Your father."

"Who are you, actually?"

The platform that they were on was beginning to slow down and Harmon lowered his arms. Now could have been Ayr's chance to rid himself of the man, if he knew where the other two platforms that had taken Elanor and Azura were. Instead, Harmon smiled at him once again.

"I've already told you, Ashbourne. I am Harmon, Keeper of the Tomb of Chilijo. However, your father discovered us and made a request of me. Despite the power and magic hidden within the tomb, I am no match for the power of a fully grown elder dragon and a rider."

"You could have come to the riders and the Commonwealth for help."

Harmon laughed and shook his head. "What, and hand over the relics that my forefathers have curated over for centuries? No, I don't think so. A small favour to ensure that this place remains safe from riders seeking treasures that they cannot understand is better than allowing open season here."

"You can stand up to him. We wanted one thing, and then we would go."

Harmon laughed again. "One thing leads to another. You are the first riders to visit in a long time. Those that venture here typically do not return to the Commonwealth."

"What have you done with Azura and Elanor?"

"Dalton has instructed me not to kill them yet. Azura is the dragon, I presume?" Harmon waited for his confirmation. "She's important to you, and so is the girl. She's the dragon rider that needs the scalebane ether, correct?" Ayr nodded again and Harmon extended his arm towards the edge of the flat ground that they had just landed upon. "Well, there is only one man here that will give that to you. Good luck."

Ayr was defiant. "I'm not going anywhere until you bring Azura and Elanor back to me."

"They will be returned to you in due course. Now go."

Ayr turned on his heel, frustrated and annoyed. He walked towards where Harmon had directed him, only to look back over his shoulder to see the platform he had just stood on moving away again into the darkness. Gripping his sword tighter, Ayr followed the dimly lit pathway in front of him.

The path felt like it continued as far as he had walked with Azura and Elanor only moments ago; the featureless walls made it feel like it would never come to an end. Just when he thought that he would continue walking further, he finally saw a turn in the path ahead. There was more light coming from it, and Ayr turned the corner, holding his breath, expecting the worst.

As he turned the corner, Ayr saw the first signs that Harmon did in fact live here. Brown canvas walls rose from the floor to the ceiling, which would provide some warmth and insulation, with another firepit right behind it. The area rose by a foot, with a blackened step that made it higher than the pathway that Ayr was on, and sitting on the step was a lone figure with a travelling cloak draped over their head. The figure was much like Harmon; however they sat with one leg higher than the other. There was no doubt in Ayr's mind who this was. A small silver dragon fluttered in the air beside him, hovering no more than a few inches off the ground. It was no longer than a cat, and just as lean.

Dalton raised his head from what he was doing. Ayr could not see it clearly, but it appeared that he had been carving a wooden figurine in his hands. As he raised his head, the hood slipped from it and Ayr could make out Dalton's face in the dull light of the fire. Dalton smiled at Ayr with a warmth that he was not familiar with. Azura could see everything.

"My son, welcome to the Tomb of Chilijo."

"What are you doing here, father? I did not think that I'd be seeing you again so soon. Your plans are surely not ready to hatch yet."

Rider! Are you alright?

Yes, Azura. It is only my father.

He is dangerous! I'm coming to get you!

I will be okay, Azura. My father will not harm me.

Dalton's smile shifted into a dark smirk. "You can stop talking to your dragon, Ayr. We need time to talk since we did not get much chance to speak when you met Sinibad, now did we?"

"Was it all part of your plan? To unveil your weapon to the world and then go back into hiding."

Dalton raised a hand, dismissing his question. "Tell me, Ayr. Can you still feel her?"

A shiver ran down Ayr's spine. The way Dalton's eyes met his was unnerving. He knew what Dalton wanted to hear, but discussing his relationship with Azura outside of Elanor was something he was yet to do. This was something that he also needed to close off from her. He could still feel her moving beneath him, somewhere within the tomb.

Ayr nodded. "Our connection is strong, just like you wanted. I got lucky. She is one of the most magically attuned dragons in the Commonwealth."

"And can you mask your emotions and thoughts from her?"

"It is hard, but I can feel her coming to me more every day. She can see some things that I do not want her to. I imagine that will only make it harder over time."

"Is this going to be a problem?"

"No, father. I will do what you have asked. Her and I will become one eventually. My goals are aligned with yours."

"Good. Sinibad grows restless." Dalton rose to his feet slowly. The small dragon rose with him, fluttering up to his shoulder to rest on it. "My plans are beginning to spread their wings."

"What game are you playing, father? You've told me about my part, but you refuse to give any more information. You revealed Sinibad to us, but that was it. Do you control him, or does he control you?"

Dalton raised his fist and a swirl of magic caressed by the firelight danced around it like a glove on his hand. "What do you think, Ayr? If I have spent the time since the war fostering a relationship with such a creature, do you think that I would be able to bend it to my will with my talents?"

"Why didn't you tell me about him?"

"And have you be examined by Crassus upon your arrival to the Seminary of Fire and the Obelisk? Why would I risk it? There's a reason why I only told you your part, Ayr. Yet yours is one of the most vital."

Ayr heard footsteps from behind him and he went to turn to deal with whoever was coming towards them, but he felt a tight cord wrap around his waist. Ayr tried to take a step away from Dalton, but instead was dragged to him. Ayr tried to free himself from the grips of Dalton's spell, but the magic was too strong. Instead, he resorted to screaming at Dalton as he was pulled closer.

"What are you doing?"

Dalton cast a side eye at him. "Leverage. Wait here."

It was like he was trapped and as the footsteps grew closer, Ayr came to a stop. He heard a whistle from beside his head and turned it to see a small needle hanging in the air beside him. Moments later, Elanor came into view. She did not have her sword drawn yet. Her eyes narrowed as she assessed the situation.

"Ayr!"

He attempted to lift his arm, but Dalton's spell was like an invisible vice, tightening its grip around him. The needle hovered menacingly, whizzing even closer to his throat with a chilling precision. Elanor took another deliberate step forward, her eyes locked on the scene, the tension in the air palpable.

"Greetings, Lady Sunfire. What a pleasure to see you again."

"Dalton Ashbourne. What are you doing here?"

"I came to the Tomb of Chilijo for its tools that I intend to use in the upcoming war."

"War? Will you listen to yourself? You're one man with a rogue elder dragon that needs to be put down."

Dalton's smirk spread across his face again. "If only that was correct. The Tomb of Chilijo harbours many secrets which the Commonwealth has long thought lost to them, Lady Sunfire. What they don't know is that I have discovered many of them, including Sinibad."

Elanor hissed at him. "Where is he?"

"That's none of your concern. What are you planning on doing without your dragon, Elanor?"

Elanor finally drew her sword and spat at the ground. "Kill you."

"I know that your magical talent has ceased to exist without your dragon by your side, Elanor, but consider the consequences."

"I have. You at the present moment are the biggest threat to the Commonwealth. I will not have us go through another war just for your pride."

Dalton laughed and raised his hand towards Ayr's throat where the needle was resting. "Do you see that? This war won't be fought for my pride. This will be fought for my legacy."

"What have you done to him?"

"Nothing. But these are the consequences that you need to consider. You can try and kill me. You might succeed. But can you do it before my needle there goes through Ayr's throat?

Elanor paused and finally Ayr could see her eyes, looking into the space beside him. She could see the needle. "I would lay my life on the line for Ayr, so he does not have to serve you for one more day."

Dalton's smirk changed into a well-practiced smile. "Excellent! That's what I'd hope you'd say. Lady Sunfire, the purpose for luring you here, was not so that I could kill my son or his dragon. No, that would be counterintuitive. What I lured you here for, was you. I have plans for you."

"You wanted me this whole time?"

Dalton sniggered. "Of course. I sent that wyvern out there with the scalebane. Onoss was far too valuable to risk for such an endeavour, especially if he was to fail. The wyvern snuck in behind your dragon and infected him with the scalebane before it succumbed to the poison itself. I already have Ayr and in turn I will have his dragon, but you on the other hand. You would be a most valuable asset that I do not yet have access to."

"So why bring us here then, father? Why not fly on Sinibad to the Obelisk and have us meet our fate? If the elder dragon is so powerful, would he not have been able to do it?"

"Because you know as well as I do, that I cannot make a move against the Obelisk whilst it remains under the protection of Crassus and his overgrown green snake. He is the one rider that can stand up to me. Until you complete your task, Ayr, nothing else can take place."

Elanor rounded on him, her mouth ajar. "Your job? What the fuck are you talking about, Dalton? You're going to kill my father and open up the Commonwealth to him?"

"It's about time you clued onto what's going on here. Yes, Crassus will die for what he did to me."

"What he did to you? You tried to court his promised and you blinded his dragon!"

Dalton chuckled. "Is that what he told you? Is that what *she* told you? I expected this and it appears that your parents have not disappointed me."

"That you're a dangerous fanatic and that you're unhinged. That you'll stop at nothing in your pursuits."

Dalton continued to chuckle. "Do I appear to be either of those things right now? I want to change the world, Elanor. The Commonwealth deserves to burn for what they've done to it. Do you really think that you're protecting it?"

"I do. I'm tired of you pretending that I'm not. I have a job to do and it's to protect the Commonwealth from people like you."

Dalton reached his hand into his cloak to reveal a small glass bottle, no larger than his palm. Elanor took half a step forward and stopped, staring at it. "Is that what I think it is?"

"This is what you came for wasn't it, Elanor? The scalebane ether?"

"Yes! Now hand it over!"

Dalton outstretched his hand slowly, before bringing it back in. He held his hand open and the dragon leapt down from his shoulder to snatch the bottle. It took off up into the ceiling. "Why would I do that? You'd run me through with your sword the first chance you got. That's also why this is not enough ether to cure Evor completely of the scalebane."

Elanor's face darkened. "Where's the rest, Dalton?"

"I ordered Harmon to destroy the rest. He can make more, of course, but he is the only person in the world that knows how. Without him, your dragon will not be cured."

"What do I need to do for you to allow him to make more?"

"I want your soul, Elanor Sunfire. In exchange for the cure to the scalebane, you will be my eyes and ears within the Obelisk anytime that I call upon you. In return, when I deem you have earned it, I will deliver you the final sample of the ether. Do you want your dragon to die?"

Elanor bowed her head. "I will do as you ask, Dalton Ashbourne."

Another smirk crossed Dalton's face. "Excellent. Chorru! Bring the ether."

The small dragon that had flown off into the darkness of the tomb reemerged, floating down from above. In its front talon, it carried the bottle of scalebane ether that Dalton had given it only moments ago. Without a care in the world, Chorru had flown over Elanor's head, dropping the ether into the empty space. Like her life depended on it, Elanor leapt for the ether, catching it in her non-sword hand. With a sigh of relief and a smile across her face, Elanor held the ether, staring at it in her outstretched hand.

"Lady Sunfire! You have what you came here for, and I have my answer. You'll be hearing from me soon. Begone from this place."

"That's fine by me. Now release Ayr."

TWENTY-TWO

The corners of Dalton's lips curled again as he laughed. "The audacity of you, Elanor Sunfire. We are moments into our new arrangement, and you are already trying to force your position. You are not the one with the power here. Look!"

Ayr flinched as the needle came closer to his throat, now hovering less than a thumbnail away from him. One more movement from Dalton would see him finished. He had been in this situation before, Dalton often using this spell to train him. Ayr took a deep breath, hoping that Elanor would make the right decision.

She bowed her head and slowly sheathed her sword. "Apologies, Dalton. I only wish to take Ayr back so that we may return to the Obelisk with haste."

Dalton stopped laughing and waved his hand. The needle faded from existence as if blown apart by a gentle breeze. The spell that constricted Ayr's midsection also fell away like someone letting go of a rope. Chorru continued to beat his wings in the air above them, circling like a shark as the palpable energy was sucked from the room.

"You may take him. It is clear to me that you care about him. Are your dragons promised to each other?"

"They are." Ayr spoke at last. "My dragon waited almost thirty years to be paired with me."

Dalton chortled. "Got yourself an older woman, Ayr? I know how that feels. If you're dragons are promised, don't let anyone come between the two of you."

Elanor's eyes narrowed. "Nobody will."

Spurred on by Dalton's compulsion, Ayr followed Elanor back down the path that they had travelled. At last, he reopened his mind, allowing Azura back in..

Rider! What happened? I lost you!

Nothing, I am fine.

Rider! You need to tell me what happened.

We have the scalebane ether. Dalton had it.

There was an influx of warmth and gratitude from Azura. *Well, you'd best hurry. I don't know how long Evor would have left.*

We will be right there. Where are you?

Near the entrance.

Elanor cast a side eye at him as they walked down the corridor. "Azura? Is she safe?"

"Yes, she waits for us at the entrance."

"Great, well I hope we're going to get out of here in one piece."

"I have a feeling that we will. Dalton isn't one to throw away assets on a whim."

Elanor frowned, letting her thoughts consume her. Ayr could see her mind whirling as she was trying to digest what had just occurred. There was nothing she could have done to prevent it. Ayr had been born into servitude of Dalton Ashbourne, but he had seen countless others bend their knee to his father. Even now as they were walking away from him, Ayr could feel the magic presence of Dalton behind him.

They were nearing the end of the corridor and, at long last, Ayr could see into the dark, empty expanse that Harmon had brought him up through. At the end of the corridor, Harmon was waiting for them where he had left Ayr. A faint smile washed over his face as he saw them approaching. He stepped back onto the platform and waited for them to arrive. As they neared, he rubbed his hands together in anticipation.

"How did it go? I assume since you are both leaving in one piece that the negotiations were successful."

Elanor puffed out her chest. "I wouldn't know about successful. But yes, I got the scalebane ether."

"I'd like to apologise for that. If he had not threatened me with the destruction of the tomb, I would have been more forthcoming. Please do as he says going forward. It will only save you pain the future."

"Like you'd know."

Harmon laughed and removed the glove from his left hand once again to reveal his blackened skin. "I wouldn't know pain? Look me in the eye and tell me I wouldn't know pain. The burnt hand is the one that teaches the harshest lessons."

"Did Dalton do that to you?"

Elanor turned to Ayr; her hand raised towards Harmon. "See, just another marked by your father's doing. We need to end him."

Now it was Ayr's turn to chuckle softly. "That's easier said than done as you just found out. He had no elder dragon with him and yet you will now complete tasks for him."

Harmon was apologetic. "Again, I am sorry. This tomb remains and the only way to do that was by serving him. If I see any opportunity to right my wrong, I will."

"You're the only one that can make the scalebane ether, correct?"

Harmon nodded. "I am, rider."

"Then you will do nothing until my dragon is cured. Am I understood?"

"If you insist on playing this dangerous game with a man like that, you will die before I have the chance to cure your dragon. You'd best be cautious. Now are you leaving my home or not?"

"Azura is waiting for us, Elanor."

Harmon sighed. "I'll take that as a yes."

He raised his hands into the air, much like he had done previously. The platform that they were on began to move once again, and this time Ayr was not as worried as he had been on the way up. As long as Harmon was taking them where he promised, everything would be fine. Azura became more predominate in Ayr's mind, filling it with her presence. She was trying to calm him, but Ayr was only thinking of what had occurred with Dalton. Harmon took his time lowering the platform to the entrance level, and it was not long before Azura came into view.

"Rider! Elanor!"

Ayr smiled up at her. She would have been smiling back at him too if it was not for her distain of Harmon. Every fibre of her presence wanted Ayr to reach out and run him through with his sword. The only thing preventing it was the knowledge that Harmon was the only person that could make scalebane ether.

"I'm glad to see you as well, Azura. We have the ether."

"I know, rider. We should depart."

Harmon grunted as he moved past them both. "Follow me to the exit then."

Elanor held out her arm, trying to prevent him from going past. "We've followed you enough places."

"I will still need to open the door in order for you to get out." Harmon tugged on his cloak. "I insist."

Harmon limped past them, swinging his cloak as he went. With no other choice, Ayr sighed and fell in behind him. The rest of their journey to the door was wordless, Harmon's face unreadable from this angle. Once they reached the door, Harmon removed his glove again and raised his hand to it. Now they were able to see the mechanics of the door from the other side. The door slid across on a rail when activated by Harmon's touch. Light started to filter into the tomb and Ayr was glad to feel the warmth of the sun on his face once again as they stepped outside.

"Congratulations, riders. You are now two of the very few people who have seen the Tomb of Chilijo and lived to tell the tale."

Elanor sniggered beside Ayr. "Not without you trying to kill us both by feeding us to Dalton Ashbourne. Thank you for the ether."

Harmon shrugged his shoulders. "You had to make a difficult choice today, rider. It's not like we are dissimilar in this situation. You will not hear me judging you for it."

"Speaking of that, Harmon. Is there anywhere else that we can find some scalebane of our own? We need to kill his elder dragon."

"Unlikely." He glanced up back towards the top of the tomb as if hoping that Dalton was not watching them and then lowered his tone. "If I knew a place, I would not look in any other tomb around here." He raised his eyebrows with suspicion. "There will be other dangers that await you in them, but thankfully, Dalton Ashbourne is not a mind reader."

"I wouldn't put it past him."

"Neither would I. Now go. Otherwise, you may not have the chance to. I can feel a shift in the air. Dalton is protecting something here."

"Like what, Harmon?"

Harmon shrugged like an innocent child that was trying to let on that they did not know what was being talked about. "Might I suggest research in your spare time? If I tell you, he'll kill me."

Ayr nodded and then noticed Elanor patting her chest just outside his field of vision. He turned to her with an eyebrow raised. "Still got it?"

"Yep, just checking. Let's get out of here."

Ayr retrieved his mask from his vest and raised it to his face. Elanor was doing the same thing and once the masks were in place, Ayr began climbing up Azura's leg. She lowered herself to the ground for both of them, and within moments, Ayr was locked into his saddle. There were no further words spoken, all three of them eager to return to the Obelisk, away from Dalton's reach.

Double checking and ensuring he was properly secured in his saddle, Ayr felt Azura turn underneath him. For a creature of her size, her turning circle was small and as she started to run, he felt less secure than ever before. Azura bound across the charcoal-coloured ground, bounding away from the Tomb of Chilijo like a giant dog. Each bound into the air made his stomach rise in his throat and each of Azura's landings on the ground rocked him. The motion was not something that he was used to.

Rider, I can feel the magic lifting.

Then take flight, Azura.

Her next bound did not touch back down to the ground. Instead, Azura's wings were unfurled in a single step, and she used the momentum to propel herself into the sky. Ayr's stomach caught in his throat for one final time, before Azura was finally gaining altitude, rising into the sky. At first, the climb in altitude was slow, but then as Azura began to flatten out, it became easier. Whatever magic lay around the Tomb of Chilijo was now fading away.

Ayr settled into the flight and was beginning to enjoy it. They had achieved their goal in at least retrieving some of the scalebane ether. As Ayr sat back in the saddle, something seemed off, coming from behind them. He turned slowly to see an indomitable form streaking across the sky towards them. The golden hue on the creature's scales from this far away and the simply gargantuan size it cut across the horizon could only mean it was one dragon.

Sinibad.

Rider!

I know! Go!

All you can do is fly, Azura! Keep going! He may not have seen us yet!

An ear-splitting roar ripped through the air, despite Sinibad only just being within the horizon. His city sized wings were propelling him forward with each beat, his figure rapidly growing faster than it had any right to. As Sinibad grew nearer, Azura was becoming more and more panicked. Her wings were beating faster, desperate to flee the larger titan. Ayr threw his head back over his shoulder just to see how much the dragon was gaining on them. Surely Dalton would have told it by now.

Regardless, Sinibad bore down on them, and upon closer inspection, dozens of wyverns were flying under the body of him. If any of them caught Azura, they would be torn from the sky. Azura screamed inside Ayr's mind. This was the first time that either of them had seen Sinibad in open flight. The wyvern were much slower, but could still be considered a threat, even though at this point they were nothing more than black dots against the blue horizon.

Azura was making good time away from the Tomb of Chilijo, but Ayr feared that it would not be enough. Sinibad's head was swelling by the second and there was only so much encouragement that Ayr could give Azura to push her faster. He felt Elanor's hand squeeze on his shoulder, but it offered little value in this situation. They had come all of this way only to be snatched from the sky by Dalton's dragon.

Just as Sinibad's head was becoming the same size as his hand in the distance, the enormous golden dragon let out another ear-splitting roar. This was much closer and forced Ayr to cover his ears. Instead of speeding up and tearing after them, Sinibad instead made a sharp right-hand turn. He was headed for the Tomb of Chilijo. Ayr was not convinced until he at last saw Sinibad touching down onto the ground. He breathed a sigh of relief that flowed on through to Azura.

We got lucky. He wasn't after us.

I know, rider.

TWENTY-THREE

Ayr had never been more grateful to see the towering structure of the Obelisk floating in the sky high above the mountains. Despite Sinibad now being leagues away from them, Ayr would have felt better if they had been flying with the protection of Evor. Azura felt the same way. None of them had slept, Azura powering through the journey fuelled only by fear and Ayr's magic when hers faltered.

As they flew towards it, the Obelisk once again seemed scarce of dragons and their riders. Rather than coming into one of the landing platforms that was customary, Azura headed straight for the courtyard in which Evor lay. As they crested the Obelisk, an all too familiar face rose over the ledge with them. Gundrag had been lying in wait. As Azura flew within meters of him, Gundrag roared, shocking Ayr properly awake.

Whilst he had not slept in the saddle, considering the proximity to the Obelisk, Ayr had opted to close his eyes. The deafening roar of Gundrag was unwelcome; Azura made herself known, bellowing back at the purple dragon in retaliation. Gundrag fell silent and allowed them to pass the threshold of the Obelisk in peace. Already, Azura was readying herself for their landing, most anxious to see the ether presented to Evor.

I hope we are not too late.

He will not have passed in the time we have been away. Elanor would have sensed it.

I am not so sure, rider.

We will see in a moment.

As Azura angled around the Obelisk, making her way to the court-yard, Baindussa quickly came into view. As he saw them, Baindussa raised his head from his roost and let loose a roar of his own into the sky. Was he alerting Crassus of their return? Baindussa's massive nostrils flared as he sniffed the air. Evor was directly underneath him and still had not moved from the position that he had been laying in days prior. There was no noticeable change to his body except for one of his scars on the back of his legs had turned a similar green to the scales of Baindussa.

"Azura! You know the protocol. Riders must come through the gate first."

"Baindussa! There is no time!"

"Turn back and place your riders at the bottom of the Obelisk! Now!"

"Baindussa, please! Evor needs them! They have the ether!" She pulled out of the dive and circled around again. "Baindussa, I am begging you!"

"Let them past, Baindussa. Evor is not allowed to perish on under your watch." The new voice that came out of nowhere was deep and familiar as it rose up from behind them. Ayr checked over his shoulder to find Gundrag rising above the Obelisk. "This is urgent, Baindussa. Protocol be damned!"

Baindussa was rising from his roost, with now more than just his head off the roof of the Obelisk. "You would challenge me?"

"I would have you see sense! Now let them past!"

Baindussa grumbled and let up, sinking back down onto the ceiling. "One time only."

Gundrag stood down, grumbling at Baindussa in his own right. "Thank you. Azura, land!"

Following Gundrag's instructions, Azura finished her loop and came down straight at the Obelisk. The courtyard was plenty big enough for her to land in, even with Evor taking up a large portion of the space available to her. Ayr cringed as he looked at the green wound on Evor's leg.

Baindussa lazily watched them from his roost with one eye open. "He has not worsened, nor has he recovered. I have kept watch over him, keeping him in a stable condition. If you have the ether, you will need to ensure that his body absorbs it properly through his mouth."

Ayr was turning in his saddle as Azura settled herself down on the ground beside Evor. "Go to him!"

Elanor was already leaning forward in the saddle, retrieving the ether from where she had stowed it in one of the saddle bags. As soon as the lid of the bottle was in between her fingers, she was removing herself from the saddle and slipped down Azura's body. There was no time to waste. Ayr removed his mask and started to pull himself from the saddle as Elanor raced across the few meters of the courtyard to be by Evor's mouth. His breathing was slow, but stable.

Ayr slid down from Azura's back, patting her on the shoulder before he left. By the time he had landed on the ground, Elanor had already climbed up Evor's jaw, tittering precariously on the largest of his scales in the area. She held the ether bottle in her left hand, ready to pour the contents into his mouth.

"How am I going to do this? There's no gap."

"I will assist you, Elanor."

Azura stood up again and raised one of her talons to Evor's jaw and used it to pry open his lip. It was the slightest movement, but it was more than enough for Elanor to get the bottle to where it needed to be. She cracked open the lid and poured the contents of the bottle into Evor's mouth. Once the bottle was empty, she remained standing on Evor for a moment, watching for any sign of movement. Azura removed her talon, allowing Evor's mouth to close again.

"Will he get better now?"

Ayr moved in underneath Elanor as she stood watching Evor, her shoulders rounded. "We probably have to wait. The magic may take some time. That dosage also was not enough to cure him, remember?"

"No, Ayr, Harmon said that this would get him up. If I was meant to put it on the wound…"

Baindussa grumbled down from his roost again. "Patience, Lady Sunfire. Evor is a large dragon and that was not a lot of ether. Anything like that will take time to work. Just wait."

"I don't have time to wait!" Elanor stamped her feet like an impatient child. "I need Evor returned to me!"

Baindussa started to hum, a welcome change from his grumbling tone. His eyes closed and a moment later he reopened them. "You are better served resting, Elanor. I have felt something stir inside Evor, but it will take some time for him to recover from his sedated state that I have put him in. Rest assured that the scalebane ether is doing as it was intended to."

"So, I haven't done anything wrong?"

Baindussa shook his mighty, magnificent green head. "No, you have not. Now attend Crassus. He comes."

Ayr turned his head to see none other than Crassus emerging from his chambers. He wore Draxion around his shoulders like an overgrown cat. Regardless of how Crassus looked, the dragon appeared comfortable. Crassus was adorned in red robes and as he stepped into the sunlight, a smile spread across his face as his eyes rested on Elanor standing atop of Evor's jaw. Most notably, he was not flanked by Kaiser.

"Daughter! I am so glad to see that you are safe. I hear the Tomb of Chilijo is a perilous place to visit."

Elanor nodded her agreement. "It is, father. We encountered Dalton Ashbourne again, father. He's growing bolder. He was inside the Tomb of Chilijo."

Crassus' eyes widened. "And you escaped him again?"

"He was the one responsible for Evor's condition. I retrieved some of the scalebane ether required that will nurse Evor back to health, but he got away. Once Evor is fighting fit again, I will hunt him again."

"Good, I am glad to hear it. Have you spent any thought towards those riders that will hunt Dalton with you?"

"I have been too concerned with Evor's condition. If Azura had not been trapped away from Dalton when we encountered him, we could very well have stopped this war already."

Crassus raised an eyebrow. "A war?"

"Dalton's words, father. He claimed that he would be fighting for his legacy."

For the first time since he had emerged from his chambers, Crassus' eyes fell on Ayr. They stared at each other before Crassus nodded. "Interesting. You should come down from Evor in case he wakes up, you know. We don't want you suffering another fall, do we Elanor?"

"No father, we would not."

"Either way, I'm glad to see you home safe. I imagine you are exhausted. The Tomb of Chilijo is some distance away. You should retreat to your chambers."

Elanor offered Crassus an informal, sloppy salute. "Yes, father."

Crassus nodded, satisfied he had been caught up on the events. With Draxion still on his shoulders, he turned on his heel and started back towards the way he came. His red robes kissed the tiled floor beneath his feet as he walked. Elanor was already on the move before Crassus had turned, making her way down Evor's scales, looking for footholds in the dragon's hide.

Azura was amused. "I could have just picked you up and lifted you to the ground, Elanor."

Elanor hit the ground a moment later. She dusted her hands off and smiled up at Azura. "Now where would the fun in that be?"

"Me not having to explain to my promised that his rider fell to her death after administering him with an ether."

Elanor shrugged. "I can see your point, Azura. Now I don't know about you two, but I'm knackered. If Evor will take some time to arise, what is the point of being here?"

Azura nodded her agreement. "Indeed. I would like these saddles off me."

Ayr ran his hand on her leg. "You did amazing. Can you fly a little more?"

Azura turned her head so that Ayr could see directly into her eyes again. She nodded gently. "Yes, rider. I think that I can fly to see the stable hands. You should return to your quarters and rest. I would not have been able to complete the journey so timely without your magic. Thank you."

"It was my pleasure. Now go, get the saddles off you!"

Azura turned her head to the sky and took a step forward to avoid collecting Ayr in her movements. She kicked off from the ground and Ayr felt himself pushed into the tiles by the first few beats of her wings. As she soared up above him, Ayr was transfixed by the sun as it caught her scales, making her shimmer in the light. He let out a sigh as Elanor wrapped an arm over his shoulders.

"Should we go, Ashbourne?"

"Ashbourne? You're back to calling me that again?"

Elanor winked at him. "Old habit. Come on."

It was clear to him that she was exhausted. Yes, whilst he had spent energy helping Azura speeding up their journey, Elanor had no connection to Evor. Ayr was happy that she was using him as a crutch, but as they approached the platform to the rest of the Obelisk, a figure moved inside the gateway.

He heard Elanor audibly sigh as she recognised who it was before him. "What do you want Kaladin?"

Kaladin moved from out of the shadows and into the light with a neutral expression. Behind them, Ayr could hear Gundrag moving into position to be closer to his rider. It was not a position he was comfortable being in, having just sent Azura away. He wanted to call out to her, but something told him that Elanor could handle whatever Kaladin wanted.

"I didn't hear a thank you."

Elanor snorted. "For what? Getting your dragon to stand up to my father's outdated safety protocols? It's something we've all wanted to do in our time, but now suddenly, you as the head of security have found it convenient to skirt them yourself?"

Kaladin shrugged with an indifferent expression. "We all have our price."

"What's yours then, I wonder?"

"I want in on the hunt for Dalton Ashbourne and the elder dragon. Gundrag and I single-handedly won the Battle of Ashenfort. You'd be stupid not to take us with you.."

Ayr raised his hand. "I for one think it is a good idea."

Elanor shook her head in silent disgust. "Just because we used to fuck, Kaladin, doesn't mean you automatically get included in every big game hunt."

"Sorry, I don't see many other riders jumping at the chance to hunt with you and Ashbourne."

"Fine." Elanor rolled her eyes. "I'll think about it."

"Thank you."

"You're not welcome."

Kaladin could not contain a sinister smile any longer. "It's always a pleasure doing business with a Sunfire and an Ashbourne. Let me know when you two want to go hunt the elder dragon. I'll ensure that we're ready for take-off when you are. I would not want to miss out on this glory. I'll be in the mess hall."

Ayr watched as Kaladin faded from sight, headed towards Gundrag. The purple dragon waited until his rider had mounted and the two of them took off, disappearing over the edge of the Obelisk within a matter of seconds. For what had been minutes of chaos and distractions, Ayr welcomed the quiet except for the sound of the gentle wind as it pushed overhead.

"Should we retire?"

Elanor flashed her teeth at him with a warm smile. "I was hoping you would never ask. I can't wait to bathe and get out of these clothes. It's almost exciting as the prospect of having Evor return to me!"

TWENTY-FOUR

*E*lanor...

Elanor jolted awake with a shock. The room was dark around her and nobody else was visible. The voice had come from outside. And there was only one place that the voice could have come from. When it called to her again, she instantly knew who it was.

Elanor!

Evor!

Elanor. What in Chilijo's name have you done?

Ensured your survival.

Elanor...

Stay right where you are. I am coming to you, Evor.

What about Baindussa? He will not be pleased if he sees you coming into his courtyard uninvited.

Fuck Baindussa. If he has an issue, he can take it up with my father. The sooner we get you out of there the better you will be.

I will come to you, Elanor.

No, you need to stay right there, Evor. Rest. I won't be long.

Before she had time to consider her decision, Elanor was already on her feet. If her dragon needed her, he needed her, and she was not going to let anyone tell her differently about it. It was late into the evening, well past the point that the moon would be rising somewhere on the horizon.

Rather than getting dressed completely, Elanor found her night gown and flung it over her shoulders. It was a dark, lush sapphire that contrasted with the stark whiteness of her undergarments, but Evor had seen her in every condition, and she was not dressing to impress. She grabbed her sword from beside the bed and carried it by the sheath in her left hand. Her hair was loose, but the only thing that mattered was Evor. She slipped into a shorter variant of the riding boots that she kept at her bedside table and without ushering another sound slipped out of her door.

The corridors outside her chambers were exactly what she expected this late at night. If a dragon and their rider were late returning from an errand or task, they would be the only beings that Elanor would sight between here and Baindussa's courtyard. The voices of the creatures that were rumoured to inhabit the walls might have followed her at this hour, but Elanor was more than ready to ignore them.

She made good progress, cutting through the corridors that she had spent her whole life traversing. Elanor prided herself on her ability to navigate the corridors faster than most other riders, if not all of them. Unfortunately for her, there were no contests in navigating the Obelisk efficiently. She reached the elevator in good time and opened the door with the hand gesture that it required. The closer she got to Evor, the more impatient she was getting.

The door opened onto the courtyard and at last, Elanor could see Evor again. He was still in a prone position, sprawled out across the majority of the courtyard, but there had been movement. Evor's front legs were in a new position, more under him as though he had tried to pull himself up. His head was no longer laying to the side, but resting on his front right leg.

Baindussa was still ever-present on his perch high above them. However much like Evor, he was laying with his head on his front legs. The giant green dragon was snoring at a steady beat, breathing in and out in almost perfect harmony with Evor. Elanor put a foot out onto the open courtyard floor when she heard a whisper on the wind.

"Elanor...Sun..."

Elanor froze. Baindussa was still asleep, but he may have been able to smell her. Much like any good guard, Baindussa still needed rest. During the nights, he opted to cast a simple sealing spell on the doors to Crassus' chambers to add a layer of protection to the Lord Chairman when he was sleeping. She had timed it just right. His magic was incredibly powerful; however, it was not infallible. The Obelisk relied on its many layers of protection to stop threats from reaching Crassus. Typically, most of the threats the riders faced also did not have access to dragons. Then there was the matter of Crassus himself, one of the most magically gifted men in the world. He had almost burst Ayr's head during their first proper meeting.

Sensing that Baindussa was still fast asleep and wanting to test her luck, Elanor placed one foot in front of the other. She stopped after the next step, glancing up at Baindussa on his perch. The guardian dragon had still not moved. Wanting to tempt fate, Elanor hurriedly crossed the courtyard towards Evor's head. Seeing him in this position made her feel just as vulnerable, but thankfully he was on the mend. Evor grumbled as she approached, and Elanor raised her hand to his head, opening an even more energy-conservative way of communicating with him.

She had not touched him in days, and felt a surge of electricity rocket through her body and into his. Elanor tried to contain a gasp, whilst Evor grunted, snorting from his nostrils. Elanor pressed her hand against his scales even more, calming him.

Shh, Evor. It's me. I'm here. We need to be quiet. Baindussa is asleep.

You have come to me at last.

From the Tomb of Chilijo no less.

Hmm, so that is where you have been the last few days. I wondered why Baindussa was healing me and not the little one. And why I saw Dalton Ashbourne in your memories.

I can explain all that.

Please do, Elanor. I do not need to take this to Crassus, do I?

I swore my service to Dalton Ashbourne in exchange for the scalebane ether.

You would help our enemy?

Look into my heart, Evor. You know my intentions.

Elanor... you should not have done what you did. Even if it was for me. That man seeks to destroy everything that we know and love.

You are everything that I know and love. Without you, I would cease to exist.

You are holding something back. What is it, Elanor?

I cannot serve him, but without the scalebane ether, I cannot ensure your survival. Your promised is also compromised. Ayr Ashbourne is working with his father to bring down the Commonwealth from the inside. We need to cure you of this disease permanently so that you may stand up to that elder dragon.

Elanor, you know as well as I do that I cannot face an elder dragon, especially one of that size, myself.

We will have a hunting party. We will bring it down.

So that solves one problem. What about the rodent within our walls? You play a dangerous game, Elanor.

I am only playing with the hand I am dealt, Evor. Can you fly to the Tomb of Chilijo?

If I have enough preparation, yes. It will be a long flight.

Can it be done?

Yes, Elanor.

Then see it done.

Elanor. What about your father? It is clear that he is Ashbourne's goal here at the Obelisk. If Dalton wants revenge, Crassus is sure to be a target.

My father is a dead man walking. I can do nothing to prevent the fate that awaits him. Either I save him and lose you, or I save you and lose my father.

Elanor, I am not asking you to choose between us.

There is no choice, Evor. Your survival is paramount. Not only for you, but for Azura and your entire bloodline.

Some things cannot be undone, Elanor.

I know, Evor. I will return to you later tonight.

You need to be careful.

He cares for me because Azura cares for you. If he is not kind, I will slit his throat where he stands.

And what are the chances of that, Elanor?

Considering he has made himself an enemy of the Commonwealth with what I witnessed in the Tomb of Chilijo, very high. Azura be damned.

You say that my survival is paramount, yet you would compromise my promised? How is that not going back on your word?

Elanor paused, frozen on the spot. *You know that's not what I meant.*

No, it is not. I know you will not threaten my promised. She would be better off without him if what you are telling me is true.

Then we need to tread carefully.

Now that I am awake and can protect you, I would see what more information you can gather from him, Elanor.

Protect me? You can't even stand, Evor.

Stand back, and I will show you my power is returning.

Should we do this with Baindussa right here watching over us?

Do you want me to return to form or not, Elanor?

Will you wake Baindussa?

I will do my best not to.

With every sound of his internalised, Evor began to groan loudly in Elanor's head. It was clear that he was still very much in pain. However, with each groan came progress. There was little that Evor could do to keep himself quiet in this situation, but as he pushed himself off to stand on his front legs, Baindussa still did not move. Elanor watched with bated breath, hoping that Evor would be able to take off successfully without Baindussa noticing. The green dragon was not typically a deep sleeper, but he may have been choosing to ignore Evor's efforts.

Evor rose, and for the first time in days, was standing on all four feet once again. He shook out his wings and his entire body looked like an enormous dog shaking itself out after being wet. Evor groaned in Elanor's mind again as he took his first step forward.

I can feel my bones, Elanor.

Good. Can you take flight?

Yes, I will return to our chambers. Where will you go?

To find Ayr and Azura.

Good luck, Elanor.

Elanor backtracked, heading towards the elevator as Evor checked himself over one last time. Now that he was able to get back in the sky and Elanor could feel his presence growing stronger, she was no longer concerned, the only problem now lay with Ayr and Azura. She slipped away from Evor and Baindussa, heading back towards the rest of the Obelisk. The ride down was as short as the trip up, and when she emerged from the tube, there was nobody in sight.

Elanor realigned the grip on her sword and made her way through the corridors, tracing her steps to her old room to where Ayr and Azura hopefully were laying asleep. She approached the familiar corridor where she had spent years of her life and went to the door. She took a deep breath and raised her hand to rap on the door. She knocked three times and was met with silence. As the seconds passed by, it was evident that nobody was in the room.

Evor, where are they?

Azura should be on the opposite side of that door. I am not sure where Ayr is. I cannot sense him near her.

Nobody is answering.

I can see that Elanor. Perhaps you should try again.

Frustrated that she was not getting answered, Elanor was ready to knock the door down. Where else could they be? It was not like nighttime flights were something that either dragon or rider would do on a regular basis. They were just as exhausted as Elanor, if not more so. Losing her patience, Elanor knocked on the door again with no response. She racked her brain, trying to work out where they would be. It was also unlike Ayr to seek out something like the mess hall with the hostility that the other riders had shown him.

Can you reach Azura?

She is shut off from me at the moment. I don't know why.

What are they up to?

I hope for both of our sakes that they are just in a deep sleep.

I don't like it.

I know, Elanor. Perhaps I should start searching the Obelisk for you?

I would appreciate it, Evor. I'm going to try as well.

Elanor gave the wooden door one final heavy slap before she turned away from it. She thought about cutting at it with her sword, but for what purpose? Elanor headed down the corridor, trying to work out where they could have gone. With Azura, Ayr could have gone anywhere in the world. Had he snuck out to consult with Dalton again? Was he meeting an agent within the grounds of the Obelisk? She turned left at the end of the corridor, deciding to head towards the mess hall when all of her questions were answered.

Ayr stopped dead in his tracks, looking like he had seen a ghost. He had no chance but to continue down this one path, knowing that Elanor had seen him. Maybe she wasn't looking for him? He continued walking towards her, and Elanor made it look as though she was not looking for him. At the last moment, she altered her path, quickening her pace and colliding with Ayr.

TWENTY-FIVE

Ayr laid on his bed staring up at this ceiling. He had climbed into it hours ago, refusing to eat when they had returned to the room and refusing to remove his boots. Azura laid in her bed as well, curled up in a ball like a giant puppy in a straw bed. There was silence in the room, one that Ayr was waiting for Azura to break.

He could not hide this from her forever, and he could sense her probing him to find out what was wrong. Ayr had given her pieces of information. Meanwhile, Azura had taken some against his will, but that was the basis of their relationship. She would eventually piece together what had happened in the tomb. He could feel her scratching around the edges of the time that he had blanked out. Dalton revealing his face had been the last thing that she had seen and now she was thinking about the interaction.

"Dalton let you go, didn't he? That's not what Elanor told Crassus."

He couldn't hold out for much longer. The strain was beginning to press on his cranium, making it feel like his head was going to explode. "Yes, he did."

"Why?"

The question lingered in the air between them. Ayr slowly sat up from the bed and Azura raised her head out of her ball. They stared across the room at each other and Ayr spun his legs to climb out of bed. Then he began to walk towards Azura. He could sense her confusion which remained until he sat down at the edge of the circle bed, with his feet hanging in the straw. Ayr stared up at her blue eyes and felt them piercing into his soul.

"I'm going to tell you everything."

"Rider, what did you gamble with when you met with Dalton in the Tomb of Chilijo?"

"It wasn't me. It was Elanor. She agreed to serve Dalton."

"And you did not stop her? Or tell anyone about this? Crassus should know at a minimum."

Ayr remained silent for more than a few seconds. It quickly became uncomfortable, Finally, Azura filled in the gap. "You've known this whole time? What has he commanded you to do?"

"I am to kill Lord Chairman Crassus Sunfire."

"Rider! You cannot do this! You would be branded a traitor to the Commonwealth. They would hunt you! Hunt us! Think about what it would do to Elanor! Please tell me you have considered all options. This is not one of them!"

"If it came between Evor and her father, Elanor would choose Evor every time. Just like I would to ensure your safety. That is now the threat that hangs over your head if I don't follow through with it. Dalton has spies everywhere. The Commonwealth would not put down a dragon of their own, would they?"

"It is rare, but they have done it before, given the circumstances. This would certainly quantify as one of those circumstances."

"We could escape and flee the Commonwealth."

"We are just as likely to do that then we are to escape your father's wrath should you fail. Ayr, the Commonwealth, the riders, they can help us."

"You've seen them. They refuse to do anything, especially Crassus. Elanor is the only rider that has bothered to help us! You and I are caught between a rock and a hard place. I am not going to choose anyone over you."

"That's not what it sounds like to me. Are you telling me if there was a choice between myself and Dalton that you'd pick me every time?"

Ayr nodded. "Yes, Azura. We are one. Our goals and beliefs will be indistinguishable from each other one day."

"I will not side with the man who sought to bring down the Commonwealth. Even if you as my rider demand it."

Ayr brushed her foot ever so slightly as he stared up into her big beautiful blue eyes. "Azura. Whilst I do not know the extent of my father's plan, everything will become more apparent once I complete this task. It needs to be done, and I will need your magic to accomplish it."

"Ayr, I can't. This goes against the oath that you and I both took."

"Does it outweigh the one we made to each other when we were bonded together as dragon and rider?" Instead of meeting her presence with a cheery demeanour of his own, persuading her to help him, Ayr was becoming more demanding.

Azura's gaze darkened. "You are making me regret my choice in rider. What else are you hiding from me?"

"Have I ever done anything to misplace your trust in me?"

"No, but..."

Ayr raised his hand to the underbelly of her jaw. "Then trust me, Azura. Everything I do, I do it for you. We will have a better life together, as dragon and rider."

Her tongue flicked out of her head at him. "You don't want the riders or the Commonwealth to exist?"

"Come closer, it would be easier to show you."

Azura hissed but lowered her head regardless. Ayr raised his right hand as high as he could, placing it against Azura's cheek. She closed her eyes as Ayr willed his memories towards her, finally letting her see everything from his past life. The transformation was slow, each memory leaking out of Ayr like it was dripping from a tap. One by one, Azura absorbed the memories of everything from his first sword fight against his brother and his training with Dalton to a dinner surrounded by his father's associates and advisors. His mother dying, a beating from Dalton and the first night he had spent with Elanor on the island in the Seminary of Fire.

As Azura drew back, Ayr fed her a memory, one that he had long suppressed. A green dragon flew overhead scorching everything in its path. The dragon was immediately identifiable, with a dark shade of green the primary colour of its scales. The dragon tore apart the city around Ayr as he watched on. There was nothing that he could do to prevent it. She would need more time to process everything.

"Ayr... you were born into this. Why did you not tell me?"

"I needed to gain your trust, Azura."

Azura's eyes flickered open slowly and at last the warmth returned to them. "And you have it. I will never doubt you again. We are one."

"We are one?"

Azura bowed her head, trying to tuck it against his body more. "Yes, Ayr. We are one. Completely. No more secrets."

Ayr hugged her tighter. "No more secrets."

He felt a surge of energy rising from somewhere deep within Azura. It pressed against him; heavier than even her weight was. Ayr felt ready to melt into her scales and to join her completely.

"We are one."

"Then let us see your task done, rider."

"Now? I can't, can I? What about Baindussa. How are we going to get past him? I need to do something that Crassus will not suspect."

"You underestimate my power, rider. I can help you implant a false memory inside Crassus' brain should he be awake. If you can handle the sealing spell on the door and unlock it without waking Baindussa, you might be able to slip inside to his library and cast a toxic spell on one of his books that he frequents."

"That sounds complicated, but that is our best chance, I suppose. The longer we can go without being outright accused of committing a crime, the better."

"Our?" Azura chuckled, clearly amused. "Yes, I suppose it is our, isn't it?"

"Are you ready for what we're about to do?"

Azura nodded her head. "I am yours, Ayr."

Ayr sucked in a massive breath of air as he pressed his face against her. "And I am yours, Azura."

"Then it is time. Are you ready?"

"As ready as I'll ever be."

"Then rise. Take no weapon with you. You will be less conspicuous. I will remain here and guide you. Good luck."

"Thank you, Azura." Ayr raised his legs from the straw bed and stood up, making his way towards the door. He slid it open with the faintest sound as it ran along the floor. He stepped through it and then looked back at Azura, one final time. "Thank you for everything, Azura."

"It has been my pleasure, Ayr."

Feeling confident with a step in his stride, Ayr shut the door behind him with a faint click. He took a deep breath and looked around, knowing the way to Crassus' chambers. It was not long before he found himself standing before the shaft that would take him up to the courtyard where Evor lay. Ayr raised his hand and repeated the cross motion that he had seen Elanor and the others do so many times before and was immediately in the tube towards Crassus.

It opened and immediately, Ayr stopped. Something did not feel right. He glanced out at the courtyard and realised that Evor was no longer there. Somehow the dragon had picked himself up and moved, despite still being affected by the scalebane. As he peered out from underneath the gateway, he could still see Baindussa in his usual spot, just above the door to Crassus' chambers. There were still lights on inside, giving Ayr hope that he would not be stumbling around in total darkness. If he made it there.

Careful, Ayr. Be quiet and do not wake him. Hopefully the scent from Evor is still overwhelming in the area.

That's not much to pray for, is it?

Fear was imbedded in every step that he took across the courtyard. His heart was pounding in his chest, even with Azura trying her best to keep him calm and moving forward. Every two steps, Ayr glanced up at Baindussa, ensuring that the green behemoth was still asleep. As he neared the entryway, with Baindussa's breath coming down upon him, Ayr slowed even more as he knelt to get a good feel for the sealing spell that was blocking his path.

Thankfully, sealing spells and how to get around them was one of the first things that Dalton had taught him as a child. Since then, Ayr had spent years practicing getting around them with increasing difficulty, in case a moment like this arose. He was also thankful for the assistance of Azura, her presence weighing heavy in his mind as he attempted to unlock the spell. He was quiet, but all it would take was one slip to alert the spellcaster that there had been a breach in their magic.

With Azura acting as a failsafe, Ayr was able to slip through the sealing spell and open the door without making a sound. Azura held the spell in place until he was able to slip through the door and reapply the lock. Ayr grinned to himself. So far it had been too easy and now only one more door stood between him and Crassus. Ayr and Azura repeated the same process with the next sealing spell and in the blink of an eye, Ayr was inside Crassus' chamber with an invitation.

His heart continued to pound in his chest as he made his way into the room. The desk stood idle, with Draxion nowhere in sight. Ayr knew what he had to do, but he needed a book that Crassus would refer to regularly. There was every chance that he could pick a book that Crassus never read. The library was enormous, with enough knowledge that could educate an entire generation's worth of dragon riders in their own right. Ayr stopped for a moment to collect his breath and think about what he was doing.

Before long, he was scanning through the first set of shelves available to him. As he perused the shelves, Ayr looked for a topic that every rider would need to know the basics of and for something that would serve as a good reference point. It took a few moments for him to make a selection.

The Biology of Draconians. He plucked it from the shelf and cradled it in his hand, examining it for a moment. Ayr ran his finger over the mahogany-coloured spine of the book as Azura sent a surge of energy towards him. The magic flowed through his veins, extending from his body into the book. Thankfully with Azura's assistance, the spell would now last as long as it took to get the job done. Ayr allowed himself a small smile as he felt the magic take hold on the book. He bowed his head and closed his eyes as he let the spell carry across the entirety of the book.

He lowered his voice. "For you, father."

"Ashbourne!" Fear shot down Ayr's spine as Crassus made his presence known. "What in Chilijo's good name are you doing here?" How did you get past Baindussa without permission or an appointment? How did you get past the sealing spell? Why are you out of bed at this hour in my own personal library?"

Ayr shuddered and almost dropped the book out of fear. He could not touch it anywhere else outside where he had it in his hand, unless he wanted to suffer the same fate as Crassus. However, Crassus being here presented the perfect opportunity, even though he had sprung out of nowhere. There would now be no risk that he would need to wait weeks or months for the Lord Chairmen to pluck the book from the shelf when he could now simply hand it to him.

Crassus was dressed in a lighter, more nighttime appropriate version of the red robes he had worn to greet them two days ago. If Ayr had brought his sword, it would have been easy to run him through with it as long as Crassus hadn't blown his brains out first. He was hoping to not see Crassus this evening - now he needed to think on his feet.

"I don't have an appointment, but Baindussa let me in regardless. I wanted to come and talk to you about Elanor."

Crassus raised an eyebrow. "Baindussa is asleep, and I do not remember giving him permission to stop the spell this evening."

"It is important, sir, please I beg you to hear me out."

Crassus folded his arms and still had not lowered his eyebrow. "I know she is your dragon's promised rider, but why would you need to speak to me about her?"

"I'm concerned about her. Ever since we found the elder dragon she hasn't been the same."

"Has not been the same, how?" Crassus' tone was balanced.

"Ever since the elder dragon and my father, it feels like she is slowly becoming more irrational. It's like her sole focus is on doing whatever she can to find him when she's not training me. It's an unhealthy obsession. I can understand Evor, but when she is not thinking about him, everything is to do with that elder dragon."

Crassus smirked at him. "That's because she is doing what I have instructed her to do. The obsession is not unhealthy, unless it is perhaps because you don't want Dalton to be found. What happened when you found him inside the Tomb of Chilijo?"

"He's a danger to the Commonwealth, especially with that dragon. I want him found as much as you do."

Crassus eyed Ayr and frowned. "Answer the question, Ashbourne."

"He gave us the scalebane ether in exchange for his freedom. Both Elanor and I were prepared to bring him in."

"And what happened then? Did you just let him go?"

"He escaped."

Crassus wasn't buying it. "He escaped? I know that Dalton Ashbourne is powerful, second only to me. But do you believe me to expect that my daughter let him escape?"

"It was either that, or he would kill me."

"So, she does have feelings for you." Crassus clenched his fist. "And do you not know where your own father is?"

Ayr folded his arms and held the book close to his chest. "No, I don't. This is the man that evaded the Commonwealth for how many years despite living under your noses for how long? If he has that elder dragon at his disposal he could be anywhere. We were fortunate to make it out of the Tomb of Chilijo with our lives."

"Hmm. I have half a mind to throw you back into a void cell for a few days to ensure that you are telling the truth, yet I want to believe you. What are you going to do once you and Elanor find Dalton again?"

"I'm going to bring him in."

Crassus sniggered. "And do what exactly?"

"Whatever you want to do with him. I know what he's done to the Commonwealth and the sooner he's dealt with, the better. Then Azura and I can get on with our lives."

"You care about her, don't you?"

Ayr nodded. "We're bonded and by proxy, I care about Elanor and Evor too. They are going to become as much a part of us as each other."

Crassus' eyes ran up and down him. "Maybe I was wrong about you, Ashbourne. Perhaps you're more like Anton. If that's the case, you'll do well here. Anton was quick to rise through the ranks as well, however he didn't fall victim to Dalton's fallacies."

"That's the first time I've heard someone here speak positively about my family."

"Outside of that, there isn't much to celebrate. Perhaps you could change that. Now is there anything else you want? You don't have an appointment, and I am a busy man."

Ayr shook his head and extended the book towards Crassus. "No, sorry for taking up your time, sir."

Crassus reached out with his long-pointed fingers and closed them around the spine of the book. Ayr let go as he felt Crassus' grip tighten around it. How long would it take for the spell to take hold? He did not intend for Crassus to drop on the spot. Would he need to hold the book for a period? Could someone else finish the job before the toxic spell took hold? Running him through with his sword would have been far too obvious, however Dalton did not particularly care about what method was used. His relentless testing ensuring that Ayr did not rely on one method of execution was a testament to that, but this was something he had never done before.

Crassus tapped the cover of the book and with a thoughtful gaze nodded at Ayr. "You should be in bed at this hour, Ashbourne. I'm still not entirely sure what possessed you to come and pay me a visit at this time. Your concern for Elanor is admirable, but foolish. She is a grown woman who will handle herself and her obsessions."

"I just wanted to inform you before it became too late."

"I appreciate the concern, Ashbourne. Now go to bed." Crassus raised his arm gesturing towards the door.

Ayr bowed his head and took a step backwards. "Thank you, My Lord. Have a good evening."

TWENTY-SIX

The collision was brief and violent. Ayr was thrust back into the nearest wall as Elanor flung him by his collar. Her eyes held him in contempt, anger prevalent on her face. There was no way she already knew what we'd done, was there? Evor was gone but had she been watching him the entire time?

"What the fuck are you doing?"

"I went for a walk. I couldn't sleep."

"Don't bull shit me, Ashbourne. What are you doing out of bed? Where is Azura?"

"She's back in the room, why?"

"Come with me!"

She still had not let go of his collar and Ayr was none the wiser as to why she was upset with him. It would have been foolish to protest, and most likely would have resulted in a beating with how she was glaring at him. Ayr took the smarter approach, opting to go quiet and to follow her lead.

How can she know?

She can't! Not unless she's been watching us the entire time. We're in trouble.

I will defend you, rider. Find out what she knows.

"What have I done? What have I done?"

"Shut your mouth or I'll cut your tongue out. You know exactly what you've done. Get to your room. I'm not going to have any more eyes on us than we need to have. I'm in this up to my neck as well."

"What are you talking about?"

"Being one of Dalton Ashbourne's agents." Elanor breathed the words into his ear despite there being nobody clearly within earshot. "Quickly! Open the door."

Geez, she is pushy tonight.

She clearly has demands she wants to make of you. Let her inside so that we can speak to her in private.

Ayr fumbled with the door, pushing it open as Elanor breathed down his neck. If she wasn't so aggressive, it could have turned him on. Instead, Ayr pushed the door open, and Elanor pushed him through it, slamming it shut behind her a second later. Elanor was incensed and as Ayr turned, she had her sword at his throat. It was still in its sheath, but it could still cause damage.

"I don't know what game you're playing at. Was Azura here the whole time?"

Ayr thrust his hands into the air. "What game? I haven't done anything wrong."

"Do you really think it is smart to be wondering around the corridors this late at night? Especially considering with what has transpired here recently? Word will get around."

"I don't particularly care for word spread by other riders. The only other one I care about is in this room right now."

"That's sweet, but it matters what they say. Especially if you don't want anyone figuring out what you're actually doing here. You have enough doubters as it is. Now you want to throw in doing tasks for Dalton? You're just asking to get yourself killed."

"He never tells me his plans."

"And for good reason. I know you might think differently, but when people usually get interrogated here, they break. If they suspect someone is working with Dalton, you can bet that they're going to try every trick in the book."

"I'm ready for them."

Elanor shook her head and laughed. "Oh, sweet Ayr. No, you're not."

"Elanor, please take your sword away from my rider."

She cast a side eye at Azura who had just stood up from her straw bed.

Elanor lowered her sword with a half swing. "Fuck! Seriously? How quickly do you Ashbournes want to do things? First the calling and now this? Ayr you don't need to sprint through the entirety of a rider's life cycle you know."

Ayr shrugged and for the first time since she had ran into him, he laughed. "What can I say, I have a talent for it."

"And an ever-increasing ego. Even riders with fully grown dragons, decades old are not this powerful. You are abnormal, Ashbourne,"

"Wow, tell me how you really feel."

Elanor sighed. "I'm just not used to someone coming through having so much raw talent. It pains me to say that you're an Ashbourne. That'll make it harder for them to strip Azura from you, unless they send you to the afterlife together."

"They will have to try."

"I should have known if it was going to be any out of your recruit crop, it was going to be the two of you. Regardless, that's not what I came here for."

"Are you going to be long? Feel free to sit." Ayr gestured to the tables and chairs situated in the centre of the room.

"I'd prefer something more comfortable."

Ayr thought she was going to tables, but Elanor pivoted at the last second and flopped onto his bed. With joyful glee, she kicked her legs up and made herself comfortable. Ayr sighed watching her move up on one side of the bed. There was more than enough room for him to join her. It had been her bed previously after all.

"Ah. That's right, I miss this mattress."

"Is the new one not to your liking?"

"Too soft. Sometimes I think that the more you move up here, the more creature comforts they give you and then less resilient you become. It's true that some of the bigger dragons don't even hunt for themselves."

"That doesn't seem productive."

Elanor waved her hand in the air. "Age, complacency. Whatever you want to call it, it will be the death of the riders. I assume our actions are going to have a big impact on them going forward."

"Have you received any word yet?"

"From Dalton?" Elanor snorted. "Unless I've missed the signs, no. Nobody has made contact with me yet."

Ayr frowned. "Hmm, and if you do, you'll only get the one part of the job."

"Like you killing my father?"

If questions had points, that would have found its way into Ayr's heart. "I haven't done it yet."

"I know, because there'd be hell to pay if you did. Kaladin is just looking for an excuse to arrest you and throw you into a cell. You've escaped him once, that won't happen again."

"I have more help this time."

"Me?" Elanor laughed. "Ayr, I am dreading when Dalton finally gets his claws into me. I have more access to things at the Obelisk than you do. I made this sacrifice so that Evor would survive."

Ayr lowered himself onto the bed beside her. "I don't blame you at all for that. I don't think anyone would. You saw one way to keep your dragon safe and you took it. If I were in your shoes I'd have done the same thing."

"Easy for you to say sitting on that side of the fence."

Ayr scoffed. "Easy? I've known nothing but hardship. I was born into this. If you think being hunted your entire life isn't hard, then by all means, feel free to let the Commonwealth know that you struck a deal with Dalton."

"That's not what I meant."

"What did you mean then?"

"I meant that I refuse to serve Dalton Ashbourne to the fullest of my abilities. I hope you know that."

Ayr rubbed his eyes. "How are you intending on doing that, exactly? Despite what you might think, he has spies everywhere. My father has spent the years since the war growing his influence and expanding his network. If you don't serve him faithfully, he'll kill Harmon and end your supply of scalebane ether. Evor could be in trouble."

"I intend to serve him long enough to free Evor from his disease. Once Evor has completely gotten rid of the scalebane, I will drive my sword into Dalton Ashbourne's throat as reparations for what he has done to the Commonwealth."

"If someone finds out that you're working for him, will they feel the same? The daughter of the Lord Chairman of the Obelisk working for Dalton Ashbourne." Ayr clicked his lips. "What a sight that would be."

"There are plenty of Ashbourne sympathisers that came over when the war was won. They still live within the Commonwealth today."

Ayr scoffed again. "Is that what your father would have you believe? I've seen with my own eyes that which the Commonwealth does not approve, does not last very long. Azura. Show Evor."

Azura bowed her head. "Yes, rider."

She closed her eyes and fell silent, swaying from side to side as she started to communicate with Evor. Ayr grew more comfortable on the bed, Elanor fell silent. It was clear that Evor was relaying the information to her that Azura had given him a moment ago. Ayr waited until Elanor blinked, finally returning to the world. Much like Azura, his memories had an effect on Elanor. A sad expression filled her face. It was clear that she was experiencing his pain as teardrops started to form in her eyes.

"You were at Ashenfort? I understand so much now. But you were born into this, you don't know any better. From where we sit looking outside, Dalton is evil."

"He may be, but an eye for an eye makes the world blind, Elanor. I can't help that the Commonwealth decided to wage war against my father."

"And you can't help that he decided to break the rules either. What is your point, Ayr?"

"It doesn't matter who started hostilities, what matters is who's going to finish it. Do you know who ordered the attack on Ashenfort?"

Elanor stared blankly at him as the realisation set in. "There was no accident was there? It was my father, wasn't it?"

She searched his face for confirmation. "Do you see why they tell you lies now? Ashenfort was supposed to be a safe haven. Thousands were lost in that massacre."

"I was still training with Evor at that point in time. I'm lucky that I never saw combat in the Ashbourne rebellion. I remember Kaladin upon his return bragging about it. They said that it was a hard-fought battle against dozens of Dalton Ashbourne's faithful."

"Most of the faithful you speak of were no older than I was." Ayr was on the verge of tears.

Elanor moved closer, sensing it, seeking to comfort him. Her arms wrapped slowly around his shoulders, from behind instantly giving him as much support as Azura did. Azura felt his pain and echoed it, remaining in her bed, but was not able to ignore how he was feeling.

"I can only imagine what that must have felt like. You are lucky to have escaped. They said they had left no survivors."

"They didn't."

"Well, I don't know exactly what you want me to do, Ayr. I can't go back in time and fix the past."

"No, but you can stay with me."

"What do you mean, Ayr?"

Ayr sat up on the bed and pivoted so that he was cross legged facing her. "Elanor. Do me a favour and sit up."

She raised an eyebrow. "Okay..." Elanor copied his movements and sat upright on the bed. She brought her boots underneath her legs, sitting cross legged as well. "What do you want to say."

Ayr slowly reached out and brought her hands into his. He looked into her eyes, and she held his gaze. Azura breathed in deeply, waiting for the moment.

"Elanor. I am going to make you a promise, right now. Ever since coming here, ever since Azura and I were bonded together, I've changed. When I got here, my mission was clear. To infiltrate the Commonwealth and bring everyone in it to their knees. Since Azura, since you, nothing else has mattered. I am promising to commit myself to you from this day on."

"Ayr..."

"What? Our dragons are promised to each other and I'm making this now to you. Whatever happens, we are on the same side, regardless of who is trying to control us."

"But what about your task. What about what Dalton gives me?"

"Fuck my task. Dalton, Anton, Crassus, fuck them all. Azura, Elanor and Evor are the only names that hold any meaning to me now."

"Do you mean that?"

Ayr nodded. "With every fibre of my being."

"Good. Then come here."

"What are you…"

Elanor's lips met his in a fiery frenzy that almost pushed him back off the bed. Shocked, Ayr responded with his own kiss, trying to melt his lips against hers. At last, they had all the time in the world, and nothing would come between them. Their embrace lasted for a few more seconds, until Elanor turned her hands over in his, submitting to him. Ayr pushed her gently and Elanor went back onto the bed, kissing him back as she went.

Ayr felt tight against her as she wrapped her arms around him, feeling his head, neck and shoulders. In return, Ayr was not worried about crushing her and put his hand in her free left one. They continued rolling around on the bed, and slowly, piece by piece, each article of clothing came off. Ayr could feel Azura's presence in the back of his mind, but this was not instigated by her, she was only encouraging the activity.

In moments, Ayr found himself completely naked with Elanor just underneath him in a similar condition. It was like being back at the Dragon's Gore all over again, except this time they had a comfortable surface underneath them. Elanor gave him an encouraging nod, her hand helping him find his way into her. Ayr groaned as he entered her, feeling spurred on as Elanor ran her hands down his back. Whilst she had no nails, the pressure from her fingertips was more than enough to excite him.

Ayr squirmed at her touch, as she reacted to his as well. Their moans were only growing loudly as their speed intensified. Elanor grabbed and clawed at Ayr, trying to pull him tighter into her. She hooked her legs around his back, driving him deeper into her. Elanor's eyes started rolling back in her head as she climaxed again and again. Ayr couldn't keep track of where her hands were. He could feel her aftermath, however. With each stroke and each new groan from Elanor, there was another kiss, another touch and another sensation to explore.

Sweat was beginning to pool across Ayr's forehead, the constant thrusting and motion of the act beginning to take its toll like he was running a marathon. His pace was starting to slow and Elanor sensed it. She tapped his shoulders.

"Don't worry, I'll take care of you."

Confused by what she meant, Ayr paused and frowned down at her. Elanor's grip tightened on his shoulders, and with her Evor like strength, she threw him off her. Ayr gasped, shocked by the sudden movement, but unsurprised at her power. He fell sideways, but before he had time to take a breath, Elanor was on top of him. Her taking the brunt of the work took pressure off him and he tried to get his breathing under control. Ayr ran his hands up her entire body, starting at her thighs.

Elanor reacted to his touch, particularly when his fingers grazed over her nipples with the faintest of touches. She kept bucking her hips, grinding on him, her hands on his stomach, her fingers digging into his skin once again. He was getting close, but he did not want to let go yet. However just like before, his upward thrusts were beginning to lessen. Elanor leaned down and breathed her hot breath into his ear.

"Come on, don't give up on me yet, Ashbourne."

With one last guttural grunt, Ayr hooked his arms around her and flipped her over on the bed. There was a wild windmill of limbs as they both tried to regain position, but as soon as Elanor's head had touched the pillow, Ayr was inside her again, eliciting one of the loudest moans yet.

She reached up with her left hand and grabbed at his nipple. The new sensation electrified Ayr and with each thrust spurred on by her encouraging him, along with her moaning as she kissed his neck. It was too much. Elanor groaned as she bucked her hips up again, and Ayr could not hold on any longer.

His hand finally left hers, grabbing onto the bed sheet as he started to feel his toes curl with pure euphoria. He had been transported to another world as every muscle in his body contracted. Ayr started to shake and there was no holding back. He groaned as loudly as he could, his head collapsing beside Elanor as he pumped everything he had into her.

Ayr finally breathed out, beginning to pant, trying to draw in as much oxygen as possible. He slowly raised his head as Elanor laughed at him. She cupped his face in her hands, sat up, and kissed him once again.

"Fuck."

TWENTY-SEVEN

Ayr puffed out his lips as he shook his head laughing softly. "Elanor, that was incredible."

Elanor leaned over and stretched up to his forehead, wiping the hair out of his eyes. His chest rose and fell in time with hers. She laughed at him again softly.

"What can I say? I aim to please."

"I think you've done more than that. By Chilijo!"

"You're not half bad yourself, you know. Although I don't know what evoking Chilijo's name is going to accomplish."

Now it was Ayr's turn to smile. "Thanks. It just seemed right to say at the time."

Sensation was now finally starting to come back into his legs as he stretched out his feet. Azura was inside his head once again, trying to calm him back down. He welcomed her presence.

As Ayr lay looking up at the ceiling, a loud knock came from the door. Elanor raised an eyebrow who in turn gathered her sword from beside the bed. In a flash she had it in her hand, ready to stand up and deliver it point first into who was at the door. Azura was also alarmed.

I'm not sure who would be calling at this late hour, rider.

Neither am I. I don't trust it.

Ayr held his hand out at Elanor. "I'll answer it. You stay here. I don't trust it."

"Neither do I."

Ayr climbed off the bed and found his pants beside it, scrunched up in a ball. He unrolled and climbed into them, taking care not to stumble over. Once he had secured the belt around his waist, he moved towards the door. Regardless of who was on the other side, he was protected by Elanor and Azura at his back. With a deep breath, Ayr pulled back on the door handle, using some of the frame as a shield. The open door did not reveal a large attacker, or someone that could have been suspected to have been working for Dalton. Instead, Ayr was met with Elanor's mother. Grace.

"Grace, what are you doing here?"

Grace snapped forward with the agility of a woman half her age and grabbed both of Ayr's hands. Immediately, he knew what she was trying to accomplish as he felt his mind getting probed. Not having the barriers in place because of Azura caused Ayr to arc up as he tried to defend himself from a possible onslaught of his mind. As they flicked into place and Ayr pulled his hands away from Grace, the other side of the door burst open, knocking Ayr to the floor.

"Did you get him, Grace?"

Ayr took the brunt of the door impact on his shoulder and as he fell almost smashed his head onto the tiles. As the door opened, Kaladin strode into the room, his eyes firmly affixed on Ayr. He had his sword drawn and looked ready to draw blood with it. Kaladin was flanked by at least half a dozen other riders also brandishing swords. Each of them wore blackened armour with a tall, full helm, unlike anything that Ayr had seen here at the Obelisk thus far. Where had they come from?

"Secure the dragon! Nobody gets in or out of here. Grace, did you get him?" Kaladin's tone was higher this time.

"Yes, Kaladin! Just!"

"And?"

"Nothing."

Kaladin grunted, inching his sword closer to Ayr's throat. "You don't have to stay here if you don't want to, Grace."

"I was given a vision. Draxion never lies. She pointed me to him. I will stay here until the verdict is past."

"Kaladin? What the fuck are you doing here?"

"I could ask you the same, Lady Sunfire. Awfully old to be in your student's room this late is it not?"

"What are you? My mother? I can see you brought her along, but what is the meaning of this?"

"This is a matter of Commonwealth security, Elanor. Something that you do not know very much about, now do you?"

"Kaladin! I won't ask again!"

"Your father, Lord Chairman Crassus Sunfire was found dead a short time ago in his chambers. His dragon, Baindussa has your scent, Ashbourne. What have you got to say for yourself?"

Elanor was the most confused person in the room. "I'm sorry, what did you just say?"

"Your father, Elanor. He's dead. Killed recently. The Obelisk has been placed on high alert. His killer may still be among us."

"And then why are you here?" Elanor paused and sighed. Ayr glanced over at her, seeing her body language change. She tightened her grip on her sword and had taken a step forward. "Right. You think Ashbourne is the killer."

"I'm glad your mother is blind, Elanor. I wouldn't want her seeing this. Have you considered putting some clothes on? How did he go compared to me?"

Kaladin cast his eye over the ruffled bed sheets that she was standing on. Elanor still held her sword out in front of her in its sheath. She was standing upright on the bed, her feet splayed out evenly, shoulder width apart. Two of the riders clad in the black armour stood at the foot of the bed, with their swords drawn as well.

Elanor spoke through gritted teeth. "That's none of your business, Kaladin."

Kaladin scoffed. "Oh of course it's not. Judging by your reaction it wasn't particularly good."

"I was enjoying my evening until you came along, Kaladin. Can you leave? Crassus isn't actually dead."

Grace's head turned towards her. "He is Elanor. Did you not hear Baindussa's roar?"

"No, I should have from here. We're not that far from his courtyard."

Kaladin snorted. His sword was still uncomfortably close to Ayr's throat. "Maybe it would help if you weren't being distracted by temptations of the flesh. Anyway, back to the problem at hand. Baindussa swears that it was Ashbourne. What kind of idiot doesn't flee the scene before they are discovered?"

"Because I didn't do it. I'm not sure what else you want from me, Kaladin."

"He lies!" Grace hissed from behind Kaladin.

Kaladin inched his sword closer to Ayr. "Tell me the fucking truth. What have you been doing tonight?"

Ayr glanced over at Elanor who shook her head ever so slightly. "I've been here all night with Elanor."

"If that's true, is there anyone else that will be able to confirm your story? Aside from your dragons?"

"Nobody saw us."

"How convenient. Grace, are you certain it was him."

"Yes, I am certain."

"Then we may need to bring this to an end now. Gentlemen."

On Kaladin's signal, the other riders moved from their positions. They encircled Ayr, all of them staring down at him from underneath their faceless helmets. None of them had their swords at the ready, merely hanging loosely by their sides. Kaladin on the other hand, raised his sword bringing it back past his head.

"It's been nice knowing you, Ashbourne. Perhaps we can bring your father to the same deserved fate."

"No!"

No!

As the sword came down, a sheathed sword crossed its path. Ayr went to roll out of the way but looked up and saw Elanor standing half naked over him, with her sword the only thing that had stopped Kaladin from cleaving him in too. Overhead, Ayr could sense Azura, but she would have been too late, only able to chomp down on Kaladin after he had landed the killing blow.

"Oh, this is too perfect. I noticed that Evor was gone from his position in the courtyard. Baindussa could smell you as well."

Elanor grunted, the downward pressure from Kaladin's sword still on top of hers. She was fighting from a compromised position, while all Kaladin needed to do was apply pressure. She struggled, trying to push back against Kaladin but he was too powerful.

Grace shook her head. "Do not lie to me, Elanor. I can see right through you."

"Yes, I went and saw Evor, but that was it. Evor has recovered and I wanted him out from underneath Baindussa. I didn't see anyone leave or enter my father's chambers."

Grace's eyes twitched. "You went elsewhere. What were you doing?"

Elanor sighed and jerked her head towards Ayr. "I was looking for him."

"Why, Elanor?"

Elanor drew back from Kaladin at last and her sword fell loosely to the side of her body. "Because he wasn't in his room."

"Aha!"

"I found him and brought him back. He had been gone for no time at all. He was barely at the end of the corridor."

Grace's eyes narrowed. "Elanor..."

"I'm not lying to you, mother."

Kaladin chortled again. "There is one more thing."

He reached into his pocket and for a moment fidgeted with something inside it. Then between he revealed a small, folded piece of parchment from between his middle and index fingers. The piece of parchment was stained with blood. Upon closer inspection as Kaladin spread it out, Ayr could make out something in the blood. It spelt something. The handwriting was almost illegible and different from his father's typically elegant scripture. It was still in his father's hand, but something was off about it. Almost like it had been written by someone else entirely.

Grace Sunfire. I'm coming for you.

"Is that evidence enough for you? If it was not you, then your father graced us with his presence this evening."

Ayr shook his head and scoffed. "Are you listening to yourself? You think that my father, somehow miraculously got past all of the Obelisk's security features, including Baindussa and then snuck out in one go without being detected? I don't know if you know this, Kaladin, but that dragon he has in his possession wouldn't exactly go unnoticed."

Kaladin remained smug. "I am still not seeing a fault in my reasoning. You are not making a very compelling argument that's going to stand up in court. And no, you won't be receiving a trial by combat again, if I can help it. I saw what you did to that innocent dragon, and I won't be allowing Baindussa to take the fight."

"It's not up to you, Kaladin. If the dragon wants it, the dragon is allowed to fight."

"That dragon is as much of a liability to us now as anyone else in this room that may be working against the Commonwealth. Are you telling me you want to deal with that?"

"Yes, Elanor. I am prepared to take that risk. Baindussa would not irk the responsibility like you and Evor."

"When have I ever?"

Kaladin raised an eyebrow. "Gentlemen. Grace. It's clear to me that both Ayr Ashbourne and Elanor Sunfire are guilty in conspiring to murder the Lord Chairman. It is by my order here as the head of security that these two are placed under arrest immediately and taken to reside in individual void cells. As are their dragons for good measure."

He can't be serious can he? You didn't do anything to harm Crassus.

No, the spell would not have taken hold yet. There's clearly something else at play, Azura. Can you stay the course with me?

Yes, rider. We are one.

"Bind them!"

One of the faceless riders from behind Ayr stepped up behind him and Ayr could hear steel rattling against steel. Another rider ripped his hands above his head as the first then clamped the irons around him. Ayr grunted at the force they used, but considering their company, he did not expect them to be gentle in the slightest. Satisfied that Ayr was no longer a threat and in chains, Kaladin at last properly lowered his sword. Two more riders were dealing with Elanor in a similar fashion, however, were receiving more of a struggle from her.

"When you're done here, bring them to the void cell." Kaladin turned away and then stopped on his heel before turning back. "And Elanor, when you're not too busy, put some clothes on please. We try to maintain some level of decorum here after all."

TWENTY-EIGHT

For the second time in as many weeks, Ayr was being thrust headfirst into a void cell. There was no point in resisting, the black clad guards that walked with Kaladin were simply overpowering. The men were no bigger than Ayr, but it was clear to him that they rode large dragons that helped amplify their power. In a one on one, he was confident he could take any one of the riders. Ayr grumbled, unhappy as Elanor walked beside him, the only solace in Azura as she trudged along behind him.

Rider, there is no point in getting angered in this situation.

I didn't even kill him, Azura. I don't know what to do.

If we're going to the void cells, we will have plenty of time to think about a plan of action. I do not like it either.

We will get through it together.

The long march was getting to him. Every step they took was another step that he wanted to leap forward and stab Kaladin in the back with his own sword. The smug aura around him irritated Ayr, but there was nothing he could do to change it. They turned down one last corridor and at the end of it was a door that Ayr was hoping he would never see again. It was large enough to fit himself and Azura inside it. However, Ayr heard a snarl from behind him.

"Follow me, Azura."

Ayr almost leapt out of his skin but settled when he saw Gundrag sitting in the corridor behind them. His tongue flicked out of his mouth as he eyeballed Azura, almost beckoning her to go with him. With no choice but to obey, Azura turned and headed after the purple dragon.

Be safe, Azura.

He won't harm me yet, rider. They just want us separate so they can interrogate us.

I understand.

Don't do anything that will cause Kaladin to lash out.

No promises.

Kaladin kept walking down the corridor towards the void cell at the end, and did not stop until he drew level with the second last doorway. Kaladin jerked his head to the side along with his thumb. "Take her in there."

There was a scuffle as Elanor was dragged forward by two of the riders. She kicked her legs off the ground, trying to provide the riders with only dead weight to carry. They had firm grips around her body, and Elanor struggle against them was futile. One pushed the heavy door open, scraping it against the floor, and the riders tossed Elanor inside. As soon as she was let go, Elanor spun, trying to get out. The second rider that had not opened the door slammed it shut and Elanor was lost from sight.

Kaladin was the next to move, grabbing Ayr by the back of his neck. If Kaladin applied more pressure, Ayr worried that his neck would snap. The void cell beckoned to him, and Kaladin carried him forward. When they were only a handful of steps away from the cell, Kaladin thrust him forward, sending Ayr sprawling into the void cell. Ayr was unable to catch himself on the wide walls and fell forward with the force of Kaladin's shove.

He groaned as he hit the ground, falling onto his elbows. A boot from Kaladin connected with the back of Ayr's leg, further pushing him into the void cell. Kaladin laughed behind him.

"Make yourself comfortable, Ashbourne. You'll be in here a while, I would imagine."

Ayr didn't give him a response as he was beginning to feel the void cell overtake him. There was nothing he could do to get himself out of the void as it clung onto him, making him unable to move. Ayr tried to climb to his feet to make himself more comfortable, but he remained stuck. With nowhere to go and nothing to do, Ayr closed his eyes, trying to get some sleep. He drifted in and out of sleep, but did not know how much time had passed, until he felt something moving behind him.

Someone was reaching into the void cell. Hoping that it would be a friendly face, Ayr braced himself for the worst. With one motion, he was hoisted out of the void cell and dragged onto his belly. Ayr was helpless to resist as the vice like grip on his ankle as it pulled him out. As he groaned, he was finally rolled onto his back, only to see Kaladin standing above him. Gundrag was further down the corridor, watching on.

There was a faint ray of sunlight behind Gundrag, indicating that the night had at least passed by. What had taken Kaladin so long and was it only the next day?

"I've got some questions for you. Get up."

Kaladin reached down and grabbed Ayr by his handcuffs. Feeling like a ragdoll, Ayr flew into the air barely having enough time to land on his feet. Kaladin grabbed him and dragged him forward, heading towards the room that the other riders had thrown Elanor into. Kaladin pulled open the door and Ayr found the room was empty, apart from two chairs and a small steel table that stood in the centre. The chair that was facing the door appeared to be rigged as well as curved in the middle, designed to be uncomfortable.

Knowing that it was for him, Ayr moved around the table, no longer being forced to move by Kaladin. Ayr slumped down in the chair, immediately regretting his decision and sat upright, trying not to push back against the curvature in his back. Kaladin slowly sat down opposite him, placing both of his hands on the table.

"You really think you're something special? Don't you, Ashbourne?"

"That's because I am."

Kaladin snorted and raised his fist, but did not bring it down on the cold table in front of them. "If you think you're special because you can call your dragon to you in record time, I've got news for you. The only one who did it just as fast was the man we threw out of here."

"He could have been a great rider if you let him be."

"That wasn't my call."

"I'm well aware of that fact that there were other forces in play. My father warned me about that and everyone that I have met since I got here has had secrets to keep."

"Even Elanor?"

Ayr nodded. "Even Elanor. You should really give up on pursuing her you know. We will be one, just like our dragons eventually."

Kaladin scowled at him. "You've been in her life for only a few months, Ashbourne. The moment you and your dragon are out of the picture, she will come crawling back to me."

Ayr laughed. "So, this isn't just about the murder of Crassus. Is it?"

"No, of course not. Yet you were at the scene of the crime. Nobody else entered or left the Obelisk this evening since sundown."

"You can admit that this is convenient for you and leave it at that. I'm not going to hold it against you anymore than I already do."

"As the head of security, it is my job to ensure that the Obelisk is secure. Now it is clear to me that it has not been secure, and you are to blame. Unfortunately for me, I will not be the one to find you guilty."

"You're in charge now, Kaladin. How much more power could you possibly want?"

Kaladin folded his hands into his pockets and a wicked grin spread across his face. "I want everything. That path has been opened up to me now because of you, so I suppose I should be grateful. However, it's not me who has the final say on what is going to happen to you. It's your uncle. Anton. He just arrived at the Obelisk this morning. Excuse me a moment."

Kaladin turned and moved towards the door, pushing it open. He vanished out into the corridor and silence filled the room once again. Ayr sat with his handcuffs firmly planted on the table, watching the door, waiting for a sign of movement. A moment later the door burst open again to reveal a heavily-bearded Anton, his hair in a mess, falling around his face. His body was covered by a rich brown tunic and black riding pants that looked like scales from a dragon's hide.

His firm expression fell on Ayr and Anton shook his head. Anton pulled the opposite chair out and flopped down into it with a heavy thud as he smacked his fists on the table.

"So, this is the chaos that my brother brings! One mention of his name is enough to send the Commonwealth into a tailspin. Frankly, it's getting tiresome and I for one will be glad to be rid of his name forever. It appears that it will start with you, nephew."

For the first time since he had been in this room, Ayr leaned forward in his chair. It was uncomfortable, the cold steel pressing into his spine, but he grimaced through the pain. "And tell me, uncle. Just how do you intend to do that? You haven't been able to manage that for the last twenty plus years. He always used to tell me that you were jealous of him. Is that why you chose to side with the Commonwealth over him?"

Anton's firm glare washed over Ayr and he suddenly felt dwarfed, even though they were sitting at the same level. "Of course I was. He was always chosen first in everything just because he was a bit more powerful than I was. Oh, and when he broke the record of calling his dragon to him? You can just imagine."

Ayr shook his head. "I can't, actually. There was no fanfare when I did it."

"And for good reason. At least that's one thing you've taken away from him, Ayr. It's a shame he had to give you the task he did. If I have it my way, I'll be the one to take you away from him."

"Why, Anton? I'm just like you. My brother is Dalton's favourite child. I don't know why I served him. I'd like to repent."

Anton cocked an eyebrow. "I'm listening. But considering you killed the Lord Chairman; I don't like your chances."

"For the last time, I didn't kill Crassus."

"And I am not the Overlord of the entire Commonwealth. The evidence points to you being the one to commit the murder. You and your father's handwriting are very similar. Do you mean to tell me you didn't leave the note on Crassus' body?"

"No, I did not. Why would I have any reason to get near Crassus? More importantly, how would I get close enough to him? What was the cause of death?"

"You're the killer. Why don't you tell me how you did it?"

"Cross examine Azura for all I care. She will hold the truth and not lie to you."

"I would. Unfortunately, our best dragon to do so is grieving the loss of his rider. Do you have any other suggestions?"

"So, you're going to forgo due process just because of one dragon? Surely there is another. Take Draxion or someone else to investigate her."

Anton laughed and shook his head. "No, I'm forgoing due process because of your father. I'm not like the fool, Kaladin who is doing that for his personal gain. As we speak, riders are making their way across the Commonwealth to spread word of your pending execution. That word will reach Dalton. I want to flush my brother out and end this once and for all. Surely, he would not give up his own eldest son so easily."

Ayr shrugged. "Clearly you don't know him that well. I'd say he's achieved a goal. Why would he need me anymore?"

"Dalton isn't so stupid as to throw away his most valuable asset."

"He's not, but you have achieved something that he has been unable to accomplish for years."

Ayr sighed. "I'm not doing this anymore, Anton. What do you want out of me?"

"A confession would have been ideal, but we can always force that out of you at a later date. I'm here to take you to the Haven. An offence like this that you have been accused of needs to be dealt with at the highest level. You will be tried, found guilty and then executed by Baindussa. I will hear nothing else of it."

"Why not just drag me to the Amphitheatre straight away then? Why waste my time?"

"Because if we are to witness his fall, I intend for Dalton to be seen by the most amount of people. There are many within our ranks that still secret harbour admiration for the man. He will be humiliated."

Ayr shook his head. "You really don't know your own brother that well, do you? He won't come for me."

Anton pushed the chair back and slowly stood up. He rested his hands on the table as thoughts ran through his head. "You're as defiant as him, aren't you?"

Ayr stuck his chin out. "I am. He taught me well."

"Hmm. We will break you. I look forward to continuing this conversation at the Haven. There's nothing more we can do here. I'll get someone to fetch you a vest so that you don't get ripped to shreds on the flight to the Haven. Enjoy your last moments here at the Obelisk, Ayr."

TWENTY-NINE

The room was quiet as Ayr sat alone in it, waiting for something to happen. He could do nothing except for bang his handcuffs on the table. Ayr had switched to the more comfortable chair as he waited. After a while, the door creaked open to reveal none other than Kaiser. Kaiser ventured into the room holding a tunic for Ayr to throw over his shoulders as well as a pair of boots. His glare was just as intense as Kaladin's and Anton's had been, but unlike the other two, Kaiser placed the items on the table without speaking.

As Kaiser left the room, Ayr scrambled to pick the items up. Knowing that if they found him slacking it would not be good news for him, Ayr quickly threw the tunic on over his chest. It was a size too small, but Ayr had no other choice. It was almost like they were trying to make things deliberately uncomfortable for him. He repositioned on the chair and started to pull the boots on. Ayr grunted; they were also too small.

There was no communication from Azura, clearly still in a void cell of her own. Time ticked by and Ayr felt like the walls of this room were slowly closing in on him. He wanted to pace, and he wanted to bash against the door, but he knew that wasting energy would be his enemy. After a while longer, the door started to open again. The hair on the back of Ayr's neck stood up.

"Let's go."

It was Anton. With a heavy sigh, Ayr kicked out the chair from behind him, and he felt a surge of energy from behind him. Ayr stood up and the energy surge died down.

"Wise choice. No funny business. If you ever thought that you beat Dalton in a display of magic, you won't win against me. I will not hold back."

"Where are we going?"

"Drementhol awaits."

A shot of fear ran down Ayr's spine. They were heading to the roof. Anton stood back and allowed Ayr to move out of the room, no more than a step behind him. He could feel Anton breathing down his neck, and as Ayr stepped into the corridor outside he was greeted by the presence of eight tall, imposing riders, all clad in similar armour to the ones that had escorted him to the void cell.

Their black armour gleamed ominously, each intricate link high-lighted by a bold red trim that traced the contours of the metal like veins of fire. The riders, formidable and imposing, were draped in long, flowing white cloaks that cascaded down to their ankles, swaying with every movement. Among them, one rider stood out, their helmet a stark white with red lines through it that suspiciously looked like blood flowing down the metal. The air seemed to shift as Anton emerged from the dimly lit interrogation room, his presence commanding at-tention. With a firm grip, he pushed Ayr forward, the tension palpable in the charged atmosphere.

"Wyrmguard Barrett. I assume that we are ready to proceed."

The white helmeted rider nodded and spoke in a distorted voice that carried like a drumbeat. "We are, Overlord. The preparations are just about made."

"Then fall in behind me. I am most eager to see the downfall of Dalton Ashbourne."

The wyrmguard formed up around Anton and Ayr, closing upon both of them like a coffin, keeping them boxed in. As one, they started to move forward, marching down the corridor with Barrett leading the way. The footsteps of the wyrmguard were heavy and weighted as they marched down the corridor towards where Baindussa and seemingly Drementhol awaited. The wyrmguard led Ayr through the Obelisk and eventually to the elevator where Barrett performed the crossing hand gesture that allowed them access. The shaft opened and the ten men all crammed inside.

Ayr barely had room to breathe, pressed between the many armoured plates of the wyrmguard. Thankfully, the trip to the top did not take long and the wyrmguard started to disperse around him. As the taller men moved in front of him, Ayr stopped, gasping at the sight before him. The entrance way to the courtyard was taken up by one massive bronze foot. Ayr started to walk forward, fear creeping into his system again.

Drementhol's size was truly shocking. Whilst still not quite as large as Sinibad, Drementhol required Baindussa to move from his roost. The dragon blotted out the sun as he rested on the spires that Baindussa usually occupied. How strong was the roof of the Obelisk to be able to contain such a colossal weight? The summit of the Obelisk was the only place within the city that would have been big enough to hold him. Ayr couldn't even see his head even as he looked up.

"Is this your nephew, Anton?"

If Ayr closed his eyes, he would have imagined thunder rumbling over the hills. As Drementhol spoke, the Obelisk shook, almost creating an earthquake in the air. It took everything in Ayr's power to stay on his feet.

"It is Drementhol!"

"Hmm, I can smell him. He smells more like his father. Did this child come from the same bloodline as you?"

"He did."

"Then that is a shame. His magical ability rivals only you and your brother."

"Even more so than the late Crassus?"

"Yes, he has more potential than the mighty Crassus. It is an untapped resource, just waiting to explode. I can sense it all over him."

"That's most interesting. It's a shame that he killed Crassus."

"For the last time! Outside of Baindussa thinking that he smelt me at the scene and the note, what evidence is there?"

Anton grabbed him by the scruff of his collar and thrust him forward with such force that he fell forwards. Considering he was in chains, Ayr was unable to keep himself from falling forward onto the ground. His hands hit first, and Ayr tried unsuccessfully to roll to the side to lessen the impact of the blow. He winced in pain, not wanting to show any audible sign of weakness before Anton.

Anton was swift on his feet for a man of his size. Before Ayr had even begun to push himself back to his feet, Anton reached down and grabbed him again. Dalton had manhandled him like this as a child, during their sparring sessions, but that had not happened since he was an early teenager. This power that Anton was displaying was something else and not even necessarily magical. As they neared Drementhol's roost, the world-ending sized bronze dragon lowered one of his front claws towards the ground.

There was a metal chain hanging from above and Ayr followed it up. The chain ended, snaked its way up Drementhol's body to his head. It was how Anton boarded the massive dragon. Somehow, with his hands still in cuffs, Ayr did not think that that was how he was being transported.

Anton shoved Ayr again, pushing him towards Drementhol. "Here you go nephew, this is you."

"Come here, worm."

Drementhol stretched out and there was nowhere for Ayr to go. Darkness began to enshroud him as Drementhol's claw closed around him like a vice. The world went black as it shut around him, and Ayr was suddenly knocked off his feet.

A moment later, Drementhol was in the air, gusts of wind swirling through the small gaps in his knuckles.

With no indication of where he was going, all Ayr could do was hang on. He listened to the roaring wind and imagined Anton sitting astride Drementhol. He called out to Azura, but she was unresponsive. Where had she gone? Was she still locked in her own void cell?

With Drementhol in the air, he had plenty of time to think despite the trip being brief. Ayr almost went tumbling around in Drementhol's grip several times, and was at the complete mercy of the dragon's movements. After what seemed like only a few minutes, Ayr found that Drementhol was slowing down. Moments later, a massive crash could be heard and felt by Ayr, signifying that they had arrived at whatever their destination was.

Ayr fell to the bottom of Drementhol's paw, and half expected that he would discover that he was back on top of the Obelisk. The difference in altitude told him otherwise, that he was somewhat closer to the ground level. As Drementhol opened his paw, Ayr discovered that his assumption was correct. Ayr tumbled from Drementhol, hitting the ground which winded him as he rolled a countless amount of times before he could finally open his eyes again. Breathing heavily, Ayr glanced up to see that Drementhol was no longer the only thing obscuring the sun from his location here.

Towering over Drementhol, however, whilst only being what seemed like double of his height was the Obelisk. They were not in the town underneath it either, but rather on the outskirts. Had Drementhol landed on anything in the nearby area, it would be crushed into powder. Half a dozen other dragons, all similar in size to Evor, soared down from the Obelisk: green, red, yellow, purple, blue, and black. These must be the dragons belonging to Anton's wyrmguard.

Despite the bulkiness of the armour, the dragons did not appear slowed. Between them however, they all carried something that seemed to be as large as Drementhol. As Ayr picked himself up from the ground, he was able to inspect what the dragons were bringing towards them. As the dragons neared the ground, it appeared to be a giant net, one capable of fitting Drementhol inside. The dragons spread out, widening the net over the landscape and they headed towards the flat plain beside the Obelisk.

The nearest edge of the net came down only a stone's throw away from Ayr and Drementhol. The metal chain that was drilled into Drementhol's face was being lowered again as Anton was finding his way to the ground..

Anton landed on the ground and let out a loud sigh. "Thought it'd be at least a few more years until we had to get the maw out again."

Drementhol shook his head, allowing his tail to splay in the air behind him. "So did I, Anton.

"Get in the Dragon's Maw, Evor."

"I am perfectly capable of flying to the Haven myself."

"If you could be trusted, this would be up for debate. Now get in." Smoke started to spill from Drementhol's jaw.

"This is absurd!"

"If your rider had not laid with Ayr Ashbourne, I would not be asking you to do this. Now get in the Dragon's Maw!"

With little more than a grumble, Evor bowed his head and made his way into the Dragon's Maw. In comparison to its size, he looked like a small kitten as he stepped over the threshold of the enormous trap. Evor was also surrounded by the wyrmguard dragons. They watched on as he moved into the Dragon's Maw, all of them ensuring that he was inside it from all sides.

Then at last, Azura returned to him, her presence filling his mind, but she was panicked. She sent him a vision, she was being carried in the claws of a much larger dragon. By the purple that was on the dragon's leg, Ayr could only assume it was Gundrag. Wanting to calm her, Ayr sent positive thoughts her way, but there was little he could do to instil faith in her. This would be an incredibly hard position to get out of. As she neared, he looked up at the Obelisk and at last saw Gundrag approaching with his prize in his claws.

I am alive, rider.

Are you hurt?

No. This is just a formality. I am not in pain. Do not do anything rash.

By comparison, Azura was small, just sticking out of either side of Gundrag's claws. Anger rose through Ayr's stomach upon seeing her in such a helpless state, and wanted nothing more than to fly into the sky himself and free her from his grasp. Gundrag lowered Azura near the Dragon's Maw and she landed next to Evor who was making himself comfortable, despite still shuffling his feet against the netting.

"Hello little one."

"Hello, Evor. It would appear that we are in this together."

"Indeed, we are. I hope that we can get out of it together."

"Touching." Drementhol stood tall over them making his presence known. "Now if you could both make yourselves whole within the Dragon's Maw we can begin our journey to the Haven."

"I can assure you, Drementhol. This is not a necessary precaution. I am capable of flying to the Haven on my own with my rider."

"No." Both Drementhol and Anton spoke at the same time, their voices echoing each other. "You will be taken by Drementhol and that will be the end of it. You are a prisoner, suspected of aiding the murderer of Lord Chairman Crassus."

Evor grumbled and sat down in the netting at last, once again right beside Azura. She in turn cuddled into him as much as she could. With the targets now clearly settled within the net, the first of the wyrmguard dragons slowly rose into the air, taking the net with it. One by one the others rose into the air as well, leaving Ayr with two questions. Where was Elanor and how was he getting taken to the Haven?

"You're with me, nephew."

"With you? On Drementhol?"

"Yep, now get up the chain."

Ayr held the cuffs out in front of him, signalling to Anton that he was still bound. "How do you expect me to climb up?"

Anton tutted and waved his hand over Ayr's wrists. The handcuffs moved in place, loosening and giving him more opportunity to move his hands. It was not a full range of movement, but he suspected that Anton wanted to deny him that.

"Now get climbing. Drementhol doesn't take kindly to stragglers."

With a sigh, Ayr turned and walked towards the massive dragon. The dragon growled at him, a low sound that vibrated the ground that he stood on. With Anton breathing down his neck and the thick chain dangling in front of him, Ayr was left with no other choice. He began climbing up the chain. Anton had made it easy so that there were divots that he could put his hands into that he would not have seen from far away.

With the handcuffs relaxed, Ayr climbed the rungs one at a time. At a moment's notice he looked down to see Anton hot on his trail. How the older rider could move so fast climbing this was beyond Ayr. Upon reaching the top of the chain, Ayr drew level with Drementhol's orange and smoky eye, which seemed as wide and tall as the mess hall. Thankfully Ayr was going past it. The climb was exhausting, especially with his arms not having their full range of motion.

As he pulled himself up onto the last rung, Ayr wiped a bead of sweat from his brow. He looked out over the Obelisk's surroundings for what may as well have been the final time. If he was coming back, it would be in a box. As he was taking in the surroundings. Ayr spotted a second rider strapped into Gundrag's back. Judging by the mask on their head, it was Elanor. He wanted to call out to her, but she would be too far away to hear him.

Remembering that Anton was right behind him, Ayr pulled himself properly onto Drementhol's back. It was unlike anything that he had ever seen before. Whilst Drementhol's lower body gave a sense of normality, stepping onto his back was like stepping into a whole new world. Anton's saddle was impossible to make out at this distance. Drementhol's spines were like ridges, that rose high above his head like a mountain range in their own right. It was like he had stepped back into the desolate wasteland that housed the Tomb of Chilijo. The only difference was the red glow that radiated from cracks in his scales on his back from the fire inside his body.

It was unlike anything that Ayr had ever seen before. He felt Anton moving behind him, and a hand was placed on his shoulder. There was something in Anton's hand and Ayr raised his own to see what the object was.

"You might need this, boy. Don't want you getting cut up, now do we?"

It was an unfamiliar mask, which Ayr begrudgingly took from Anton's hand and began to pull it over his face. It smelt old and mouldy, as though it had been in water for weeks on end. Regardless, it slipped onto Ayr's face and he was now safe from the potential dangers of flying on Drementhol's back. Anton stepped past him and headed towards Drementhol's snout. Anton was like a man half his age, moving with a grace and agility that would have only come from knowing the best routes to take on Drementhol's uneven scales. He used the larger ones that stuck out from Drementhol like barriers so that he did not slip and fall over the edge of the dragon. Ayr did his best to keep up with him, but ultimately fell behind before Anton reached his destination.

There was indeed a saddle, however this saddle was seemingly drilled into the back of Drementhol's head and made of metal compared to the normal saddles that dragons were equipped with. There was enough room for Ayr to slide in beside Anton. Anton turned back and gestured towards Ayr, urging him to hurry as the winds began to pick up, the closer he got to the saddle.

The bronze and black metal blended with Drementhol's scales, giving it a seamless appearance against his body. It formed a somewhat protective dome from the wind, and it gave plenty of coverage for a rider sitting in it. As Anton sat down in the saddle, he gestured to the seat beside him with a grunt.

"Strap yourself in, otherwise you will be in for an uncomfortable ride."

Ayr hurried to do as he was told, heeding Anton's instructions. As he strapped himself in, Drementhol lurched into the sky, Ayr still surprised that the gargantuan creature could still move with so much weight. He saw the wyrmguard dragons rise around them, each now with their riders on their backs. They were raising the Dragon's Maw up to Drementhol's level. Azura opened her eyes and he could see through them. The Dragon's Maw was stretching high above the ground, supporting both her and Evor. The wyrmguard were bringing the maw closer so that Drementhol could take hold of it. His claws wrapped around the rope like structure, and he continued to rise into the air, supported by the wyrmguard.

"I have it! Fly with me to the Haven where we can see these traitors brought to justice."

THIRTY

The flight of dragons quickly left the Obelisk behind in their wake. Even with the Dragon's Maw in his clutches, Drementhol still moved at a terrifying speed. The other dragons were still all assisting him, carrying their share of the load. Ayr wondered how much Azura and Evor weighed between them, and how it would have looked from the ground as they passed over what was sure to be smaller settlements and other cities. Not that Ayr could see them from the position on Drementhol's back. The dragon was simply too big for Ayr to see where they were headed.

They chased the sun, heading north over the Commonwealth. For the first time in his life, Ayr was finally getting at true understanding at just how much land the riders had access to. There was nothing to do in the saddle, except look at the back of Drementhol's massive neck, comparing the different scales to each other. He talked to Azura throughout the days as the leagues passed underneath the dragon wings. With nothing else to do, Ayr tried to keep himself occupied, eating and drinking when Anton provided him with the little food and water he was given.

As the sun started to set, Drementhol and the other dragons came to rest, finding a large, open, flat piece of ground that could safely house them. Drementhol released the Dragon's Maw and the wyrm-guard lowered it to the ground. As Evor and Azura rose, Ayr could feel the discomfort radiating through Azura's body as she tried to shake out her body.

Anton and the wyrmguard alone were efficient. Within moments of landing, each of the riders dismounted from their dragons and had a camping space set up beside their dragons, who made themselves comfortable in a large circle around the area. One at a time, the different dragons would leave to hunt, only to return with full bellies. Some dragons brought food for their riders. However, the white helmeted wyrmguard, Barrett, was sitting beside a small campfire that he stoked with his sword. A slab of meat that his dragon had returned to him with was on the point of the blade. Strangely, he was among the only rider that Ayr had seen who preferred his meat well-cooked.

Whilst the wyrmguard and Anton seemed somewhat comfortable with their setup, Ayr was not able to dismount from Drementhol. Instead, as the wyrmguard made camp every night, much like he had done the previous two nights, Anton stepped out of his saddle and tied Ayr's hands to it. Ayr winced as Anton tightened the grip on his handcuffs, magically shrinking them back to a size that made them uncomfortable to wear. Ayr could do nothing but accept his fate.

"Don't try anything. Just remember where you are."

As Anton walked away from Ayr, he turned to make sure that Anton was leaving Drementhol's back entirely. Anton slipped over the side of Drementhol and vanished from view moments later - now was Ayr's chance to make a move. He siphoned a small amount of magic into the handcuffs, trying to reverse the effects of what Anton had just done to them. They started to stretch, but as soon as he had made them stretch an inch, he heard a loud rumbling from underneath him.

Ayr stopped, and the moment he did, the rumbling also stopped. He frowned, trying the spell again. This time the rumbling was instantaneous. Drementhol shifted underneath him, and he realised that it was the dragon rumbling.

"That's your last warning, Ashbourne. One more drop of magic and I will crush you."

Ayr froze, not willing to pour anymore magic, risking his life or Azura's. Defeated, he slumped into the saddle.

It's no good trying anything..

I know, rider. Are you at least more comfortable?

I am. I might be able to get to sleep tonight.

Have you not been able to sleep, rider?

Not without your help. It has been very uncomfortable.

Then I will continue to help you rider. You know that I am more than ready to do it.

I do, Azura. I appreciate it. How are Elanor and Evor doing?

Just as well as we are. Elanor remains on Gundrag tonight and Evor's presence keeps me calm. If we were to try and escape the wyrm-guard would destroy us. Zephyr is the fastest dragon in the Common-wealth.

It's too late, isn't it?

It is, rider.

I am sorry for dragging you into this, Azura.

You are my rider, Ayr. There is no other place that I can be apart from by your side. Do not be sorry. My choices are yours.

Ayr slumped his head as Azura cut the communication. She reverted to humming inside his mind, trying to calm him as the sun set over the mountains in the distance. If he was not in the predicament that he was in, he would have asked Azura to take him to the nearest mountain peak to watch it set. There would be peace, maybe even with Evor and Elanor with them. Sighing Ayr slumped down into the saddle, waiting for the time to pass.

He was in and out of sleep, tossing and turning throughout the night. The amount of sleep was at least more than it had been in the previous night, but it still was not enough. As first light broke, there was noise and movement from the camp below. Ayr tried to keep sleeping, but unfortunately for him, the rumbling from Drementhol was far too loud.

Eventually, Anton returned to Drementhol's head. He was looking worse for wear and tired, but otherwise was in good spirits. There was a different aura about him as he strode across Drementhol. Azura had not alerted him to anything happening, so he was confused as to why Anton was in such a good mood. Anton's smile became apparent as he came closer and finally sat down beside Ayr.

"Morning, nephew! How are you? Did you sleep well?"

Ayr scowled at him. "You don't care."

Anton laughed and slapped Ayr across the shoulder blades with a ham like fist. "You're right, I don't, but I'm in a good mood this morning."

"And why is that?"

"I forgot how much the Dragon's Maw slowed us down. However, with any luck we will reach the Haven by this afternoon."

"Great. I can't wait."

"Thought you'd be ecstatic about that. Can't imagine you're too thrilled to have been up here for an entire two days straight."

Ayr rolled his eyes. "I just want this over and done with. The sooner I can prove my innocence the better."

"We're not interested in that."

"I know."

Anton chuckled. "I for one am most interested in sending you back to Dalton in a body bag."

"At least I know where I stand."

"And so did Dalton. Put your mask on, boy. The sooner we return home to the Haven, the better."

Anton reached down from the saddle and patted Drementhol. Their silent conversation undoubtedly discussing their next move.

Around them the wyrmguard and their dragons were rising with the Dragon's Maw between them. Ayr could feel Azura growing uncomfortable.

The sooner we get this over and done with I will be much happier, rider.

What if it is not a good result for both of us?

Then we will live with the consequences.

Are you hearing everything that's going on? Anton does not want me to survive.

Have faith, rider. You did not kill Crassus. They cannot find you guilty.

I know, but I still worry.

The Dragon's Maw was closing around both her and Evor and they were slowly rising up into the air for what would be the final time. As the wyrmguard rose on their dragons, Drementhol then rose into the air along with them. The dragons repeated their process that they had done in the past days and once Drementhol had a grip on the Dragon's Maw, they were underway once again.

Ayr relished being in the skies once again. However, every part of his being he wanted to be on Azura's back. He missed their closeness; all he wanted to do was snuggle into her warm, white scales. There was no sense of calmness and as they kept flying north, instead he was feeling more anxiety coming from Azura.

There was no reason, but it flowed onto Ayr as well. He kept shifting in the saddle, agitated by the straps that held his wrists in place. Drementhol continued to rise higher and higher into the air with an increased pace. Ayr could only judge by Anton's reactions as to how far away they still were. For most of the morning, they flew in the one direction, until there was a shift in the winds. Whilst Ayr could not see underneath Anton's mask, he could gauge their progress by the best of his bodily reactions.

Anton leaned back in the saddle and crossed his arms. Dremen-thol's pace increased, as did the wyrmguard flying just above them. Time slipped away and as the first hints that the sun was going to slip over the horizon, something started to come into view on the horizon. As each wingbeat from Drementhol beat down behind them, Ayr could make out the structures more clearly. They were larger than any castle or town that he had ever seen to date, with the tallest of the black spires in the distance reaching to the clouds. It was their destination.

For as tall as the Obelisk was, it appeared that the Haven reached the same heights and then some, despite the Obelisk being suspended in the air. The Haven was built from the ground up, sloping up the hills, following one singular long and wide path. For as wide as the Obelisk was and how wide its city sprawl was, the Haven was easily double it, stretching far past what the eye could see, diving deep into the holds of the mountains.

Despite being in the dizzying heights of a mountain range as tall as Ayr had ever seen, there was the feeling that the Haven was nothing short of a fortress. The one winding path that led up to it seemed as long as the length of the Seminary, a brown and black snake cutting and twisting through the surrounding greenery of the forests that bordered the Haven. Ayr did not see anywhere that they could safely land with the Dragon's Maw intact... if that was indeed the intention. In order for Evor and Azura to step out from the dragon trapping netting, the airborne structure needed to be flat to ensure their safety.

Instead of landing somewhere within the city, it appeared that Drementhol was coming into land far outside it. Just like with the Obelisk, there was no place for him to land safely with the Dragon's Maw within its walls. Instead, the wyrmguard and Drementhol all began to descend well before the city. Ayr was most anxious to be on solid ground once again, and was ready to have his feet underneath him. He waited patiently as Drementhol released the Dragon's Maw from his grip.

The wyrmguard dragons took over, controlling the descent of the cage all the way to the ground. Azura was growing increasingly less patient as the Dragon's Maw took the wyrmguard forever to lower to the ground. Ayr was sharing her frustrations, waiting for them to be finished. At last, the Dragon's Maw touched down onto the ground, and the wyrmguard brought down the four walls. Drementhol touched down just after it with a rumble so loud that it could have shattered the earth.

Anton stood up from the saddle and glanced around at their surroundings as he removed his mask. He nodded as if speaking to someone which was obviously Drementhol. The dragon lowered his head as if bowing, but it allowed Ayr to see more of what was in front of them. The wyrmguard dragons were all now beginning to move away from the Dragon's Maw, with one dragon right beside Evor and another beside Azura. She felt uncomfortable.

What are they doing?

Guarding us. The thought is that if either of us were to fly away, they would be able to grab our tails and pin us down.

You're not going to go anywhere, are you?

No rider. My place is with you. Come down from there when he lets you. I have been absent your touch for far too long.

THIRTY-ONE

Elanor shook out her hair as she tore the mask off her face as they came into land. The sooner that she was off this dragon and back on solid ground, the better. Gundrag stalled and was waiting for Evor and Azura to step out from the Dragon's Maw. Elanor was sitting behind Kaladin in his dual saddle and not the place that she wanted to be. In fact, there was no place she would rather not be.

Watching Evor step out of the Dragon's Maw was painful as he stretched out for the first time in hours. In no world should he have been able to go through that pain. Elanor wanted to grab Kaladin's head and pin it against Gundrag's back, grinding it into the purple scales of the dragon.

Evor mirrored her feelings, his yellow eyes glaring at Gundrag. Elanor could feel his anger growing inside his throat, but he knew as well as she did that, they could do nothing without putting each other in danger. Gundrag rumbled underneath her in response to sensing Evor's anger, and the former began walking towards the Haven. The two wyrmguard dragons on either side of him were escorting him towards the city and away from the Dragon's Maw.

Kaladin turned in his saddle, with his all too familiar, snarky grin on his face. "Come on, you going to follow your dragon?"

Elanor rolled her eyes at him. "You might need to untie me for that to happen."

"Never thought you'd say that."

"Shut up, Kaladin."

Kaladin laughed as he set about loosening Elanor's restraints. There was not much difference between the two levels of tightness; Elanor could barely move her wrists, but it would be enough for her to climb down Gundrag's neck and make it to the ground. Kaladin was the first of them to slide down Gundrag's frame, with Elanor quickly following. It was a struggle, and whilst she could not control her descent as much as she liked, Kaladin was there to help her.

"You're welcome."

"I didn't need your help."

Kaladin raised an eyebrow. "Uh huh. You know you can ask at any time."

"I'm never asking you for help again in my life!"

Elanor pushed away from him and could see Ayr making his way down Drementhol. A fall from that height could be fatal with no return, even if Azura was nearby with her tears at the ready. Hopefully Anton had loosened his restraints enough so that he could climb safely. A few moments later, Ayr finally touched down on the ground with Anton only a few chain links behind. Before Ayr could take a step away, Anton had grabbed him and was retightening the restraints. With a guiding hand, Anton guided Ayr towards Elanor and Kaladin.

"Right, now that we've finally got the two of you here, I think it's time that we discussed what we're going to expect of you."

Elanor glanced around at the wyrmguard who all stood watch over them, apart from the dragons that had been assigned to watch Azura and Evor. Their shadows were long, covering the ground and blocking out the sun. She wanted to fold her arms badly, but could not as Kaladin retightened the restraints the moment she touched the ground.

"What games are you playing, Anton?"

Anton's hearty laughter filled the air again. "There are no games here, Lady Sunfire. We cannot have our reputation lowered in the standings of the people. If someone has been accused of killing the Lord Chairman of the Obelisk, they will have assumed that we have done something to them."

Kaladin moved around in front of her and his smirk was apparent. "What did you have in mind, Overlord?"

Anton drew his sword in a single fluid motion. He held the blade in front of his face for a moment, marvelling at the steel in his hand. "Theatrics. We need to make this believable after all."

Kaladin's smile widened as he turned to Elanor. His eyes were swimming with glee. "Of course, my lord. You'll bear witness to this won't you?"

Realising what was happening Elanor surged forward. "Don't fucking touch him!" She was stopped by Kaladin, pushing back against her. "Stop it! Get off me!"

Kaladin pushed her again with more force this time. Unable to catch herself, Elanor stumbled and fell to the ground in a heap. Kaladin pounced upon her like a dragon would have on its prey. Kaladin's power came down on her more, pressing her shoulders down into the ground. Elanor kept trying to buck him off, using every ounce of her power. He had her pinned. Kaladin hooked his legs around hers, and Elanor felt like she was being constricted by a massive, thick snake.

"Stop resisting!"

Kaladin kept shouting, but all Elanor wanted to do was keep fighting. Gundrag stood over the two of them and all she could sense Evor wanting to do was charge at them as to break it up. Even with his enormous size, Evor had enough precision to rescue her from a situation like this. She continued to struggle, but slowly, Kaladin was taking the fight out of her. She felt powerless as he continued to choke her, even with Evor watching on. Elanor could feel the air slipping from her lungs and with no other choice, she went limp, unable to tap out as a sign of submission. Kaladin moved her from side to side a few more times, ensuring that she was no longer moving.

He lessened his hold on her and Elanor breathed deeply as his legs finally slipped off her. She gasped up at the sky, feeling the cool air surge back into her lungs. Kaladin was already up on his feet. In the next motion he was pulling her up by the back of her neck.

Elanor, do not resist, this will only make it harder on us.

I can't just stand here and let them do it.

Ashbourne will be fine. Until they want to kill him, no real harm will come to him. They're putting on a show. They want to illicit an emotional response from you.

They're not going to get it from me.

Then pull yourself together.

"Kaladin, have you got control over her yet?"

"Seems like it."

Anton's wicked smile returned to his face. "Excellent. Lady Sunfire, this will be a lesson to you as well. Pay attention. I would recommend staying extremely still, nephew."

"What are you! Ah!"

Anton lashed out with his sword, cutting through the air. Elanor saw it come down and then Ayr fell a moment later behind it. He let out a loud cry, Azura issuing a similar sound from her own lips as Ayr hit the ground. Elanor wanted to surge forward, but Kaladin's power was stopping her from moving. Anton, however, was not opposed and he took a step forward, pointing his sword point straight down at Ayr.

With another thrust, the sword entered Ayr's chest, a howl ripping from his lips. His trying to grab at the blade. Anton's sword was in and out of Ayr faster than a lightning strike, but the pain was still there. Both Ayr and Azura roared as Anton's sword flicked down at him again, cutting him three times. Elanor bucked against Kaladin again, but his grip was far too strong.

Anton had not taken his eyes off her the entire time. "This is just a sample of what awaits anyone that would dare move against the Commonwealth."

"We didn't kill Crassus!"

Elanor's plea fell on deaf ears. Anton struck again and Ayr cried out again. Even with Azura nearby, Ayr was reduced to a crumpled, bloodied mess on the ground. His vest was in tatters, his pants split in the multiple places where Anton's quick sword work had cut him. Ayr bled from head to toe. Only now did Anton's eyes revert to Ayr as he lay on the ground. None of the wyrmguard had moved, all silent onlookers to the slaughter. Anton knelt beside Ayr, brushing the hair away from his sweat and dirt covered face.

"You know, considering you're Dalton's runt, I expected more fight from you. He never gave up, always scratching and clawing to get what he wanted."

A brief silence passed between the two of them as Ayr slowly turned his head to face his oppressor. From the struggle on Azura's face standing over them, she was doing all she could to power Ayr into action. He raised a struggling, shaking arm, but then no sooner had it gotten to shoulder height, it dropped, slapping against the ground uselessly.

"Fuck you, Anton."

Anton rocked back on his heels, the smile still on his face. "That's a bit better. Is that all you can muster?"

Ayr tried to grab at Anton again, and this time, his arm did not stay down. Anton took half a step back, almost laughing at him. "Fuck... you!"

Anton kicked at Ayr's hand, his heavy boot colliding heavily with Ayr's palm. Another cry of pain tore from Ayr's lips. He sobbed as his hand hit the ground. A fire surged in Anton's eyes as Drementhol rumbled behind him. He glanced up at Azura who remained unchanged in her expression.

"That's better! Where was this before? Is she giving you something?"

Ayr started to grunt, and his legs were moving underneath him. He found solid footing and shuffled to try and get his legs underneath him. Anton tutted, watching Ayr as he tried to stand on his feet. Anton rocked back on his heels, his sword held in front of him like a spear. As Ayr's knees rose, Anton lashed out with the sword again. More screams ripped from Ayr's mouth as the sword was impaled into his foot. Anton's wicked grin did not let up until he removed the sword.

"Fuck! Ayr!"

Kaladin's grip tightened on her throat again. "You're not going anywhere!"

With the sword removed from Ayr's foot, Anton stood tall, his shadow only dwarfed by that of Drementhol. He looked incredibly pleased with himself, as he stared down at his handywork.

"He's been through enough!"

"He's been through enough when I say he's been through enough!" Anton paused and then chuckled before sheathing his sword. "No, that will suffice. His dragon will be pained trying to keep him alive."

Elanor let out a deep breath as Kaladin slowly let go of her throat. "Do you expect him to walk into the Haven like that?"

Anton folded his arms and nodded his head, satisfied. "You will walk into the Haven under the watch of the wyrmguard. You will be put on display for all to judge. It's not every day that another Ashbourne, one that is a sworn enemy of the Commonwealth is presented before the crowd. Then word will spread, drawing his father out from whatever hole he is hiding in."

"And what of our dragons?"

"We will not harm them. Not yet at least. But just remember, if you are found guilty, we will put them to the sword. They will walk behind you, allowing the world to see how you have corrupted them."

"Azura and Evor are good dragons. They do not deserve this."

Anton scoffed at her and shook his head. "Then they both should have picked better riders. It's not my fault that they were incompetent when it came to the bonding."

Elanor's mouth fell open. How could he stand there and insult both dragons, both of whom had done nothing wrong?

Elanor... I am surrounded by unfriendly dragons. Do not do anything. We will follow the proceedings. We are not guilty of any crime.

Of course, Evor. I am sorry. For you.

"Go to him." Kaladin's mouth was right against her ear. "Go to him. Comfort him. Get him ready for the long march."

A swift kick from Kaladin sent her scrambling forwards and Elanor fell onto her knees. With a grunt, Elanor pushed herself up off her knee and stumbled towards Ayr again. With the dozen wounds that Anton had inflicted to various degrees, it was hard to see just exactly what part of Ayr had not been cut open. His breath was coming in laboured gasps and as Elanor drew closer, his eyes slowly filtered towards her. He tried to raise his hand, but he only managed to bring it down over his chest.

Elanor stumbled again and fell to both of her knees. "I'm here, Ayr. I'm here."

She heard a retch from somewhere behind her and she snapped her head around to see Kaladin dry-heaving. Kaladin realised she was staring and stopped almost immediately, beginning to laugh.

"Oh sorry, I didn't realise that traitors to the Commonwealth got special treatment."

If she could have leapt up, grabbed his sword and pushed it through his chest, she would have. "Ayr Ashbourne did not kill my father!"

Anton took a step towards them and Elanor backed away instinctively, even though he did not have his sword drawn. He reached down and grabbed her by the collar, pulling her to her feet.

"We will see what the people and the tribunal has to say about that. On your feet, Lady Sunfire, we go to the Haven."

THIRTY-TWO

The screaming had not let up. From the moment Anton's sword had entered his body the first time, Ayr had been in a world of pain. All that filled his head was Azura as she tried to comfort him, unable to heal his wounds directly. Anton's sword burned like it had been dipped in scalebane, a poison filtering through his blood flow. Even with Azura and Elanor comforting him, it was not enough to stop whatever burned within him to cease. He could feel his blood exiting his body wherever Anton's sword had struck him.

You're not going to die, rider. You're not going to die.

Ayr's anger started to surge. The initial shock of the wounds was dying off, and whilst she could not heal him, Azura's energy was keeping him in a stasis.

No, I will not. I am here for you, Azura.

Then get up. Show the Overlord that you will not be taken down so easily. I am with you, Ayr.

We are one.

Elanor had been taken away from his side, wrestled back to where she now stood struggling against Kaladin. There was nothing that she could do to help him. Feeling Azura's energy surge through him, revitalising him, Ayr rose at the feet of Anton. It was slow progress, but inch by inch, Ayr willed himself to stand. With each small movement that upset the deep wounds that Anton had inflicted, he grunted, full well knowing that Azura would not let him bleed out. With one last big breath of air, he rose to his full height as Anton glowered at him.

"Well, there it is. You did have more fight in you, after all, Ayr."

Ayr maintained his stature, not wanting to speak in return, in case his willpower fell from his mouth. Anton continued to stare as if waiting for it to happen. Ayr felt like he was under scrutiny, even from the looming mass of Drementhol from behind Anton. Anton clicked his tongue and then turned away towards the wyrmguard.

"Barrett! Are your men and their dragons ready to proceed with the march?"

"Yes, Overlord! We are just waiting on you."

"Very good! Fall to formation!" Upon giving the order, Anton turned on his heel again and crossed towards Drementhol's mouth. Ayr could barely make out the dragon's eyes, only partly open most of the way towards the back of his skull. He cooed, however the coo was more of a rumble in comparison to Azura's. Anton reached out and patted what he could of the dragon's scales.

"See yourself to your roost, my friend. I will attend you there once I have dealt with this."

"Yes, Anton."

Drementhol unfurled his massive wings and started to rise from the ground. The deep shade that had extended over the area thanks to his massive bulk was now tripled as he rose to his full height. With a singular motion, Drementhol leapt into the air, his enormous wing-beats thumping down on the immediate area surrounding them. Ayr was nearly barrelled over by the strength of the dragon's wings, only saved by Azura reinforcing his mind. Anton had turned back to him and his smile had returned.

"Right, let's go, Dalton spawn. Walk."

The wyrmguard dragons were already walking up the pathway. Two of them walked side by side, as the remainder waited around. As he started to walk, slowly taking each step at a time, Kaladin pushed Elanor towards him. She stumbled but quickly fell into line beside him, uninhibited by any physical injuries. Elanor adjusted her pace to keep time with Ayr, as Barrett and half of the wyrmguard swept past them.

They were surrounded by the dozen riders, all of whom were silent in their thick, blackened armour. Their dragons were still scattered around the area, with each of their reptilian eyes focused on the point of interest. All it would take would be one word from Anton or Barrett and they would all be fried, Evor included. With the wyrmguard closing in around him, there was nothing he could do.

What are they doing with us, Azura?

You're being made an example out of. They expect you to perform the long march. Do not be surprised if people within the city are hostile to you.

Great. What's new?

Azura chortled in his mind. *I'm glad you have a sense of humour still.*

We're in danger, Azura.

Yes, Ayr. Yes we are. Keep focused on the path ahead of you and do not let your mind deviate. I will keep giving you strength.

Thank you, Azura.

With the circle tightening around them, Ayr began to feel more constricted. Elanor must have sensed his anxiousness, because she reached down and grabbed his hand, holding it tight. Whilst the gesture did nothing to ease his pain, he appreciated it all the same. Like Azura, she had been through it all with him and wherever Anton was taking them, they'd see it together. With the wyrmguard behind them, Ayr was kept to a certain pace. If he slowed down they'd shove him, urging him along.

Besides the backs of the heads of the wyrmguard, Ayr could not see much of what was in front of them. Several of their dragons were side by side with Azura and Evor, with more behind. The two in the rear of the pack launched themselves into the air and followed Drementhol's trajectory towards the Haven, following the winding path from the air.

Instead, he was focused on what was in front of him and what was keeping him upright. Azura kept a constant flow of energy seeping into his body so that he did not fall over at the faintest of breezes. The wyrmguard and their dragons wordlessly followed the path stretched out before them, their footsteps the only sounds that passed between them. The silence was starting to annoy him as they made their way closer to the city. Flying in on dragon back would have made more sense, but it was clear that Anton had other ideas. He was level with the last of the wyrmguard in the back row. Ayr could almost feel his sword poking into him, even though it was not drawn.

The first wyrmguard dragons were nearing the enormous gate that guarded the Haven. It loomed over them; however, despite its impressive stature, the black wall of stone and mortar would have only been useful for stopping ground forces belonging to mortal men. If the attackers had dragons, it would have fallen in an instant. The wall would do its job as a dragon would be impossible to contain. The Haven, however, would have had dragons of its own to defend it.

They continued to near the wall, and the massive black gate opened, slowly swinging backwards. Whoever was on the wall was well and truly aware of their presence and what their purpose was. With the gate swinging open, the wyrmguard dragons were allowed through, still able to fit through it side by side. The gate only just surpassed their heads in height, meaning Drementhol would have towered over it. He was still within view as he soared over the city, casting it in shadows as he flew. As the humans began to pass through the gate, Barrett called for them to stop, raising a fist in the air. He turned back, his helmeted face remaining expressionless.

"Overlord, do you require us to do anything further with the prisoners?"

"I don't think so. They are bound and restrained enough. What are they going to do? Fight their way through you?"

The wyrmguard chuckled, the voices echoing from within their helmets. "No, sir. I would assume not."

"Then we will continue on. The sooner we have these two in the cells, the better."

The way forward into the city was crowded. Through the gaps in the shoulders of the wyrmguard, Ayr could just make out the path ahead. The Haven was much like any other city he had been in during his time in the Commonwealth. Whilst the Haven was larger than anywhere he had seen before, the towering buildings on either side of the wide path were cramped and small in comparison to the dragons. It was clear that not everybody here was a rider, much unlike the Obelisk.

Instead, dozens of plainclothes townspeople hung from their windows, trying to get a view of the precession below. Men, women and children of all ages and sizes stood silent as the wyrmguard moved into the city. More townspeople lined the sides of the road, many of them standing with wooden buckets in hand. Despite seemingly being well-fed, the people looked downtrodden and afraid. Was it the dragons?

Ayr felt the hairs on the back of his neck rise. Something was not right. The only sound that he heard was that of the dragon's feet all around him, bashing down on the path, as well as the boots of the wyrmguard. He kept looking around at his surroundings until he felt Anton's hand pressing into his shoulder, asserting more weight than he needed. Ayr shuddered as he felt Anton's hot breath in his ear.

"No funny business. Nobody in this crowd is going to risk their life for you. They know exactly who you are and what you've done. See the look on their faces? They don't want you here."

"My father has spies everywhere."

Anton laughed. "Yes, he does. And let's hope they run back to him and tell him what has transpired here today. There's more fight in you now, isn't there? What happened? Did she give you energy, did she?"

"She did."

"And yet Drementhol would crush the life from her soul."

"She has more fight in her than you would possibly know, Anton."

Anton's laughing bark ripped into his ear. "Ha! A dragon that small. Whilst she may have all of the magical talent in the world, if I sent Drementhol to hunt her, she would be taken from the sky in moments. Don't push your luck boy. Be grateful that she is still alive. If I were the Council of Dragon Lords, Azura may not find herself so lucky."

Ayr swallowed hard, not wanting to show any signs of weakness. It was hard not knowing what Anton was doing behind him. Dalton had warned him that Anton was volatile at the best of times, and the cuts that Ayr currently carried proved it. He was still breathing slowly, the long march into the city taking its toll on him. Azura remained a constant presence, trying to keep him focused and motivated.

"Azura has done nothing wrong."

"A dragon is just as guilty as their rider. Keep moving."

Ayr received a shove for his trouble, almost forcing him into the wyrmguard in front of him. He stumbled and the wyrmguard turned in a flash, reaching for his throat to push him back. Ayr held his ground, and the wyrmguard's hand connected with his throat. Azura held him steadfast against the blow as did his anger. Ayr puffed his chest out.

"Don't get out of line!"

"Or what?"

Barrett had heard the exchange behind him. Within a step he had raised his hand. "Stop!"

The wyrmguard that was in Ayr's face drew closer. "You've done it now. Last chance."

Ayr focused on the blackened helmet of the wyrmguard, his left eye twitching. He felt Elanor turning, her hands reaching for his even though they were in her constraints. He could feel his anger bubbling just below the surface, a fire rising in his heart.

Rider... that was not smart.

I don't care.

Please do not do anything foolish.

Lend me your power.

Ayr! You can hardly stand! What are you going to do? We are both surrounded by the wyrmguard and the strongest dragons within the Commonwealth!

We are one, Azura.

As he broke the communication, from somewhere above him, Ayr heard a loud, angry female voice shout across streets. "That's her! That's the white dragon that chose Dalton Ashbourne's son as her rider! And that's him amongst the wyrmguard!"

Shouts of alarm echoed this first call and they quickly became a chorus. Someone unseen hanging from the windows unleashed a projectile. The rotten tomato splattered against Azura's otherwise perfect white scales. Azura was unfazed by the first tomato, but then in the blink of an eye, the lone projectile became a torrent.

Ayr was incensed. He could see fruits of all shapes and sizes being flung from every angle at Azura like she was a criminal being held in a stockade. Now Azura was starting to become affected. She turned away from the barrage and was clearly uncomfortable as rotten fruit after rotten fruit splattered against her scales. Ayr couldn't take anymore. His anger that had been bubbling just beneath the surface was rising.

Ayr!

They can disrespect me, but I won't have them disrespect you.

Ayr...

Azura! They can't!

Ayr!

The wyrmguard he had been facing raised his fist again, ready to strike him for a second time. Everything was moving slowly. Ayr raised his hands to block the wyrmguard's attack. With his hands still in the restraints, the grab was swatted away like a fly. The wyrmguard's body was turned, not expecting the resistance. He was close enough and struck one of the right hand wyrmguard in the side of the head. The offending wyrmguard recoiled, as his colleague responded. Taking advantage of the situation, Ayr pushed the first wyrmguard towards Barrett, using his enormous body as a shield. In the chaos, the wyrmguard split apart, one of them already drawing their swords.

Ayr picked up his pace, but before he had taken multiple steps, he felt a yank on the back of his collar. Ayr immediately fell backwards, not expecting the sudden movement of his clothing being pulled from behind. The crowd was starting to become rabid, working themselves into an even greater frenzy. The rotten fruit was still flying in thick and fast, with no way to avoid it. It came at him from every direction, but as he was pulled backwards, so did the fists from the wyrmguard. They had all turned, beginning to attack him. His clothing offered minimal protection against the armoured fists and boots of the wyrmguard as they landed. A fist came flying into his side and Ayr faltered. He buckled over, the blow feeling like it had cracked his ribs.

Ayr! Ayr! Ayr! Get up, rider!

There was another yank on the back of his neck, this one more powerful than before. Ayr's feet were taken out from underneath him.

Even if Azura was pumping magic into his system to numb the pain, he was feeling every blow like they were a new cut from Anton's sword. A moment passed and the blows lessened with the wyrmguard less determined to get their hits in as he fell. Ayr collided with the ground, his head ringing from the contact. Ayr blinked trying to recover, wanting to stand but could not as rising above him was the imposing figure of Anton. Anton readjusted his grip onto the front of Ayr's collar, applying pressure down on Ayr's throat.

"Fucking idiot. Trust you to try something. You're just like your father."

Save me, Azura!

Anton's right fist went up and stopped just underneath his chin. Then it fell.

THIRTY-THREE

Ayr groaned; it was all he had the energy for. His entire body feeling like a dragon had sat upon him. He was unsure if his limbs were intact. He could barely feel his feet and fingers. Ayr groaned again, protesting against whatever state he had found himself in. Ayr rolled his head from side to side, slowly, glad that it still worked.

Rider...

Azura's voice was faint in his head, nothing more than an echo. Ayr raised his arm, trying to reach towards her, but instead of finding a dragon's scale, he found something else. It linked in with his fingers, feeling like soft, but calloused skin brushing against his. Ayr moaned again, reaching for it. He felt the warmth and rolled his head towards where his hand was.

"By Chilijo you make some noise, Ayr."

Rider! Wake up!

Azura? Where are you?

Nearby, but we are weak. We are being held in a softer version of a void cell. I cannot rescue you.

I feel dead.

You are not. I won't be able to speak to you after this. Let me help you.

Okay, please be safe.

I will, Ayr. Now rise!

A powerful surge of energy coursed through Ayr, forcing his eyes to snap open with a sudden intensity. Hovering over him was Elanor, her presence both commanding and gentle, her hand the thing that Ayr was touching.

"What happened? What did I miss?"

Elanor laughed at him. "You've looked better, Ayr."

He laughed back at her. He had no doubt that he looked like a half chewed up dragon's dinner, but Elanor had also seen better days. Whilst she had not been cut to pieces by Anton's sword, she sported multiple blackening bruises on her face that was covered with a thick layer of dirt and grime. Yet covered in the shadows of their surroundings it was clear that she still held her regal beauty. "Yeah, so have you."

Elanor sniggered and pushed off from the ground, rising to her full height. She brushed out her hair with her hand and raised her nose towards the ceiling. In the faint flicker of sunlight that beamed down from above, Ayr could see a splatter of a dark matter across most of her face. Upon second glances, it was certainly not dirt.

"I don't know what you're talking about. I feel fabulous. This is just where I wanted to be today."

"I'm surprised they've put us in the same cell."

Elanor shrugged. "Yeah, well, you're not much fun to talk to when you're taking a nap."

Ayr rubbed the back of his head again. "Well thanks, I guess. I can't believe the townspeople didn't decide to help us."

Elanor chuckled again. "The townspeople. You're joking right? You saw them. They egged this on. I don't know what you were thinking striking out like that. They're fanatics, they're obsessed."

"Obsessed? Why?"

"Welcome to the heart of the Commonwealth, Ayr. These people will believe just about any bit of propaganda that Anton feeds them. He protected them in the rebellion, after all. Once all was said and done, Anton made this place his seat of power. Luckily for him,

Drementhol was one of the only dragons that could stand on their own against Dalton and his horde."

"Was it really that bad?"

Elanor leaned her head against the cell wall. "Honestly, because I didn't see any active combat, I cannot say. The tales that my father told me were more than enough."

"Ha! And what stories have you heard, Elanor Sunfire?"

Ayr jolted upright, his heart racing, as an all too familiar voice pierced the dimly lit room outside their cell. The darkness cloaked everything in shadows, making it nearly impossible to discern what lay beyond the bars. He strained his eyes, attempting to pierce the black veil and catch a glimpse of the source. Judging by Elanor's sharp intake of breath and the way she stiffened beside him; she had also heard the voice. It was clear he was not hallucinating; the voice was real and unmistakable, reverberating through the oppressive gloom.

"Dalton Ashbourne! Show yourself!"

Dalton's deep laughter filled the room. "I've told you before, Lady Sunfire that you are not in the position where you can make demands of me."

"Where are you, father?"

"Right here, son."

Dalton materialized from the void, his hand gliding smoothly down past his body as though he were drawing back a curtain to reveal a hidden world. His entrance was marked by a lopsided grin that seemed permanently etched onto his face, a grin that Ayr immediately found irritating.

"What kind of spell was that?"

"Invisibility, of course."

"You never showed me how to do that."

"You didn't need to learn it, Ayr. A great man once taught me how to do it. Said it would be useful one day. Now he was a true master of his craft."

"Who?"

"Never you mind. That is a story for another day. Now I came here to see my two favourite troublemakers. I never thought I'd see the day where you knocked off Crassus, Ayr. I'm proud of you. Congratulations."

Ayr's jaw fell open in disbelief. "What are you talking about? Are you delusional? I didn't do it. Why does everyone think I killed Crassus?"

Dalton's grin still had not gone away. "But you opened the gates to make it happen." He cast a side eye at Elanor. "And no, Lady Sunfire. For your reference, I did not kill your father. I did order his execution, however."

"You piece of shit! I'm in here because of you! You killed my father!"

Dalton raised his arms in a casual shrug. "Crassus had to die. He was well past his expiry date."

"Do you know what you've done?"

Dalton nodded, his smug expression still prevalent. "Created a power vacuum within the confides of the Commonwealth? Ordered the execution of one of my greatest rivals and one of the few men that could stand up to my power?"

"You're filth!"

"I did what had to be done! Be the change that you want to see in the world. With Crassus gone, the Commonwealth and the Obelisk are weaker. You should be happy with this Elanor."

"Happy? Crassus was my father."

Dalton opened his coat and put his hand into the top pocket. From it, he retrieved a small black bottle, no bigger than the palm of his hand.

"Do you want this?"

Elanor frowned. "What is it?"

"You don't recognise the scalebane ether? I would have thought for sure you'd want another dose to give to poor Evor when you see him next. I've already popped in to see him, Elanor in case they don't want you to go to trial so quickly. Evor has received another dose of the scalebane ether. Consider it a courtesy, despite the fact you've done nothing for me yet."

"I refuse to."

Dalton wriggled the bottle of scalebane ether in front of her face, almost pushing it through the bars. "If you would prefer, I can just drop it."

Elanor took in a deep breath of air and sighed. "What do you want me to do?"

Dalton frowned, thinking about his response. "Hmm. Killing Anton would be a suitable act in my opinion, but I have other ideas in store for him. I will tell you soon. For now, to get your next bottle of ether, make it through the trial. Ayr cannot die either."

"Then you'll just give me the bottle?"

"Sounds like a fair deal to me, Lady Elanor. I will not have need of your services for much longer and Evor will be whole again."

"I'm glad to hear it. Now why are else are you…"

Dalton raised his hand, cutting Elanor off. He turned his head over his shoulder, his eyes darting from side to side as he inspected the room in front of him.

"Shh! Who is it? Stay still. I was not here."

With a swift, fluid motion of his hand in front of his face, Dalton disappeared into an unseen mist right before Ayr's eyes. The air seemed to ripple momentarily, like the surface of a pond disturbed by a pebble, leaving nothing behind but a faint, ethereal shimmer that flickered briefly before fading entirely from view.

"He never told me he was that powerful."

Elanor was still unimpressed. "I guess you're seeing it on display now."

"Shh! Shut it you two!"

Dalton's hiss came from somewhere in front of them, but he was completely invisible. Ayr stared at where he thought Dalton had vanished to, and he caught the faintest ripple of movement in the air where nothing was present. He blinked and it had gone. An uneasy silence filled the room, and it was slowly replaced with the growing loudness of footsteps approaching. They echoed down what seemed like a hallway outside, and Ayr dragged himself closer to the bars to get a better view.

As more seconds passed by, and with the more he listened, Ayr could hear the sound of the footsteps now being separated into three sets. They were so close to each other that they overlapped. He drew in a deep breath, waiting for the arrival of whoever it was entering the room. As his wide cloak swirled into the room behind him, Anton was flanked by two wyrmguard. Both of the wyrmguard were silent and both of them wore bone bleached white masks, identical to that of what Barrett had worn on the journey here.

Anton stopped just within sight and placed his hands on his hips. "Let there be light."

He smacked his left hip and Ayr shut his eyes as a blinding light filled the room. A moment later and he could see the light was fading, back to what could be considered a normal level. The light sat above them in the ceiling, casting down shadows in every direction. Anton stepped towards the cell and Ayr saw something shimmer underneath the harsh light behind him and the wyrmguard.

Ayr followed the shimmer and as Anton approached the cell, the shimmer shifted, a short knife extended from the shimmer. It plunged into the neck of the wyrmguard on the right first, before in the blink of an eye, made its way, deep into the throat of the wyrmguard on the left. Both men clapped their hands to their open wounds, trying to stop the bleeding. Ultimately, they fell to one knee, the sound eliciting a response from Anton. He turned, his hand on his sword hilt, but he was not fast enough to block Dalton's advance. With a violent shove, the back of Anton's head slammed against the steel cell, a groan escaping his lips. The short knife had not left his throat and Dalton dissolved the invisibility spell that was around his body.

"Hello, brother."

"Long time, no see, Dalton. I would have thought that you were buried somewhere in the desert by now. Why are you here?"

"Thought I owed you a visit. I heard that you had my son prisoner. My spies told me that it was your plan to lure me here."

Now was Anton's turn to smile. "I wondered how long it would take you to come back and strike at us, however this is longer than I would have thought."

"All good things come to those that wait, Anton."

"Yet here you are, sneaking around the Haven because of the criminal you are. What's changed, Dalton?"

"Nothing has changed. I could say the same about you. No man is ever truly good, Anton. With this being said, no man is ever truly evil either. I went and did the things that you never could. But you and I, we will never be equal."

"No, we will not be. One of us has a dragon. Drementhol is on his way."

Dalton sniggered in Anton's face. He was so close to him that Ayr could see one of Anton's beard hairs sticking into Dalton's face. "Is he? And what's that overgrown lizard of yours going to do, Anton?"

"Bring the roof in on your head."

"You're in here as well, you fool."

Anton pulled his head back as much as he could and unleashed a ball of spit at Dalton. Dalton was far too close to avoid the projectile. It landed square on his nose, splattering his entire face.

"Fuck you! I don't care as long as you die like you should have done all those years ago!"

Drementhol announced his arrival with an ear-splitting roar that shook the jail cell around Ayr, but much of the sound was dampened by the thick walls that surrounded them. The giant dragon must have been close. Dalton still held the knife at Anton's throat.

"If Drementhol couldn't kill me when I had Zyro at my disposal, what makes you think he will be able to kill me now?"

Anton's eyes widened. "Ah yes, I assume that you are referring to your new pet, Sinibad? I haven't seen it. Where is it?"

"Sinibad will appear when he is ready."

Dalton pulled back from Anton, the knife slipping into Anton's neck, parting his flesh. Anton shouted and pushed back Dalton even further, his powerful arm striking out. Drementhol let loose with another powerful roar above, echoing Anton's cry of pain. It was clear that the large dragon was getting closer. As Dalton backed away, flicking the knife in front of his body, Anton raised his right fist. The wyrmguard that had fallen to their knees were now rising again. Dalton's smug expression had not changed.

"Thank you for the blood, brother. But your magic, and their dragons, do not impress me, Anton."

"You will fall, Dalton!"

Dalton continued to back away from Anton. He shook his head and the wyrmguard remained in their positions. It was as if they were struggling against his power as they tried to stand. When he was behind the wyrmguard, Dalton dropped his knife to the floor. As it clattered against the cold, hard tiles, the wyrmguard fell face first, their helmets cracking against the floor alongside the knife.

"I'll see you later, Anton."

In the blink of an eye, Dalton was gone, vanishing like he had done only moments ago, his magic shrouding him in a cloak. Anton leaned back against the cell, still cupping his neck, his free hand ready to grab his sword in case Dalton decided to reemerge. After a second, he grunted and lowered his hand from his neck, moving away from the cage. Anton attended to the wyrmguard in their crumpled forms, checking their pulses, but the growing pools of blood on the floor told Ayr all that he needed to know.

Anton sighed and grabbed the knife off the floor. He stood to his full height before glancing back at Ayr in the cell.

"It would appear that your father has shown his face again. He will pay for his latest crimes as well."

For the first time since Dalton had entered the room, Ayr smirked. "We'll see about that."

"I'm sure you won't be saying the same thing at your trial tomorrow. I will ensure that the Council of Dragon lords bury you."

"You will try, uncle."

Without another word, Anton turned, clutching Dalton's knife in his fist. His silhouette and footsteps quickly faded from sight and hearing, entering the way he had come from. Once Ayr was sure that Anton was out of earshot, he breathed heavily, turning back to Elanor who was standing with her arms folded at the back of the cell.

"We need to get out of here, Elanor."

"Have you ever been to the Haven before, Ayr?"

Ayr shook his head. "No, but if we can get out, just melt the bars or something, we should be able to escape, right?"

"You can't hear Azura anymore, can you?"

"No. She said that she would need to cut communication with me. We're in a variant of a void cell."

"Exactly, so what makes you think that your magic will be powerful enough to see us from the cell, especially if you wanted to melt the bars?"

Ayr stopped and rested his hands back on the ground. "I can at least try."

"Then we'd need to find our dragons, free them and then get past the entirety of the wyrmguard and every other rider that calls the Haven their home. You might not have seen the enormity of the city, but I have. I'm telling you it is impossible."

"They'll be too busy trying to find Dalton! We can escape!"

"No." Elanor was stern.

"Then what do we do in the meantime?"

"You can answer a question for me."

Eager to please, Ayr nodded at her. "Yes, Elanor. What do you want to know?"

"Did you do anything to my father? I find it convenient that he just died when you were unaccounted for, despite what Dalton said. What part did you play in his death?"

"I did nothing that should have killed him straight away. I find it suspicious that neither Kaladin or Anton could not tell me his cause of death. Clearly it was either Dalton or he was working with another agent of his."

"How did you want to kill him?"

"Poisonous magic. If it's anything but that, then I did not kill your father, nor did I play a part."

Elanor folded her arms, a frown prevalent, creasing her forehead. "I find that very hard to believe. You and I need to be very careful going forward, Ayr."

THIRTY-FOUR

"Wake up, scum!" Anton's voice ripped through the steel bars like it had been Drementhol that had roared it.

Ayr's eyes snapped open, and he found himself on his back. He could feel Azura's presence nearby, but it was no more comfort to him than the cold, hard floor that he lay on. It was dulled and felt flat like a constant loud droning buzz in his ear. Ayr groaned as Anton rattled the cell beside his ear and rolled his head to the side. Anton was standing above him, as were at least a dozen wyrmguard standing behind him. They all watched on, each faceless head unremarkable from the next. Half of them stood with their swords drawn, all waiting for Anton to direct them.

Anton held a large silver key in his hand, and he proceeded towards the cell door. He rattled the key and then put it into the lock. Anton pushed the door open and beckoned to them with his hand.

"Come on, we've got places to be."

Ayr rose slowly; Elanor was already on her feet. With no other choice, except to go to Anton, Ayr followed Elanor out of the cell. The wyrmguard's bodies had been cleaned up, their blood washed away by a cleaner who had visited in the middle of the night. Their comrades were now waiting alongside Anton with new restraints in hand. Ayr lowered his head as he stepped out of the cell for the first time in what may have been days, yet his sense of freedom was cut off as the restraints fastened around his wrists.

"Is this really necessary, Anton?"

Anton nodded and beckoned for the wyrmguard to surround them, just like they had done upon entering the city. The wyrmguard were wordless, and now that both Ayr and Elanor were in chains, Anton moved his way to the front of the group. A sense of foreboding washed over Ayr as they started to move. As they left the room, Ayr realised there was more than just the original dozen wyrmguard waiting for them. The corridor leading away from the cell room was full, with more men, each of them wearing the armour, helmets and billowing cloaks that he was learning were synonymous with the wyrmguard.

Each guard kept falling into line as the precession moved through the corridor, only increasing the volume of the marching footsteps that echoed in his ears. They rounded what seemed like one final corner and Ayr saw bright sunlight breaching the tunnel. He stared at it, squinting, trying to allow his eyes to adjust. The corridor was drawing nearer to an end, and the city was opening in front of him. As the sunlight started to hit his body, Ayr felt Azura's presence wash over him.

Rider. Are you safe?

I'm not sure. We're being taken somewhere.

So are we. I fear that we are being taken to the Dragon Lords. It is time for the trial.

Do you like our chances?

Honestly, no. If the Overlord has gotten in the ear of the Dragon Lords, then we are doomed, I am afraid. Whatever the Overlord wants, the Overlord gets. He has the final vote on the council.

Can you see my memories, Azura?

He heard Azura pause as she started to delve into his mind. He was not used to the unfiltered probing, but it was something he needed to get used to. Azura was efficient, digesting the memories of his time in the cell. Azura drew breath.

Your father. What did he want? I can see just how powerful he is. Taking two wyrmguard down like that permanently is no easy feat. They are powerful as well.

Clearly not as strong as my father.

No. We need to be careful. Was he just springing Anton's trap?

He was.

Then, should the worst happen, we may find ourselves with an un-expected ally within the Haven. Pray that he is able to assist us.

Don't worry, Azura. I am.

We have arrived, Ayr. This is the hall of the Dragon Lords. I will see you shortly.

Yes, Azura.

Not knowing what awaited him, Ayr sucked in a deep breath of oxygen. Elanor glanced over and she walked beside him.

"Azura?"

"Yeah. Has Evor spoken to you?"

"He has. The Dragon Lords await."

One of the wyrmguard reached out, slapping Ayr across the face with his gloved hand. "No talking!"

This journey through the Haven was much quieter than what they had received at the gates to the city. Ayr was trying to take it all in, bewildered by the sheer size of it. They were elevated, high above the gate where they had come in with the city stretched out below them like a maze. Dragons of every size and colour littered the city lounging on the roofs of the buildings, stretching out like cats in what appeared to be the warm morning sun. Spending time in the cell had distorted Ayr's sense of time.

The multiple levels of altitude that the Haven exhibited, undoubt-edly hid its true size and expansiveness with many pathways cut off, hidden behind the orange and brown stucco and tiles of the buildings that were sprawled across the city. The wyrmguard continued to push

Ayr and Elanor along one of the topmost paths. Most dragons would not be able to walk along it without scraping their wings on the cliff wall. They continued following the path as it veered up and to the right, beginning to slowly level out.

Ahead of them was a tall building, much in the dome-topped, mushroom shape of the Obelisk. It stood imposing against the backdrop of the blue sky behind it, with five dragons laying on top of it. Drementhol was instantly recognisable, his size imposing, taking up most of the space on the building, however he was not alone in his massive size. Right beside Drementhol lay a blue dragon half of his size. Beside them was another green dragon, along with a slightly smaller black and a second blue dragon.

Drementhol was the first to react. He rose up from the domed roof, hissing. "Ah about time, Anton. I was getting bored. The worms survive."

"They do, Drementhol. The trial will begin once we are inside."

"Good. It is overdue."

The other dragons, all peered down at the ground. Ayr felt small as their eyes rested upon him. If any of them willed it, he would be cinders within the blink of an eye. Wishing the wyrmguard would move faster, they quickly passed underneath the judgemental gaze of the dragons through the tall doors that were already open for them. Most dragons besides Drementhol would have been able to fit in these halls, however cramped they may have been.

This building reminded Ayr of Crassus' chambers. Rich tapestries covered the walls, ranging from the floor to the ceiling. Any words on them were written in a strange cursive text that Ayr did not recognise, with the majority following the colours of the dragons that lay on the roof. If he was not being guided by the wyrmguard he may have stopped to appreciate the art that was splattered against the otherwise plain walls.

The wyrmguard continued marching down the long corridor that seemingly took up the majority of this building. After walking for minutes, another tall door that was a replica of the outside came into view. Ayr trudged towards it, and as the wyrmguard approached, the door began to slide open. The open door revealed a large circular room that seemed large enough to fit Evor in his entirety inside it. As they approached, Ayr realised just how wrong he was. It kept going back further than Ayr could see, more than high enough to fit Drementhol inside it.

In the foreground stood a grand semi-circular table, reminiscent of the one found within Crassus' chambers, yet this one was more elevated, commanding a lofty position above the ground. Five majestic, high-backed throne-like chairs flanked the table, mirroring the regal seat that Crassus possessed in his own quarters. Each chair was crowned with an intricately engraved headpiece, sculpted in the likeness of a dragon's head, exuding an air of power and mystique. These engravings soared above the individuals seated in the chairs, casting a watchful gaze over the room below, as if the dragons themselves were overseeing the proceedings.

Upon closer inspection as they drew nearer to the raised chairs, Ayr could make out the faint outline of a large dragon paw that was engraved into the floor. He traced the outline of it as the wyrmguard started to fan out in the room. If he had been looking at it from the top down, he imagined that the chairs were all aligned with where a dragon's claw was. Ayr was also beginning to realise just how many wyrmguard had escorted him and Elanor to this place.

Elanor leaned in now that they had some space and whispered into his ear. "We're in the Praetorium of the Dragon Lords, and these are the Dragon Lords. They will be sentencing us today."

"Great. Just who I wanted to meet."

The chair in the middle of the room stood vacant for now - as Ayr could only assume that it belonged to Anton. Sure enough, once they had come to a stop, Anton moved around the group and headed towards the chair. Along the way he greeted the other dragon lords with firm handshakes before taking his position.

As Anton clasped the hand of a gruff, heavily bearded man beside him, he spoke loudly and clearly for all to hear. "How are the efforts going with tracking your brother, Anton?"

"Dalton is an eel. We will find him, rest assured, Roderick."

The woman on the left-hand side of the arrangement leaned forward in her chair, glancing across to where Anton now sat. She was adorned in a deep sapphire robe that mirrored one of the dragons outside, rising up into a headdress that caressed the back of her head. Ayr peered closer at her and thought that he saw a small horn protruding from either side of her head. "I am glad that the efforts to bring your brother to justice are going well. Are you ready to begin, Overlord?" She even sounded like a dragon, her tone smooth and almost a hiss as it escaped her lips.

Anton brought both of his hands together. "Of course, Lady Alexandria. Let's lure Dalton out of hiding once more."

Alexandria clapped her hands together. "Wonderful! Adonis, will you do the honours?"

The older rider at the far right of the table that resembled Crassus rose slowly from his chair. He placed both of his hands on the table in front of him, trembling ever so slightly. He looked ready to fall over, but unlike his counterpart in Alexandria, had no horns on his head.

"Vorrax, give me strength."

A dragon roared overhead, somewhere from outside. Ayr glanced up at the ceiling and saw an opening, large enough for a dragon slightly smaller than Evor could fit their head through. The black dragon that had been perched on the roof with Drementhol made his presence known, and Adonis straightened his back, standing fully upright. His voice was raspy and sounded faint, yet the Dragon Lords hung onto his every word.

"My fellow Dragon Lords. We are gathered here today to investigate the murder of Lord Chairman Crassus Sunfire. The accused are Ayr Ashbourne and Elanor Sunfire who have come before us today. By association, their dragons will also be punished if they are found guilty. Ayr Ashbourne. Step forward!"

Do not give them any more information than they require. They will use it against you.

I wasn't, Azura. I can feel them already trying to probe my mind.

Can you resist them? Do you need help, rider?

Your presence is always welcome, Azura. It will help keep me sane.

Then I will protect you, Ayr.

Adonis' eyes passed straight over Ayr's head as he stepped forward. His lone footsteps echoed throughout the praetorium and even though Azura was in his mind and Elanor was only steps behind him, he felt very much alone. Azura steadied him as he stared up at the podium, waiting for those above him to begin speaking. Adonis peered over his nose down at Ayr before continuing.

"Are you Ayr Ashbourne, son of Dalton?"

Ayr nodded in response. "I am."

"And did you, Ayr Ashbourne, murder Crassus Sunfire?"

"No, I did not."

"And what evidence do you have to prove your innocence, Ashbourne?" The otherwise quiet Roderick spoke up over Adonis. "Baindussa has identified you as present at the scene of the crime on the night that Crassus was killed. There was nobody else there on that night. Baindussa has been probed extensively in the past day and he is telling the truth."

"Elanor is not a suspect. She was helping Evor that night. He was in Baindussa's courtyard. How was Crassus killed?"

"I ask the questions here, boy. Not you."

Ayr bit his upper lip in annoyance. "How was Crassus killed?"

At last, Anton shook his head and rolled his eyes. "He was stabbed in the back by a blade."

Ayr raised an eyebrow. "Really? Just like the two wyrmguard that Dalton killed when he came to visit you."

Anton's fist slammed down on the table. "Speak his name again and I'll have your tongue cut out!"

"Yet you want to feed me to Crassus' dragon. What's worse? If Crassus died by my hand, he would have been poisoned. That's how you know I did not kill him. Probe me. I'll let you see it."

Anton waved his hand, dismissing him. "There is no need for that. Any evidence you will be able to bring to us will be refuted."

"Do I get a chance to speak?" Elanor spoke up from behind Ayr. "Crassus was my father after all."

Anton waved his hand dismissing her as well. "You are compromised, Lady Sunfire. That is why you are here. You have bought into the Ashbourne web of lies. Your dragon is promised to his. How can you be impartial?"

"I am faithful to the Commonwealth! I have served you for years, Overlord! My father was the Lord Chairman of the Obelisk for Chilijo's sake. What more do I have to prove? What reason could I have for helping an Ashbourne kill my father?"

"Dalton is a master manipulator. If your dragon is compromised, you would do anything to preserve him. Speaking of which. Major Kaladin, step forward. What evidence do you have to present the council? I believe you are knowledgeable on this subject."

Anton raised his arm to the side, and Ayr groaned. Kaladin slinked out of the darkness towards them. He was among the last people that Ayr wanted to see right now.

"As the head of security at the Obelisk, I was privy to an incident that occurred when Ayr Ashbourne and Elanor Sunfire went away together on a training exercise. Elanor's dragon, Evor was injured by scalebane. They undertook a venture to the Tomb of Chilijo in an attempt to find a cure for his condition. Yet, Elanor, you returned empty handed. What happened in the tomb? And don't lie to me."

Ayr could sense Elanor's hesitation in her answer. "He gave me scalebane ether to help Evor."

"At what cost?" Kaladin's question cut through the room like a blade. Elanor remained silent, unable to answer. "That's what I thought. You have been unable to stop Dalton because the two of you are colluding with him."

"What my father does is his business! I had nothing to do with his plans here."

"Yet you did not stop him! Why is that, Ayr?"

Ayr shook his head, infuriated. "Because his own brother is not powerful enough to stop him! What makes you think I can do it?"

"We've heard enough, Ayr. There will be no more from you. Excuse us a moment."

The Dragon Lords exchanged glances, their eyes flicking from one to another, a silent conversation unfolding between them. Anton, however, remained an exception. His piercing gaze was fixed unwaveringly on Ayr, as if trying to bore into his very soul. Ayr felt an uncomfortable heat rise within him under Anton's intense scrutiny, wishing he could shrink away or summon a spell potent enough to sever Anton's head cleanly from his shoulders. The air was thick with tension as the lords leaned in, whispering in hushed, conspiratorial tones. Their deliberation was brief yet intense, a fleeting moment of consideration before they collectively turned their attention back to Ayr, their expressions unreadable but charged with decision. Ayr was growing impatient, waiting for the decision to be passed down.

"And what have you all decided?"

The remaining Dragon Lords all nodded in unison, their eyes turning expectantly toward Alexandria. With a graceful rise, she stood up, her presence commanding the attention of the room. Leaning slightly over her ornate podium, she acknowledged each of them with a deliberate nod, her gaze moving methodically from one face to the next. Her eyes, sharp and discerning, did not need to seek out Anton, as if she already sensed his silent agreement. The air was thick with anticipation, the weight of her authority palpable in the chamber as she turned her gaze to Ayr and Elanor.

"Keeping with our traditions, your punishment will be simple. We were informed that Baindussa has requested the chance to face the accused in the Colosseum. He will arrive there shortly."

Kaladin raised his arms in alarm. "Wait! I do not think that it is wise. Ashbourne has already conquered one dragon of a rider that he has killed. Giving him this second chance along with Elanor would prove to be foolish if he won again."

Alexandria raised her hand slowly, calling for an end to Kaladin's protest. "I understand your concern, Major Kaladin. Bersos was a hatchling. Baindussa is a veteran of many wars, with Crassus having ridden him for centuries. He will be arriving to the colosseum shortly."

Anton leaned forward in his chair. "Kaladin, take them both to the colosseum. Keep their dragons separate from them. This will be a most entertaining battle. One that I pray has the desired outcome. Lords, if you are ready, we will begin preparing for the execution. Major Kaladin, if you would not mind escorting our combatants to the colosseum."

Another grin spread across Kaladin's face. "It would be an honour, Overlord. I look forward to sending a message to Dalton Ashbourne."

THIRTY-FIVE

*I*t was to be expected, Ayr.

What are they going to do with you?

I imagine it will be much like the first time we have gone through this. I will aid you where I can. We are being transported now.

Thank you, Azura.

As they left the Praetorium of the Dragon Lords behind, a sense of déjà vu found it's way into Ayr's mind. Only this time, he was not going through it alone. It was the same eerie feeling that he had when Crassus had ordered him into the Amphitheatre to fight Bersos. They walked back exactly the same way through the corridor. Ayr could practically feel Kaladin's breath against the back of his neck as they walked down the corridor. As they came into the daylight, an all too familiar enormous purple leg made its presence known. Ayr groaned, knowing exactly what was coming.

He wanted to resist, despite Azura's pleas. He had won one fight against a dragon but was now doubting himself against the power-house that was Baindussa. Even if he had Elanor's help, Baindussa was a monstrosity. Kaladin and the wyrmguard behind them pushed them into the outstretched claws of Gundrag.

"I don't believe that you will escape this time, Ashbourne. It would be a shame for one of the greatest dragons of all time to fall to your sorcery."

Elanor scoffed underneath her breath. "Greatest dragons? My father gave Baindussa half of his power."

"Be that as it may, Baindussa would challenge even me to this day. He may now be riderless, but that does not make him any less dangerous, especially to rodents like you. Now come. The colosseum awaits."

Gundrag wrapped up Ayr and Elanor in his talons, pressing Ayr awkwardly against Elanor. Obviously, there were worse places to be than crammed inside a tight space beside her, but given the situation, Ayr wanted out. Elanor looked defeated, the casual dismissal from Crassus weighing on her mind. The wind rushed through the gaps in Gundrag's foot as they gained altitude. Ayr had not seen the colosseum from his time at the Haven, so he could not gauge where it was and how long the journey would be. He sunk into where his body fell, trying to shut out the rest of the world.

You can do this, rider.

I know, but Baindussa is a much larger threat than Bersos.

I can still help you.

Will it be enough? We barely resisted Crassus when he was still alive.

We are one, Ayr.

I know, Azura. We are one.

Gundrag sped through the air and was already descending upon what Ayr assumed was their destination. He could feel Azura growing closer to him, but she too was unaware of her surroundings. Azura wrapped herself around Ayr as much as she could, trying to shield him from the corrupted thoughts that entered his mind. Their only pathway forward was clear. Kill Baindussa.

With an enormous thud, Gundrag hit the ground, finally landing. Having experienced falling from his foot before, Ayr braced himself. Sure enough, Gundrag dropped them a moment later, his foot opening like a trapdoor. Even though he was bracing himself, Ayr still hit the ground with all the force of a mace to the side of the head. He folded immediately, Azura trying to do whatever she could to comfort him. With shaky legs, Ayr stood, trying to stretch out.

Nothing felt particularly damaged, outside the cuts that still remained from Anton's blade. Ayr was hanging on by a thread, but with Azura's magic coursing through his veins, he still felt alive. He winced as he pulled himself to his standing base, putting pressure on his foot.

"Fuck."

Elanor was scrambling to her feet as well, significantly less hurt. "What's wrong?"

"My foot."

Elanor grimaced, glanced down at his foot, and then up at the steel cell around them. "Fuck."

"What's wrong?"

"My magic won't be strong enough to push through these restraints, even with Evor helping me. Is Azura helping?"

Ayr nodded. It was all he could do. He took pressure off his foot, rising more onto his toes. "Yeah. I hate this."

"So do I."

Gundrag chuckled overhead. "You won't have to put up with it long. Good luck."

Without another word, Gundrag rose into the sky, his wingbeats almost knocking them to the ground. Most surprisingly, Kaladin had no final snide remarks. He turned as he heard a rattling key behind him and saw six wyrmguard all standing outside. All but one of them were armed with polearms, standing twice as tall as they were. The gate clinked open, and one by one, the wyrmguard entered with their weapons lowered. This was not a situation that they could fight their way out of.

The wyrmguard in the white helmet that was last to enter had a gift for them. With a deliberate motion, he extended his arms, revealing two glistening swords. He remained silent, his presence imposing as he stared at them through the impassive, dark eye slits of his helmet.

"Thanks."

Ayr reached out and grabbed the sword that was meant for him. He groaned upon seeing the edge of it. Just like it had been the time he had entered the arena with Bersos, the sword was blunted with no real edge or point. They would need to improvise. Their backs were well and truly against the wall.

"Is this going to be it?"

Elanor nodded slowly. "I never thought this would be the way that I'd go out. Dying as I fought against a dragon in the colosseum. I always thought that Evor and I would live long and happy lives together before we died of old age together."

"That sounds like a peaceful retirement."

"Yeah, well it's funny how life never pans out that way." She took his hand in hers and squeezed it. "If this was most other dragons, I'd say between the two of us, we'd be okay. But considering Baindussa's size and magical prowess, we're out of options unless you've got more of a reserve trapped in there somewhere."

"I can try, but without Azura's full assistance, I don't know if I can make it happen."

"Well, we've got one chance, Ashbourne."

The iron gate in front of them started to clang open. As each bar passed over the threshold above them, another loud clang filled Ayr's ears like a hammer dropping on an anvil. It was nerve wrenching, but at the same time, he could feel his blood beginning to boil. Azura didn't deserve the fate that was coming to her. If he was guilty of killing Crassus, he would have been less angry about it.

"I'll give it everything I've got."

"I know. Come here."

Elanor pulled him close towards her and Ayr bent his neck for one last kiss. The dirt and grime that had accumulated on her face was no more or less than the mess he had on his. He lost himself in the kiss, indulging in her every touch and taste. There was nothing more that he wanted than to hold her and keep her within his embrace. Bersos had been one challenge, but Baindussa would be another entirely. He cast the thoughts from his mind, wanting to enjoy the moment. Whilst Elanor was bitter and dirty, Ayr gave everything he had until a spear caught him in the thigh from behind.

"Get a move on you two!"

Aggravated, Ayr spun, rounding on the wyrmguard, wanting to boil his head inside his suit of armour. Instead, Elanor squeezed his hand again and led him through the gate. Ayr took in a large breath of air as he tried to calm himself. The colosseum was much larger than the Amphitheatre had been, with double the seating and also an arena floor that could fit larger animals like Drementhol inside it. Just like the Amphitheatre, it was rocky, filled with many crevices that appeared to run down to a lower level below. As they strode through the gate, a loud drum beat filled the stadium, one beat for every two steps they took. It was a simple rhythm, but it still felt foreboding to Ayr.

He had flashbacks to the Amphitheatre, fully expecting to see Crassus in the orator's box, standing before them, delivering an address, accusing him of his crimes. Instead, as they strode out into the colosseum, he saw Alexandria still dressed in her oversized sapphire robes, glaring down at him from the podium. Anton, who had been insistent on witnessing their entrance into the death pit, however, was nowhere in sight. The other Dragon Lords were present, however, each of them looking just as impressed as the last. Kaladin lingered over their shoulders like a bad smell that had no right to be there.

The crowd was already packed into the colosseum, with many townspeople in nothing but plain clothes in attendance. They seemed to make up the bulk of the audience. However, dragons and their riders were also all crammed into the mixed seating of the colosseum, an array of colour that covered the spectrum of the rainbow. Ayr ran his eyes over them, trying to pick out a familiar face in the crowd. Suddenly, Ayr spotted a tiny dragon resting above the colosseum on one of the shade sails.

"Chorru?"

"What?"

Ayr pointed up to where he had just seen the dragon. "Look."

"I know Dalton was in the city, but you're seeing things, Ayr. His companion dragon isn't here."

"I saw it!"

"Get your head in the game, Ayr we have a fight to win. We're not getting rescued."

"You've changed your mind from a minute ago."

"Evor wants me to live. I'm doing this for him, Azura and you."

A smile came to Ayr's lips for the first time in days. "I know."

At long last, they stepped out onto the floor of the colosseum properly. The rocks continued to rise around them, much like they had done in the Amphitheatre. The colosseum, just like the Haven, put the Obelisk to shame. As did the enemy that was inside it. Baindussa was laid out before them, his body coiled across the ground, wrapped around one of the mountainous rocks that jutted out from the centre of the arena. Even with Elanor beside him, he felt insignificant.

Elanor inhaled through her mouth. "He always looked smaller inside his courtyard."

Her words did nothing to calm Ayr's nerves. A new chill of fear raced down his spine. "I'd hate to agree with you, but you're right, Elanor."

A heavy crack blasted Ayr in the back of the head. He reeled forward, Azura crying out in pain in his mind along with him. Ayr stumbled, unable to support his weight and dropped to a knee. He turned, snarling to see the source of his frustration. The wyrmguard were not happy with his progress.

"Get a fucking move on."

Ayr groaned and hurried to catch up to Elanor. As they walked out further into the colosseum, the crowd started to react. With Azura in his mind, Ayr was able to block most of it out. His only concern was the blind green dragon, now rising above them. Baindussa was stretching out to his full height and the crowd was reaching a fever pitch. They wanted to see blood. Ayr tightened the grip on his sword as a roar split the sky. It was not from Baindussa.

A dragon flew overhead, flying into the colosseum from behind them. The crowd gasped in awe and pointed. As the familiar golden dragon passed overhead, Ayr looked up and saw something dangling from one of its claws. Onoss was carrying someone in his claws and had two riders on his back.

Ayr... why is he here?

I don't know...

"Dalton Ashbourne. Why have you come here?"

A human scream ripped through the air. "Put me down! Put me down!" Anton's voice did not need magical enhancement to be heard over the sound of Onoss' wingbeats. "Put me down!"

Dalton's voice on the other hand did. He wanted to be heard. He stood up on Onoss' shoulders, hanging from the saddle that kept Gable in place. Both of them wore masks over their faces and as he extended his arm, Dalton removed his mask in a single fluid motion.

"People of the Haven. I come before you today to remind you of simpler times. A time when these riders did not make the rules for you. A time when your Commonwealth was governed by men that you could reason with. My name is Dalton Ashbourne, and although some of you might not know me, I almost made this place yours again.

Now this man you see in my companion's grasp would call himself your Overlord! He cast me aside when I needed him the most. I've waited decades for my revenge, and I will now take it! You will all have to pick a side!"

Riders were scrambling everywhere in the colosseum, desperate to get to their dragons. Some riders were already climbing up their dragons as Onoss began to beat his wings faster.

"No!"

A mighty roar ripped through the sky and from out of nowhere, Drementhol let out an ear shattering high-pitched shriek of panic. It was unlike any roar that Ayr had heard from him thus far. It was pained and startled like it had come from a banshee. The enormous brown dragon was nowhere in sight. Onoss put his front claws together, and he brought Anton up towards his face, holding him like a piece of meat. With one final nod from Dalton, the golden dragon pulled back and opened his mouth as Dalton cried out on his back, his laughter spreading over the colosseum.

A torrent of flame gushed from Onoss' mouth, completely engulfing the small portion of Anton that Ayr could see. Drementhol continued to scream, and a moment later Onoss' flame stopped. What was taking Drementhol so long to get here? Onoss opened his claws and what little cindered remains of Anton remained tumbled from his grasp. More gasps reverberated from the crowd, all of the onlookers helpless in aiding the one man that had supposedly saved him from the villain. As what remained of Anton's body tumbled towards the rocky surface of the colosseum, Onoss' wings started to beat upwards as he angled himself back towards the south. Dalton let out one last final scream with his magically-enhanced voice. He waved his hand out in the air like he had just finished performing an enchanting circus act.

"Dragon Lords, Sinibad sends his regards! I wish you luck without your Overlord at the helm! Release my son and his companions, otherwise the rest of the Haven will burn!"

Acknowledgements

Crazy how time flies when you're having fun, right? It's been a rough year already. I feel like it was only yesterday that I released Shadows of the Dragon. I definitely had a lot more fun with this one, building upon the already existing lore and fleshing out where I want to take this series. We're not done by any stretch of the imagination. All I know at this point is the ending. No, I won't give you spoilers. But if you're reading this, I hope you had fun with this one and I will not be apologising for any cliffhangers. Sorry.

That being said, this is the part of the book that everyone wants to see their name in! Firstly to my readers. If you're still loving the Ashbourne Saga at this point, thank you so much. We're still in for more of a wild ride. Ayr and Elanor still have plenty of exploring left to do, and what about that Dalton, huh? Think he needs some more screen time. Did any of you spot the easter egg? Either way, if you're loving Ayr, Azura, Elanor and Evor, there's plenty more where that came from. So thank you for sticking with me as I try and pump this series out. If you're reading this when the whole series is published, congratulations! Get onto the next book and enjoy the ride.

Now my circle is small, and this is almost a one-man operation. So secondly, I'll thank my parents, Mr. and Mrs. Mememaro senior. They've been a massive help this year. I hit rock bottom earlier on, and I don't know how I'd have gotten back on my feet without them.

Hopefully one day I can pay them back because my books have shot to the moon.

Thirdly, there's Ajay. If you're on my socials, you'll know her. A random author friend that is now the book bestie and sometimes (most of the time) who I'm going to for life advice and support. She doesn't have to do it, and I don't know why she does, I'm just a random dude, but I swear she solves more of my problems than her own. Sometimes I don't follow the advice and tell her things she doesn't want to hear, but we've all got that one friend that is there for us regardless. Then there's everything else she does as a number one fan. When she's not working on her own stuff, chances are she's doing something for me. If I listed out everything that she does, there'd be a whole new novel about it. Maybe I should do that? Who am I kidding, I don't need more novel ideas already. Either way, if you're having a hard time and are struggling, just having that one consistent person who shows up for you time and time again can be all the difference to helping you get back on track. Reach out to someone if you are not in a good place.

Fourthly will be the biggest group of people that I talk to regularly. This includes my PA, Autumn, who is constantly sending me messages, trying to get me to do stuff for these damn books so I can get them in the hands of more readers. I honestly need Autumn full time, but we're making good progress. One day Autumn. Along with Autumn there's also my street team that are constantly giving me encouragement and motivation to keep going, despite them wanting me to switch it up and write some vampire smut. Soon ladies, I promise. Nana, Kal, Heather, Chandi and Momma T and the rest of you all are vital to me getting stuff done. The street team is just a cool little group and is always open to more applicants.

I think we're nearly done, so I'll wrap this one up. Fifthly, there are a couple of gentlemen that I'd also like to thank. There's John who's wit and humour I definitely appreciate, especially when he's giving me feedback and finding errors in the books that I send him. His razor sharp eye definitely means there should be less typos in these masterpieces. Also in this category is my main editor, Mr. William Burkhandt. I call him the advanced version of John mainly because he goes a lot more in depth, pulling out issues that I have not foreseen. Without William combing through the books, they'd certainly be in a worse off state and without all of his hard work I wouldn't know what to fix. The man however has complained that he's got more credits with my name on them than his own lol. What a bad problem to have right?

Anyway, I've taken up too much of your time with real life words, rather than something that's in a fantasy fictional world. So with that being said, if your name isn't in here, I would love for it to be next time. Just reach out. I am always open to new ideas and plot points as well. If the Ashbourne Saga is also the first series of mine you have read, I highly recommend checking out my other dozen plus books too. They're a good read! Until the next one, stay safe and enjoy your life! Live in the moment and find something good to cherish every day.

ABOUT THE AUTHOR

Matt Mememaro is an Australian author that exists somewhere in the void in Australia, as he battles with the unsettling fact that he is no longer a true spring chicken and is experiencing grey hair growth all over his head. He constantly stresses about his books and whether or not the meaning of life is in fact fourty-two.

In his spare time when he is not at his day job that he wishes to retire from, he is probably writing, playing paintball or trying to grow his forearms. Matt wishes to one day soon become a full time author, but he cannot do that without your help.

If you enjoyed Revenge of the Dragon, please consider leaving a kind review and or checking out Matt's other works and social medias in the QR code below.